THE
TWO WIVES
OF CUDDY
RANSE

ANNA HOUSEGO

This novel was written on the island of lutruwita/Tasmania, on the southern land of the muwinina people, with the mountain slopes of kunanyi on the skyline. I pay my respects to the Traditional Owners and acknowledge the Tasmanian Aboriginal people as the continuing custodians of this land. I honour their Elders, past and present, as the keepers of deep knowledge and culture spanning more than 40,000 years. They and their story live on.

For the Connor women, who baked strength
and resilience into our DNA.

PROLOGUE

Que cada palo aguante su vela.

May every mast hold its own sail.

Spanish proverb

MELVA
GIBRALTAR, 1776

THE OLD CATALAN TURNS THE card and squints, black pebble eyes disappearing into her head. Milva shifts uncomfortably before her, turning her gaze to the empty chair set out for the adivina's spirit guide.

If her mother had not insisted she come, the girl would be scrambling up the lower slopes of The Rock, enjoying the freedom of its soaring fourteen hundred feet of elevation, the blessed release from the confines of the narrow strip of land where she lives. She'd be pausing to take in the view from the toe of the Iberian Peninsula across the bay to Algeciras in the west and Morocco to the south, staying there as long as she dared. Then herding their two goats through scattered palmettos on rough tracks, down steep passages and alleyways to the doorway of the patio for milking.

Her mother is a determined woman, though, and Milva is now of marrying age. It is time to seek answers in the search for a husband.

Mama has expectations. Papi is a trader, has orchards, a market garden, and a fruit and vegetable shop supplying the British military. Like many locals with such good connections, his children have been raised to speak English, to understand the customs of those who rule this place.

Though the British expect those with darker skin to step off the pavement when they pass, it is her mother's hope that she will marry an officer, spurred by the fact that Milva's skin is not coffee dark like her own but a sun-kissed shade of olive.

'Eight of swords. A long journey winding away into the future, where hasty action may call down a curse upon your head.' The wrinkled face leans forward, crumples. 'Beware impulse, girl, for it is a foe to the beneficial.'

Melva flinches at the intensity of the adivina.

'I see affliction, misfortune, lest you be watchful. Hold fast to wisdom, for you will be called to account for poor choice. Tread carefully, obey when you should, dare only when you must.'

The warning means nothing to the girl, who smiles, but only on the inside. She has faith, knows her future shimmers, beckons in the golden light of promise. Yet she remains silent, does not need to irritate the adivina, for her mother would hear of it.

The woman now raises one hand in a grand gesture before turning another card. Red, so much red on this card.

'The Rock of Gibraltar is washed with the blood of your ancestors. You are called to honour them, work hard, make your own home.' Milva doesn't need to be a soothsayer to know what will come next from the slack lips of the wizened woman.

'You will wed soon. Your husband is at hand, I see it. There will be many children, strong sons and loyal daughters.'

Minutes later, Milva is hurrying down to the bay, desperate to feel sand under her bare feet, to shake off the cloying air of the old woman's room. On the beach, she throws her hands in the air, bursting into wild laughter. Her mother could have saved the precious silver real dropped into the adivina's hand, for all the good it did.

The Old Catalan must be bird-witted. Ha! Didn't even know Papi was a Minorcan, came here as a young man in search of fresh opportunity. Mama not Gibraltarian either. Her family arrived from Tétouan when she was a girl. Moroccan jews, Milva's been told, but not by Mama, who slaps her ear if she dares ask questions. No blood of ancestors here.

As for marrying? Mierda. What good is being a wife? Fourteen years she's lived on the red sands of Gibraltar, and all she sees is hard work, duty and babies for mothers still growing up themselves.

The youngest daughter, the only one of three unmarried, Milva sweats alongside her mother day after day, cooking, washing, cleaning, while her brothers Patricio and Biel work with soil and seed. They have the reward of fresh air, not for them the dark, ill-ventilated rooms of their apartment, the unholy stink from filth in the courtyard latrine. They see fat fruit ripen; the glossy leaves of vegetables growing from their labour. She, on the other hand, slogs through her day's chores only to see the same messes, the same empty pots begging for food to be prepared, the same dirty dishes tying her to the washing bowl.

What woman with her head on straight would want that destiny? She laughs again, stopping when a chill pricks her bare arms, though there is no breeze, merely thoughts cooling the fire of her outrage. They bring images of her sisters with their grizzling children, of the friend who will marry before the month is out. Escaping that fate would surely mean shaking off life here, leaving family, fleeing across the spit to Spain, or hiding on a ship to Morocco. Then what?

She shakes her head, turns for home. She is no adivina. While her heart says she is made for more than this, when she imagines stepping forward into her future all she sees is grey sky above, below, all around.

In the next street she skirts a pedlar carrying a set of scales, his donkey loaded with huge saddlebags full of vegetables. He gives her a grin as she hurries past and she flashes him a smile, is still smiling when she gets to her door.

Her mother is waiting impatiently on the other side, hands smoothing a bulky garment folded in a parcel. She shakes it out as Milva steps through the doorway.

'For you, daughter.'

Crimson fabric falls in deep folds to the floor, revealing black velvet trimming the edges of a generous hood, front opening and armholes of a new cape.

'Your walking out cloak. The time for running through the streets with skirts flying, hair wanton, is done. Now you must be a respectable young woman.'

Each afternoon, Milva toils from the family shop in Whirligig Lane, up the steep Calle Comedia, her bulky basket full of onions, pumpkin and potatoes for the family's evening meal of berza. The cloak confines her, requires movement that is measured, weighs on her body and spirit.

She longs to go to the street's end, high above at El Castillo on the side of The Rock, but her mother will be angry if she is late. The British call it the Moorish Castle and though it is centuries old, use it for their own purposes. Its Tower of Homage rises from the rock face to look over the whole town and the Mediterranean Sea. Massive walls, hidden passages, a soaring stone gateway protecting the entrance to the kasbah, they beckon such that Milva yearns to explore it all, to walk where men with skin the colour of hers have been. The British, though, prevent entry.

The Moors were creatures of this land and so is she, no less than the Barbary macaques scrambling over rocky ridges above, grunting, screaming, picking at scorpions, gobbling berries. Layer upon layer of history has burrowed into this place, the only land she's known, a glittering prize for whoever seeks to control shipping in the Mediterranean.

Papi has stories, shared when darkness rolls down and he can take rest. It's said that deep caves near sea level, over on the steep eastern flanks of the Rock, have strange human bones from a time before any town existed, before even the Moors. Heavy skulls and short leg bones unlike any ever seen. Milva imagines these stocky people bending large heads, teeth stripping flesh from fishbones, faces shining in the light of campfires long gone cold, their souls now deep in the earth below.

She wonders what else may be hidden beneath her feet, tapping at the crust of cobblestones, searching for a weak point, a tiny gap through which it might emerge, hungry to claim what's in its path.

Instinctively she looks to the ground, fearful of what might rise up, grasp her by the ankle.

A voice interrupts, moving through the air with no sign of a body. Alarmed, she spins sharply, shaking loose three onions from her basket, and watches as they bounce and roll down the street.

'I'll catch the wee buggers.'

She hadn't seen the man behind her and now he's running, red jacket flapping, arms askew. She watches the onions disappear around a corner and his tall black boots after them. The absurdity of it builds in her belly and soon she's laughing so hard that the rest of her load is at risk. She sits the basket down, and as she straightens the fellow appears, hands held high, triumphant, bearing the runaway onions.

'At your service, ma'am.' He bows as he hands them over, but for the life of her Milva can't stop laughing.

'I were a fine sight, to be sure.' He laughs too, a great gulping sound rising to a bellow, tears rolling down his face.

When he catches his breath he introduces himself. She offers her name in return.

'Melva. How was it you come by such a fine Irish name, like?'

'No, M-i-lva. Genoese. Mama met one of the fisher wives many moons past. She carried the name.'

No matter how he tries to say it, his tongue can only manage the sound of Melva, which he promptly decides is the name for her, despite her smiling protest.

'Aargh, am not big blue fish, slippery tuna. That's what it stands for in our tongue. Family, friends would laugh at the joke.'

He feigns disappointment, lips she sees are thick, luscious, turning down in a mock frown. With one of his palms he pats powdered reddish hair tied behind, then tilts back his head, flaring the nostrils of a thin, long nose for extra drama.

'I'll thank you not to bad mouth such a beautiful name, for it means graceful lady.' His eyes lock on hers. 'Though it may well be that you're a slippery one?'

The question rising at the end of what he says is quite direct, requiring her to declare any interest, unlike the way the shoemaker's boy has circled around in his attempts to court her. For once in Milva's life any words crackling through her mind don't make it to her throat.

That is not what she notices most, though. What commands her attention is the way her feet remain rooted to the spot instead of carrying her away from this saucy fellow.

Three onions, how can it be that a person's life can turn on such a humble thing, can change direction with the loosing of a few vegetables? It is a question she will ponder for all her days to come, for she cannot know it yet, but all that will befall her, hold her up, give her love and take it away, all those years spill out from this one, simple moment in the sun.

For this is how Milva comes to meet Private Cuddy Ranse, Irish by birth, English by regiment, and one of only thirteen non-native men in Gibraltar to be a Catholic, though he keeps it secret from his Commander.

This is how her name turns Irish and she grows into it, how her mother tongue is gradually cast aside, how her life surges forward, and she barely able to hold her grip on its coattails.

She discovers much later that in this fellow's homeland the name Cuddy is slang for a jackass, though he will often remind her that his proper name is Cuthbert, 'which me dear Ma back in Derry favoured, for it means bright shining one'.

CHAPTER ONE

GIBRALTAR, MID-1779

ELVA HOLDS TIGHT TO THE memory, runs it through her mind again. Was it only yesterday the boy was crawling on the narrow beach, clutching fistfuls of sand then scattering them towards the water?

The peace of it ran deep, Rogelio happy while she gazed across the vast bay as she had when she was his age, towards Algeciras where, out of sight, Spanish warships were quietly massing.

She keeps the memory close, even as her son's screams reach fever pitch and the patio shakes with each pounding. Pulling him tightly against her chest with one arm, she drops to her knees and crawls under the table.

"Shh, I keep you safe, chiquito. I here for you, always."

It's a promise only a barely seventeen-year-old mother, whose entire life has been contained between the limestone monolith rising fearsomely behind her and the sea ahead, would dare to make.

The floor shakes, dust fills her nostrils. She hears wood splintering above on the top floor, stone split asunder, stucco tearing away from outer walls. One storey down at the building entrance, vivid tiles crack from the walls, flower patterns falling in a mounting rubble of blue, maroon and cream petals.

The cannons lined up on the isthmus are finding their mark. Spain, emboldened by its alliance with France and early success towards taking back its territories in the Americas, wants Gibraltar back.

Melva clutches the rosary Cuddy gave as a promise in those first weeks, his pocket rosary that's been hers for three years, the green beads once easily hidden up his sleeve or tucked inside a shirt where the Protestant officers wouldn't see it. The beads dig into her skin and press painfully against the boy's sweating, squalling face, but she cannot move.

Papi would never have given his consent to the union had it not been that Cuddy, like him, was one for the Pope. Mama, on the other hand, had protested that a lowly enlisted man was not the right prize for her last daughter, let alone a fellow twice her age who saw humour where there was none. Melva did her best to show her mother that in Cuddy she'd found her true half orange, that he was the right match, though it was Cuddy, bless him, undeterred, who worked on Mama, charmed her, kept it up until she agreed to the marriage.

Now her brothers, sisters, their families, Papi and Mama are all gone to Minorca, leaving on supply ships the British organised for civilians. Mama begged her to leave with them, take the boy, but she knew better, trusted Cuddy to see them right.

Before the fighting, the British men often went to harlots on the border in La Linea. If that was Cuddy's habit until they married, she prefers not to know. She is enough for him now, and in the midst of this siege she needs him to be enough for her and their son, to keep them from harm.

Above the rumbling she hears a different thundering. Her old neighbour is beating on the door, roaring like a banshee. 'Bring the boy. Now! Go south, get to ground where the shot don't reach.'

By the time Melva opens the door her neighbour's skirts are disappearing down the stairs. She takes nothing except her son and runs, straining to keep her legs moving and mind empty.

As if by a miracle, the Spanish land batteries momentarily cease their barrage. Melva picks her way through smoking buildings, shutters torn away, past walls peppered with large holes, following women and children who were screaming a moment earlier but are now eerily silent.

Local legend has it that St Michael's Cave, on the Upper Rock, is an entrance to the underworld and now it's as though the doorway has opened, letting chaos and devilry into their town. Black magic, surely.

Even Rogelio has gone quiet on her hip, perhaps touched by his mother's numb calmness.

They straggle to the area above the Naval Hospital, where tents have already sprung up alongside a few rough huts built by those with more foresight than her and Cuddy. They thought their apartment at the far end of town would be safe, that Spanish guns could only reach the northern end, where their shot has already pounded Papi's fine gardens to muck. She has trusted Cuddy's assurance that the enemy couldn't target the rest of town, even as the Spanish built fortresses closer, got their hands on better ordnance.

Melva sits on a rocky ledge, studying the backs of her hands as they clasp the boy, looking at them as though they belong on the end of another's arms. Who has she become? Where is the girl who craved freedom, saw the hope of it in a man who dances on the Earth, his spirit light and easy?

Still shaken, she feeds her son, comforted by an old rhythm that runs deep in her, through every woman who ever birthed a child. Her milk is slowing and he will wean soon; she hopes not for a time. At least if she can still suckle him he won't starve.

She lost the first one before her belly began to swell, bleeding before dawn, bloodied pulp on the sheet to greet the light of day and only tears to show there'd ever been a baby growing inside. The second went the same way, then Rogelio was born early, a mite who survived on the hope she poured into him. He must have sustenance, cannot come to harm.

When signs of impending siege began, the garrison insisted that civilians who stayed must maintain six months of provisions. A fool's errand. Who could hope for that? She berates herself just the same for failing to make preparations, keeps scolding herself until she can't stand her thoughts a moment longer. She is still sitting there at dusk, spent, when Cuddy appears out of the smoking gloom.

'Thank the Lord. Bin lookin' for you everywhere.' He is panting, strands of hair have escaped from his hat, sweat beads on his lip. 'Let's get this set up.' He nods to the tent he carries against his hip.

They climb higher, to a strip of cleared land on Windmill Hill that, despite the slope, already has a row of tents pitched in neat triangles, dark mouths facing the sea.

Once their shelter has been hastily pegged and propped up, he makes to leave.

'No, Cuddy.' It explodes from her, a violent sound.

'I'll come back soon, with food for you and the boy, promise. I'm under orders to get back to my post. If they catch me here I'll get a flogging.' He takes in the sight of her wretched face and decides it's best not to say why every able-bodied man is on duty. Spanish gunboats, they've been told, have been seen approaching, testing how close they can get, and the hasty camp scattered up the southern slopes of The Rock could well be within their range.

Melva waits for food, sitting at the mouth of her tent and cradling the sleeping boy, the taste of terror cold as hammered copper in her mouth. Water, dear God, she will need to drink. No doubt the barrels and tinajas full of rainwater in the courtyard will have been smashed, and who knows what's happening to Cuddy's ration of two and a half gallons a day.

Cuddy. He's unlike any man she's known, partly why she loves him dearly. His regimental Commander refused to agree to their marriage so she is not on the strength, doesn't qualify for Army rations, use of the military's married quarters, medical care, any of the privileges of an Army wife. They must keep up a pretence, so he sleeps in the barracks with the single men.

He married her in anger, an act of rebellion they might both live to regret, declaring that he'd done what they demanded for twelve years, but damned if he'd let them choose who and when he wed.

They'd relied on Papi's gardens and shop to get by, with plenty of food to go with Cuddy's rations. Now the gardens are a wasteland and the shop is likely in ruins or looted of anything worth taking.

The crowding thoughts are wearing her thin. Melva crawls into the tent with the boy, curling around him on hard ground, exhaustion pinning her there till she gives in to a ragged sleep. She wakes when the boy stirs at dawn, to find no food and no Cuddy. The guns will start up soon, she must get water at least or the boy will get little milk today.

One of the big water cisterns, at a house on the edge of town, has eels to keep it clean. If the cistern is undamaged she might secure water, even catch one of the slippery creatures. She goes looking for her neighbour, a friend, anyone to take the boy. With him safe in other arms, she hurries towards the town. The British guns already blast from the north face of The Rock and within minutes the Spanish return fire, ending any silence.

Soon twenty-six heavy guns and mortars at the King's Bastion on the waterfront join in. Somewhere down there, in the casemates near the barracks, a battalion has swung into action, and Cuddy among them.

Melva suddenly pauses, struck as though by a blow, yet there is none, just the shock of grasping how precarious is her situation. She sees what Cuddy didn't, that this a fight with no end for months, till the British win or the population is starved into submission.

Cuddy will be little help, at the whim of his officers. She is on her own.

To her right, three local men are tearing timber from the doorway of a broken building to use for a rough hut in the camp. Fire billows from a top floor window, sending out black smoke that bites her eyes. Four or five doors down a pair of soldiers have found a supply of spirits in a ground floor apartment, and stagger along the street clutching a bottle in each hand, heedless of the gunshot.

For a moment she freezes, empty of thought, unable to believe her world has fractured faster than a shattered spine, no longer able to hold its form or anything that relies on it.

It is then she hears the boom, speeding closer, reverberating. In front of her the cobblestones fly up in a deadly spray. She flings her arms across her eyes and drops to her knees, but before she hits the ground the force of the shot knocks her sideways. Shards of stone rain down on her body, on her arms still covering her face. She tastes blood.

No, no, no. I can't die like this. Get up, get up.

She scrambles to her feet, bent over from shock, bleeding through a hole in her jacket sleeve. Her ear hurts, her legs shake. She must get back to Rogelio.

She remembers nothing till she reaches the camp, as though the hands on every clock have stopped. Only when she finds her son, takes him in her arms, does she tremble. Mama was right. She is witless, fat headed as an Andalusian donkey, telling herself she's different, that she's sharp, smart as a honey buzzard diving for larvae in a bee nest, when the joke's on her.

Mama's voice rises up in her mind, speaking the truth. *Stupid, stupid girl. Head on your shoulders, learn to use it.*

A water cart has arrived. She joins the throng jostling around it, pushing forward for a turn drinking deeply from a ladle.

At one o'clock the Spanish stop firing. Siesta, it seems. The Jewish merchant Belilo, also the local butcher, calls his brother to his side. 'It's safe for now. Make haste.' They begin striding towards town. Melva ties Rogelio to her back and joins the line of women and children who follow, hurrying to collect what they can and secure their homes.

At the patio her shoes crunch on broken tiles. The stairs are intact and she climbs to her apartment, the door still open from when she flung it aside. She loads her basket with all the food she can carry: bread, jamon, cheese, leftover calentita, spinach pie, and a few oranges and figs. So much food it seems she's ready for a feast – if so, the last she will have for years.

She reaches to the back of the cupboard, feeling around behind empty jars for the bag of coins used for household purchases. Rogelio, fed up with being confined in the sling, begins to squeal as she leans forward, fingers finding empty spaces.

'Aye yai yai, we've been robbed, little one.' Panicking, she shoves jars aside. Money matters more than ever. At last her fingers touch the velvet of the coin purse.

She is still leaning over, scrabbling in the cupboard, when she hears heavy boots on the stairs. 'Hush, Rogelio.' Melva knows only too well that she's of no consequence to the British soldiers if they're intent on taking what they can. The boy, sensing his mother's fear, cries harder.

Melva stands, swiftly turns, looking for a broom, but the wooden washing beetle is closer. She won't give up their money without a fight. Stepping closer to the doorway, she raises the pounding tool above her head, set to swing it hard, but a hand shoots out and grips her wrist before she can.

'Jesus, Mary and Joseph, you could crack a fella's head with that thing.' Cuddy's grin makes her want to hit him with it just the same.

'Where you been? We needed you.'

'You know how it works, darlin'. Even when we be in a bloody siege the Army's after first call on us men.'

Melva shakes her head. It's not fair, but he's right, though she's too distracted to suspect the game of cards that kept him up well past midnight, causing him to sleep later than he should.

'I come to get food and provisions for you and the boy, and to be sure no one's disturbed our things. Here, you take a few clothes, blankets. I'll get the rest.'

With both of them loaded up, he shutters the windows and locks the door behind them. They walk back to the camp soon after four o'clock.

'I gotta go. The sarge says most of us will be moved up here, out of range, in the next few days. It'll make it a bit easier to see you.' Mercifully the gunboats have not materialised.

He kisses her on the cheek, rubs his hand over the head of their son and is gone. Within the hour guns from both sides are booming again.

Day after day the rhythm of caring for her son is punctured by the sound of shells exploding, tearing the flesh of her town, splintering the only world she's known, and she must check her arms that she doesn't bleed, for it feels as though each volley pierces the frail protection of her skin.

She cries herself to sleep some nights, scooping Rogelio against her chest. Then in the daylight must crawl from the tent and do what has to be done to keep her boy well and herself strong, elbowing away others at the water cart, scrabbling in the dirt for spilled food, foraging for sea campion or a few late spears of wild asparagus.

At siesta she joins the crowd of women and civilian menfolk as they enter the streets, weaving their way around rubble, each hoping their home will be intact.

Her apartment has some external damage, but so far has withstood the bombardment. On the top floor a section of roof has been knocked in, and a shaft of sunlight shines on the top landing as though God beckons from his place on high, giving a sign of hope.

She lifts Rogelio onto her lap in the rocking chair, soothing herself with its gentle motion, a brief experience of predictability. What she would give now for ordinary domestic routines, for the safety of the walk to Papi's shop to collect vegetables and chickpeas.

A sharp sense of loss stabs her, but not for him. For Mama, of all people. She longs to see the familiar set of her face, the dumpy body moving purposefully, always committed to a task, plates piled high with raisin fritters. Growing up, any thoughts of Mama were about sharp words, a quick slap when she got things wrong. How calming it would be to have her here, even for a few minutes, her presence telling Melva what she needs so badly to hear. *Be strong, you will get through this.*

She shakes her head. What madness. Mama is hundreds of miles from here, no doubt fussing over a boiling pot, not worrying about comforting a wayward daughter.

Melva locks the apartment well before the end of siesta and walks back towards the camp. Civilians are now allowed to grow food on the side of The Rock, and she must weed the small vegetable patch she's scraped with a hoe, young cabbage shoots growing from Papi's seeds.

She needs to start thinking ahead, stop being the girl waiting for Papi or Mama to tell her what to do, and certainly not Cuddy, for he is caught up in the Army's demands.

The December day isn't particularly warm, maybe sixty degrees, but her son seems unusually red in the face. He is light against her hip, does not grow as fast as he should. The Spanish have succeeded in their blockade and some days, now the boy's largely weaned, all she can find to feed him is seaweed and wild onions cooked as a salty broth.

With the garrison running low on provisions, the Purple Death is rife. She has seen children at the camp with blackened skin and teeth fallen out for want of proper nourishment, their round eyes full of pleading. While occasional North African ships risk smuggling in food, only few succeed and the cost of what they sell is out of reach, such pain for the mothers.

In the shade of her tent she examines Rogelio's skin. He is a little hotter to the touch, but she tries to convince herself that he's fine. 'Sweet boy, grow strong like wild fig, roots reaching down into the earth.'

Cuddy's regiment is now camped nearby and at dusk he appears at her side, falling to his haunches, exhausted.

'I think Rogelio sickening.' Melva looks to her husband, willing him to know what to do.

He takes the boy in his arms, squeezing him first, then tossing him up in the air.

'Cuddy, stop it. He getting ill.'

'Looks like a fine young lad to me.' At the sound of his father's voice, the boy begins to cry miserably and does not let up, even after Cuddy returns to his camp. The crying continues all night, regardless of shouts from a nearby tent to 'shut that child up'.

Melva takes him from the tent at first light, walking and rocking her son, trying to settle his fractious state. Her easy-going boy is no longer. He cries piteously during the walk, waving starfish fingers as though shooing off invisible insects. As she pauses to catch her breath, the full glow of morning light touches the back of his hands, illuminating bright red spots spreading fast. Soon they appear on his face.

By early afternoon, her son has a fever and arches his back in pain. His open mouth reveals spots on his tongue and within hours welts spread along his arms and legs.

Water is tightly rationed, enough to spoon into his mouth but not to cool him. She resorts to fanning him with her shawl.

'The pox, no doubt about it.' The old neighbour gives an opinion from a distance. 'You'll be seeing blisters popping up soon enough.'

Melva knows children have already died. She has been counting each time she hears of a new death. Twenty-two so far; Rogelio must not be twenty-three.

When Cuddy next returns, two days later, the boy has agonising pustules covering his body, including his face, and despite a small respite his fever is back. Her precious son is a fragile bird she lays in the shade, his breathing laboured.

'Do something, Cuddy. Medicine, a doctor, some help?'

For the first time she sees fear in her husband's eyes. The Army will not spare its medicine for civilians, nor treat those not considered its own.

'Nothing any of us can do except pray, Melva. Here, give me your hand.'

They fall to their knees. Melva knows her man is bound to Catholic ways but he's not been a praying kind. His way is to laugh in the face of whatever God sends, and this fellow beside her, humble, earnest, trying to find the right words, has set off a band of pain across her chest, squeezing so hard she can't breathe, feels faint.

'Lord, I know I've not been to church in a long while, but I beg you to hear me out. This boy, he's innocent as the day, and don't deserve to die this way. Take me instead, if you're for taking someone, for I'm but a useless wretch. Dear Lord, spare our son, heal him, free him from pain. In the name of Jesus Christ, amen.'

Before Cuddy can finish crossing himself Melva's panic has peaked and she collapses against him. He throws an arm across her shoulders.

'Have faith, my girl. It's all that will bring him through now.' A few minutes later she sends a reluctant husband back to the soldiers' camp. It won't help any of them if he faces the lash because his commanding officer discovers he's married.

Though night creeps in, Melva sits wide-eyed, dry-eyed with her son, unable to feel anything but the incessant willing of him to fight. She chants it aloud to keep herself alert, certain it will be the end of him if she gives in to dozing. 'Keep fighting, little one. You can do it.'

A friend brings a precious bowl of water, laying it down at a distance because she doesn't want her own children to get the pox. Melva rips a strip of cotton from her petticoat, soaks it in the cool water and presses it to her son's forehead again and again.

There is no priest for succour, for blessing. She bends to the bowl, then to her son, back and forth with the cloth in her hand, the ritual of every mother with a feverish child. He is holy, this boy, he is holy. Lord have mercy.

CHAPTER TWO

GIBRALTAR, 1779-1783

HOW DO YOU MEASURE ONE night in a person's life? A few minutes, an eternity? Or a line marking before and after and there's never any going back? One night can be the difference between a girl and a woman, the slim margin between innocence and insight.

It is in the long night where Rogelio teeters on the brink of life and death, where a single breath is enough to shift such a delicate balance, that the substance of the girl Melva once inhabited is burned in the fire that comes, in the end, to every person. The woman who clambers from the tent next morning, her son's limbs dangling as she hugs his limp frame to her chest, will never again be unknowing. She will see the world as it is, in all its glory and its many horrors.

The speckled monster spares the boy, but only just. He is weak at first, doesn't turn his eyes to follow movement around him, not even the outline of his father when he arrives later that day, and Melva fears he has lost his sight.

Next morning, though, he is more alert, reaching out for the stale bread she holds up in front of his eyes. The weeping sores turn to scabs in the following days, healing slowly into pock marks that scar his face and body, the sign that God has touched him, drawn a map on his skin showing the way to a grave long distant, or so his mother hopes.

Melva, for her part, goes quiet for a long time. Cuddy is unchanged, just as much the lad he's always been, only now more confirmed about the power of his prayer.

'Make deal with the Lord, Cuddy? Who think they do that.' She tries to hide the disdain in her voice, though it is plain enough.

How she longs to sit at the table with Papi, hearing his stories as night quickened. The steady beat of his voice as he told the story beloved by Greeks and Romans, of how the Rock of Gibraltar was one of the Pillars of Hercules, holding up the sky at one end of their known world.

She has married a loveable man, jovial, not visited by worries. She has been drawn to him willingly, cares for him deeply, but the true nature of what she has chosen is now laid bare and she can think of nothing else.

Her husband is no pillar holding up her sky. He can surely make the sun shine down with his beaming face and tomfoolery, but she is the one called to grapple with clouds and rain.

She was giddy stepping through the days of the courting dance, and only now does she remember the knowing looks that passed between Mama and Papi, who surely knew this day would come. Time is the friend of the truth.

Now as she walks her feet strike the earth a little harder, each step bearing down as though her shoes have iron soles, yet she feels less sure-footed than in the days of scrambling after goats.

If Cuddy notices the change in her, he says nothing.

After the smallpox comes yellow fever and influenza, both mercifully passing over Melva, Cuddy and Rogelio, though she is weakened twice by dysentery coming from open troughs used as latrines, which contaminate water. She has stopped counting how many have been taken by the speckled monster, more than five hundred in the end, and why waste time with all that counting?

Melva wakes daily from fitful sleep with only one thought on her mind – how to find food. The New Year is two weeks under way, the beginning of the new decade of 1780, a round, fat number that does nothing to fill a belly when you and your child starve.

She looks out towards the long finger of the harbour wall, reaching out into the bay, with nary a ship to unload there for months. A tiny movement catches her eye, as though something approaches from the sea. She shakes her head sharply to rid herself of hope, a harmful thorn that will dig in and poison a soul in circumstances like these. Far better, she thinks, to keep your mind on the immediate necessity of staying alive.

Within minutes, others have seen it too and are shouting. Gradually it hoves into sight, a Royal Navy brig that's made it through the Spanish blockade. As it moors at the end of the New Mole breakwater, out of reach of cannon fire, a crowd begins to press down the hill towards it but are waved back by a regimental officer from the nearby Army camp. Melva can't hear what he shouts but it's clear they must wait.

Impatient and needing to soothe herself, she walks Rogelio through rows of tents towards the east, in the direction of Europa Point, desperate to see the place where the Atlantic Ocean is defeated by the Mediterranean Sea. Nature trusting itself to yield in saltwater, tides and wind, while she must fight and struggle.

Her son staggers like a tiny drunkard, still learning steadiness on his feet. Usually it would be amusing, a small pleasure taken in a dreary, anxiety-ridden day, as any mother might when doting on a child. The boy looks up at her, waiting for a smile, but there is none, only a furrowed brow as she fights the desire to believe the end of the siege is nigh.

She longs for salt-moist air in her lungs instead of the acrid bite of gunpowder, can hardly believe that through the wreath of gun smoke the tongue of Gibraltar still laps at the sea, the same as always, while all else has been rent asunder.

Back at the tent she studies the ramparts below, the red specks of sentries on guard, the cluster of officers gathered near the gangplank of the brig, trying to discern what their movements might mean for the future.

Hours later Cuddy turns up, brimming with news. 'We're saved, we'll have food again, Melva.' He wraps his arms around her waist and scoops her high, swinging her around.

'Put me down,' she demands. 'What happening?'

He's breathless with excitement. 'Told you they wouldn't let us down. A great victory's been had, ships with new copper bottoms, they overpowered part of the Spanish fleet and got through the lines.'

His voice is rising, unstoppable. 'Fought them even at night, a moonlight battle they said. In a storm, would you believe.'

She has heard enough, cuts him off.

'Cuddy, forget battle. Tell me, what this mean for us?' She tips her head towards their son.

'The Royal Navy's got a convoy of ships heading this way, bringing supplies, tomorrow they reckon. You and the boy will get meat, vegetables. We'll all get to eat proper again.'

She grips his arm. 'This the end, is it over?'

His grin fades. 'Why would you be thinking that? The enemy's not done with us yet.'

To his surprise she sobs into his shoulder.

The following evening the ships begin to arrive. The guns have fallen silent and Melva and many of the women walk into town, a ragtag group with not one clean walking out cape between them. The garrison is already celebrating, and wine shops closed to prevent disorder have reopened, doing a roaring trade.

Through the door of one Melva sees Cuddy laughing with other soldiers, swilling a dark drink. She pauses, shifts her toddler from one hip to the other, uncertain whether to join in or to step up and berate him. In the end she does neither, turning quietly and retracing her steps to their tent. Once Rogelio is asleep she cries again, for surely tears are the only sane response to a world gone mad.

During the next month or two Gibraltar's luck holds. A Newfoundland ship gets into the harbour with a cargo of salt fish, then a Danish ship is boarded under the cover of fog and a cargo of lemons captured. Melva's coins ensure she has citrus to ward off scurvy for Rogelio, though as the weeks pass she sinks into the knowledge that it has only been a brief reprieve.

She has been born into the tumult of a place where Italians, Arabs, Jews, Englishmen, sailors from all nations, have spilled through streets, shops and bodegas, a place where anything can happen. She learned the stories at Papi's feet, of the Barbary pirates who favoured the town for raids, taking hostages to sell into slavery; the conquerors who lost and won. Yet she's just as shocked as her fellow camp-dwellers at what unfolds next.

In August she is in their tent under a clear, starry sky. Cuddy stayed till dark, when he left for the military camp, and the lingering sense of comfort from his touch shepherds her gently towards sleep.

A few guns fire listlessly from the Spanish lines near the isthmus and she hears the British guns respond in short bursts. The sequence is hardly welcome, but it has become familiar, a strange scaffolding to her days and now her nights.

The next sound has her sitting bolt upright. 'That was close,' she says aloud, involuntarily. More shots quickly follow. Around her screams erupt, and by the time she throws back the tent flap a moving mass of women, children and the few civilian men are running.

The firing comes from the water near the town's sea walls, aiming for the soldiers' encampment and the civilian shanties.

Cuddy. Ay Dios mio, let him be okay.

She clutches Rogelio and runs, hitching her nightshift past her knees to gain more speed, looking for the nearest hollow or cave in the rocks. Some of those fleeing are half-naked, others with only a blanket thrown over them, as shells and balls rain down below.

'What do they want from us? Do you know?' Surely the butcher, panting nearby with his family gathered around him, can explain the attack. No answer comes. He is staring, mouth open, to the edge of the camp, where a wooden hut explodes and burns.

The gunfire peppers the area above the Naval Hospital, while little response comes from their side.

'Gunboats.' The butcher seems pleased to have worked it out. 'They've sneaked in with small gunboats.' He looks at his fearful wife. 'General Eliott won't let them get away with it.'

Down in the casements, Eliott has a different view. If little damage is done, then he's not willing for the garrison's ammunition to be wasted.

The firing continues for hours, while Melva and hundreds of others scattered up the hill watch in horror, too afraid to rest. 'Perhaps,' they reassure each other, 'the butcher is right and Eliott will put a stop to it'.

They would be better served, however, to forget Eliott and think instead of Spanish Admiral Barceló, corpulent as only a man with a history of military success can be. Tonight is just the start of his new cunning plan.

At dawn the townspeople emerge from their rocky shelters and return to survey the damage. Other than the burnt hut and a few damaged tents, all is still as it was.

Melva resists the urge to go in search of Cuddy, well-schooled as she is in the role of secret military wife. When Rogelio naps late morning, she curls up with him and sleeps as well.

In the coming nights, she and all inhabitants of the camp come to grasp that they've entered a fresh hell. Within an hour of darkness descending the gunboats often return to bombard what they can reach from the sea, night after night sending everyone scattering for safety. Harassment is the weapon Barceló's wielding.

Tempers fray from lack of sleep and anger rises. When Cuddy next visits his wife is one spark away from an explosion.

'Eliott has a plan, you can be sure of it.' Cuddy's attempt at reassurance supposes that his wife would be fool enough to believe the General shared his tactics with him or any enlisted man.

Melva is strung out, fraught. 'What is this Army of yours, Cuddy?' She flings an arm out to encompass the camp. 'Us with dark skin, good enough when we grew food, mended boots, sewed uniforms. Don't count now, do we?'

She is shouting, tugging at his sleeve.

'Now, now dear girl. Eliott will have a reason he's biding his time.' He folds her into his arms, holds her close. 'Just you wait and see.'

Waiting is all Melva seems to do, months of it slowly grinding into years. She exists in a void without time, hope or purpose, fear as thick as the gun smoke that shrouds the sea, obscuring its dazzle so that some days she wonders if the tide has run out and kept going, leaving The Rock to its fate.

Eliott has finally acted, though it took the deaths of Belilo the butcher, a regimental sergeant and two civilians before he ordered that a pair of double-fortified sea mortars, newly fixed to the old harbour wall, fire on the main Spanish camp whenever the gunboats visit.

Cuddy's smile-creased face has become grim these days, not just because the siege continues unabated. Troops have been ordered to find and destroy alcohol supplies, and strict discipline is being enforced. He shows up more often at her tent without the temptation of drink, cards or dice.

'Must be a comfort to have your man here more often.' The old neighbour, face stern as ever, has dropped by to check on Melva and her son. Her remark is harmless enough, Melva knows, but it touches a raw spot in her chest.

'No comfort at all,' she spits out.

The old woman smooths her skirts and looks out to sea, beyond Europa Point, taking her time, while Melva feels the sting of shame for snapping at her in such an unprovoked way.

'A husband can only be what he is. Most choose to see their woman as the weaker vessel. They refuse to look in the mirror, not wishing to gaze on where the true weakness lies.'

The neighbour turns to Melva. 'Take heart. A wife forged in fire is stronger than iron. Like iron, she bends to bear any weight coming down.'

Weary to her marrow, Melva could slap the old one there and then for pretending that difficulties could possibly be a boon. She is so tired she wonders how blood even bothers to flow through her veins.

'Deny it to yourself if you will, but I've seen you grow up. Aye, you're no weak vessel, so maybe it's time to stop acting like you are.'

The old woman puts a palm on the ground, pushes herself up from where she's been squatting and wanders off without a backward glance.

Rogelio, wary of the neighbour, watches her leave and wanders over, still not too big to fall into Melva's lap. She rests her chin lightly on his shoulder, feeling it rise gently with each breath he takes.

'Have I given up?'

If Rogelio heard the question he gives no sign, tugging on a few dry blades of grass that have miraculously survived hundreds of boot-heels.

Every day, Melva hoists Rogelio on her back and walks without destination, mostly to Europa Point, but anywhere it's safe. Often she repeats her route several times, despite stares from onlookers, passing through the rows of tents and out to open space, returning only to leave again.

The act of walking has become its own purpose, each footfall striking the ground like a match to flint, setting off a charge from the earth that surges through her. She imagines a storehouse deep in her chest where she holds the energy, locks it tight, without knowing why.

She walks and walks, dried grass stuffed in worn-out boots to cover the holes. Battles rage at sea and on land, yet she steps out, keeps going during the weeks it takes to finish the wholesale destruction of her childhood town. She walks while scavenging for wild berries, or handfuls of oatmeal from a cask burst by a shell, keeping herself and Rogelio alive in the long months between two more relief convoys carrying supplies, with the little of Cuddy's rations he can sneak to them.

Driving rain swamps the camp and strong wind flattens her tent, yet she goes on. Like a lost traveller starting the long road home, Melva sets her sights on moving, one leg then the other, one minute after the next, one day at a time.

Cuddy doesn't see the point of it, though he has long stopped trying to discourage her. He is recovering himself but not from an ailment of the mind or spirit. He has come from a week in hospital with enteric fever, which has swept through the ranks. Still weak, his head throbbing, the vomiting has abated and fever broken, but he needs to check on his wife and son, dragging himself to the camp to let her know he's recovering.

Melva barely knows the year. Walking has given a rhythm to her days, marking time better than any calendar she's known.

'Seems this is it, love. Word has it a truce will be signed soon, heard it from the mouth of my own Commander when he were talking to the surgeon.'

He is standing back, keeping his distance so any sick fumes can't reach her. She lifts her eyes to his gaunt face, wants to stroke it.

'What month we in, Cuddy?'

His heart aches with all he has not given her or done for her in these years, let alone the boy now four years old. This is one thing he can manage, though, offering up a date pinned in the steady forward march of time, hoping it will bring her to rest.

'Tis near the end of January in the year 1783, Melva. A good time to end the siege, end the war … and maybe call to a halt your walking.'

She nods as though agreeing, not believing a word he's said about peace, and ignoring the suggestion about coming to stillness.

Even when news comes through the following month of a signed truce, Britain keeping Gibraltar, the Franco-

Spanish taking Menorca and parts of the West Indies and Florida, she refuses to believe it.

All around is destruction and ruin, yet the sea lavenders bloom from crevices, larkspurs and candytufts dare to flaunt purple and pale violet flowers on rockfaces, and native thyme insists on flowering. Melva wants so badly to feel joy at the signs of spring but is dogged by gloom.

On the tenth of March the frigate, *Thetis,* moors in a harbour full of such unaccustomed silence that it swells in Melva's ears, and she thumps them to shake it loose. The vessel brings dispatches confirming the end of the siege and the American War.

Late that afternoon Melva joins the celebrations, watching a military parade followed by the rapid fire of a twenty-one gun salute. When no answering fire comes from the Spanish line she finally allows herself to receive the certainty that the fighting is done.

She stands in the main street, where rows of patios still smoulder, and watches people dance and shout in newfound freedom. As she lifts her eyes to The Rock's limestone cliff-face, a shadow crosses it as though wiping a blackboard clean. She looks for the cloud that sent it, but there is none.

CHAPTER THREE

GIBRALTAR, LATE 1783

C LEANLINESS, PROPER DRINKING WATER AND food, shelter allowing decency and dignity. Peace brings none of it. With most remaining civilians fleeing in the months after the siege, the ruins of the town are inhabited only by a growing population of black rats and cockroaches.

Cuddy is alive while hundreds of soldiers have died. Melva tries to be grateful, but he is still poorly, tired most of the time and continues to be on the regiment's sick list, making him on half pay.

Half of nothing. Melva doesn't say it aloud. It hangs in the air between them, an unwelcome guest in the hut they have cobbled together for her and Rogelio. Cuddy's eight pence a day was, in any case, whittled down to sixpence thanks to the Army's stoppages for rations, clothing, shoes, and the semblance of medical care given to the men. The threepenny bit they get now is barely enough for a pound of cheese and a half loaf of bread.

Famine has flattened Melva's curves, though she's no thinner than others. She leaves the boy with Cuddy and takes work at the military washhouses near the cemetery, ignoring her husband's objections.

'Money is needed, Cuddy, for buy food.' The patio is uninhabitable and little of their furniture or belongings, let alone what her parents left behind, has been salvageable.

At the washing huts where troops' bedding is laundered she barely notices the filth as she skirts large pools of stagnant, foul water. How Mama would have rolled her eyes that she has been brought so low.

Melva has no desire to work at the huts, but aside from the money, the strength stored in all the days of endless walking is bursting through, demanding expression through useful action.

By the end of the week her hands are red, cracked, and fit to bleed. She returns to their ramshackle hut, pushing open the crooked door, where Cuddy greets her with a smile, the corners of his mouth turning up for the first time in weeks.

'There'll not be a need any more for you to be up to your elbows in hot suds.'

She sits on a box they use as a stool and is barely settled when Rogelio rushes over and buries his head in her waist.

'Come by pot of gold, have we?' She smiles back.

'Got news, Melva. We're getting out of this busted up place, going where we'll have a home, a future.'

A pain starts up at the base of her skull, spreading through her jaw, her teeth aching as though they've been clamped together in a vice.

'What you say?'

'They've no need for us, what with the war being done. We be sent back to England in two weeks.'

Melva's spine stiffens against the words that seem to travel so lightly, bubbling from her husband's mouth. The hand that's been rubbing Rogelio's shoulders freezes mid-air.

'A new life, me darlin'. A fresh start for all of us.'

She studies his face, her own devoid of movement.

'Say something, Melva. I'll get a pay-out, find work, you'll see.'

She should feel something. Maybe dismay at never seeing Mama and Papi again, sadness at leaving the place of her birth, or should it be hope for a better life for their son, who has seen more dreadful things than a child should? She searches within, finding barely a ripple of response as her moorings loosen and she floats, eyes no longer seeing her husband but the hunched body of the adivina. *A long journey. Misfortune.*

How little she knows of the world or the way life works, the girl who thought fate was for others, never her. Yet here it comes to claim her, willing or not, laughing in her face, cackling with glee. *See? I never let you go. You're mine, all mine.*

'What comes out my mouth is dust in the wind, Cuddy.'

She pushes aside the dull mood that cloaks her and, ignoring her husband's urging against the work, keeps going daily to the washing huts. Where once she walked away the hours of waiting, now she labours at the washtubs to defeat them.

Only when the transports moor in the harbour and loading begins does she abandon endless wet bedsheets, walking alone next morning to Europa Point. The big sky stretches forever across the Mediterranean, and she watches the sun steadily rise, willing it to warm the husk she has become, to mend what has been crushed.

Even when she gouges fingernails into the soft underside of her wrist she remains numb, as though pain no longer has the means to reach her. She scans the sky again, silently praying at first, then begging for release from the cage built not by bricks but by gunshots, explosions, starvation, terror.

As she tips her face skyward a movement catches her eye, a dark dot coming fast across the strait from Morocco, and as it gets closer it splits into ten, twenty, then so many she loses count. By the time she recognises the Griffon vultures, hundreds, maybe a thousand wheel, dive, soar above her. A vast mass of claws, sharp beaks and feathers ride the thermals, cumbersome, heavy bodies made gossamer light by wide wings and the lift of air.

Their unexpected grace, appearing from nowhere, frees the tension under her ribs. Her body softens, throat opens, and a rush of keening flows through. She wails out fear and grief to the vultures, lets them take it, never once taking her eyes from the birds, though tears blur her vision. On and on the sound goes, despair without end, rising to meet the mass of life drifting, sweeping above.

Soon the vultures stretch long necks, gather into a tight formation that faces towards their destination, and head inland over Spain.

As they leave, Melva's hands reach high in a gesture of benediction, though she cannot tell if it is a blessing given or received. Once the birds have disappeared she is spent, sinking onto stony ground to recover. In the peace that floods through years of emptiness, a message arrives unbidden, an understanding she has blocked for weeks.

Though starvation has stopped her monthly bleeding for more than two years, a child has miraculously taken root in her womb.

She weeps anew, for this, she knows with every breath, is no miracle at all but a burden that may be too great to bear.

Reckless, that's what she and Cuddy have been. It's yet another truth that slaps her in the face during the month.

Her husband, funny, mostly cheerful, sometimes childish, can't see the ears of the wolf. He has been blind to the dangers hidden in their marriage, and now they are about to bite.

He arrives home to fess up that there's no place allocated for Melva and Rogelio on the transports to England. They wed without the Commander's approval so the Army does not recognise her as a wife, bears no responsibility.

'We rot here or die when you gone. That it?' She's done with pretty words that forgive her husband's ways, especially with another baby on the way.

'Dear no, my love. We get you a passage, mebbe on a merchant ship.'

'You making coins these days, Cuddy? Any not needed for staying alive are long gone to drink and tobacco.'

He pauses, unsure how to handle the stern woman who's materialised before him.

'You tell your officer, I just the same as him, belly empty through siege, worse even, no rations. You tell him I washed, mended clothes for you, cleaned bedding for others. Least he can do is get me and the boy on a ship, treat me like proper wife.'

She reads what crosses his mind without him needing to open his mouth.

'If it comes to a lashing, you pays the price.' Her chin points upward, in a show of strength that belies the weak sensation in her gut. Right now she doesn't care about him getting caught out for being married, the drum major with the cat-o-nine-tails likely to meet him at the flogging frame in Grand Parade. The lives of two children are at stake.

'You're not meanin' that, darling. Them's angry words and I'm not blaming you, but a thrashing will do me no good.'

She's so riled it is all she can do not to ball up her fists and beat his chest. Why did Mama never tell her? Where there's love in a marriage, hate hides there too. She bristles with it, overcome by its urgent, sudden arrival.

They argue loudly till Rogelio starts screaming and covers his ears with his hands. Cuddy leaves soon after for the barracks, before evening roll call.

His health has gradually improved and he has been placed on invalid duties, returning at midday after morning sentry duty.

'Squabbling will na do, wife. We have to stick together.' She lets him wrap his arms around her, squeezing her close. When he lets go, he breaks into a grin.

'I chanced some words with the Commander a mite earlier. He's disposed to us, though not official like. He's of a mind to get you two on a ship.'

Her hand flies to her chest. 'Thank the Lord.'

'Won't be on the same transport as me, darling. One that leaves a week after.'

Cuddy, flushed with relief his wife and son will not be left behind, has chosen to forget what he overheard as he left the Commander's quarters. The war-weary officer turned to the secretary holding the regimental discharge book, not even bothering to whisper. 'Another dead loss we're clearing out.'

The days blur into one, as though Melva wakes to live the same day again and again, stopping with a jolt on the day Cuddy must board his ship.

Despite informing the Commander he's married he feels obliged to maintain the pretence of being single, 'for the fellow has spared me a floggin'. They hug their goodbyes in the privacy of the hut, Melva holding herself tight, not wishing Rogelio to see her distress as Cuddy walks off to the barracks.

When dawn breaks she takes the four year old's hand and, head tight from lack of sleep, walks to the harbour. The transport's deck is a mass of movement, men lashing down final casks, ropes being readied, orders shouted. She searches for a glimpse of her husband, though there is none. As the vessel is dragged from its mooring and sails begin to catch the wind, there is still no sign of him, and she fears he is already lost to her. She begins to cry quiet tears of despair, wiping her eyes when Rogelio tugs on her hand.

'Papa, Papa.' The boy waves excitedly. Cuddy has come to the rail. He cups his hands around his mouth, shouting something to her, but the words scatter before they reach her ears.

She blows him a kiss, waves with a vigour she doesn't feel as he pulls away, slowly shrinking until he is a mere hint of red, then nothing. She watches until the ship grows smaller and is swallowed by the grey of fathomless ocean, ignoring Rogelio pulling at her to leave.

When her turn comes there is no one to wave her off, no family, not even the old neighbour, gone from this world a month before the siege ended.

Melva walked the day before up the slopes of The Rock, where once she chased goats and tasted freedom, Rogelio grizzling and needing to be piggybacked from time to time. Her eyes remained steadfastly on the sea, distant mountains and coast. She would not allow the broken town, her shattered beginnings, to be the final memory leaving with her.

She knelt beside her son, drew him into a hug, then held his face near hers. 'No more guns, no more hunger, dear one. Papi says where we go you have good life'. She has no vision of this place across the Atlantic, must trust that Cuddy waits there, that at last they can live together as a family.

The sloop, a merchant ship hired by the Navy, is small, made more crowded by extras carelessly added to the manifest at the last minute, she and Rogelio among them. With no seafaring experience, even she can see how worn and ill-kept it is.

The sea all her life has held her in its embrace, enfolding her town and the enduring companion of The Rock. Now that she must give herself and her son over to it, the vast expanse of water seems less of a friend.

Standing at the rail, Rogelio quiet in her arms, she chooses to keep her back to the sea as their ship swings out towards the north-east, where its two square-rigged main sails are slow to catch prevailing winds in the Bay of Gibraltar.

At first The Rock seems to follow her, looming tall as ever, but gradually it wanes, until it is a shrunken lump by the time the ship turns its bow towards the coast of Spain. She wants to stop watching its diminishing peak but cannot.

Rogelio is squirming now and she puts him down on the deck, holding fast to his hand. Her heart aches, for she is Llanito no more, and who is she if not Gibraltarian? Will she be somebody, with the bindings of place torn away?

The boy pulls free and she is forced to look away from all that represents her past. He is squealing, a delighted sound, and she begins to smile despite herself, until she sees that the object of his amusement is a rat that he and two other children are chasing, while seamen roar with laughter. After she has caught her son and given him a scolding she takes one last look back towards the harbour, then turns to face the open sea.

It is over. The horizon draws a pale line between all that came before and all that will be. The ship rises and falls, and she wonders if dying is like this, travelling the in-between, the hand of another at the helm, not knowing if heaven or more hell is yet to come. She shifts uncomfortably, sitting with her back against a water barrel. Fear will change nothing so best to imagine she sails towards a better, happier life.

As if to reinforce the thought, when darkness steals down a trio of English sailors, free of tasks till their midnight watch, pull out a fiddle, fife and banjo to sing ballads, slapping knees and calling to each other in the chorus rounds. Melva rocks Rogelio on her lap as the trio launches into a song they call Spanish Ladies, the fiddle player winking at her as his bow races up and down the strings to lusty words.

When they start the Song of Solomon her heart responds as their voices soften, singing in harmony. 'Many waters cannot quench love, neither can floods drown it.' She feels the music work its way to her core, a warmth melting what has hardened against her man, and by the end of the song she senses again the strength of the love that ties her to Cuddy. Praise God its flow will never cease again.

Soon the men shift to bawdier rhymes, and she takes Rogelio below to the dead air of their bunk.

Despite worries about the ship's safety, their journey up the coast of France is uneventful and a flush of excitement at seeing Cuddy, at starting anew, begins to creep in.

Near the Isles of Scilly they sail into a rogue gale. Passengers are battened down below in darkness, the vessel's seams leaking water that is soon putrid with vomit and piss. Several times Melva is knocked from her bunk, losing grip on Rogelio as her feet slide on wet planking. She can't tell if what thumps against her, knocking her down time after time, is her boy, a wooden pail, or one of the other women.

'Rogelio, Rogelio.' Her screams join those of others, and in the chaos it is astonishing that she and the terrified boy find each other again.

On the second day the leak is so bad the crew must pump the ship every half hour. Melva tears the hem from her patched skirt and ties her wrist to her son's. The gale does not abate till late on the fourth day, and when they are finally allowed on deck, dragging their wet bedding with them, she emerges squinting, daylight hurting her eyes. She is filthy, hair and clothes stinking. Rogelio, cowed by the ordeal, has purple bruises from head to toe.

'It over, my love. Soon we see Papi.' She clutches him against her, the boy gripping her legs.

Though England is in sight they are far from landing when they arrive in September. The sloop must ride six days' quarantine at the Motherbank, off the Isle of Wight in the English Channel, where at least they are given food.

A strange haze fills the air, through which the sun burns oven red yet throws no warmth. Melva stares, unable to understand the strangeness of it or the reason why her eyes and nose sting. While she was reeling in Gibraltar at the end of a long war, a volcano in Iceland was erupting, spewing sulfuric fumes that have spread in a slow, deadly spiral across Europe, reaching England a few weeks ahead of her. Corn has withered in Norfolk, and in the south, blades of wheat have turned brown as though scorched by frost, and labourers have died from the poisonous air.

'Looks for all the world like Judgement Day be comin'.' The wife of one of the Gibraltar Governor's footmen laughs nearby, pleased with her joke.

The eerie light has made navigation difficult, though the sloop is one of two fortunate vessels to get a small window in the glowing fog to moor at Portsmouth. As the ship is warped from the harbour to the wharf, six men straining on the capstan as the rope pulls tight, she surveys the waterfront with eyes already red-raw, hoping for a glimpse of a familiar figure in a red coat. When there is none, she chides herself for expecting him to be there. *Hardly knows when we arrive.*

From the time she boarded the vessel she has forgotten the fear he might vanish, that she and her son will land in a foreign country with no home, no means of support. Now it rears up in her. She begins to tremble, her stomach churning.

'Mama, Mama.' Rogelio is pointing. For a moment she thinks he has caught sight of his father, but it is a small monkey on a chain, dancing on a man's shoulder, that has captured his attention.

A new thought startles her. *What if he got sicker, not better, and is buried deep in the ground?*

Her panic is interrupted by orders for all passengers to collect their belongings and prepare to disembark, the shouts barely audible above the din coming from wharves and piers that appear and disappear in the dry fog. She gathers her bag and pulls her son against her hip as passengers surge towards the gangplank, desperate to be free of the ship's confines. Melva hangs back, unsure what to do when her feet reach dry land.

'Go, Mama. We go.' Rogelio takes the lead.

She and her son are pushed and pulled, jostled this way and that, and in the thick gloom she loses her bearings, doesn't know which way she's facing or where to go. With one hand outstretched she finds a timber wall, feels her way along it to a shallow doorway, where she and Rogelio shelter from the crowd.

Each minute stretches into an eternity. She remains there, unable to decide what to do, who to ask for help.

'Hungry, Mama.' The boy whimpers, then begins to cry in messy gulps.

A man's voice booms nearby. 'What's this, missus? Need a place to stay?' His face appears from the haze, wet lips, leering gaze. He is barrel-chested, broad-shouldered. With her back against the door she is trapped.

'The little 'un. He be needin' bread, mebbe cheese. Come with me.'

He towers over her, blocking the way as he reaches out to grab her arm. Immediately, with no thought, only instinct, her knee jerks up and strikes him in the softest place she can.

He staggers back, clutching the front of his britches, roaring in rage.

'Filthy darkie whore. You be payin' for that.' He raises a fist to smack her in the face, but she is small, light, and ducks under his arm, running and dragging Rogelio behind. Her bag is abandoned.

She hurtles slap bang into another woman, the footman's wife. 'Crazy to be running in this fog, girl. We gotta wait at the end of the wharf. The rummagers gotta go through our goods afore we leave. As if any of us got anything worth troubling customs.'

'Have nothing, no bag.'

'They be still wantin' to check you two over, know you're not sick.'

The woman seems to know where to go along the wharf. Melva follows close behind, checking over her shoulder when she dares.

The queue is long and the boy becomes fretful again. Melva hasn't a crumb to give him. She had foolishly put the ship's biscuit she'd saved in the bag left behind. She lifts him onto her hip, drawing him close, the comfort doing nothing to soothe his grumbling belly.

At last they reach the customs desk. 'Name?'

She identifies herself and Rogelio. The officer quickly scans his list, then fixes her with a hard stare that takes in skin far darker than his pallid face.

'Can't see that surname here. If you're not on the list, you're not allowed in.' He purses his mouth, pleased he's spotted a rock scorpion, what the British lads call the Gibraltar locals, a foreign alien sneaking into the country.

Rogelio is still on her hip, the weight of him sending a pain down her leg, and she swings him to the other side to stop herself collapsing. She summons her best English.

'Please, look more. Husband a soldier, came before.'

He looks down, considers the list more slowly while she waits, Rogelio whimpering 'mama, mama' into her shoulder.

'Where's your baggage?'

'Haven't any. It lost'

His eyebrows lift, but his finger slows then rests on their names. He makes an entry in the passenger book, and waves them through. Beyond the gateway she steps to the side, away from the stream of people moving by. There is nothing to be done but wait.

In the strange, stinging fog she cannot see the movement of the sun, does not know how much time passes. One hour, two, maybe three. The business of the port continues around them, not heeding the mother and child, and begins to wind down. No more ships will berth today.

She sits on a low bollard, Rogelio dozing on her lap after exhausting himself in crying for want of food. Watching him, tiredness overcomes her too, and her chin begins to drop to her chest, the hubbub around her dimming as she rests. Through it comes a recognition, a sound that seems familiar, though she cannot say how.

She jerks upright. It is her name, Cuddy calling her name.

'Here, Cuddy. Over here.' She shouts it again and again as she and Rogelio get to their feet.

'Call for Papa, Rogelio.'

They call his name, wait for an answer, then call again. Suddenly the haze parts and he is upon them, flinging his arms around the pair.

'Bin comin' every day since you was at Motherbank. So glad to see the pair of you.'

At last she can slump against his chest, relief washing through. Cuddy is here; all will be well.

They stop at an inn for bread, a little fatty mutton, and cheese. As she tucks into the food Melva can't tell if Cuddy has recovered full health or is simply fired up with excitement. He looks different without the red coat and its forty shiny buttons, which he hastens to say he sold back to his captain for a tidy sum. He also sold the woollen breeches, gaiters and hat, keeping only the linen shirt from his uniform, some of the money used to buy the kind of brown jacket seen on every rough workman in London.

'Got us a room, Melva. What with the pay owed me and a few shillings they give me for the bayonet, we can eat well, start gettin' ahead.'

Perhaps it slips his mind that he also got fourteen days subsistence, a sum given to encourage discharged men to go back to their home parish. In any case, most of it is already gone on dice, bets on bare-knuckle boxing, and grog.

Cuddy reaches over and tweaks his son's chin. 'Bin thinking, Melva. Best to call the boy Roger from now on. Easier for him.'

She stiffens. 'Ro-gair? Not his name.'

'Rog-er. He be settlin' in better with an English name. Won't draw notice to bein' from elsewhere.'

She pushes a lump of bread into her mouth and chews, then shakes her head at her husband, though her silence is taken as agreement. The boy will always have a coloured mother, which Cuddy can't deny. If she gives up her son's proper name, surely there's little else left to give away?

She lets the question go, comforting herself with the thought that her family is back together, stronger in reuniting. She is still young, unaware that it wasn't wise to ask such a question, even to herself, that sacrifice is a deep well that some must plumb further than others in giving up what they value for what may be more important.

CHAPTER FOUR

ST GILES IN THE FIELDS, 1783-1788

THEIR ROOM IS DOWN A narrow alleyway in St Giles in the Fields, about a mile west of London's city walls. Unlike the streets of Gibraltar there are few glimpses of sky and no shimmering sea, only a sluggish brown river out of sight. When winds finally disperse the sulphuric haze, tall buildings throw shadows that darken doorways and corners, and Melva coughs as chimneys belch coal smoke that clings to fog vapour, making a filthy pea-souper.

She hasn't heard the term 'slum' before coming here. Where she grew up, there were poorer parts of the town but none so ugly and rife with despair as the place where she now lives. Cuddy comforts her with the knowledge that at least they've not been forced into The Rookery nearby, where Irish folk live with open sewers running through basement rooms, and up to twenty people might rent two-penny beds, if they're lucky enough to get something at ground level or higher.

Their room has a stump bedstead, a flock mattress for the three of them to share, a sheet and two blankets. Two chairs sit against the wall, alongside a small table near a grate. Melva sees no sign of a washbasin, cooking utensils, kettle or means to light a fire. The building has no courtyard and no garden, with steady clouds of dust rising from a timber yard at the rear.

This is all she has to make a home for her family.

What little money Cuddy was paid is soon gone. He is thirty-six years old and London is teeming with younger, stronger men who've not lived through the ravages of war, along with thousands of discharged soldiers returning from the Americas. Some weeks he picks up work hefting bags of malted barley at a brewhouse near Crows Alley or labouring at warehouses lining the Thames. In others, they have little to eat.

Cuddy hears that Army wives can earn a few shillings collecting urine from soldiers billeted in small groups throughout London and surrounds. Melva goes daily to the nearby Maiden Head Inn, collecting a bucketful and carrying it to the foul-smelling tannery in Harrow Lane.

Her belly is growing and Roger, nearly six, helps lift the bucket to pour its reeking contents into the vat where cow, goat and sheep skins are soaked to strip away the remains of fur and meat.

Winter has torn up the calendar, coming in harsh, cold and a month early, so they need money more than ever for coal. Twice Cuddy has been forced to beg at the alms house for charity.

Travellers are freezing to death by the roadside, snow swirls in thick flurries that turn to brown mush when they land, and frost splits trees in churchyards, clean as if struck by a lightning bolt. Melva has never known such cold, biting deep in her bones, making her glad for the small ball of heat growing at her centre.

She and her family huddle tightly on the mattress, fully clothed, often with damp boots on to stop them freezing overnight. What she'd give for a blast of the hot easterly Levante winds from the Sahara in Africa. She'd even be willing to forgive the summer humidity it brought to her town.

As ice on the Thames thickens to almost a foot deep, a frost fair springs up. Cuddy has befriended some of the watermen and earns six shillings for setting up tents for food stalls, drinking and gambling. Next afternoon he declares his family could do with an outing.

'Time for a bit o' fun.' He spins Melva around, her feet lifting off the floor as she squeals in protest.

As they walk towards the river, the heavy years drop from Melva's shoulders and she smiles at Roger, skipping beside them with excitement. They ignore their breath turning to tiny ice drops on their faces as the smell of spit-roasted ox and hot chestnuts draws them on. At last they leave Thames Street and head down Old Swan Stairs, close to London's medieval stone bridge.

As the view opens up, Melva gasps at the spectacle on the frozen river, a thousand feet wide before them. Groups skate on a rink in front of rows of market booths. Musicians, jugglers, puppet plays, and games of skittles bring laughter, while a handful of children take turns pulling one another on a small sledge, others queuing for a turn on a donkey ride.

She ignores the makeshift brothels, the drinking and dice booths, for the oddity of men and women strolling beneath the bridge's trapped narrow arches, nineteen of them.

Cuddy is smiling at her. 'Know'd it would cheer you.'

They stroll arm in arm as they did when they first met, Roger leading the way, pointing enthusiastically to one new sight after another. Melva's heart aches a little, watching him. Most of his childhood has been a trial.

Darkness soon wraps the scene in softness as lamps are lit and candles flicker, turning the ice into a fairyland. Cuddy buys each of them a sausage and a pennyworth of spiced gingerbread, with a dark ale for him and Melva to wash it down. He lifts the tankard in a toast, gesturing towards the bulge of her skirt. 'To new beginnings, me darlin'.'

As she lifts hers in reply she finds, to her surprise, that a sense of possibility is blooming within, of change for the better, stirring in her imagination as though the night has sprinkled magic dust all about.

The baby is born well after the great thaw, going full term, a spring arrival with jet black hair and her mother's olive complexion. Melva sips the caudle without asking how Cuddy got the money for it, enjoying the warmth of the wine, spices and sugar in the egg gruel. She wants to call the girl Saffea, but Cuddy isn't so sure. After a day or so they settle on Saffy and the babe gurgles as though she's happy with the choice.

Melva is delighted that Roger takes to the little girl immediately. 'Be good boy and look out for her, my son.'

Cuddy has found steadier work, with a saddler cum returned soldier over at Seven Dials, where livery stables abound. The regular income means they fare better as another harsh winter sets in. The ground is covered in frost from late December through February of 1785, when Melva again quickens with child. Like the first time, her body cannot hold the baby and within three months her womb is empty.

'Gives us a better chance to look after these two, proper like.' Though he attempts to console her, Cuddy knows his wife feels the loss keenly.

In early summer the following year another child takes root, and she is determined this one will hold on. Cuddy worries that she will feel she's failed again. 'Aye, my darlin'. Best we leave such things to God.'

Whether or not a divine hand is at work, the baby stays put. A month before it arrives the saddler who employs Cuddy drops dead in the workshop among the leather strips, harnesses and saddles. The business is sold and Cuddy is no longer required.

He gets work at stables run by John Edwin in Soho, mucking out stalls and doing any labouring that's required, while aristocratic clients are busy building fancy houses nearby. It only pays half-days and he must search for other means to earn money.

'I do charing, washing, once the baby born, grows bigger,' Melva promises, uneasy about another child being more than Cuddy's pocket can handle.

Still, the boy born in February the following year brings great joy. An easy-going baby, Melva wants Daniel as his name, or Danny. Cuddy wants it to be Donny, a name with a touch of the Irish, maybe because the little 'un has the same red gold hair as his. Melva refuses to budge, will no longer tolerate him changing names to suit himself, and insists that Danny it is.

When she's strong enough she makes rosto as a celebration of the new arrival, though in England macaroni is only for the wealthy upper classes and she must make do with some sinewy beef, tomatoes, a few mushrooms, carrots, and cheese to melt on top.

They are in straightened means now, and the responsibility of four dependents weighs heavily on Cuddy as another year slides by, bleeding into the next.

One morning he arrives silently at the stables at his usual time, a little after seven o'clock, when few are about. He goes to the storeroom to fetch a shovel and barrow, but when he sees a crowbar leaning against the wall an impulse seizes him. He leaves the barrow and takes the crowbar instead, carrying it to a barred window at the side of the stables.

He is not a common thief, no more a shyster than those in silk hats at the stock exchange in the city's Sweetings Alley, conjuring money out of thin air without the need to carry a jemmy bar.

He prides himself on being a street-smart schemer, a fellow canny enough to see an opportunity and take it. It's meant he can buy extra food and coal, or sometimes join soldier friends at the card tables, with Melva none the wiser. Wouldn't want to bother her with such things. A dropped silver crown, a pair of boots snatched from a stall and hidden in his jacket, once even an undressed fowl lifted from a hawker's basket. Oh that one were worth a pretty penny.

And anyways, this country owes him. He fought for it, sacrificed health, only to be tossed away while the officers with their clean hands got half-pay pensions. What matter he takes a little to balance the scales?

He checks to his right, then his left. The coast is clear. He works the crowbar into the mortar below one of the iron bars covering the window. He must lever it back and forth several times to loosen the seat of the bar, but soon he can pull it forward, and with a sharp tug down the bar comes free.

It has a heft of twenty or so pounds, should be worth a couple of days' wages to the right buyer. Cuddy grins, imagining the relief on Melva's face when he takes home the money.

Intent on the pleasure of the moment, he fails to see the face of Peter Alverton looking out from an upstairs window on the far side of Compton Street. This is not any man but one whose carriage was robbed only the week before. Alverton is incensed at what he sees, rushing down the stairs two at time and across the street.

Cuddy is thinking the storeroom will be a good place to squirrel away the bar till he can get a chance to take it later in the day. Pleased with his plan, he turns to find his way blocked by a large man barrelling towards him in a fury of greatcoat, bulging eyes and a mouth with spit flying from it.

'How dare you. Stop thief, stop.' The screaming catches Cuddy by surprise, as though his dream has suddenly become a nightmare and him swept along in it. The fellow slams into his shoulder with a thud and Cuddy, still gripping the bar in his left hand, staggers a little and raises his right fist, fighting back, even as his hat falls to the ground. The pair scuffle, too close together for either of them to land an effective blow.

Cuddy pulls free and sprints into the street, gripping the bar tightly, unwilling to let go what it promises for his family. He flees, feet barely touching the ground as he flies up Charing Cross Road, turning quickly into a narrow street, twisting onto another to shake off the man.

He runs even as his breath burns his throat and his lungs are fit to burst, legs straining, into Great Russell Street. Five minutes have gone since he left the stables, and he smells freedom as he approaches the corner of Bloomsbury Square.

But if the Irish have any luck, his runs out right there in front of leafy gardens and sandstone mansions, on the sixteenth day of March in the year of our Lord 1788.

Alverton catches up, seizing Cuddy from behind by the arms, and he drops the bar as the local watch patrol, dashing from the other side of the square, comes to see what causes the shouting. It's too late; the two patrolmen are upon him.

Alverton fills them in as he hands Cuddy over.

'How come you by the bar?' The watchman making the arrest shakes the object in Cuddy's face, already seeing himself in the courtroom, looking impressive as he draws himself up to his full height, testifying before old Justice Ashurst.

Cuddy knows the game's up, though in his panic he tries a kneejerk reaction. 'I found the bar. When I heard the cry of stop thief I ran because I feared I'd be taken, it be lookin' bad.'

'Too right.' The watchman bundles him away to the lock-up at Newgate prison.

Over in St Giles, Melva has fed baby Danny and started cooking soup with mussels bought that day at the market.

Usually Cuddy would be home by now, and she hopes he's not caught up at the dice or card tables.

By nine o'clock she's sick with worry and prepares to leave ten-year-old Roger in charge of the infant and four-year-old Saffy while she goes in search of her husband. As she throws a shawl around her shoulders there's a bashing at the door.

'You Mrs Cuddy Ranse?'

She drops the shawl. 'Yes. What happen? Where is he?'

'He's been a foolish man, thieving. He's in Newgate and will stay there till his trial.'

'No, he a good husband, father. Not Cuddy.'

'Afraid so, missus.' He should tip his hat, show respect for the wife of an ex-soldier, but he sees she's a darkie the fellow must have picked up somewhere overseas, and he leaves without even the courtesy of a nod.

Melva is still standing there after the man departs and the door's been shut.

'What we do, Roger? What we do now.' She whispers it to herself, though the boy hears what she says and is troubled by a lack of knowing how he should save his father.

Next morning she takes the children, baby Danny dozing in her arms, and winds her way through back alleys and narrow laneways onto Holborn Street, walking three miles to the entrance of Newgate. At the steps she hesitates. The three children have their faces turned up to hers. She must pull herself together, go in.

Inside the doorway where she's let through, prisoners run a drinking cellar, openly selling cheap spirits to anyone who can pay. It suits the turnkeys as more grog means more stupefied inmates, less trouble.

Melva is told Cuddy has been taken to the stone hold, a dungeon so dark and dirty that no matter what money the physicians are offered to see the sick, none will enter. She is sent away to get an entry permit from one of the Sheriffs at the nearby Old Bailey Courthouse, returning almost two hours later, close to tears.

When the family finally enters the stone hold, Cuddy is stunned to see her.

'Please, dear wife. Take the children. This be no place for them, no place for you.'

He turns her around towards the exit and despite her attempts to stay insists she leaves.

'I'll send word when I go before the beak, promise.'

She presses a small bundle into his hand, a little cheese, bread and an orange; sees the deep lines on his face, the purple rings under his eyes, the tangled hair. Has to be prodded by him before her feet will carry her away.

Outside, Saffy grizzles miserably, snot running as she begins to cry pitifully. Roger wipes a sleeve across his nose, dabs his eyes in the hope his mother won't notice they're wet. 'Da be fine, ma. He be comin' up with something, a way to sort this out. I know he will.'

'For sure, my boy. Papa come home soon.'

Roger can tell there's not an ounce of conviction in his mother's voice.

Two weeks' later Melva is informed that Cuddy will appear in court next day. She goes alone to the Old Bailey, her mind trapped by a cruel image of the man she loves swinging from Tyburn gallows.

It's common enough for thieves to get the death penalty, what with crime rates climbing as rapidly as poverty grows. Melva has seen the size of the crowd that gathers every hanging day, thousands leaning out windows or lining the route from Newgate to the scaffold, people flinging food, shit or stones at the condemned as the cart passes by. Let it not be her Cuddy's fate.

She pays the court official the last penny she has to get into the public gallery, along a wall above the seething business of the court, the jurors immediately below. Nosegays and sprigs of rosemary, thyme and crushed mint have been scattered around the judge's throne to prevent gaol fever. Melva smells the herbs' sweet scents through the stench of unwashed bodies.

She is still waiting two hours later as the case of a highway robber is wrapping up, court officers and lawyers down in the pit looking restless, wanting it over.

'He be dancin' the Tyburn jig afore you know it.' The court officer standing at the nearby door of the gallery laughs at the prospect of the spectacle.

From the corner of her eye she sees the next group of prisoners brought in, Cuddy in front. He is blinking in strong light pouring down from windows up high despite the film of filth covering the glass. His clothes are soiled, gone is the smiling fellow who charmed her into marriage. She wants to get to her husband, hug him, somehow make it right. But she has come to understand, down to her boots, that some things cannot be made right, no matter how hard she wishes for it.

He is shoved into the dock, harsh light reflecting on his face from a large mirror positioned above, angled so the court can gauge every expression on the faces of the accused.

Alverton gives evidence briefly, then arresting officer Smith. George Gaddy, blacksmith, is sworn in and testifies that he put up the bars, that each is worth a shilling.

One shilling. Melva sees Cuddy recoil at the knowledge that he's risked his family for such a paltry sum.

The trial is over in less than fifteen minutes. She hears the verdict, guilty, but can't fathom the sentence as her husband is dragged from the dock, with one beseeching look in her direction. Only when she begins the walk home does she grasp that he got transportation to the colonies for seven years.

She sobs all the way to her door. Seven years. No-one ever returns. The judge has delivered a death sentence for her and the children. She is ruined.

In the fog of shock she puts out the word that she's available to take in washing and mend clothes. If she can work at home or close to their room, she can still take care of the youngest two, relying on Roger to help sometimes. She does it even as she knows that not a soul around here can afford to pay another to do their dirty work.

At least in the siege they had Cuddy's meagre rations, a patch of land to grow a few vegetables, the chance to forage for whatever grew on The Rock. She curses the Army, stealing Cuddy's best years with no offer of care when they were rid of him, but cursing doesn't fill her children's bellies.

The lodging houses scattered throughout St Giles and the grand homes over on Gate Street turn her away the moment they see she has a babe in arms. Roger is a year too young to be bound to a master, even if she found one willing to take him.

She sells their table, and two weeks later their chairs.

At the end of April she returns to the prison to see the broken man that is her husband.

'What I do, Cuddy?' Despite her resolve to stay strong in front of him, she breaks down.

'Oh Melva, I be such a fool gettin' you and the wee ones into this mess. Regret burdens me, every minute of every day.'

He puts an arm around her shoulder, pulls her shaking body close. 'Go to the parish office, ask for charity.'

'Already been there, husband. Got a little food, nothing more.'

He has no words. There is nothing more to be said in their shared sorrow and distress.

Not yet eleven, Roger has the wits of a much older lad. He manages to persuade a furniture-maker to take him on as dogsbody, sweeping floors, carrying timber on delivery days, running and fetching, packing away the chisels, saws, planes at the end of the day. Dust clogs his lungs, his back aches, but he gets on with it because he must. Each week he hands his mother a few coins, the only income between them and the workhouse.

In early May the boy is at work, the baby and Saffy at home with Melva, exhausted after fending off the landlord because the rent is overdue again.

The door bursts open without a knock and she can scarcely believe her eyes at the person standing there. Cuddy grins from ear to ear, while she splutters, unable to speak.

'Walked out the gates, easy like. Followed the visitors leavin', no one hindered me, doubt the turnkeys even saw.'

He holds her tight against his chest. 'We be alright now, darlin'.'

The stink of him is strong in her nostrils, overpowering, but she keeps her arms around him, leans against him for a long time, the boniness of his chest and shoulder the proof that he's really home.

'They come for you Cuddy, know where you live.'

He steps back, hands on her shoulders, looks deep into her eyes. 'No need for worryin', my love. When they let us out for exercise they never bother counting heads.'

Within a day or two he gets labouring work on a building site at the edge of the parish, which pleases him because he's out of the way, where nosy parkers or watchmen are unlikely to pay much attention to one of a ragtag of working men.

Melva feels she can finally let out her breath, as though she's been holding it in all these weeks. Danny, who hasn't seen his father for nearly two months, cries at first when his Da approaches but soon gets used to him again.

With Cuddy and Roger both bringing in regular money, the family settles back into a routine. Melva, the girl who hated domestic chores, finds newfound pleasure in having the means to buy and cook food for her family, even if they must eat it with bowls balanced on their laps.

She reminds herself every day to keep faith in Cuddy.

Six weeks pass as a particularly mild summer gives the family the freedom for Sunday strolls towards the river or the occasional picnic under a tree in a churchyard, ignoring the way the warmth of the sun unleashes a greater funk than ever from pisspots emptied into the street and horse dung curdling in the sun.

After all that's unfolded in her twenty-six years, Melva sits one afternoon under an old, soaring oak, watching her three children laughing with their Pa, and is deeply content.

Life is nothing like in Gibraltar, a salty breeze blowing through the town, abundant food from Papi's market garden, neighbours and families she's known all her life saying hello in the orderly streets. She has been uprooted, and in all honesty can never feel that England is home, but she can find belonging in her family.

Better to love what comes than live miserably wanting what cannot be. Papi's words, spoken often as she grew up, ring true in her ears. 'That which a year does not bring us, a moment may.'

As the family enters July, happenstance approaches. It can be a fine thing, bringing bounty and reasons for gratitude or, as occurs on the blue sky day of the tenth, dragging behind it a cart full of sorrow.

Cuddy is busy shovelling mortar into a barrow while two masons shout at him to hurry with it, they have fresh stones at the ready. He takes no notice of the stranger who arrives to strike up a chat with one of the masons, a man known to be a braggard when it comes to the quality of his jobs. The stranger, John Owen, is brother to the braggard and on a day off, invited to inspect his sibling's fine work on the grand arches for the windows.

Cuddy sweats as he swings the shovel with its heavy load, not bothering to lift his eyes to the man as he passes in front of him towards the stone wall.

As he reaches into the mixing pit to scoop up another shovelful, being careful not to disturb the rhythm of the fellow stirring it with a large paddle, a blow lands on his back. He loses balance, pitching to one side, dropping the shovel. Cuddy can't see the face, struggles to free himself without understanding why he's been so baselessly attacked.

The man is yelling for his brother, who scrambles down the scaffold and helps pin Cuddy by pulling one arm up his back in a painful angle.

'Remember me? Cos I surely remember you.'

John Owen stands in front of Cuddy, who tries to marshal his thoughts, get them back into an orderly pattern.

'What damn business is this? I done you no harm.'

Owen seems to enjoy the exchange, waiting for the penny to drop. But Cuddy, in his fury, has no recollection of the man.

'Let me enlighten you, good sir.' Owen is laughing now, a full-throated rattle, while taking a kerchief from his pocket to mop his brow.

'I were the court bailiff who put you in the dock at the Old Bailey, not yet two months ago. And I never forget a face.'

CHAPTER FIVE

LONDON, 1788-1790

THE OLD BAILEY COURTROOM LOOKS the same. Melva glances down, where the faces of the Second Middlesex Jury, the lawyers at their table, the court officers, all seem familiar and just as stern.

Cuddy is brought in, a Recorder bearing the name of Lightwood sitting in judgement today, for this is a more serious case than larceny. Before Cuddy pleads to feloniously being at large, the Recorder addresses him.

'I think it right you should be fully informed of the consequences of your plea. If you expect to receive any favour from the court, or your King, on account of you pleading guilty, you may probably be deceived in that expectation.'

He stops to draw breath. 'You must decide whether to abide by a plea of guilty or take your chance of acquittal by a jury of your country. How plead you?'

Cuddy knows what's at stake. He looks up to the gallery where Melva sits, white-knuckled, trembling.

'Gentlemen, I am guilty. When I found the gates open, I walked out, I went at my liberty. I have three small children and a wife. They have no support. My wife had visited me, her and the children were very much distressed.'

If he had hoped to find a little sympathy from the Recorder, there is nothing in his expression to show it.

'My Lord, I did serve my King and country abroad during the time of war, and I thought it very hard to be kept there.'

He can think of nothing more to say, except that his master is willing to be fetched tomorrow to speak to his character. 'They told me I was to be here on the last day of trying, you see, not today.'

The Recorder clears his throat, ignoring the suggestion of a delay. Unfortunate as it is, this is a straightforward matter and the plea of guilty means a verdict can be given immediately, with no need of the jury conferring.

The situation requires evidence, though. John Owen is sworn in and gives his statement, followed by the arresting officer. A tedious process, but the law requires it and the Recorder has been assiduous in his legal studies and practice as a barrister, determined to prove he has more substance than his surname suggests.

When the officer steps down from the witness box the Recorder composes the muscles on his face to reflect the gravity of the moment, taking his time to reach up and place a black cap on top of his powdered wig. He summons his most commanding voice.

'Cuthbert Ranse, upon your plea of guilty the only thing the court has power to do is to give judgment of death against you. So be it.'

Up in the gallery Melva watches, hands clenched, life draining from every limb as her husband is bundled away. Ill-gotten gains never prosper, but this, this is cruel, heartless, worse than shot raining down, destroying whatever it strikes.

She stumbles home, dreading the terror she will see in her children's eyes when she gives them the news.

The system has no care for Cuddy Ranse, one of endless felons sent to English gaols that are bursting at the seams. Rural workers have left struggling farms for the city, where newfangled machines in factories means fewer jobs and crime spreads faster than the pox. The government's harsh penalties are no more use than wielding a wooden pail to hold back a flood tide.

Melva and the three children have been tossed like scum into the gutter. The desperation of it worms its way into her marrow, darkens her thoughts. She lies for wakeful hours on the mattress, now on the floor with the bed long sold, and berates herself that she can't find a way forward.

The bitter thoughts that come some nights are far worse. She tries to fend them off, belly rumbling. The sour notions that Cuddy's shown himself to have a hollow head, his recklessness bringing them all undone and her the one who willingly, blindly entered into a life with him.

Her man has been a cork bobbing on the water, going wherever the current takes him, sweeping all of them along with him.

She puts a stop to such ideas, must save her energy for immediate matters, not just food and coal but now water. London has had little rain during summer and autumn and by late November a severe frost has begun, which will persist till early January. The city and surrounds are suffering a shortage of water, which must be bought at the high prices demanded by profiteers.

The pittance that Roger earns, and occasional charity, is all that stands between the family and utter destitution. Melva gives thanks to the Holy Father for the miracle of the four of them surviving the long winter.

She goes to the gaol every few weeks to see if Cuddy has news of his hanging, a sorry meeting that leaves them both suffering beyond words, her in abandonment and him stewing in a hot mess of guilt.

The delay goes on for months, so unbearable that the next time she visits he is in a different mood. 'I be ready, dear wife, to get it over and done with. It's not in me to keep going like this.'

She has little food to spare him. Gaol conditions have worn him ragged, his dirty clothes hanging off his bones, teeth coming loose, even his nails losing their grip on his fingertips and toes. It's such a miserable business that she has also begun to wonder if it's better to end his suffering, not something she would say to his face. Her head tells her that surely it's the right thing for a wife to hold hope.

In the coming days her heart insists otherwise. Every time she pictures her shrunken husband, his torment, she leans towards a merciful end. Better than a snapped neck. How she wishes she no longer loved him, could see him as merely a ragged wretch, leaving him to his fate. Yet they are linked together, and whatever power passes between them, a depth of care bigger than her pathetic thoughts, it sends her to the apothecary with the last of the week's food money.

The shop is bright with light from windows set in a high wall on one side, where the apothecary sits, stirring a smelly brew in front of a double brick oven that's burning.

His apprentice lad, wearing a long leather apron, is at a bench filling bottles with a large funnel. Baskets hang from long hooks and one wall has shelves with jars all in a similar size but filled with different dried herbs and strange-shaped fungi.

The apothecary looks up with interest. 'What can I do for you, missus?'

The witches' favourite, that's what they called black henbane where she grew up. He will know she means mischief, demand she leave the shop, maybe call to the watch. She should turn away, give this up, but Cuddy's haggard face floats before her and won't let her leave.

'Henbane seeds, if you please.' She has mustered her best accent, though has stammered with the words.

The man shows no reaction, placing his bowl carefully on the table beside him and reaching up to a dark jar on the highest shelf. He'll give her no grief. Another desperate wife looking to be rid of a nasty husband, though she'd be better with arsenic or mercury, less suspicious when it's a slow death.

He doesn't ask for the required weight of it. She'll need enough to stop a heart, and he shakes the measure out on the scale, then pours the seeds into a twist of paper.

'Take care not to let children near it.' She pays him the money and hurries out of the shop, the small parcel digging into her closed hand.

Over in the Palace of Westminster, far from minor concerns such as trying to find the next cup of water, Prime Minister William Pitt has called his Cabinet together. News from the first fleet of ships to establish the far-flung colony of New South Wales is encouraging, but more labour is needed to clear land, build farms and a new society.

'It is imperative that we secure a strong foothold, show the French, the rest of Europe, that it is our continent and we will not let it be for the taking.'

Cuddy, slumped on the floor in the dark and damp of his dungeon, has no idea that he and hundreds like him are the subject of discussion.

'We have many able-bodied men languishing in gaols, so many that soon the prison system will have no way to contain them. Gentlemen, the moment is upon us. We can surely solve two pressing problems at once by doubling our efforts to send as many as we can, to the limits of our budget for ships, to the Great Southland. We must begin at once.'

They all nod, murmuring agreement, unwilling to acknowledge it's no cure, will not change the root cause of growing crime.

The Home Secretary, Lord Sydney, speaks to the necessity of marriage and families in the new colony, a bedrock of stability and a steadying force, and for this, women will be needed. He proposes that one ship be dedicated to female convicts. Almost as an aside, the suggestion is made to try an experiment, allowing a small number of convict's wives to join the second fleet.

As the Ministers compete in oration behind their safe walls, Melva grows dispirited, weak with worry and poor sustenance, and Cuddy withers away. She has hidden the seeds under the mattress, waiting for the courage to grind them, slip them into a little honey, and deliver them to her husband.

She won't visit him again till she has the nerve to see it through, though she wakes day after day to find she is not. At night she imagines the seeds pressing through the mattress, taunting her that she is weak, useless. They torture her soul. She cannot decide if it is a purer love to give him his end and spare him anguish or a deeper love to let him have life, desperate though it is.

She stares into darkness, sees her outstretched palm handing over the potion, him swallowing then falling to the stone floor, his heart stopping, severing the union with her, the Devil marrying him to death instead. And she in league with it.

A month later, more than a year after his final sentence, Cuddy is in a batch of the condemned dragged back into the blinding daylight of the Old Bailey court. It is the twenty-eighth day of October and with no consultation, for any opinion of his counts for nothing, his verdict is reprieved to transportation for life.

Within weeks a naval agent offers Melva the chance to accompany her husband to New South Wales, but there is no time for mulling it over. 'You must decide now, but of your own free will,' he warns.

What mother has the freedom to choose, when destitution and starvation snap at the heels of her three young children? She agrees immediately, unaware that only five other wives are willing.

In early November she farewells Cuddy. Next day, he is loaded onto a wagon and taken seventy-four miles to Portsmouth, where the *Scarborough* is slowly filling with more than two hundred men, including some of the most dangerous in British gaols.

Melva and the children leave their room at St Giles in the dead of night, hurrying into darkness with two weeks rent owing. Becoming a sloper who runs from debt is the least of her concerns, and she musters a smile that, too bad, the landlord will have no satisfaction in seizing scant belongings left behind. She scattered the seeds in the river the day before, glad to be rid of them.

It has been made plain that the wives and children will be treated no differently to the convict women and their offspring. The nervous free families cluster at Newgate, waiting to be loaded onto one of the prison carts to follow the men to Portsmouth.

As daylight spreads grubby fingers across rooftops, Melva keeps the children close. It occurs to her, standing in half-light in front of the closed doors, that she has been holding herself in a perpetual state of waiting since Gibraltar. It has become an end to itself, making her always departed, never arrived.

The *Neptune* rides at anchor in the shelter of Spithead strait. The surgeon examines them before they are rowed to the ship, concerned at Saffy's barking cough. The last thing he wants is an outbreak of typhus or cholera at sea.

'Weak lungs but strong, strong girl.' The surgeon hesitates at Melva's reassurance, checks his papers. He has rejected a few convict women, sent them back to gaol, but is uncertain what authority he has to send away a free woman and her family.

Melva draws breath, and in that moment of mere seconds her destiny arrives in all its immensity. It teeters, falters, unsure which way to swing, and then suddenly is set in motion.

It will haunt her for the rest of her days. Only later, months later, does she see it for what it was, does she grasp that this was, after all, the journey the adivina foresaw, and that Melva stands at the centre of this moment, holding it in her grip so that her family may turn back, face away from danger.

She says again how strong the girl is. Then the moment moves, already shaping the future, and it is too late. The harried surgeon waves them through.

The fleet sets sail at the start of a new decade, Melva glad one minute that Cuddy's on a nearby ship and panicked the next about the future, a brief moment before any chance to worry is knocked out of her by events that call for blind reaction.

In all the brutality of war and the ugliness that London has thrown her way, sticking like muck to a wall, she is not prepared for the unspeakable journey to follow, in a ship with rotting sails and lack of caulking, already abandoned by several sailors.

For now, though, strong winds force the fleet to wait off Motherbank for nearly two weeks. Melva is with the convict women in a boarded off section of the upper deck, lice jumping from head to head, foul language burning her ears, while the convict men are chained on the orlop deck, three down.

She must see the best in the situation and offers up a silent thanks for fresh air on the poop deck, where they can escape overcrowded quarters, and the rations of bread, pork, pease, rice, even a little sugar to go with the tea. She is especially glad for the new jacket, flannel petticoats, stockings and shoes provided. Never mind the rough cloth and shoddy workmanship, she has warm clothing for a change.

She looks over the water, girlish hope rising, pleased she's had the courage to follow her husband, unaware that innocence and ignorance make dangerous bedfellows. For this is no bargain in her favour – hiding in the British Government's offer of free passage is a high price.

When finally they leave the English Channel they are but three days out when they sail into a fearful storm in the Bay of Biscay, mountainous seas causing former slave ship captain Donald Trail to order the women locked in their quarters.

Melva, flung this way and that, a rag doll with limbs flailing uselessly against the juddering and lurching, empties her stomach again and again into putrid sea water swirling around her ankles. She must help Danny and Saffy, leaving Roger to fend for himself.

When the storm finally recedes, she tells herself that the worst of it is done. But Trail has no interest in wasteful welfare, is intent on making the *Neptune* a house of horrors. A man who finds pleasure in inflicting pain and harm on others, he withholds rations, and is an abomination with convict, soldier and seamen alike.

They are five days out from fresh food in Cape Town when purple blotches of scurvy bloom on Danny's arms and legs. He grows weak and moans, complaining of pain in his bones. The two year old, rigour drained by poor nutrition before embarking, is gone within a day of port and fresh fruit. So fast his Mama is left gulping stale air, mouth open, a landed fish wrenched from the waters of mothering.

More than sixty bodies, almost all convicts, have been dropped with little ceremony off the side of the ship so far. Yet the sight of this small one, stitched by his mother into scraps of blanket too small to cover the top of his head, so that curls of golden-red hair break free, brings heavy stillness to the busy deck.

And it brings Melva to her knees, clutching the stiff parcel of her son to her chest, iron weights belying his light form.

The soldier trying to coax her to release the body has no hope. Roger is the one who hooks an arm under his mother, gets her to stand, and after some minutes gentles her into handing over the bundle of his brother.

The Chief Mate mutters a few words of committal then the soldier drops Danny from the gangway. Melva leans over, watches him fly for a moment, then start to fall, feels the cord between his heart and hers tug and stretch, straining as though she might reel him back, somehow save him. Then it snaps completely as her son reaches bottomless ocean, so light he disappears without even a splash and there is nothing to be seen but churning water.

Saffy cries against Melva's skirts while Roger stays close, puzzled that he can't see a single tear on his mother's face. He is too young, yet, to know that a person's wellspring of sadness can be scoured to the bottom by pain too great to bear, emptied into numbness.

For many days Roger remains vigilante with Saffy while their Ma remains adrift, giving him no choice but to take her place in their mess group where they've been assigned for rations. The group's pudding bag with salted meat, pease and rice is a free-for-all when it's retrieved from the boiling water and he must fight for their share. It's the same with the keg of water passed around to each, the strongest taking all they can, leaving little for a boy, a toddler and their ailing mother.

It is not the first time he has felt the powerlessness of being unable to save a parent, but this time it comes with a hot fire of rage. He uses his fists on some of the other boys with little provocation, until one of the seamen catches him at it and gives him a thrashing of his own.

Melva has no interest in going ashore when they land, keeping Saffy and Roger with her in a shady spot on the deck. When *Scarborough* arrives in port to resupply, Roger demands to go over to his Da, give him the news about Danny.

'No, son.' It is almost a shout, shocking him after days when she's barely spoken.

'He in a bad place, like men in chains here. No good dropping that stone in his lap for now.'

Less than a week's sailing from port she is struck down with fever, leaving Roger helplessly trying to care for her and keep an eye on six-year-old Saffy. Some of the women are kind, give him occasional help, but disease is everywhere and they have little effort to spare.

As Melva recovers, Saffy develops dysentery, water running through her as fast as she swallows it. They have been at sea for five months and are skirting the coast of

New Holland, within weeks entering the heads of Botany Bay. Saffy seems a little improved, or so Melva tells herself, and dares to leave her for a few minutes to stand on the poop deck and catch sight of their new home.

'We made it, Ma.' Roger punches the air in excitement, a pretence of youthful exuberance for a lad with hollow eyes and shrunken stomach. His mother can only nod before returning to her daughter's limp form.

The *Neptune* has been anchored off Garden Island for two hours, awaiting warping closer to Sydney Town, when Melva looks down at Saffy lying spent on their bunk, and sees her chest is perfectly still.

Roger, leaning over the rail, absorbed by activity across the water at the settlement, is ignoring the dead being tossed into the harbour, where they refuse to sink, a silent, ghastly flotilla condemning Captain Trail. The boy hears the awful animal wail from the convict women's quarters and knows immediately what it means.

This time Melva will not let her child be consigned to water. She clings to the warm body as she and Roger are rowed in a crowded longboat to the wharf near a rough hospital building, where emergency tents sprout like mushrooms.

In the chaos on the wharf, where bodies of the dead and near-dead line up like fallen gravestones, she refuses to hand over Saffy. Roger is the one to explain when an assistant surgeon insists she lay the body down.

'Come with me.' The man is abrupt, aggravated, but he sees this woman is not going to budge and he must get on with help for the living.

He shouts to a convict woman near the top of the wharf. 'You, here. Lead them to the burial ground.'

Up the hill a grave detail is busy dumping bodies stretchered up from the wharf. One of the men takes pity on Melva, leading her to the side of the pit being used as a mass grave. 'Here, missus, this be a nice spot for the wee one.'

He climbs in and Melva hands down her daughter, one leg coming free as though the girl kicks against leaving her Ma. The fellow lowers the body gently onto a bare patch in the hole, while corpses thump down from stretchers emptied on the other side. When he climbs out, scowling at the men to stay away, he hands her a handful of thin grey soil, 'to send her on her way'.

Melva scatters it in. Some of it lands on the girl's face, near her open eyes, and she must turn away at the sight of it.

She should say a prayer for her dear daughter's soul and desperately searches her mind for the words, but it's as if everything she learned in church has been stolen away. This is the underbelly of the land that birthed her conejita, her sweet little bunny. No words she could possibly summon will help, for the burying place can hold no peace. Ashes to ashes, dust to dust. This dirt cannot recognise her daughter as its own, so how can it take her back, how can she truly be at rest?

'Come away, Ma. It be Da we need to find, see how he fares.' Roger shepherds her with a hand on her elbow, fearful she may not make it to the wharf.

What he can't know is that something strange is beginning to happen to his mother. She senses it first in the soles of her boots, as though a tingling heat courses up from this strange land, pouring into her feet so they seem outsized, and she trips over them, stumbles.

It travels up her legs, muscles knotting a little against the flow, then relaxing with the warmth of it as it passes through, slowly flooding her belly, chest and throat, bursting into her head with a force that takes her by surprise.

She is her own pyre, sweeping all into flames. She stands in the cauldron of all the wounding, the grief, the terror, gives herself over to it, ice meeting fire. She lets it have its way; it is not the first time such a force has visited, and she knows there is nothing to be done except wait to see what will remain, who she will be when it has finished with her.

Roger feels her wobble, misunderstands it as weakness. 'Sit for a bit, Ma. No hurry.'

She is consumed by what is happening within, unable to reply, though her body keeps taking one step after another without any intention on her part. After some minutes the sensation begins to abate, leaving her chilled. She pats her son's hand. 'Keep going, dear boy. We find Papa.'

It is late in the day before she searches one of the last of thirty hospital tents and finds him. Or rather, he finds her, weakly calling her name after she has passed, having failed to recognise him.

How much can a body take? The ravages of gaol, a cruel ship, disease, are etched on the bones visible through his skin, translucent like he's a human jellyfish. Her husband is a man as close to death as one can be.

Her hand flies to her mouth to stifle a groan at the sight of him and the smell of rotting flesh, ankles stripped of any meat from months of manacles.

Her first thought is not one of sympathy. Unspeakable grief is forging a tougher woman and though she is shaky, arms longing for the son and daughter she'll never see again, Melva has only one concern.

'Mierda, no dying on me, Cuddy Ranse, after I follow you to the ends of the Earth'.

CHAPTER SIX

SYDNEY TOWN AND PARRAMATTA
DISTRICT, 1790-1804

ROGER CAN'T BEAR THE MOANING, the putrid smell in the tent. Melva doesn't notice him lift the flap and slip away to sit on a rock like a stone himself, even though the heavens open and he is soaked through.

She tries to get help from an assistant surgeon, but he brushes her off like one of the circling flies, demanding she leave. One of the nurses walks up, a bloodied basin in her hand. 'Best you wait outside. Just gettin' in the way here, dearie.'

Melva ignores her, clutching at the next woman who comes near, begging, pleading with her to help Cuddy.

'We be doin' our best, promise. You being here just slows us down.'

She tries again. 'Oats, where I get them? Make poultice for pus on ankles.' Within minutes two orderlies strong arm her out of the tent.

She goes back every chance she gets, sneaking in, forgoing sleep to stay by his side. When one of the nurses returns next morning, the one with the kinder face, she tries again, lack of sleep leaving her on the verge of hysteria as she begs for mercy.

The woman lowers her voice, tells her if she has a garment to sell to go to the stone quarry, trade it for sugarbag honey one of the men gathers from a secret place in the woods. 'Bring it back, cover the wounds Mrs Ranse.'

'Thank you, bless you. Melva, call me Melva.'

The woman whispers. 'I be Maggie. Not a word, I get caught meddlin' there be hell to pay.'

Melva takes Cuddy's jacket past the tents, the barracks and beyond the Governor's house, asks for the fellow called Rocky, sneaks back into the tent an hour later. She waits for a moment when the surgeons are distracted to wipe honey on the wounds, pleading with Cuddy not to make a sound in his agony at being touched on raw flesh.

She repeats it each day till the honey runs out.

The tents empty rapidly morning and night as more bodies are taken to the pit. No one thinks to raise an eyebrow when convict Cuddy Ranse rises from his bed of straw and, supported by his wife and son, staggers from the tent.

Weeks pass before Cuddy can walk freely, throwing away the thick stick he has leaned on, though his gait will always be a bit lopsided where scar tissue has wrapped around the bone on one ankle.

He grieves his son and daughter, weeping openly, marked by sorrow that he draws around his weakened frame as a cloak, bewildered that his wife's grief spurs her instead to action, fighting for a fair share of victuals in a colony close to starving, foraging for shellfish on the waterline or wild celery on the edge of the woods.

The three of them sleep in crowded convict huts with stamped earth floors, Melva in one at the women's camp, Cuddy and Roger in the men's.

At muster one morning Cuddy is called aside. Melva watches him walk over to the soldier, alert to what may be unfolding. Her husband tries to be a good man, though no one can deny he's impetuous. He has been a swill-belly and gambler at times, but not a cheater, fist-happy, or the worst kind other wives must endure – the men who flee in the night with nary a glance over the shoulder.

Ojalá, God willing, no more punishment.

She forces herself to look away from him and back at the soldier, who finishes speaking to Cuddy then gestures Melva over, glaring at her as he speaks.

'You will be given a plot of land upriver, tools, and enough seeds and grain for the first season.'

The Corporal can barely bother with the effort of delivering the words. The dullness of his eyes says he has already decided that, though a free person, she is a mere woman and will fail. That her husband is not worthy of this chance to remake himself under a brighter sun.

Cuddy is no farmer, that much she knows. She meets the soldier's gaze but holds her tongue because there's nothing to be gained in telling him that her husband is more than a lifer, that he has been a soldier and a labourer who doesn't shy away from giving sweat to effort. Better still, he has a wife who will keep his nose pointed to purpose. Together they will till the soil and toil for their survival.

The Corporal informs them that Cuddy will work in one of the convict gangs, allowed one day off a week, when he can join his family. Melva tries to jolly herself into imagining her husband with her, shoulder to shoulder as they plant and grow, but instead she must stiffen against the urge to turn away and collapse on a nearby mound.

Surely the arrangement is no different to a fiddler's pay, with much work and no return for many years. Her limbs feel weak and she but a puppet with cut strings. She sucks in a great breath of this new air, full of strange moisture and a mix of smells she cannot name, then draws herself up as tall as she can while the soldier hands her the papers.

Master to her husband, now that is a first.

Melva looks over the shoulder of the soldier delivering the news that her convict husband will be assigned to her once his term of Government work is completed. She sees the muddy wasteland meant to be a town, the scattering of rough wattle and daub huts, then glances beside her to Roger, intent on his father's face.

Cuddy Ranse is looking up at the clear, white sky, as if he might see a higher authority, a God who grants him back some dignity.

Melva's not looking at the sky but down at the ground, to a land that makes her feel more alien than London ever did, where she's been washed up by the slop of unknown waters, told by others who she will be.

Her torn heart is another matter, for it cannot begin anew. It will never mend, the beating at its centre that belonged to her darling boy, Danny, or the quiet corner that was Saffy's. It is something Melva knows with certainty. Mysteriously, her heart still pulses and that will have to be enough for now.

The soldier has lost interest, dismisses them with a flick of the wrist.

It is as if one woman was rowed from the *Neptune* and another has taken her place. Though she faltered at first while in Sydney Town, sixteen miles away at the head of the Paramatta River, Melva becomes a woman of the soil.

The block she's been allocated is half an acre or so, nothing more than a large allotment above mangroves and saltmarsh on the river's south bank, the site of the Guv's plan for a town where saltwater gives way to fresh.

She has been given a hatchet, narrow grubbing hoe, spade and shovel to clear and dig ground for vegetables and maize. There's no hope of getting chickens, a pig or a milking cow when the colony's entire livestock comprises two stallions, six mares, two colts, sixteen cows, two cow-calves and one bull-calf. Still, Melva dares dream of fresh eggs, home-made cheese, even bread baked without the mark of dead weevils.

She and Roger are greeted the first morning by a laughing jackass perched on a nearby branch, brown and cream feathers fluffed up from the dawn cold, big head thrown back, cackling as though their arrival is nothing but a joke.

Roger laughs back. 'He be fat enough for the cooking pot, Ma.' He shouts up at the bird, at last something he can control. 'Watch out mister, I got you pegged for grub.'

In their tent, Melva wakes daily to an ambush of grief, a rope looping around her neck, choking each breath, or tying itself to an ankle so that she must drag the leaden weight of misery through the hours.

Soon they are given a draughty hut, one of many a convict gang hastily throws up, thatched roofs lined up neatly, two long rows spilling away from the Governor's house being built at the top of a nearby rise. The huts are sixty feet apart, not for the benefit of privacy, for Lord knows no felons or their low-life wives deserve that, but as a means to stop any fire from spreading.

They have two rooms, one to sleep in, another with a brick fireplace and chimney, and a wooden box against the wall in which to store the primitive wooden bowls and plates they've been given. She rests on the shady side of their hut in the early afternoon, watching her son practising his whittling, and looks across the sparse settlement, its rickety granary, storehouses made from rotten canvas, military barracks, and overlooking the river, two adjoining thatched sheds they call the convict hospital.

Surrounding them are gentle hills and dales that are lightly wooded, grassy slopes forming parklands that to Melva's eye are an astonishing natural feature. For all her looking, she is blind to the fact that the natives, inhabiting the area for thousands of years, have long cultivated these open areas through careful burning, and made pathways along the river, eel traps, timber and stone river crossings, all manner of things created by human hands.

She and Roger soon find their rhythm, catching eels, leatherjackets and snapper in the river to supplement Government rations, and scuffing patches of ground to scatter seeds for peas, broad beans and turnips, some sprouting so that soon they have a few fresh vegetables for the cooking pot. No herbs, though, which doesn't surprise her. The English have no respect for flavour, not like Mama, dishes steaming with oregano and thyme, or turmeric and saffron in a fisherman's stew. Her mouth waters at the thought.

She begins to live on her own terms now, the taste sweet as nectar on her tongue, easing the tightness under her ribs. Not even the griping of a fellow free wife can stem her optimism. Sarah Smith has invited herself over for tea, causing Melva to lay down her hoe.

The woman complains in a noisy string of words, tightly gathered so there's no space to pause, how the heat is unbearable, the primitive housing appalling, the absence of her convict husband a punishment she shouldn't have to suffer. Suddenly, she pauses mid-sentence, turning her opinions on Melva.

'You're wastin' yerself for nothing. You know that, don't you? The Guv won't be rewarding you for growing a garden, no matter how hard you work at it.' She sniffs as if the stating of her position has resolved the matter.

Unlike female convicts who serve their sentences, the free wives will never be given land in their own right, however productive they are, something Melva knows only too well. Working the soil, the green shoots of something growing, are pleasures all of their own, something beyond this woman's understanding.

'It worth it. We barter what we don't need ourselves, maybe get shoes, clothes, other food.'

The visitor leaves soon after. Such determination leads to back-breaking, filthy work, and what woman, other than this foreigner heathen, can be bothered?

Cuddy's been spared the rock-breaking gang and works in the Sydney Town lumberyard for several weeks, before the need for more labourers on Parramatta's fertile ground sees him sent upriver. He's been doing Government task work from seven o'clock till the bell rings at half past two then carousing the rest of the time, something Melva intends to change.

'Good for Roger to have his Papa here, show what to do,' Melva tells him, encouraging the felling of two scrubby eucalypts on the edge of the allotment. It's her way to keep the rein on the horse that is her husband, for Roger needs no supervision.

Cuddy still goes to the grog when he can, but knuckles down, taking care not to attract the wrong attention from the overseers or the constables. This life in a new colony is his last chance.

Their first maize crop is days away from being harvested in late November when Melva steps out the cottage door at first light. The morning is already sixty degrees, promising a hot day. She hopes Cuddy isn't made to sweat too much in the gang sent inland overnight in the hopes of rounding up cattle escaped from the Government Farm.

Gradually her eyes make out the Indian corn patch, the first row a line of broken, empty stalks. O'possums, greedy rotters. Fat ears of corn all gone. Then the breeze picks up and carries women's voices to her in words that don't make sense, though she hears the unmistakeable sounds, the laughter heard whenever women gather to work.

A rush of anger and she's snake-headed, leaping towards the second row, rustling as cobs are ripped away. She waves her arms wildly. 'This our food, get away.'

The three women are darker skinned than the Moors, hair curlier and features broader. Each has a woven bag slung over her shoulder, no different to Melva when she walked Gibraltar's streets to Papi's shop.

One of the women flaps her arms, copying Melva, howling at her own joke. Melva tries to push between the women and the corn but their hands are everywhere, ignoring her.

Roger comes up behind them. 'Oi, begone with you, bloody robbers.' He lifts a hand to strike one of them but his mother stops him.

'No, only make it worse, Roger.'

The trio ignores the pair of them, sauntering off with bags full of corn Melva's worked so hard to grow, confident because this land has always offered up what their clan, their ancestors need, and food is there to be shared.

Melva watches them with a sinking heart, their brazenness unsettling. She was Llanito, at the mercy of the British in Gibraltar, a person required to accommodate invaders. Now she's an invader, but the trio have shown these people are adapting, not backing down.

Roger is still incensed. 'Da woulda given 'em what for if he'd been here.'

Though Roger works as hard as any man, the family's progress is slow for seven long years of Cuddy working in convict gangs, made even slower by Melva giving birth to dark-haired William in 1794, and three years later another healthy son, Luis, pale-skinned like his father. Though Melva loves both her babies dearly, neither boy heals the heart space for the son who was Danny.

Soon after Luis' birth they have cause for celebration when Cuddy gets a conditional pardon for good behaviour;

released from Government work as long as he never returns to England.

Melva cradles newborn Luis, stroking his sleeping face, whispering. 'Free at last, mijo. We make a new world for you.'

The spirited girl who once scrambled on The Rock has tapped into the accidental education given by Papi and her brothers as they sat around the kitchen table in Gibraltar. While she dreamed of liberty, the pores of her skin were opening, soaking up what the men knew, how to manure and care for the soil, read the vagaries of weather, limit the damage of insect pests, experiment with crops to see what fetched the highest price.

Most of it lay dormant, like the nubbly seed pods of old banksia trees, waiting for wildfire to crack them open for germination, a force that came to Melva in the unlikely form of lightly built Cornish rascal, James Ruse.

She meets him within weeks of arriving at Parramatta, drawn to his Experiment Farm, not a mile to the east of her plot. She has noticed him many times, at a distance hard to spot with his dirty clothes and soot-smeared skin giving the impression he's a moving pile of soil himself.

She approaches nervously, admiring his field of wheat.

'They never listen,' he grumbles. 'Keep telling the Guv, farms will never bear if folks just keep scratching at the surface. Gotta dig deep, that's the secret.'

He sizes up Melva, the dirt under her nails, and decides he can risk a scathing remark, as any decent Cornishman might dare. 'City-bred, most of 'em. Factory work and labouring don't make you a farmer.'

Every bit of shared advice she puts into practice, even when Cuddy gets in a huff that she is talking to the fellow.

'Not proper, you down there talkin' to him, setting tongues flapping. Best stay away.'

He is standing on the far side of the washtub while she scrubs his shirt. Something about the sight of it in her hands makes her snap, and she hurls it into the suds, splashing soapy water up his chest.

'Enough.' It bursts out of her mouth in a roar, and he steps back at the onslaught.

'Everything your way, Cuddy. Not this time.' She stomps off, leaving him marooned, open-mouthed.

How she wants to run, never come back to this man who always wants more. He takes her love, wrings its neck and throws it down limp in the dirt. She can't be with him a minute longer.

Rage propels her down to the river, where she stops, shaking uncontrollably.

Two men row a dinghy laden with cabbages, going easily with the tide flowing out. Oh that it was so effortless to love Cuddy, for she does, even when the fury builds in her and she fears it will destroy one of them. She will not give in this time. She must have this one thing for herself or the mother, the wife, will eat her up till she's hollow, fit to crumble.

'I need to learn, Cuddy.' They're both a little wary when she returns. 'It help us. You'll see.'

Soon the garden flourishes, and when Ruse marries it settles Cuddy's mind about a rival, though not about his wife's new wilful streak. She no longer cares what others think about her bending her back day after day on the land, dust in her hair, dress sweat-stained, and he dare not let himself wonder if she's stopped caring about his opinions, too.

As for Melva, she is finally in the right time and place. She gradually becomes a farmer.

She takes ashes from the bonfires of felled timber and digs them deep into the soil, along with grass, weeds, any manure she and Roger can gather, letting it lie for as long as she can before turning it up again and chipping at the clods, breaking them up to sow seed. The result is messy where they've had to hoe around rocks and stumps. Papi, proud of the order in his gardens, would be disgusted.

She tries new crops of barley, haricot beans, turnips, and at last, herbs grown from seeds bought with her produce. Through it all she leans on what she learned at her father's feet and the success of Ruse's farm and kitchen garden.

Cuddy watches her on their allotment one day as she hoes a furrow ready to sow potatoes, remembering what farming folk said where he grew up – in choosing your wife or your grain, be careful. He smiles, assuring himself that he's chosen wisely.

As if to underscore his confidence, the autumn winds blow in with a reward after he gets his pardon.

He can be a hard worker, a fact not in doubt, and if he is given credit for Melva's successful garden what does it matter? The authorities see it as proof of his agricultural skills, earning him a land grant east of Parramatta, eighty acres at Kissing Point on the northern side of the river, at the edge of the wild unknown. He does a jig when he returns home with the news.

'Me, a common labourer and lumper ...' He affects a posh tone. '... now I be the landed gentry, an' you shall all bow down to your master.' He thumps Roger's shoulder playfully and they all fall into a mad circle, dancing along with the joke, though four-year-old Will and Luis, recently turned one, have no idea what any of it means.

Melva's swept up in the joy, though a small burr of resentment digs in, that her husband hasn't the gumption to say that their windfall might be down to her.

Soon the dancing figures in the Parramatta hut settle for supper, and as darkness falls the lamps are lit.

In the Northern Hemisphere, day is dawning over thousands of miles of dark ocean and huge Atlantic swells, finally reaching the mouth of the Thames, where morning light struggles through a bilious fog.

The yellow pall is particularly thick around the London Foundling Hospital, where a muttering woman drags a small girl past the porter, towards the reception office. The woman is rehearsing what she will say to convince the hospital to take the child. It's time to be rid of the girl, not yet two years old, least until she's old enough to be of use.

The moment is one of great significance to the Ranse family, though they know nothing of it as they tuck into their mutton stew, the lamps throwing shadows as they talk and eat. If a shiver crosses Melva's shoulders soon after, she doesn't notice the chill, intent as she is on serving thick slices of panpudin, the spiced bread pudding she makes once a week as a reminder of Gibraltar.

On the other side of the world, at the Foundling Hospital, the woman is striding back out the hospital gate.

Had the child still been with her, the incident would have been of no consequence to the Ranse family, but whatever words she managed to summon have succeeded, and she leaves empty-handed into the day.

Despite a hardened heart, the woman is forcing away memories of another morning, over at Limehouse near London's docks, when she groaned in pain on a bed. It was in the garret at the top of a tenement squeezed tightly between two others, worn stairs to the door, where she forced a fist into her mouth to stifle the sound of her scream, then gave a final push, the bloodied, slick baby shooting out between her legs.

For a moment on this foggy morning, as she gets her bearings on the street, she's back in the garret, hair strewn on the pillow in a tangled mess, pale as sun-bleached wood, the same as the unknown sailor her own mother had lain with in the bawdy house. The newborn has different coloured hair, golden brown, could have been fathered by the country squire, bootmaker, clergyman, any of forty or more men who visited the harlots nine months ago.

She remembers the smell as the babe is wiped down and placed in her arms, where she looks down on it with barely concealed disgust.

'What use is a child to me, nothin' but a chain round me ankle.'

Her friend contemplates the girl, peaceful against her mother's chest, not even searching for milk. 'She be worth it when she's ripe. Good coin to be had for untilled soil, just like yer old Ma got for you at twelve.'

The mother looks on at the child with new interest. 'Mebbe I'll call her Thomasin, after me Pa, Tommy.'

Her companion frowns. 'How 'bout Tamsin? She be called Tam, easy to get yer mouth around.' So Tam it becomes, a scrap of a name for a girl not meant to take up much space in the world.

And now, nearly two years later, the mother has given up the burden of the child. 'Good riddance. Might be I come back and might be not.' She strides away towards the docks without even a backward glance.

At Kissing Point, in a slab house thrown up on the new land, three years have passed and Melva is in the birthing business, too. She is playing the button-hide game with her young sons, a rare moment of laughter as they hunt under cooking pans and look beneath chair legs, when the first pains grip. The pregnancy has strained her thirty-nine-year-old body and she is mightily glad when it's over and another son arrives, a year into the new century.

Something deep in her belly stabs as she twists to take the baby in her arms. The midwife, a Scotswoman arrived on the most recent convict transport, sees the pain cross Melva's face.

'Yer lookin' a wee bit pasty. Rest now, lassie.' She reaches over to lay the infant on the nearby table.

'Let me hold him, will help afterbirth come.'

The boy they name George has arrived at a blessed point in the Ranse family's life, born into fortunate circumstances of secure shelter and ample food.

The farm has proven productive, uphill from the river bend where heavily laden boats brush against a shallow rocky outcrop as they pass at low tide, giving the place its name. Six other land grants, maybe more, spread below them to the winding water, but they have a small, meandering creek to supply the water barrels.

It's 1801 and twelve acres of wheat have been sown and another twelve in maize, while chock and log fences contain thirty-five pigs, seven sheep and two goats. They need little by way of rations from the Government stores, a sure sign of their respectability as settlers, and the swaying field of wheat marks out their success when so many fail to grow more than lowly maize, now considered the food of the poor.

All should be well. Yet it isn't.

Cuddy, at fifty-five, is getting old to be flogging himself starting a new farm, and truth be told he likes the idea of having the land more than working it. Melva could rail against who he is, keep trying to change him and get bitter in doing it. Instead she cajoles, lets him see her ideas as her own. What matters these days is that her family thrives, for they are her whole world.

She's long since given up on having friends. The petty pretences of polite society in Sydney have followed officials and soldiers to Parramatta, and even convicts turned settler are apt to ape the ways of the respectable, at least in public.

It's not just Melva's accent that betrays her at St John's Church, its brick walls slowly sinking into a swamp while settlers' wives shuffle away from her in the pew. No matter how hard she has tried to befriend them, she will always be a foreigner, held up as different.

She is the means by which others can comfort themselves that they are somehow better, can be assured of the bond of belonging, for without a scapegoat to shut out they might have to face their own smallness, their insignificance.

Meanwhile, Cuddy may be illiterate, yet the chancer in him has found its time, for thieving's not required here when advantage can simply be taken.

The success of the farm spurs him to petition the Governor for assignment of convict labour. 'We can clear more land, wife, grow more grain and sell to the Commissariat, and more vegetables for Sydney Town's market.' Within a month he's sent two men.

In the wee hours of morning, Melva feeds baby George and reflects on their good fortune, with a farm paying its way and four healthy sons, even the money for a new dress if she needs it.

The baby pulls off the breast and stares up at her in the light of dying embers in the fireplace, as though he has seen something his mother does not. Perhaps he senses what she ought to have reckoned, that fate loathes perfection.

The birth has done no favours for the hernia that's gradually pushed through her abdomen wall, the cause of frequent pain so that she must leave the heavy lifting to her convict workers or her sons. More troubling is that what she eats makes her uncomfortable, so she starts to cut back on her food.

Even Cuddy finally notices. 'Yer eatin' like a darn sparrow, wife.'

'Getting older, I expect. Not needing big dinners.'

Cuddy, ever restless, is now seized by land hunger. Within weeks he is home, waving wildly to Melva as she weaves through tall corn in the bottom field.

'A surprise, my love. Here.' He thrusts a piece of paper into her hand when she reaches him. She can't read, it means nothing.

Cuddy clearly expects a joyful response, but she can't summon it when she knows her husband can be like a fish dallying with a hook, to the sorrow of them all.

'What is this?' She frowns, despite the effort to compose her face until she can decide if it's good news or not.

'A bill of sale, Melva. We be new owners of the chaplain's place, Porteous Mount, over in the Field of Mars.' Rev Richard Johnson's rheumatic pains are sending him back to England, his property regarded as one of the best in the district.

Cuddy's excitement grates on her. This is the first she's heard of it.

'A fine hundred and twenty acres, Melva. We gone up in the world … so many marines got land there they named it after a God.'

Cuddy's on a roll, hasn't noticed her concern.

'Mars, me dear. They called it after the Roman god o' war.' He is still waving his hands about.

'Think of it. Me Da were a hardscrabble farmer, worked to the bone by one o' the English toffs who owned half of Ireland. He'd be mighty proud, were he alive.'

Finally he draws breath and she can cut in.

'How, Cuddy? How you pay?'

'The money we put by o' course, from the Commissariat for our grain, and selling eggs and potatoes at Parramatta market. Also a loan agin what we have here.'

Melva's mouth falls open. So much work she does, in their cottage cooking, washing, tending to children, in the vegetable garden, and out in the fields all weather. Yet she's not worthy of him sharing his intentions.

Cuddy is too wound up to notice his wife's face stiffen with anger.

'We be givin' our boys a fine inheritance when they all grown. Fancy, even the oranges picked there fetch a shilling apiece. An' we get to keep two of Johnson's convict men.'

Melva's head is whirring, but she can see the sense in it for their family. She feigns a little excitement to disguise the shudder that comes with the thought that she will be stretched even more thinly.

It's not the end of it for Cuddy, though. Giddy with greed, he wants more land. He enlists in the New South Wales Corps, encouraging Roger to do the same. Though they'll be garrisoned in Sydney, away from the farm for weeks at a time, 'it be worth it, my love, they give rank and file good land grants at the end'.

In the face of such ambition, Melva is left standing in the echo chamber of her own thoughts, all distilling into one. *What about me?*

George may be a babe, but soon after first light she is in the fields with him in a basket close by, digging, weeding, supervising their two convict labourers. Seven-year-old Will and four-year-old Luis must work too, milking goats and feeding the pigs and sheep.

Cuddy's absence makes little difference to the farm, though Roger's labour is a great loss to his mother, for no convict worker will give what a grown son can when he's finally got the power to save his parents, unlike the child who could not. Fortunately, her eldest, now twenty-two, has been garrisoned at Parramatta and can oversee the Porteous Mount labourers in his time off.

In this way she goes on for two and a half years, one day melting into the next, till the Home Secretary sends orders to reduce the strength of the Corps and Cuddy is discharged.

He gets a further one hundred and forty acres, two miles or so to the north-east of their existing Kissing Point farm. When the grant comes through, Cuddy promptly sells the original farm to William Kent to clear debts they've carried since buying Porteous Mount.

Melva knows the first farm has been their stepping stone, though it saddens her to leave the place where she has grown into herself. Surely this will finally satisfy her husband.

Any sadness is swept away by dismay later that year when she is pregnant again at forty-one, a burden that threatens to overwhelm her body, the tiredness seeping into her bones, often keeping her from time in the fields. Her daughter arrives two weeks early by her reckoning, about the same time their autumn apples are ready for picking, but mercifully the birth is uneventful. The hernia bulges further, protruding as though her body is trying to turn itself inside out.

The baby's features are darker than Saffy's, with the glossy black hair and brown button eyes of her grandmother. Melva is glad of it; does not want to be reminded every day of olive-skinned Saffy, the girl she couldn't save.

Rosanna is the babe's name, though she is only ever called Rosa, a little girl who screams at the shock of drawing in her first lungful of air and hardly seems to stop crying in the months that follow.

Melva can't shake the sense that the girl has been sent to carry the family's grief, though whether it's past sorrow or yet to come she cannot say. She tells herself not to be so foolish and gives thanks instead for the gift of another daughter, one who wears the mark of Gibraltar in the colour of her skin.

CHAPTER SEVEN

TAM

LONDON, 1805

The best fish swim near the bottom.
Old English proverb

TEN IS A GOOD, ROUND number, she thinks. Makes a pleasing sound as it rises from the throat then fades to land without fuss on the roof of the mouth. She'd be that age now, by her reckoning, though no one in the Foundling Hospital knows what day she was born.

Even her name, Tam, she must keep secret. She was just shy of two years old, it's said, when left at the hospital. Like all the others, they destroyed her clothes and anything that came with her, then baptised her with a new name, Josephine. And a number, lest she dare think herself special. Ten thousand and twenty-seven. Another lovely ten, says so on the metal disc she must wear round her neck at all times.

She has a mother who birthed her, likely pretended a man had promised marriage but abandoned her, so the hospital would take Tam. The woman showed up once or twice a year with a few coins for the Matron. She pulled her daughter close one time, hissed in her ear. 'Tamsin be yer name. I called yer Tam, always remember that.' There's been no mention of this Ma for a while, no suggestion of who she is or whether she still lives.

The real Ma, the one who wiped her little bottom, fed her bread and honey, loved her till she was five and had to be given back to the hospital, she's the one Tam longs to be with. One of the hospital's many nurses who care for foundlings till they are returned for schooling and training, Elizabeth Kent travelled nearly forty miles from Berkshire to collect Tam after she was given over.

She curled in Mrs Kent's lap for the long, rocking coach ride to the busy market town of Reading, such was the hunger in her to be cared for the proper way. It was the first affection she could trust, not that she remembers much about life before that.

She is tall for her age, the high foundling cap emphasising the fact. Her shiny brown hair is long enough to be tied back, a rare opportunity for gratitude after the locks were shorn off a few years earlier to stop lice. Soon she will be old enough to go out to service, sent to be a housemaid in some fancy house. She is being trained to take orders, know her place, which always seems to be on the bottom rung. Oh that she could run away, get back to Mrs Kent.

Her thoughts are interrupted by the whack of a ruler on the back of her hand, a reminder to get back to her sums, but even as she feels the sting of it her mind is finding its way to Reading.

She goes there often, to a quiet refuge within, where peaceful thoughts of the town and Mrs Kent's welcoming cottage wrap her in calm, give warmth in the bare dormitory decorated only with a large wooden cross, protect her from the soul-less lectures and discipline telling her she's barely human. In the blunt barrage of routine, the identical dark uniforms and white pinafores that turn the girls into rows of wooden skittles, her secret place is a shield against their attempts to kill character and disposition.

She answers to Josephine when required, avoids the cane by following the rules, but the miraculous gift of her real name is a tiny light that shines within, keeping something alive that she cannot pin down, for which she has no words.

Tam. She is a person, not a pawn.

A child, yes, but those three letters give her hope of a future that is more than the one laid out by the teachers, the stewards, the moralising Reverend on Sundays, or the toffs that come at Christmas to hand out oranges and harp on what good fortune the children have.

Oh there's truth in it, she knows, that she is one of the lucky ones, with far more foundlings dead before reaching ten years than alive, but cross your heart and hope to die, she will do more than that. She will show them.

Winter has come in hard this year, the hospital pumps frozen some mornings so the boys must fill pails the night before or there'll be no water for washing faces at six o'clock or making gruel slopped into bowls at half past seven.

In the sewing room, Tam's stiff fingers are working on the fiddly rolled edging of a pocket handkerchief, one of many the girls stitch daily, along with night dresses, aprons, boys' shirts and caps the hospital sells.

Her friend Becca sits beside her as she usually does. Though silence is required, the girls always manage a careful whisper back and forth as they work the needles. Today, though, Tam hears not a word from her friend, whose brow is beaded with sweat despite the room's chill.

When the six o'clock supper bell rings, Tam scans the lines of children, but Becca isn't there.

'Please ma'am, where be Rebecca?' It's risky to ask such a question of the Night Assistant, but Tam is desperate to know.

'Take your seat, girl. Do not concern yourself with others or you'll regret it.'

For five days Tam worries about her friend, until a whisper comes down the row of beds after lights out. Becca is in the infirmary, got scrofula bad. 'Blood and pus pourin' from lumps on her neck.' The girl next to Tam passes on the information with a tone of glee, briefly important for once.

It is impossible to get into the infirmary. Every minute of the day is accounted for, but even if Tam could sneak to the entrance there's a guard at the door to prevent unwarranted visitors causing spread of diseases.

All Tam can do is take Becca with her into the warm kitchen of Mrs Kent, imagine the two of them stepping through the doorway, her friend healing through the love and care that lies there.

Towards the end of the month, Tam has taken her turn reading the catechism when the teacher tells her to stay behind. The woman, heavy gown rustling, lowers her voice to a rasp.

'I'm going to tell you something then it will never be mentioned again, and if you say I told you I will deny it.' She looks towards the door, in case Matron is passing. 'I know you and Rebecca were friends, so it's only right you know that she's gone.'

Tam studies the teacher's bony fingers, clasped in front of her.

'Gone, ma'am?' An odd buzzing has started between her ears.

'To heaven, girl.' The teacher is regretting the rash decision to do this, hasn't the stomach for a scene. She summons her normal harsh tone. 'Now run along.'

This isn't the first friend Tam has lost. Girls are wheeled away every week when smallpox strikes, or measles, the bloody flux, lung ailments. This death is worse, breaks through the wall Tam has built brick by brick around her heart. Becca, with her gentle ways and bright smile, had a softness that nothing of hospital life could harden.

The feeling that surges through Tam is too big to contain. Becca gone, keeper of the flame of tenderness, a twin to the toughness Tam's been forced to grow, making it easier to bear. It's as if part of Tam has died. She can't understand it, panics at the strong pull of emotion that pins her down.

In the exercise yard she goes mindlessly to the wall and begins banging her head against the sandstone. More pain is the answer. Thump, thump, thump. Blood trickling down one eye. Thump, thump. Boys cackling. Thump. Empty me, God, make me unfeeling. Thump, thump. Arms pulled roughly behind. Boots dragging as she's carried off.

Weeks later, after the beating has thrashed any grief from her, Tam drifts as a phantom trapped between worlds. She has lost her friend, but far worse, can no longer find the doorway to the secret room within where Mrs Kent's arms open wide and a place waits for her beside the fire.

The emptiness haunts her in class, where the teacher extols the wonders of new-fangled iron-making factories, telling them all how proud they should be that their country has invented the process to make a product far superior to pig iron.

Tam sits in the middle row, rolling her eyes as she waits for the moral of the story, because in this place lessons always lead to virtues. She is barely listening when a thought flashes in. She is the pig iron, full of impurities that no amount of hammering, puddling or rolling can remove. It's the only explanation for why she has been brought so low. It is down to her, with faults that run in her veins. She is no good.

It's a thought likely to be disturbing for any other child, but not Tam. She rolls it around in her mind, at last understanding there's no point fighting it. She is bad by nature, as destined to grow the way she's made as a stream must wend its way to the sea, or an apricot kernel grow into the tree. She lets it rise into the void, fill her to the brim.

What is bad begets worse of its kind, will meet with greater punishment. Still, she must not be afraid, can only be what she is, hasn't the power to stop it anyway. The realisation brings a whiff of freedom. It is different to the cosiness of imagining Mrs Kent's cottage; is rough, pushy, will not bow and bend to what comes because now she knows who she is, and it sure isn't sweetness and spice.

The seed has been sown. It signals its presence in Tam with irritation in response to the timetable and the rules, leading her to answer back to teachers, attracting another beating. When she hides under her bed instead of going to her seat for afternoon lessons, she is thrashed again, this time with the whip instead of the cane.

A better idea comes to her. She will break out of the place that is her prison. From that day on she watches carefully for any weakness she can exploit. The gardener's barrow might be somewhere she could hide, maybe get wheeled through the gate, but he leaves every day empty-handed, storing it in a shed beside the kitchen garden. The big wooden gate on Ormond Street occasionally swings wide to let in a carriage carrying some official or other, but there's always a footman and driver on duty, beady eyes looking this way and that.

Months pass and her frustration builds. Early one morning, Tam and the older girls are helping the younger ones dress when the dormitory steward taps her on the shoulder.

'Matron's office, now.'

She doesn't question the order. Likely some trumped-up wrongdoing, a misdeed by another girl who's blamed it on her. She trudges through light snow to the office, but when she is ushered in, Matron stands to one side and two men sit stiffly behind a table.

'Where are your manners, girl'. Matron needs a display of discipline and Tam, in her confusion, obliges by dipping her head before the men. One of them speaks briefly, introducing himself and his companion as hospital governors.

'We are led to believe you are a spirited child.' The fellow is accustomed to being in charge and pauses for effect.

'As you are now eleven, it has been deemed in your best interests for your excess energies to be directed to a productive purpose.'

It begins to dawn on Tam that she is being placed in a position as housemaid. She will be tamed by servitude.

The two governors, dressed in white shirts and dark jackets like matching salt and pepper pots, nod in unison. The one speaking holds up papers. 'Your indenture will be with a man of good standing. You will be bound for four years with Mr John Bainbridge, a draper in Red Lion Passage at Bloomsbury.'

Matron now feels the need to assert her authority. 'As you have shown aptitude for arithmetic, this will be a most fortunate placement for you. Your responsibilities are to include keeping his accounts.'

Nothing is required from Tam. She is irrelevant to this stilted ceremony, which seeks no agreement from her save doing their bidding by signing her name on the last page of the papers.

By the time the other girls are seated in class, Tam is following Matron across the icy yard, carrying her packed bag to the side gate. Any farewells have been hurried, no time for tears, no last hugs for the little ones.

Out on the street the gate clanks shut behind her. A coach would be wasted on a foundling, of course, even though it's freezing cold and she must walk at least a mile to the address on the slip of paper she clutches.

This is Tam's first time in London outside the hospital walls, and she is dazzled by merchants hailing one another, the rattle of passing coaches, squealing ragamuffins running hither and thither. People spill from doorways, carters' horses drag loaded drays up the street, hawkers carry onions, old boots, dead rabbits. The commotion has no rhyme or reason, at least to her eye, accustomed to the order and enforced quiet she's left behind. The excitement of it causes her to smile, makes her light-headed when she should be paying attention to her surrounds.

Soon she must admit that she is quite lost. When she asks for directions she finds she has been walking for a good hour the wrong way. The weak sun is riding high through chimney smoke when she finds herself at Red Lion Square, surrounded by tightly stacked terraces three storeys high, flaunting decorative doorcases and stucco walls. In the centre a railing fence hems in four square grass plots, marked out by rows of trees.

The square looks dull, bringing to mind a country churchyard missing only the sound of the parson's cow bellowing to be milked. She laughs as she wanders along one side, chuckling between the mooing sounds she makes as she walks.

Her bag is dragging heavily against her thigh, and she is thirsty, must get on with finding the draper's. At the north-eastern corner of the square, she almost misses the entrance to the diagonal laneway, one of a nest of narrow foot passages leading away from soaring frontages to meaner buildings packed in behind.

Red Lion Passage is busy at this time of day, people browsing at a table of second-hand books outside a bookseller's, studying chairs outside the furniture-maker's, going in and out of the candle-maker's premises, the shoemaker's, a peruke maker. The lane bristles with shops, their proprietors living in rooms above.

More than half-way along she spies the sign for Bainbridge Draper's, above a green door separating two dirty display windows. She steps inside, seeing rolls of faded fabric forsaken by customers. The air reeks of neglect. Tam shivers nervously, for it's a seedy establishment.

She waits in the gloom, staring at the unattended counter and wondering how to summon the owner, when the door is abruptly flung open. A young man sprints past, swiping aside a curtain and disappearing into another room.

She hears the fellow say something muffled, hurried, and a man's voice curtly reply. Then the fellow rushes past and back out the door as though she's no more than one of the flyspecks on the wall.

She can't stand there stiff as a washboard, and calls out hesitantly, not wanting to get off on the wrong foot.

'Mr Bainbridge, sir. It be Tam Pummell, sent to work for you.'

The curtain rustles and a balding head appears, followed by a squat body. His face is tight, one side of his mouth pulled up in a puzzled expression. Silly girl, he's expecting someone called Josephine.

'They named me Josephine at the hospital, though folks call me Tam. At your service, sir.' She bobs a little, unsure how much respect she should show.

'Ah, yes I see. Don't much care what you're called, long as you work hard, keep a careful tongue.'

He gestures for her to pass the curtain and trots behind her into the other room, which is even more dim than the shop. 'Wait here. I'll call Mrs Bainbridge.'

The woman who appears is no taller than her husband, perhaps a little wider. Tam sees how unfortunate it is, given the woman is wearing a pale blue dress in the new empire fashion. The garment attempts to bring shape under the bust but fails miserably, the gown flowing to the floor in a straight line so that Mrs Bainbridge looks rather like a bollard.

'Bring your bag. It's nearly midday, so you can unpack and then I expect you'll be ready for a bit o' dinner.'

Mrs Bainbridge moves towards the stairs, dropping the friendly tone as she speaks to her husband over her shoulder, not bothering that Tam's right beside her. 'Dear me, bit younger than we was led to understand.'

Up two flights of stairs, Mrs Bainbridge ushers her into an attic, the space so narrow it can only fit a bed against the wall and a low table beside it for a candle. A long shelf has been nailed to the opposite wall. The saving grace is a window at the end with a view all to herself, even if it is the roof of the building opposite and a small patch of sky. What luck just the same.

Tam should be polite, thank the woman, make an attempt at pleasantries as she's been taught.

'No bell on the shop door, ma'am?'

The woman studies Tam's expression then sighs in a manner that shows the girl she already thinks she's a dunce. 'Course not. No need to telegraph the neighbours whereupon folks enter.'

A shop not bothering to attend to customers. Tam is so muddled that Mrs Bainbridge is on her way out of the room when she remembers her manners.

'Thank you, Missus Bainbridge.'

The woman gives a curt nod. 'Come down quick as you can and we'll eat.'

A few minutes later Tam goes down to the next floor and knocks at the Bainbridge's rooms. The door opens into a modest parlour with a wall covered in red swirling wallpaper. In front of it are two winged chairs and the first sofa Tam's ever seen, while the pendulum on a large clock on the opposite wall ticks soft as a heartbeat.

Unlike the shop, the room is spick and span, furniture carefully polished, no dust on the mantel above the grate. They go through to the kitchen, where the table has three place settings and an abundant selection of bread, cheese, cold meats, butter and two pots, each containing a different jam.

'Sit yerself down. Mr Bainbridge is on his way up.'

As the three of them eat, the Bainbridges reel off the duties expected of Tam: shopping, help with cleaning and cooking, lighting the fire, keeping an eye on the shop door on the off chance a customer enters, and looking after the ledgers.

'No talkin' to anyone 'bout our business.' Mr Bainbridge slaps the table as he says it.

Tam bites her tongue. She may be just a girl, but surely the more people who know about the shop the better supply of customers they will get.

The Bainbridges prove to be fair, sharing food generously with Tam and buying her a set of servant clothes, though she is shown none of the warm-heartedness of Mrs Kent.

Unschooled in the ways of the world, Tam is slow to unravel the mystery of where the Bainbridges get the money she writes in the accounts three times a week. Each day, except Sundays, the same three young men dash in and out of the room behind the shop until mid-afternoon, when Mr Bainbridge puts on his hat and departs till supper time.

One afternoon Tam is sent out later than usual to the market. She spies her employer at the top of the laneway and hurries to follow him as he walks at a clip, turning right onto Red Lion Street and continuing down to the corner of High Holborn.

He disappears through a throng of well-dressed young men, pots of ale in hand, into a narrow inn with a sign above the door, The Red Lion.

She pretends to look at scented waters, soaps and hair powders in the window of a nearby perfumery while keeping watch. One of Mr Bainbridge's young men, head down, hurries into the inn. He has barely left when another scurries through the door.

'Oi, you girl.' The assistant in the perfumery has noticed her loitering and suspects her intentions. 'Be off with you.' He claps his hands as if scaring off a stray mutt.

Within the hour she is back in the Bainbridge kitchen, unloading the shopping while her mistress tallies the change, pleased it is correct.

'You do well with sums, young miss. Mr Bainbridge and I approve of your work. He plans to send a letter, let the hospital guvs know we be keeping you on.'

Sundays after church, Tam is free to go where she pleases. Many folks are out strolling, including lawyers and students from nearby Gray's Inn, where they study to practise law or become legal clerks.

The toffs hold little interest for her, and in any case they are oblivious to the slip of a girl wandering this way and that. It's the street urchins that draw Tam's attention as they run and climb, sometimes in pairs, others in small gangs looking to practice the light-fingered arts.

They seem free as a flock of sparrows, flitting here, alighting there, unafraid when men shout at them or box their ears when they get too close. The girls, some not six or seven, bring a smile to Tam's face as they feign injury to beg for ha'pennies and pennies.

She pauses near a girl close to her own age, ready to give a greeting.

'Bugger off.' The girl jerks her head, has spoken without moving her mouth. 'This be my patch.'

'I've an apple, cheese, bread.' Tam gestures to the brown paper parcel tucked under her shawl. 'Wanna share?'

'If this a trick, you be a dead one.' The girl takes the splint from the supposedly broken leg and stands, spitting on one hand then holding it out. Tam shakes it. On the steps of a nearby church they share the food, and Tam finds herself talking about the Bainbridges.

'Odd, ya know, lads comin' and going.'

Her new friend, Nancy, chortles. 'Mebbe you have nice clothes, lovie, but you a muttonhead fer sure.'

'Watcha mean?'

Nancy arches her fingers together, as she's seen learned folk do when they have knowledge.

'Your master, he be a bookie, takin' bets while the law looks the other way. Mebbe even payin' off the police, who knows.'

Tam's never heard of such a thing. 'But the men dashin' hither and thither?'

'They be your master's runners, lads who can outrun the traps, collecting bets, payin' off winners, being lookouts.'

Tam takes a deep breath, grasping that a new education has begun, the kind you only get on the streets. Nancy fills her in on how the odds work for cricket matches, card games, cock fights, bare-knuckle prize fights. 'Anything where grown men want to throw a wager. All of it agin the law.'

At last the dingy draper's shop makes sense, and her master's stint most afternoons at the inn where students of the law mill about, their father's money jangling in their pockets.

The fat tallies of pounds, shillings and pence in the weekly accounts, while nary a bolt of cloth moves from the shelf, are the gains of illegal gambling. A chill passes through Tam, as though someone's walked across her grave.

CHAPTER EIGHT

MELVA

PARRAMATTA, 1805

THE COW IS THE FIRST sign that something is amiss. Eleven-year-old Will comes running into the house, panting, shouting that the Drakensberger has collapsed in her stall. Luis, at eight years, is keen to seem useful and is at Will's heels, echoing what his brother says.

Melva shuts the door behind her on George, playing with rough cut wooden blocks, and little Rosa napping in a corner of the kitchen. She follows the older boys out to the barn where she left the cow, confident it would be some time before the labour resulted in the birth of a calf that promises to expand their herd.

Now, though, the cow is lying on her side, tongue lolling in the hay, drool bubbling and hanging in strings around her mouth.

'What be wrong, Ma? She alright?' Will turns a hopeful face up to his mother.

Melva ignores the question and kneels beside the cow, running a hand along her flank. Her sides are heaving and her breathing rapid.

'How long she like this?'

'Dunno. Found her in this state a few minutes ago.'

Melva sees the cow won't make it. They must save the calf or waste the ten guineas they paid for the beast.

'Get Pat. He in bottom field. Quick, run.'

Will is gone in a flash to fetch Pat Kennar, the convict who's been with them for nearly two years. Melva trusts him more than the other fellow, and Pat grew up on a farm in Devon, knows about animals.

By the time he arrives with Will the cow is almost gone.

'Must get calf out.' Melva has a large kitchen knife at the ready, but is uncertain how to cut or where, not wanting to harm the young one.

Pat hesitates. Convict masters look for any reason to stop good assignees from getting pardons, wanting to keep them on their farms as long as possible. Playing a part in the death of a cow and calf is a dangerous business when it's their word against yours.

'Help, Pat. You save calf?'

The cow gives a brief shudder and goes still. Pat makes no attempt to take the knife, instead pulling the cow's left leg out straight to tension the dorsal, and gesturing with his head. 'There, start there, missus.'

Her hand is shaking as she pushes the tip of the knife into the skin. 'Bit higher. They got two horns on the womb. The calf be up there, in that one.'

She makes a second cut, working as quickly as she can through muscle and fat to the shiny, slippery coating around the calf. Pat spies the hooves. 'Quick missus, take it wider, an' I can get 'im.'

Will has fetched a rope and Pat breaks the water bag, looping the rope around the pair of hooves. The strain has taken it out of Melva, who's thinner than ever, and she sits back against the barn wall, the bloodied knife in her hand, as Pat pulls the black calf free.

For a long minute there's no movement as the labourer tears the sac free and begins vigorously rubbing the calf. Then an eye flickers and from it a pulse passes through the newborn, which starts struggling, wobbling on front legs as it tries to stand. As life floods into the calf it seems to drain from Melva, and she looks down at the hay, as though it's her own blood in the straw and not the cow's.

She is dragging her feet back to the cottage when she hears one-year-old Rosa bawling in bursts. Closer to the cottage, she hears in short intervals the sound of the baby choking. The door bangs open to the sight of Rosa against the wall and four-year-old George holding a large bread crust, vigorously trying to force it into the girl's mouth despite her gagging and fighting to turn her head away.

'No, George.' Melva slaps the crust from his hand. He begins squalling, making Rosa cry even harder.

'Ma-maa. Rosie want eat.' George is gulping back sobs, distressed his mother is angry.

Melva kneels on the floor, pulling Rosa into the curve of one arm, it dawning on her that the boy was trying to help his sister. 'Oh George.' She scoops him into the other arm, holding them both against her chest, salty tears wetting their heads.

So much sadness in the kitchen, the floor is awash with it, and she doesn't know why she cries.

Roger is still in the Corps and divides his time between Sydney duties and farmwork at Porteous Mount, while Cuddy took the river ferry the day before to have their wheat milled in Sydney, requiring him to stay overnight. She hopes he doesn't fall into a dice game or get drinking at one of the sly grog shanties and be late returning.

As it happens he is back mid-afternoon, dismayed to find the cow is dead. Such is the import of it that the *Sydney Gazette* reports the incident the following week, lamenting the 'weighty loss to the circumstances of the large family'.

Melva is quite worn out by the turn of events. With four youngsters still to be cared for, as well as farm work, she is flagging more than ever. Since Rosa's birth she has strapped the hernia daily, using a truss made from a timber hoop Cuddy steamed into shape, with pads she stitched, stuffed with sheep's wool and attached to the ends. It hurts just the same to lift Rosa when she's fretful, or wet sheets on washing day.

After all the hungry years the family now has an abundance of vegetables, grains, eggs, meat, and fruits including apples, peaches and lemons – so much that even their two convict labourers are off Government rations. Yet no matter how her belly rumbles she must nibble as little as possible or the griping pain sets in. Strangely, old yearnings have returned for Gibraltan flavours – the salty smack of anchoas on the tongue, the heat of ras el hanout, the smokiness of paprika on pinchitos.

The farm is in need of rain. Their new Kissing Point land is twice as far from Parramatta River, and Lane Cove River, beyond their eastern boundary with the Field of

Mars common, is saltwater up this far, so they rely on a trickling creek that now barely flows.

Melva is relieved two days later when dark clouds begin massing from the north-east. Soon the cottage is so dark she must light a lamp to see the knife she's wielding, slicing cabbage thinly for the pickling barrel. The two youngest children are restless, agitated by the charge in the air, while the older two are out in the fields helping their Papa on the labourers' day off.

Something will happen soon, the brooding air says so. It's a pressure of waiting that gets too much for George. He snatches Rosa's peg doll from her hand, hiding it behind his back while she squeals at such a pitch that Melva's nerves snap.

'George, enough! Come here.' She gives him a spoon and sets him to work stirring a boiling pot over the fire.

Rosa quietens. The only noises in the kitchen are Melva's knife smoothly slicing the cabbage with a pleasing crunch, and George clattering the spoon on the side of the pan to signal his displeasure at the task.

Suddenly, a flash of brilliant white light throws every dull corner into sharp relief. With a deafening bang Melva is knocked against the wall, the outside door thrown open to hang by one hinge.

The lightning strike has hit the chimney stack, travelled down it, found the metal spoon and George holding it. He slams back, flung to the floor in a stupor.

Melva crawls to him as a more distant bang sounds. George's hair on the right side of his head, the same side as the hand holding the spoon, is singed, stinking. She takes him in her arms, shakes the limp body to rouse him.

'George, wake. Please, George.' She slaps him on the cheek. No response. Puts her ear against his mouth, feels a faint breath.

Then she realises Rosa is strangely quiet. On the other side of the table she finds her, unharmed, her mouth open in shock.

Going back to George, Melva kneels and pulls him onto her lap, rocking him, crooning. Several minutes pass before he comes round, complaining of a terrible pain in his head.

'Thank you Lord, thank you.' She says it over and over as she continues to rock him.

He is like the newborn calf, struggling to come to life. When he does, he needs her help to get to his feet. He takes a step and falls down, the right leg lacking strength. While the use of it will return in the coming days, the foot will always turn out a little.

Melva is catching her breath, rubbing her sore chest when Will appears, purple-faced, gasping. 'It be Da. He's no good.'

She runs with him to the bottom of the wheat field, where Cuddy sits, legs splayed, stupefied, Luis sitting close by, helpless.

'What happen Cuddy, tell me.' He doesn't seem to hear her or register her presence.

Luis pulls at her sleeve, covering his terror with a voice pretending authority greater than his eight years.

'The lightnin' Ma, shot out of nowhere in a ball of fire, split the rock next to Da. He swayed a bit, dropped to the ground like a sack o' potatoes.'

'You hurt, my dear?'

No reply.

She passes her hand back and forth in front of his eyes. He doesn't blink, staring vacantly.

Will is at her elbow, wiping his snotty nose on the sleeve of his jacket when what he wants to do is sob.

'Help get Papa up.' They each get under one arm and try to lift him but can't budge his dead weight.

Melva sends Will to the house for a blanket and a pannikin of water, then sits beside Cuddy, stroking his arm, his hair.

'Return to us, my love. I beg you, we need you.'

She takes his hand, noticing for the first time the raised veins, knotty fingers, coarse palm. Her Cuddy is getting old, but God has just had his chance to shatter his bones, strike him down for good. Surely he does not intend him to die now.

A thunderclap shakes the ground, then another booms overhead, a crashing sound that bounces in waves around them. Rain begins to fall, a few drops at first but within minutes a steady rush of water has them soaked.

She sees her son running towards them. 'Your boy, he go fetch a neighbour, we get help soon. Promise.'

'Melva.' Cuddy whispers her name, staring ahead.

Yes, my darling. I here.'

'I've a terrible ringin' in my ears.' He starts to cry. 'It's all dark, wife. I can see nothing at all.'

Nature has turned against them, and Melva can't help but think it's the jinn, for Mama feared them and wore a red cord around her wrist to keep them at bay.

'The natives, more like. They be the ones who curse us for gettin' in the way.' Cuddy's not one to believe in the evil eye, and he attempts a smile to show he's joking.

Melva, though, has no time for humour as she nurses her husband, his sight slowly returning, while taking on some of Cuddy's farm work. George, too, needs care. He is recovering, growing stronger, though has a more nervous disposition these days. Even Rosa is different, hungry for her mother's touch and attention, clinging on so that Melva fears the toddler's needs will eat her up.

Their misfortune continues when their newly sprouted wheat crop is struck down by blight, its reddish powder weakening stems and leaves, shrivelling the seeds.

'It be bad luck, wife. Nothin' more.'

Nothing more? If he weren't so weak she would remind him that the earlier planting was almost in full bloom when hailstones the size of pigeons' eggs sliced it down.

Cuddy runs through the list he loves to chant out loud. 'Two hundred and sixty-five acres we own or lease, forty-five of 'em planted in barley, maize and vegetables. Thirty bushels of grain in store. Then there's the horse, seven cattle, forty sheep, as many pigs, and not forgettin' the two damn goats.'

He claps his hands, rubbing them together. 'No need to be worryin', Melva. We not motherless broke, starvin' like we did way back in London.'

She nods, agreeing with the soundness of what he says, careful not to point out that they've acquired some of that land from farmers who failed, the ones who don't have a wife with a nose for what the soil needs, fingertips that sense what crops to rotate after harvest, hair that signals with a strange tingling when the rains are about to come.

Still, she can't help the queer feeling that keeps her out of kilter, one hand often ready, reaching, as though she will need to brace against a wall or door at any minute.

If any good has come from the lightning strikes it's that Cuddy stays closer to home, often within sight of Melva, trusting the work at Porteous Mount to the convict labour, overseen by Roger.

She has never doubted her husband's love, but now he is on the mend he shows his affection more readily. A squeeze on the shoulder, a touch of the hand, a stray hair brushed back from her eyes. In bed he curls into her back, one arm flung across her waist, holding tight so she is not lost to him in sleep. Dozing off, he whispers words of endearment she has not heard for years. 'You be my beating heart, love. The best o' me.'

She reassures him as she might one of her children after a calamitous event. 'Shh, no need for fretting. All is well, mi amor, all is well.'

As she relaxes, the door to sleep swinging open, she smiles at her good fortune despite everything, amused that the innocent girl of Gibraltar saw a bright soul in this man. She may be forty-three years and he nearly sixty, but she cherishes him still, not least because he has allowed her the freedom to be a sower of seed. If she stood still in the fields for long enough green shoots would sprout from her feet, for the earth and all it grows is in her, as the apple is in the pip and in time will become the tree that bears the fruit.

They are through the worst of it. There is no curse, the old adivina was wrong. Yes, there has been misfortune aplenty, but it has led to a prosperity for her and the family that she could never have imagined as she stood in the narrow, cobbled street watching a man catch three onions.

During the next few weeks Cuddy's sight returns, though it will always be a little blurred. He is useful again, hoeing the fields with their convict men, Will and Luis close by, learning, helping when it's time to thresh grain or cut timber for another outbuilding.

Melva is grateful for it, and the fact that her husband no longer goes to the Malting Shovel Inn next to the riverbank brewery, drinking cloudy ale with watermen waiting for the tide to turn.

The family's peace is largely undisturbed as Christmas approaches, despite the pair of free-booters, escaped from a road gang, who break in. The adjacent common, six thousand acres of it along Lane Cove River, hides desperate people in its tangle of forests: bushranger convicts, smugglers, illegal timber-cutters, men who've jumped ship, anyone with something to hide.

The Ranses are fast asleep in the dead of night, their men snoring in their hut, when Cuddy is stirred by an unfamiliar noise. He cocks his pistol and pads quietly to the bedroom door, opening it a crack. A shadow moves outside the front door, swinging on its hinges.

'Stop or I'll shoot.' The figure runs towards the closest outhouse, where a horse and rider waits, and mounts a second steed with a bag clutched in one hand, riding off swiftly before Cuddy can take aim.

'What is it?' Melva stands in the doorway, a candle in her hand.

'Bastards. So quiet no one heard. Let's see what they got away with.'

A bag of flour, a pie cooked that day, the clock on the mantle and a tin with a few coins. They have lost very little, unlike their two thieves, caught soon after, pleading guilty to breaking and entering. Within two weeks they are swinging from the gallows.

Meanwhile, the Guv has taken a hard line upriver with the original people, a few years earlier ordering that guns be fired at natives around Parramatta to drive them back from settlers' habitations. The natives' warrior leader, Pemulwuy, has now been shot, beheaded.

Melva's glad that natives who show up sometimes around farms at Kissing Point are no bother. Some still fish on the river, others emerge from the woods occasionally to ask for food. They give them a little meat, perhaps a sack of flour or basket of vegetables and let them camp awhile on the edge of the house paddock, where they light a fire to cook and eat before they move on. With local farms so far from the garrison at Parramatta, Cuddy has directed his men and family to follow the example of brewer James Squire, who encourages cordial relations.

She tells herself it was the smallpox a decade earlier that reduced their numbers, doesn't want to believe there's blood in the soil where she walks and works. Yet stories of conflict in the outer areas pass from neighbour to neighbour, spread like a vine that grows to grip farm after farm. Some days she worries it will choke her.

None choose to examine what acts have been committed to provoke the natives or wonder at why they would be content to give up their land, their hunting and gathering places disturbed by hooves, guns and fences. She tries not to think about it, wants to forget the women who came more than once to raid the maize, the mothers and children who went to the riverbank at Parramatta when the golden wattle flowers bloomed, carrying digging sticks and woven bags, gathering yams, cockles, mud whelks. Or the ones on the river, balanced in bark canoes with a small fire in the centre set on a mound of soil, singing as they threw out their lines, cooking the catch as they went.

Her mind, though, fails to bend to any act of will, intent these days on throwing off locks on sealed boxes of memory and knowing. The frailer she becomes the deeper it seems to be drawn into contemplating what has been lost in order for her to gain.

She tells herself that this is no different to Gibraltar, invaded by Muslims, overthrown by Spain, and finally claimed by the British. The way of the world.

So when the news comes of another outbreak of trouble, two hundred or more natives taking a farm downriver, then a settler killed not a mile away, terrible things done to his body, it shouldn't crush her spirit.

'Why does it bother you so? We be havin' no trouble round here.'

Melva has no reply for Cuddy. It's a mystery to her, the sinking sensation making no sense.

Next day she takes George and Rosa down to the wharf near the brewery to fetch a pot of mud oysters. Cuddy has his heart set on a beef pie for Christmas Day and the oysters will add good flavour. Roger will join them, a chance to get him to open up a bit, see if he'll let on if he's courting yet. Maybe he still has an eye on the girl over Windsor way, deserted by the Papa they say, then the

Mama killed in a cart accident, the girl left to run a small farm and look after siblings. Not of age yet to wed. Yes, maybe that's the one her son waits for.

The colony has so few women that girls get snatched up at the earliest opportunity, some as young as ten or eleven if the Papa and Mama agree. She worries about the future for Rosa, a churning backwater her mind goes to if she's awake in the wee hours.

As Melva and the children cross towards the water's edge, a voice calls to her from the shadows beside the wharf. A native fellow staggers to his feet and waves her towards him with one hand, holding up the other to show he means no harm.

Melva has seen Old Jimmy before and steps towards him.

'Baccy, missus. You got 'em baccy?' He gestures with a clay pipe.

She shakes her head, ready to move on. The old man, dressed in the remnant of a jacket and convict slops with filthy cuffs above silt-covered bare feet, stumbles a little from the grog, weaving towards her. He stops a few feet away and turns to face the river.

'Hear, missus. You hear 'im?' He waves an arm slowly in a wide arc, as though gathering in the sky, the water resting at the end of its ebb tide, and the riverbank opposite.

'Ai yai, wallumai there, he swim. Star ... moon ... tree ... bird ... wallaby, all animal friend.' He draws himself up tall, dignified, thumps his chest, eyes filling with tears.

'Disfella country plenty spirit come in.'

His hand still rests on his heart as he turns his face to the sky, alone in his sympathy with nature around him, and for a fleeting moment Melva glimpses the depth of belonging that holds Jimmy and his kind in land, water, sky and all they contain. Though farms, towns, guns block his freedom, his kinship with this country has not been taken from him.

George doesn't like the look of the fellow and tugs at his Ma's arm for them to get away. His mother, though, is taking in the old fellow's words, her own eyes misting.

It is no accident Old Jimmy is on the riverbank when she arrives. He has been sent to remind her that her flesh and bones, the very roots of her, are still called somewhere else, a land denied her, and he stands in the power of it despite ragged clothes, a mind dulled by grog.

She doesn't belong here, no more than did her first daughter, Saffy. The land that lays claim to Melva Ranse is a long way over the seas, in a place where the setting sun throws long shadows of time across the face of The Rock. The remembering stabs her in the guts, such that she is caught off-guard, must bend a little to catch her breath.

She turns for home with the oyster pot, hasn't the stomach for foraging today, the children grizzling about the change of plan.

Up at the farm, four screeching black cockatoos, tails flashing yellow, rise as one from a she-oak. Instead of flapping off they circle above. Melva strains, eyes glancing across thin clouds then scanning the fields to catch sight of what disturbs them. She sees nothing in the emptiness, the cause of their disquiet invisible to her.

CHAPTER NINE

TAM

LONDON, 1808-09

CHURCH IS AN ORDEAL RATHER than a revelation. The sitting still, the endless sermons on piety and vigilance against temptation, it's enough to set Tam's teeth on edge. Yet, perched in the pew beside Mrs Bainbridge and her husband, she can bask in a little of the respectability bestowed on shopkeepers and merchants, even the phony ones.

St George's itself is vast, its ceiling soaring two storeys high, light flooding in from arched windows at ground level and above, while those at the front glow with rich colours on painted glass. It is the lofty space, the light pouring onto her head, that speaks to Tam of her immortal soul, of promise in eternal life, not the priest's urging to barter your way to it through tithing to pay penance.

They walk there every Sunday; Mrs Bainbridge insists on it. What Tam at first thought was pretence has given way to an understanding that her mistress truly believes the invention of herself as the wife of an upstanding man of business. Tam has learned to be careful about discussing any details of what she does downstairs in managing the bookie's ledgers, aware that the fantasy must be maintained or her mistress will fall apart.

She is not a motherly woman but treats her well enough, and her master has responded to Tam's work with a degree of respect and trust, a new experience the girl appreciates but finds difficult to take in, as though the hospital sent her out the gate with a crab-like crust instead of skin.

The workday is long and Mrs Bainbridge is particular about the way domestic chores must be done, prone to lecture Tam on the way she speaks and carries herself, determined to make her more of a lady than the girl cares to be. Yet there is the lure of a good reference in a year when her time's up, and for now the freedom of her day off each week.

'Look at yer, busting outta that dress.' Nance is laughing, pointing at Tam's tight bodice. 'Gettin' big coker-nuts now, me girl. Have to watch out fer the fellas, fer sure.'

Tam tugs at the dress, annoyed to be reminded that her shape is filling out.

'Best you ask yer mistress for some coin, get yerself to the market for something that do a bit less advertisin' of yer wares.'

Nance is mightily pleased with her jest, though her crowing belies the fact that she fears her own curves and works hard every day on her skills as a thief, cut-purse and look-out for the charleys because they are the threadbare line, slight as a strand of silk, that separates her from having to spread her legs for money.

When she sees the flaming face of her friend, she gets serious.

'I know you not like that. Them strumpets and dollymops, they be stupid as wooden spoons, need no smarts for that line o' work. All you gettin' is the pox, or brought low by the gin and yer puddy-house dumped to rot in the Thames.'

Tam gives her a grin. 'Got no mind to get into that line o' work anyways. You know me, Nance, I got plans.'

Her friend is quiet for a bit, thinking about what good fortune it would be to have learning, to read a book, use a pen for words or sums.

The moment is broken when Tam pulls out the food she brings each week, brandishing the rarity of a ripe peach.

'Well, you outdone yerself terday.'

Nothing, neither the chilly spring breeze nor the swearing of the cat-meat costermonger hollering about the appeal of his boiled horse meat, can ruin the enjoyment of the two girls as they sit on the step, shoulders rubbing, wiping sticky mouths.

Tam's heart feels light. A friend such as Nance is a salvation, a guardian angel. She is yet to discover that human nature is messier than that, for the same person can also be your undoing.

The weather has taken a sharp turn for the worse, a strange contradiction to the July heatwave that hit ninety-five degrees in the shade, carthorses dropping dead in the harness. Now it's December and grimy fog has hung low to the ground for ten days, so thick the Maidenhead coach lost its way to London from the west and overturned, seriously injuring at least three people.

A northerly wind clears the pea-souper, only to announce it's an Arctic messenger carrying a frost so thick it weakens masonry walls, shards of stone falling into the street where the few foolhardy venturers skitter and fall.

Tam helps Mrs Bainbridge nail old quilts across the windows, but even with the coal fire burning brightly they must keep on their caps and coats.

'The cold's no excuse to be idle,' she snaps, insisting that her charge still go out to do errands and buy food.

Tam is not offered pattens. Had she been given them, the iron ring below the overshoes would have given extra grip, essential for the ice. Mrs Bainbridge, nonetheless, makes one concession to the weather, roasting an extra potato at dinnertime so that Tam has a hot one for her pocket when she leaves in the early afternoon.

She is not five steps from the door when she lurches, landing heavily on her rump.

'Ooh, elegant as a dumped basket o' washing.'

Nance shelters in the doorway of the shop opposite, smiling though she shivers in an oversized men's overcoat tied in the middle with old rope and wears fingerless mittens and a greasy woollen lumper's cap. The thought flashes through Tam's mind that her friend has taken the clothes from some fellow found dead in the street.

'Help me up or you'll get a clip under the ear.' The mouthful of cheek covers the shock at her friend's purple face, skin peeling where the frost has bitten in. When Nance leans down with her hand, Tam sees the ends of the fingers are waxy white and bloodless.

Standing, she hooks one arm though Nance's and reaches with the other hand for the potato.

'For you. I don't be needin' it, just had dinner.'

Nance stuffs it against her mouth ready to take a bite.

'No, Nance. Eat it in a bit when yer hands are warmed.

It's plain that her friend has lain in wait, desperate for help in the big freeze, though Tam says nothing of it. No need to make Nance a charity case.

'C'mon. Let's go to the market together.'

They slip and slide to the end of Red Lion Passage, relieved that when they get to the square the ice-cart is there, a team of men cracking sheets of the stuff to load, making way for carriages and carts to pass.

The market is slim pickings, closed roads having prevented the usual supply of vegetables, fruits and meat from reaching London. Tam chooses the best she can, already feeling Mrs Bainbridge's disapproving eyes on the bruises and brown marks on turnips and cabbages.

Afterwards she slips Nance a shilling from the change, but her friend tries to give it back.

'You be gettin' a beating. Can't have that. Too busy, me, to be going to the old priest an' make confession.' Her cracked lips attempt a smile.

Tam smiles back. 'I be alright. Got hide that knows how to take a thrashing.'

Back upstairs with Mrs Bainbridge, Tam reports on the limited goods and hands over the change.

Her mistress counts it, knotting her face. 'You a shilling short, girl.'

Tam flinches, expecting the woman to raise her hand and strike her. 'Short? Sorry mistress, it be so cold my thinkin' was out when it were counted to me.'

Mrs Bainbridge keeps her gloved hands in front of her shawl, standing stiff as the Tower of London, the pain in her arthritic bones making it hard to decide on a punishment. She sucks in air through an open mouth and it is white when she breathes out.

137

'Your luck is in this time. I'll take into account how reliable you been these past few years. Be warned, though, I'll talk to Mr Bainbridge, make sure it's taken off the wages you get when you done your time.'

Mr Bainbridge is also forced to leave the shop on occasion. The bad weather has put a stop to the bloodsports and other competitions men are willing to bet on. He must try to get the benefit of any small wagers to be made on such mundane matters as when the frost will break. He takes to standing near Gray's Inn, over near the brewery chimney stacks, or down on the docks where ships are frozen in the river and out-of-work coal-heavers, lumpers and stranded sailors sit around firepits and guzzle hot toddies or mulled wine.

When the frost gives way to a stinking, slushy mess that sprays from cartwheels, business remains quiet and he has little need for runners, leaving him still chasing the street trade.

On Christmas Eve the three of them go to a watch-night church service, then Tam is allowed the bliss of an extra hour's sleep in the garret. Part-way down the stairs in the morning she pauses to straighten her apron as voices float up. The parlour door is open.

Mrs Bainbridge is grumbling, though Tam can't catch her words. Mr Bainbridge replies in harsher tones than usual.

'I be careful, wife. There's no need of you telling me how to run my business. You done alright from my efforts all these years, and I be looking after you for a darn sight more to come.'

Tam coughs and takes the next stair loudly, not wanting to be caught loitering.

'Ah, here she be. Merry Christmas, girl.' Mr Bainbridge is a red-faced from the argument with his wife, as well as the mug of spiced wassail in his hand.

'A little something for the season for you.' He points to a small cloth bag on the table. Tam opens it, ready to exclaim about the present.

She pulls out a few hard humbug lollies, two fresh pencils and a printed scripture card. *The Lord is a refuge for the oppressed, a stronghold in times of trouble. Psalm 9:9.*

Tam clears her throat awkwardly to choke back laughter. The oppressed. Her place is made clear.

Mr Bainbridge misunderstands, sees it as an expression of feeling. 'No need for thanking us. 'Tis a day for all to mark our gratitude.'

The following year swings in swifter than the one before, hurrying through January so fast that Tam must keep her wits to write the year of 1809 in the ledgers. Mr Bainbridge is not one for crossings out or corrections, prides himself on having neat books, even if the entries are for spools of thread and yardage of cloth that never move from the shelves.

Tam considers it a game, the code she must follow, counting the profits of pounds, shillings and coppers that come in, then through sleight of hand turning them into sales of draper's stock without a trace of activity in dust on the shop counter.

Her master is not one for gambling, says he doesn't deal in hollow lady luck hovering at card and dice tables, preferring to run a betting house, where skill and the artful design of prediction determine the winner of a contest.

The Government ignores the golden hells where lords and peers lose fortunes in posh gambling halls or wealthy men gather to play hazard late at night, instead hounding the copper hells and the bookies, claiming they are nests of vice. Mr Bainbridge, like others with a dusty shopfront hiding their true enterprise, is content to be small fry. 'Do nothing to attract attention.' It's the motto he often repeats to Tam.

Seven more months and she'll have her papers and a recommendation she hopes will get her a job helping run a proper shop. She even dares imagine a day when she might be an assistant at a school or better still, to a governess in a grand mansion.

On Fridays she goes to Mrs Bainbridge's favourite fishmonger at the markets near London Bridge. She keeps an eye out for Nance, who's known to appear out of nowhere and give her a fright just for fun. Her friend seems none the worse for wear from the frost, has said she still works largely alone, though has let slip she's started running sometimes with a gang from over Glass House Yard way.

Today there's no sign of her, but she's bound to be about when Tam gets her day off. Nance has changed, is older for sure but there's more to it than that. Maybe she's joined a flash house after all. The question of where Nance sleeps, what she does for shelter, has been brushed off every time Tam's asked, and she suspects her friend is under someone's thumb.

Tam is still worrying about Nance as she enters Red Lion Passageway, lifting her head when she registers a louder hubbub than usual. Most of the shopkeepers, their assistants, even the customers are gathered in small groups outside shop doors, talking excitedly, gesturing with hands to make their point.

'Too good to be true.'

'Yair, only a matter o' time afore they see there's nary a customer there.'

As she passes the scattered gossips, it dawns on her that they're talking about her master. She breaks into a run.

The shop and the office behind are quiet. She takes the stairs two at a time, bursting into the parlour, not caring how unseemly her behaviour. The room is empty, as is the kitchen. Then she hears quiet sobbing from the bedroom.

'Missus Bainbridge, it be Tam. Can I fetch you tea?'

The sobbing stops, all is quiet. Tam fills the kettle and puts it over the flame, then readies the teapot with an unsteady hand. Once the tea is made she knocks softly on the door. When there is no answer she stands frozen, holding the tray. It's ridiculous to dither, she turns the handle and steps inside.

Mrs Bainbridge is seated at a small dressing table, patting a few stray hairs back in place. Tam glides to her and places the tray in front of her mistress, then straightens, set to be sent from the room.

'I am ruined.'

Tam has never seen her like this, unguarded, unravelled.

'Surely mistress, it not be so bad.'

'Worse, Tam. Mr Bainbridge has been found out, arrested. A disgruntled fellow blew the whistle, revenge for a big loss it seems, claims my husband cheated him. All lies, of course, though it is the least of our worries now.'

The older woman pours the tea, a gesture that attempts to bring a shred of purpose to the moment. As she lifts the cup to her lips, she needs to steady it with both hands. She has an unpleasant task to fulfil right now and will not be the only one to suffer in the sudden collapse of her circumstances.

'He will be gaoled, six months at best with hard labour, not to mention a fine so sizeable there will be no monies left. I cannot keep you on. You will have to go back to the foundling hospital in the hope the governors can secure you another placement.'

Tam gives a nod and takes her leave, making no effort to deal with the stranded fish stretched out in a dish on the table, one dead eye staring up. She goes up to the garret and curls on the bed, hugging her knees tightly.

No recommendation, no reference from Mr Bainbridge. Her past rises up to destroy her future, a mere dandelion puff knocked aside. She lies there for maybe half an hour, till Mrs Bainbridge calls.

'Come down, girl. Supper won't prepare itself.'

They work beside each other in the kitchen as they have done so many evenings, Mrs Bainbridge giving orders and Tam working fast to follow them. She steadies the fish with one hand to stop it slipping about in the dish. Its one eye stares up, searching her face. She feels the cold shine of it as a trespass, full of condemnation.

'What are you waiting for?'

She lifts the slimy creature and slaps it down on the chopping board then reaches for the narrow filleting knife. As she sticks the point into the gut sac under the fish head, the eye still seems fixed on her, urging her to action, accusing her of weakness. She withdraws the knife and sees blood smeared on the tip of the blade. At the sight of it she plunges the knife in again and twists a little, then just as suddenly is shocked by the urge to do the same to Mrs Bainbridge, to force the knife through flesh, let blood show.

It's a fearful idea, made worse by the lack of malice from her mistress. Tam quickly withdraws the blade, bringing it to rest against the chopping board where it can do no harm.

Mrs Bainbridge is behind the girl, looking over her shoulder, so close it would only take one movement to clutch the knife, spin around and stick it in her.

The woman, ignorant of any risk, speaks in an uncharacteristically soothing tone. 'Today's been a shock, I know, but we need to eat.'

It's enough to shake the chill that has gripped Tam, and she gets on with using a hand to scoop out the entrails, the jarring of her callous thought pushed aside by a message coming to her, slow as letters scraped one by one across a clean blackboard.

There it is. The realisation that recent years of steadiness have done little to root out the hospital's true legacy, a demon black as night crouching at the back of her heart, ready to pounce. It has taken a cold fish, scales glinting in the lamp light, to look into her essence and show her the sum of who she is. She has not escaped what they've done to her.

She makes a promise to herself right then, watching the knife glide smoothly under the fish skin. She will not set foot back in that godawful place no matter what. It will be her own wager, staking all that is known for a chance in the unknown.

The edges of the fish bubble and hiss as they hit hot oil in the pan, though it's not the tempting smell or the sound that captures her attention, but the raw flesh that's been laid bare.

CHAPTER TEN

MELVA

KISSING POINT, 1805-1806

ROGER IS THE ONE TO collar his Ma about her state, after the family leaves dirty plates on the table and, groaning with the pleasure of over-full bellies, goes outside to catch a cool breeze in the shade.

He's argued with himself all through the Christmas spread. Should he pin her down or let things slide? So busy is he with the inner wrangle that when she tries to plumb his intentions in getting a wife, he obliges by giving an honest answer.

'Yeah, the girl up Windsor way's a safe bet, just need to wait till she's old enough. Not wanting ol' Marsden to send me to the flogging triangle.' He laughs. The good Reverend needs little provocation to demand extreme counts of the lash from his Magistrate's bench.

Roger watches as the woman who's been the steady light in his life turns her back on the messy table to go outdoors, a troubling sight when she's always so quick to make the place tidy. It settles the matter. He must get to the truth about what's going on with his Ma.

He draws her away from the others, lined up on a long bench like geese stuffed for the oven. No point talking in front of them, with everyone acting like they've been struck blind.

'Did us proud with the food, Ma,' Melva nods, clearly pleased.

'Though you hardly ate as much as half a spud and a few mouthfuls o' pie.' He pauses, hoping she'll take the bait and save him the need to be direct.

His mother sighs, giving him hope, then pats his hand. A minute passes before she breaks the silence, pointing down the track leading to the house. 'Turned into gluepot last heavy rain. Might need logs thrown in ruts before winter.'

'Geez, Ma. You're not makin' this easy.' He doesn't mean to get crabby, just wants to know what's what without having to poke and pry.

Melva rests her hand on his arm. 'You good man, son, want best things for your old Mama, always looking out for me. No need for worry.'

'Then why the bejesus are you burning down faster than a candle? Every time I come there's less of you to see.' The words are harsh, though he has managed to deliver them with enough lilt so he doesn't feel bad.

'Woman problem is all. You find out soon enough, when you have wife and she give you babies.' She smiles at him, gives his arm an affectionate rub and stands. 'Now go get another rum, while I make pot of tea.'

'Wouldn't hurt to get the surgeon to look you over, Ma, mebbe that D'Arcy Wentworth fellow from when we was on the *Neptune*? Irish and all, Da be for that I reckon.'

He cocks his head, eyes narrowed on her. Surely the right thing to do.

'Papa got him over from Parramatta a while back. Gave me medicine, it helps. Now no fussing, off you go.'

Melva won't be taking that stuff again, Gregory's Powder, dried rhubarb Wentworth said would clean her out. That it did, a painful and messy business she won't be repeating.

She shoos her grown son off like he's a pesky lamb and heads back into the cottage.

Dismissed, Roger wanders towards the barn, needing to clear his head. The hollowed out face, the lack of flesh on her arms and legs, the story she's spinning, what's to be gained by getting his Da or the boys on her case?

Soon after, Cuddy calls to his eldest. 'Come on, got somethin' for you.'

He disappears into the cottage, reappearing with a rucksack. From it he pulls a small wooden music box, a shiny handle on the side, and gives it to a squealing Rosa. He has whittling knives, each in a leather sheaf, for the three younger boys, and a new tobacco pouch for Roger.

'For you, me darlin'.' A grin splits his face as he pulls from the bag a grubby small parcel for Melva. She opens it expecting to find a scented soap, perhaps a new set of sewing needles. Instead what lies in the palm of her work-hardy hand is a small silver brooch, its fluted edge surrounding a delicate stamped rose in full bloom.

Roger can hardly bear to look at the brooch, shiny, smart, mocking his Ma's sagging cheeks, her cloudy eyes.

'Beautiful, Cuddy.' Melva summons the energy to pin it to her bodice.

Her husband pushes his hand deep in the bag. 'Last of all, for me.' He flourishes a silver watch on a chain, boasting that his initials are engraved on the outer case.

He pulls it from his pocket at every opportunity that afternoon and every day, a talisman that magics away the sneering and insults. Stinking bog-jumper, Irish ratbag, saphead. With the heft of the watch in his hand he is no longer sullied but master of his domain, a man to be reckoned with.

The watch is proof that starting in a dirt poor Irish family, trapped on a treadmill of poverty by English corruption and cruelty, does not have to decide your destiny. His children, Cuddy is certain, will do even better than their ol' Da.

Melva tries to forget Roger's questioning, as though her son's attitude is the problem, not the truth of what he has seen written on her flesh. It's not his job to worry about her, not the proper way of things. A mother is the one to do the worrying, never stops being concerned about her child, even when he's getting close to thirty.

She's managing very well, all things considering. Cuddy's petitioned for a convict girl to help in the house, likely assigned in the New Year, not that Melva thinks the expense of feeding her, building sleeping quarters out the back or providing basic clothes is worth it. They can do perfectly well without a house servant; besides, in a few more years Rosa will be five, old enough to start doing regular chores.

There's no way she'll admit, even to herself, that she rarely works in the fields these days, or that it takes far longer to churn the butter, hoe the kitchen garden, pick fruit in their small orchard. She's forty-four, about the same age as Mama when she bade her a last goodbye, and if she remembers her mother full of vigour, stepping quickly through the apartment, throwing wet washing over the line with twice the energy of her daughter at the same age, then it's to be expected. Mama never knew starvation or spine-breaking toil on a farm.

Yet even a spider watching on from the corner of the kitchen can see that George does more to care for Rosa than her Ma, who often needs to rest on a chair for long periods between stoking the fire, chopping and cooking; or against a fence in the garden, leaning to catch her breath after bending to pick beans or dig potatoes. She tells herself she'll come good, her young ones need her and she'll see them grow. She is a woman who has risen to meet life's challenges and this will be no different. She just needs a little time.

As it happens, the Ranses don't get a convict girl, due to a hold-up with the deed of assignment. Cuddy is pretty wild about it after all the money he's spent on the notary to prepare the application papers.

'Bet she's gone to one of the officers or bigwigs and they keep us dangling till the next transport comes in with women. The buggers are always ridin' us, wanting us to chafe.'

In truth, much of his fury is to do with his wife not getting what she needs to ease her load, which only deepens his sense of inadequacy. What sort of a husband is he that he can't fix what brings her low?

He should go see how the men are doing on the sickle, work alongside them, make sure they're putting their backs into harvesting the hay. The hog pen, as he passes, reeks of rot and pigs who've rolled in their own dung. He changes his mind; heads left towards the road and the inn. The river will be churning back about now to the harbour down at

Sydney. The ferrymen will have worked up a mighty sweat on the oars, fighting the tide. They'll be pleased enough to raise a rum with a friendly face, and he can help with hay-cutting later.

Melva's given up trying to manage Cuddy's ways, especially his return to the drink. If anything she's inclined to indulge him these days, knows that behind the crow's feet, the squint in his eyes, is a brooding fear and she the cause of it.

The surgeon, a bit of a charmer, couldn't tell her more than she already knew. Wear and tear, the strain of heavy lifting and childbirth has torn a part of her belly, so a bit of her insides has popped through. Clever fellow, that D'Arcy Wentworth, had a fancy name for it that she can't recall, too busy trying to remember the old gossip passed on, how he came from society kin, took up medical training, then turned highwayman they reckon.

Word has it her good doctor, who took a convict mistress on their ship – no bad thing because he stuck by her, kept her better fed, belly swelling with a son who'd go on to have more care than she could give her own boy Danny – seems he came as a free man to save his skin from the noose. Done alright for himself, he has. Plenty of slurs about him, yet a grand two-storey house at Parramatta, land all over the place, at least a thousand acres Cuddy reckons.

Wentworth has a silver spoon in his mouth. It gives him a different standing to Cuddy, led him to be a Magistrate, but the two men are the same in ways that count in this rickety colony, which her husband says is spun together with twigs, mud and spit. The doctor is a gambler and like her man, a fellow who sees opportunities and grabs them with both hands.

Melva smiles despite the ache in her back, the awful, sharp pain that's become worse in her belly. Her funny, maddening, soft-hearted husband can be ill-disciplined at times but has proven himself a loyal partner, a good provider, and a father to give his children a prosperous life.

She hopes Papi, despite exile from Gibraltar, was able to do the same for Patricio and Biel. Her brothers, where would they be now? She carries a pail of peelings out the back to the fowls, scattering scraps of vegetables and apple cores as the hens squark, feathers flapping, dust flying in the fight for the biggest share. Unforgiving white sun beats down as the run of dog days continues. She tilts her head up to a blinding clear sky, a vast roof that covers the globe, sees all, knows all.

Questions rush from her throat. 'Are my brothers content? Papi and Mama, do their hearts still beat?' She has tried so hard to forget, over the years, to avoid the pain of being severed from them, yet here it is.

'Who you talkin' to, Ma?' Luis, with Rosa trailing behind, screws up his face to look up where his mother gazes, puzzled that he sees only emptiness.

'Thinking out loud is all. Papa ask you at breakfast to pull weeds in the melon patch, you done it yet?' She waits till her boy has walked off before swiping a sleeve across her eyes then reaching down for the girl's hand to lead her back to the house.

During the next few days Cuddy stays on the farm, sweating beside Will and their two labourers to cut the last of the hay so it can dry and be tied into stooks, then forked onto the wagon for stacking in the barn.

Late morning Luis turns up in the field with soda bread, warm mutton stew and a flagon of cider, the signal for the men to down scythes and move into the shade of spreading branches on a red gum against the boundary.

'Where's yer Ma?' Cuddy was expecting Melva, usually the one to bring their midday meal to the fields if they're busy.

Luis shuffles uncomfortably, scuffing the toe of his boot in the dirt. 'Said to say she were busy.'

Cuddy fixes him with a glare. 'Always bin able to tell when you're fibbing. What's she really up to?'

'Said not to tell ya, Da,' He starts to walk off but Cuddy grabs him by the neck. 'I know something's wrong. Now tell me before I give you a clip round the ear.'

Caught between loyalty to his Ma and a thrashing from his Da, the boy weakens. 'She's sick, started throwin' up her guts about an hour ago. Came on sudden, like.' He wriggles free and runs off.

Cuddy shares the food with his two men and Will, afterwards setting them back to work before he goes to the house.

Melva's not in the outhouse, nor the kitchen. He finds her, flat as a playing card on the bed, a terrible pong rising from a pail on the floor beside her. Rosa sits on the bed close to her mother, snivelling and rocking.

As he leans towards his wife she lifts the back of a hand and wipes away sweat beading on her forehead and across the top of her lip. She wants to speak and struggles to summon the energy but can't.

'You look real crook, my girl. What's wrong?' He rests his big hand on the back of hers, the bones so slight he would break them if he squeezed.

Before she can answer she doubles over then lurches to the edge of the bed and vomits into the pail, flopping back in exhaustion. Cuddy touches her forehead. 'You runnin' a fever. Could fry an egg on there.'

He goes to the water barrel, returning to lift her head gently, bringing a tin cup to her lips. She swallows two sips before convulsing again, spitting the water into the pail before lying back on the pillow. She is worn out, spent, has nothing left to give when there is much yet needing to be given … the young ones, her husband, the farm. Panic tightens its grip and she must lurch to the pail again.

She has spent decades holding on and now her body is laying down its load, unburdening itself of responsibility, even the act of digestion. After a lifetime of changing, refashioning herself to hold on and meet whatever circumstances have come, the letting go has caught her unawares. She searches within for the familiar energy of struggle, but its place is empty, she is empty.

George has come in from feeding the goats and stands, open-mouthed, in the doorway. Cuddy shouts for Luis. 'Get yer brother and sister outta here. Leave yer Ma in peace while I go for the doctor.' He is gone from the house before Luis can coax Rosa from the bed, resorting to the offer of a ripe plum to lure her away.

'My beautiful boy,' Melva murmurs to him. 'Look after her for me.'

Half an hour later the neighbour's wife turns up. She's never been one to befriend Melva, but Cuddy has stopped at the farm to declare an emergency and urge her to attend his wife till he returns.

Bella Riddlesbury sets foot in the house for the first time, surprised at the tidiness of the kitchen, the sprig of native flowers in a jug, clean dishes and pots stacked neatly, as though she expected different from a woman not white-skinned like her, but a barbarian with a touch of the blackamoor.

George, interested in the day turning so eventful, pipes up before Luis can speak. 'Ma's in the bedroom. She's sick.'

Mrs Riddlesbury has seen her share of heartache and illness, yet she gasps at the sight of the wretched woman, then must cover her mouth and nose to the stink. She calls to Luis. 'Fetch a dish of water and a cloth. Your Ma has a fever.'

A mother herself, three strapping sons, two bonny daughters, and another two in the graveyard at Parramatta, Mrs Riddlesbury is overcome by the necessity to do what she can in the hope it will help restore this woman, or at least make her comfortable.

Gently she sponges Melva's face and hands with cool water and slowly, carefully eases her out of her skirt and blouse and into a nightshift. Melva tries to speak, though the words are soft air, without shape. 'Hush now, neighbour. Save your strength to drink this.' She fills the tin cup and gets a little water into her patient's mouth before Melva dozes, letting go for now in the knowledge that a woman is there to look out for Rosa and George.

The barn and outhouses are throwing shadows in long stripes when Cuddy appears with Dr Wentworth, who ushers Mrs Riddlesbury out of the room, removes his jacket then sends Cuddy out, too.

Will turns up, hay seeds clinging to sweat-damp hair, as the woman is leaving, his dad giving her a tin of treacle and a piece of corned beef for her trouble, along with his profuse thanks.

'Walk Mrs Riddlesbury home, Will. There's a good lad.' The boy opens his mouth to object after a long day in the sun, but thinks better of it, what with the faint tremor around his Da's mouth.

Cuddy takes Rosa on his lap and the two of them sit on one side of the table, Luis and George on the other, and wait. 'Should go and give the sheep fresh water,' Cuddy says without stirring, as though the idea itself is enough to defeat him.

Thirty minutes pass, maybe more, before the doctor opens the bedroom door and gestures Cuddy in.

'Your wife has been in a great deal of pain, has considerable swelling of the abdomen. I've given her laudanum, also a quince oxymel for the liver and spleen, which may bring the fever down.'

He retrieves a bottle of barbery syrup from his bag. 'Once she's rested a little she'll be able to take some broth. In the meantime give her a teaspoon of this three times a day for the blood poisoning.'

The doctor reeling off so many symptoms has momentarily left Cuddy stupefied. How could he not have known how sick his wife had become?

Wentworth has years of experience in reading faces, knows what is crossing this man's mind. 'Internal strangulation. You couldn't have known,' He squeezes Cuddy's shoulder as though it marks a full stop, the end of something.

'Will it fix itself, she get better?'

Wentworth is well versed in the art of giving hope, even when there is none. 'Unfortunately, the hernia sac is blocked, likely the blood supply cut off, causing a severe stagnation that is travelling through her system. If she is able to fight it, though, she may well recover.'

Cuddy squares up to the doctor. 'And if she can't fight it?'

'It will spread through her body, make it difficult for her organs to function.'

The doctor is thinking, as he snaps his bag shut, that all the signs are there with the vomiting. The poor woman's kidneys are already failing.

As he makes his farewells in the kitchen, promising to return the next day, his eyes keep straying to Rosa, for his youngest son is not much older than the girl, a thought that brings on a shudder.

Cuddy waits till the drumming of hooves from Wentworth's horse has begun to fade, then steps outside into twilight, away from his children's unsettled faces, to suck in deep breaths of air. His feet are lumps of old lard, congealed and stuck to the ground. He looks over at the rising moon, muttering to himself. 'Don't matter how you feel, old fella, get back in and care for her like she did for you.'

CHAPTER ELEVEN

TAM

LONDON, 1809-1810

NANCE TURNS OUT TO BE a surprisingly good teacher, tutoring Tam in the finer points of thieving and begging, avoiding the charleys, and how to stash or fence what she gets her hands on.

She shows Tam hidden corners, church porches, stairwells for curling up to sleep, and narrow gaps to squeeze against leaky factory walls, where a warming blast of steam can save a girl from freezing to death.

One thing she never shows Tam is where she sleeps. Though it's never said between them, the girls now have an uneasy understanding that Nance is running with a flash house these days, the master forcing all his recruits to sleep there, ready to do his bidding or cop a thrashing.

'You be too smart for this lark. Need to get on yer feet and find better work.'

Nance's half-hearted attempt to deter her friend has little effect. Soon the back alleys and narrow tracks used by the night carts, the crawling paths through slums, are a map that lives in Tam's brain, patterns no less fascinating than the ones formed by numbers. She learns fast, not wanting another black eye like the one she got for straying onto the patch of a young pilferer over at Salt Petre Bank, his fist hard as a man's.

The thrill that comes with the first guinea she lifts from a pocket, spirited away without being chased, excites her for the whole day. Yet she is sensible, not trying again while such a charge of energy runs through her veins and may spur the impulse of a wrong move.

'Never tasted better pie,' she tells Nance that evening, as they share the spoils of Tam's success.

Now the freeze has thawed and warmer days are bringing bankers, lawyers, merchants and clerks back into the streets. She tries her hand for a while as a shoeblack but sells the blacking polish and stool to a loud-mouthed street boy after one too many sly remarks from men and a few who try to paw her, wanting to lure her to a blind alley or force her against a wall.

Her luck is in today. Outside the hatters in a street running down to St James Palace she spies a swanky carriage that's been left unattended, a tan carpet bag on the seat. Tam steps back to let a brewery cart clatter past, then checks the pavement in both directions and in one fell swoop has her arm in the carriage.

'Not bloody likely, girlie.' The footman, who has been on the other side of the carriage, bending to adjust a shoe buckle, grips her wrist as her fingers reach the leather straps.

He climbs through, at the same time yanking her hard towards him so her shoulder strains in the socket and she's pinned. Tam twists to get free as he jumps down from the carriage step, turning his head to scream down the street for the watch.

Panic blanks her mind for a moment till Nance's tutoring kicks in. She jerks up her knee hard as she can and he cops it in his cods. Yowling in pain, face redder than a blacksmith's fire, he bends over and she slips free.

Round the corner she has the good sense to slow to a ladylike pace, head held high and steady thanks to Mrs Bainbridge's nagging, as the watch runs past to the hatters. Once he's out of sight she tears off full pelt, ducking into one alleyway after another till she's wound her way back to the grass of Red Lion Square.

The shock of the close call has stripped away any sense of a childish adventure, and she pants, still shaking. Street life's a dangerous business. She flops on the green, determined to look for more gainful work.

'They're after girls I'm told, scrapin' hides in the Smithfield tanneries.' Nance delivers the suggestion that evening with a tone that says the work couldn't possibly have more appeal than thieving.

'Lordy no,' Tam agrees. 'Best not in a factory, neither. Jobs like them can cut yer life short, only takes the wrong move on a machine or nasty vapours from some poisonous stuff.'

They toss other ideas around, a game of pretence as if Tam might be a girl with prospects. The masquerade drains her, leaves her spirit low, a tide gone out to mud and stirring in the thickness of it the terrible ache of wanting to be someone who matters. It rubs worse than pumice on tender skin, bad as when she was still at the hospital, a desire bigger than the narrow life she's locked into, and she wishes it would leave her alone.

Nance is still talking, has narrowed it down to two choices – washerwoman or milkmaid. Tam decides to try the dairies. No point going to one of the small-time cowkeepers, a couple of animals tied up behind a shop, the milk watered down with God knows what, and only a few hours work a day, not even enough for a tuppeny room in a dosshouse. Not for her, she has a better plan.

Come the morning she shakes out her russet Sunday dress that's been rolled in a ball and stashed above a beam in a church porch. She dons it, tying on the apron Mrs Bainbridge gave her at their leave-taking, and walks into the coal-darkened half-light.

The Whitehall area, where most of the trade happens, nurses bringing children from posh houses nearby, is out of the question. She sets her path to Green Park, a featureless triangle of grass squeezed between St James Palace and Hyde Park, lacking the elegance of the former or the popularity of the latter. The stalls at Green Park will be a better fit for a milkmaid with Cockney pipes and stains on her hem.

She arrives early to nothing more than a large field, grass cropped low, with a few trees dotted near paths winding through it. In the still air she smells the first of the cows being driven through nearby streets, earth and dung their calling card. Soon they appear, groups of three or four, some brown, some black. Welsh girls and a few Irish carry switches, shouting to each other as they separate the cows of each master, tethering them in a row of stands along the park's eastern end, close to the Palace.

The girls are easy with each other, teasing, swearing, their companionship solid as a sheltering glass pane, Tam with her nose pressed against it. She longs to be on the other side, calling 'milk below, mi-o' as a handful of soldiers arrive for their penny mug's worth.

One of the girls kneels beside a cow, pulls smoothly on the teats, warm milk frothing into the bottom of a pail for pouring into two of the cups. The third fellow wants syllabub, stirred quickly by her companion, the wine, sugar and spice mix waiting in a flagon on the bench for those who like their milk with a kick.

Tam sidles up as the soldiers walk off, addressing the one with legs like a Munster heifer.

'Good work, is it?'

'Good 'nuff, if you don't mind being up before the sun and out all weathers.' The girl wipes the morning damp from her dress where she knelt and searches Tam's countenance, her rumpled clothes.

'In need o' work are you?'

Tam holds back a moment, not wanting to sound desperate, which only serves to make honesty burst from her mouth when she opens it. 'Aye, been on the streets, a hard life.'

Hastily she tries to present herself in a better light. 'Did proper work before, keepin' the books for a shopkeeper till he moved on.'

The girl cleans one hand, still purple from the cold, with the corner of her apron. 'Get plenty lookin' for work. Why should my Da bother with you?'

It's a test worse than in the schoolroom, and she bristles like she once did. 'Mebbe that's a question for your Da.'

The girl cracks a grin. 'Catrin. An' you'd be?'

Introductions complete, Catrin tells her to follow when they take the cows back to grazing pastures on the city's edge soon after midday. Tam can talk to her father then, no promises.

Custom is slow for the first hour, so she stays to chat. Catrin has pride in her voice as she explains how her father, seeking opportunity, drove his cattle a hundred and sixty miles or more from their farm in the Vale of Glamorgan not a year gone.

'Got a right head for business, he does. More than most Cymry.' She sees Tam is puzzled. 'We don't like being called Welsh. Your lot do it to make us sound foreign.'

Tam is fascinated, not puzzled. Mr Bainbridge and this girl's Da going against the grain to better themselves, except the dairyman is smart enough to stay within the bounds of the law.

Catrin hasn't time for more talk. Her younger sister is milking the second cow into a large chestnut wood pail and she goes to their third beast to do the same. When both pails are close to full she puts on their lids and hoists a wooden yoke onto her shoulders. Her sister lifts a full pail onto either end of the frame.

'Let me help.' Tam can see the weight must be damn near a hundred pounds.

'Na, easier with two, only time I has good balance.' She nods at her sister, laughs. 'Ain't that right?'

Tam follows as the girl heads into Milkmaids' Passage, the ends of the yoke almost touching the Portland brick wall either side. It opens into the Palace stable yard, then an archway that Catrin passes through, entering a courtyard with a green door marking the servants' entrance.

A maid answers the knock, thrusts a few coins into Catrin's hand then lifts the pails inside, slamming the door behind her.

'Closest I be gettin' to a gander inside a palace,' Tam grumbles, as the maid reappears with the empty pails.

The girls hurry back to the park, where Catrin's sister has a queue waiting as she milks on demand. Tam leaves them to it, filling in time by walking the lane along

Constitution Hill and the edge of nearby Hyde Park, not a place for the likes of her.

A few early fops are strutting, making sure to be seen by each other. Tam goes in search of a food cart, breakfasting on a piece of fried cod and a penny slice of plum pudding, all the food she'll have today.

Wandering back, hands still sticky despite having licked them, she sees carriages and gigs arriving to do the park's roadway circuit. She watches open-mouthed as bewigged coachmen, seated on richly embroidered hammercloths, drive duchesses and ladies in pairs. Dukes, lords, maybe a marquis or two, she can't tell the difference, ride grey or white horses, a few holding the reins of their curricle, a woman by their side.

The women, oh their finery, dresses and ribbons in glowing jewel colours, ruby red, sapphire blue, emerald green, and carefully curled hair swept up under huge hats stuck with feathers and flowers. Every one of them a perfect porcelain doll parading, posturing in their carriages as Tam shrinks back outside the park, sensing every inch of her is chipped china, broken for all the world to see.

Suddenly, into the order of it a tilbury flies, the hood thrown back, its driver leaning forward on a seat that sits precariously high, taller than the rump of the horse pulling it in full stride. Two tall wheels spin and blur as the coachman flicks the whip, the servant beside him holding on for dear life. Tam can't take her eyes of it as her footsteps slow, failing to see the couple coming the other way.

'Oi, watch yerself.' The woman's breath is foul. Tam sees they're common folk like her.

'Sorry. Got carried away watching that gig. Who's the fellow drivin'?'

The man is already pulling his companion away. 'Don't you know nuffink'? That be the Prince o' Wales showing off. Don't care if he kills his groom, that kind never do.'

The gig makes two passes, forcing carriages to the side, before the Prince disappears out the gateway at the corner of the park, heading at high speed towards the Palace, leaving Tam breathless at the freedom and boldness of his display.

It sticks with her, that the Prince has been blessed with good fortune in birth and sex, while she's been born a bastard, and a girl at that.

Come one o'clock Tam follows Catrin and her sister as they herd their cows along Piccadilly Street, the roadway crowded with shabby growlers, hackneys and carts. The girls keep up a steady shushing and low whistles, alert to the dangers of their cows being spooked and trampling pedestrians or tossing a carriage.

Beyond the north-west corner of Hyde Park they take a right turn and head inland, past a stone pest house, the walls saying nothing of the cholera or typhus that's been contained within. They follow Black Lion Lane north for nearly two miles as the cankerous lesion of London falls away behind them. Tam takes big gulps of air – despite the smelly heat coming off the beasts in front it's cleaner by far than what she's known.

The cows pick up pace as they reach Westbourne Green, trotting onto fields as far as the eye can see, sweeping across to a manor house in the far corner.

Other herds are arriving on the common and the girls shepherd their three cows beyond a canal, where their father waits with another six beasts. The Welshman's not happy about a stranger turning up.

'What you thinking, Catrin? You two's all I need.'

'Maybe she be handy for the short milks, when we busy with the pails.'

He's not having it, but sees his eldest has her heart set on helping the girl. 'I'll speak with some of the ones rentin' my other cows. Come back in a few days and see if I got news.'

Catrin hugs Tam, who manages to paint on a smile as she leaves. Hope, having perched on her shoulder since morning, has shaken its wings and flown off.

Early that evening she waits at Aldgate Pump for Nance, hunger more vicious than the mean look on the brass wolf's head that is the waterspout. It's almost dark when her friend emerges from the gloom.

'Got any coin, Nance? Could do with a feed.'

The girl shakes her head. 'Tell you what, come with me.'

Tam follows, hurrying to keep up as Nance dives down one alley then another till they reach a grubby inn, paint peeling on a hand-drawn sign for the Goose and Gander.

'In here,' Nance hisses, leading down a tight access to a small courtyard strewn with rubbish and empty barrels.

'Stay here. Do just as I says, ok?'

The girl quietly opens the door and disappears into the sharp smell of frying lard. Within seconds she's back out, thrusting a pewter tankard into Tam's hands. 'Run, go that way.' She points to the left as they tear out of the passageway, Nance peeling off to the right, past the inn's front door.

Tam hesitates for a moment as she hears the door open with loud shouts, looks over her shoulder to see if Nance is clear, then starts to run. Too late, the cook springs from the passageway and knocks her face-down, the tankard clattering on the cobblestones.

He's a fat fellow, heavy, bellowing in her ear as he yanks her arm behind. She tastes blood coming from her nose. Strangely, she is not alarmed. Her body has gone limp, the effort of surviving month by month, day by day, minute by minute, bleeding onto the pavement. She is done for, and relief is all she feels that it's out of her hands.

July 1809. In the week after Tam's arrest, the truth of who she is becomes a matter for the public record.

She is a monster.

The Magistrate does not say it but it's in the scorn of his words and the disgust of his manner in uttering them, barely bothering to move his mouth as he speaks. Tam Pummell must be made to pay, he intones.

She wants to shout up at him; to scream that it's nothing new, she's been made to pay over and again in her fourteen short years.

Up in the public gallery spectators who paid their shilling for entertainment are restless, bored with another larceny case, murmuring and poking each other, hoping at least for a bit of daring do, or better still a murderer. Tam scans the rows above, for surely Nance is among them, wanting to see what becomes of her friend. All she sees are strangers' faces.

She turns her gaze up higher, towards grey light struggling through the soot-speckled windows of the Old Bailey courtroom. Centred in the soft glow, behind the safety of his bench, the judge wears a strange wig that sits awkwardly on the peak of his head, a bedraggled bird that has landed too heavily after a long flight. Tam resists the urge to let out a shriek of laughter, lest it flap away.

The gavel lands. 'Guilty. To be transported for seven years.'

Hysterical laughter bursts free. No longer simply Tam Pummell, a girl with few skills and many dreams, she has become a criminal. She is still laughing as she's dragged away to the squalor of gaol, no different to the filth she's walked in, slept in, wiped off her hands since farewelling Mrs Bainbridge.

Within days she is taken from her Newgate Prison cell, where there's so little space the women have had to take turns lying down, and loaded with twenty or so others onto an open cart for Taunton Gaol in Somerset.

They bounce and jostle, sunburnt, sweating in seventy-five degree heat, for two long days, not stopping till it's almost dark, then leaving the barn where they've slept at first light, to a cart with fresh horses.

Though Tam has an elbow digging in one side and a mouthful of rotten teeth squeezed up close on the other, she can't help but marvel, as they travel, at her first sight of the horizon, always obscured in London.

Soft hills and spreading pastures stretch away on both sides of the road, cows graze peacefully, smoke spirals up from stone chimneys on the side of cob farmhouses. She closes her eyes for a moment, pretends she's in a fine carriage with a family that's going on holiday. When she opens her eyes a town is coming into view, and at the heart of it a medieval castle, turrets soaring above the houses.

The cart pulls up close to the castle and she is dragged down, all of them herded like beasts of the fields into the gaol, through the women's day room where gaunt faces watch every move, hawks sussing out their prey in the gloom of the shuttered space.

They sleep in two rooms above, one with beds for those who can pay a shilling a week, the other with straw strewn about. The gods of thieving, Tam thinks, are mighty mean, giving only a hard floor with a foot in her face, half a quarter loaf of bread a day, one meat meal a week, and enough idleness to sour the souls of those cooped up.

The monotony of the following days is broken only by fist fights, spitting duels and a pair who express their hate by rubbing shit in each other's hair.

She is neither the youngest nor the fairest caged here. Not the cleverest, the most bitter, the kindest, and certainly not the most violent. The women size her up, don't like the way she holds back, keeps to herself, even if her eyes are full of shock not distaste. One of them announces her nickname. 'Mistress Fancy Prancium, whore of Taunton Manor.' The others hoot and cheer, baying bloodhounds out to catch the fox.

If they believe she's the weakest, more fool them. The demon from the Foundling Hospital has woken from slumber. Let them try to harm her, for he will have his way.

CHAPTER TWELVE

MELVA

KISSING POINT, 1806

F AMILIAR VOICES RISE AND FALL. Melva wants to go to meet them but can't summon the effort. A hand squeezes her fingers, or is it her arm? She is a featureless mound, its weight pressing her down.

'There, there, wife. Easy does it, rest now.'

Cuddy. With great effort she lifts her eyelids to see his face floating above her.

'Hello, my love. You been out of it for a while.' His smile is brittle, and even in her weakened state she knows him well, that his face splits near in half with the stretch of a genuine grin, and this is not one.

'Come and say hello to your Ma.' Will and Luis hang back, but George and Rosa push in alongside their Da, little faces screwed up at the sight of their mother stuck in bed, not chasing them out from under her feet, or hugging them when they fall. For two nights they've gone to bed with no songs from her, and they sense there'll be none tonight either.

'Give your Ma a kiss, then let the other two come over.'

George kisses her papery cheek, but Rosa grips her mother's face, a plump hand firm on either side, and Cuddy must prise her off.

Will and Luis are at a loss. If she danced with them in the kitchen or called them to dig turnips, maybe chase the ewe escaped through the fence, they'd know what to do. This, though, is something new, baffling, as though they are the sheep with no rails to hold them in.

Cuddy nudges Will. 'Yer Ma needs to know you been prayin' for her, we all have.'

The boy nods. 'We been prayin' you'll get well soon, Ma. It's not the same without you about the place.' His voice cracks, the dead giveaway that tears are close.

Luis unexpectedly saves him from making a fool of himself. 'Yeah, Da's a shocker of a cook. Yesterday's pork were tough as shoe leather.'

Everyone else laughs, relieved to have a light moment, though the nine-year-old's face remains solemn.

Cuddy speaks again, continuing to talk as though Melva is participating in the conversation when she hasn't the wherewithal for it, a fact that her husband is determined to overlook.

'Roger came by yesterday, Melva. Sat with you awhile. He'll be mighty pleased to hear you've come round. A few folks bin asking about you, too.'

His voice goes on, a rhythm that rushes to the end of each sentence then rises a tone or two at the end, up and down, a gentle singsong as much a part of her day as the pulse in her wrist.

She wants to keep listening, to mouth a few words, tell him, tell them all what a good life it's been, but any struggle in her has gone and with it any sense of having control. At first she seemed to become empty, a nothingness. Now a force is pulling at her, a letting go that is quietly dissolving any ties to the dear ones she senses nearby, and she is slipping away.

She has done all she can. It floods her being, the certain knowing that purpose, the polestar she's relied on to power her life, drive her to strive, is of no consequence now, maybe never was. She summons Rosa's face, then George's, tries to fight one last time to stay, but instead is met with a peace that tells her they will be okay.

A bliss beyond family or farm, bigger than rivers, mountains, even sky, is tugging at her, drawing her on, and it is greater than her body, than Cuddy holding her, than all of them gathered by the bed. She goes alone, taking nothing, not even pain or discomfort, into all she has ever been, will ever be, the fullness of it at her centre all along, so beautiful she can hardly bear it.

She floats for a time, watching her husband, her sons and daughter, all bathed in love, cannot understand why they look so bereft, wants them to know she is complete, all is well, that their turn will one day come.

As they fade, the room dissolves into motes, dancing through a shaft of light that grows strong as a sunbeam, shining down on a shape that forms from the dust, tall before her, glistening in the brightness, beckoning. The Gibraltar Rock, such a sweet sight, telling her she is on her way home.

Cuddy, panicked that she's closed her eyes and let out one long sigh that seems to empty her out, gives a gentle shake to rouse her. When she doesn't move he shakes her arm harder, then half stands, gripping both her shoulders, more vigorous in the shaking so that her head bounces on the pillow.

He keeps shaking, the children watching on, eyes round with horror, till Will can't take it anymore and pounds his back.

'Stop it, Da. You'll hurt her. Let her go!'

Grief lies sticky on every surface of the cottage, clinging to the apron waiting on the hook for a woman who no longer needs it, coating the table, the windows, damping the fire under the cooking tripod.

The sheep bleat piteously, perhaps because no one has noticed their water trough is nearly empty, and the cows in the field seem to low mournfully from dawn to dusk. Autumn has arrived, the season of ripening and harvest that can only lead to winter.

Cuddy and the children are planets spinning away without a sun to hold them in place, uncertain about where to be, what to do, caught in the fullness of understanding, muddied before by the daily business of living, that their wife and mother has been the shifting weight on the set of scales keeping balance in their home and on the farm.

Neighbours drop by with food, then two days later huddle in the pews at the Kissing Point Chapel. It's their duty to attend the funeral. They must band together at difficult times, even though they were only on nodding acquaintance with Ranse's foreign wife, but the glow of friendship can be pretended on such a day.

Cuddy sees it, knows the rules of this game, doesn't care for it anymore. At the burial ground, Rev Marsden shakes his hand. 'Lean on the Lord in your sorrow, Mr Ranse, and your neighbours. In Him, and in community, you will find the strength to endure.'

'Where were they, when she needed them? Not a friend among 'em, the lousy buggers.' Cuddy wants to spit on the ground there and then, right on the uppity minister's polished shoes, or maybe give him a quick right hook for his sanctimony. This is the man who preaches forgiveness from the pulpit one day then delivers a hundred lashes, sometimes more, the next, showing no mercy from the Magistrate's bench.

The reverend lowers his voice, touches him lightly on the shoulder as he might a wayward boy. 'Bitterness is a bad companion, Cuddy, believe me. I'm sure your wife, a fine woman by all accounts, would not want it for you.'

Cuddy opens his mouth, ready to cut the man down, especially for the pretence of knowing his Melva, but Roger grips his elbow and shepherds him away.

'Don't go makin' a scene, Da. Hard enough without turning everyone agin us. Come on, I'll get you all home.'

They pile onto the cart, Will and Luis quiet as mice, stealing glances at their Da as Roger drives the horse home, where a local girl is minding George and Rosa.

As the horse finds its stride, Cuddy looks back at the mound of soil where Melva lies and can't bear to think of her alone in the graveyard. He fights the absurd urge to dig her up, take her back to the farm.

Their two convict labourers and a third man, now free and paid wages for his work, fortunately aren't slackers. The men are not stupid, they benefit from the grain, vegetables, meat and eggs the Kissing Point farm produces, but they have no call to flog themselves silly on a plough or hoe. They let things slide, and why not? No one notices that the absence of proper planning means they're not put to best use, except maybe the eldest son when he drops by from the other farm.

The one blessing for Cuddy is that the assignment of a house servant has finally been approved. The young woman is Scottish, ruddy-faced, with hands already work-hardened. It's her second placement, Cuddy's been told, though not why the first didn't work out.

Maisie Brown stands in the kitchen, hands on ample hips, a frown creasing her face. She surveys the dirty pots, the cluttered table with breadcrumbs scattered across it, the two snotty-nosed kids watching on, and draws in a huge breath to loudly sigh.

'Dearie me, what a mess. S'pose I should get on with it.' The girl reaches for the apron on the peg.

'Leave it alone. Don't touch it.' George is at her side, pulling fiercely at her skirts. 'It's our Ma's, it's Ma's, not yours.'

Maisie's far stronger than the five-year-old, could throw him off as easily as kicking a stray cat, but the fervour of the boy stops her from giving him a whack.

'Alright, alright. Suit yerself. But if you ever grab me like that again I'll gi' you summat tae make you real sorry.'

She turns her back on the lad and his sister, grizzling at the menacing tone, and sets to cleaning the fireplace, where she'll need to get coals hot enough for cooking. No doubt the bloody lot of them will expect a hot dinner.

Maisie Brown might be cruel but she's also a cunning one, relishing the power of taunting the little ones with nasty slurs, twisting an ear, hitting them on the back or shoulders with the leather knife strop or a wooden spoon. She loves to see George and Rosa recoil in pain or cry out, though is careful to give the appearance of female care when Will and Luis are about, not wanting the pair of them to blab.

Cuddy, in the aimlessness, the void of loss, can't see what's right under his nose when Rosa cowers if Maisie comes near, or the two-year-old stiffens, eats little, if the servant girl sits next to her at the table.

George has taken to shielding his sister, standing between her and their tyrant to take the blows, which only seems to incense the servant girl further. He cannot fathom what is unfolding. They have known such kindness from the woman who was their Ma. Sure, she gave them a smack now and then, but always for a naughty deed, never out of the blue, and never with the twisted, mean smile on the face of this woman.

The little ones grow quiet, hide out in the barn or the sheep paddock unless she fetches onto them to take a pail of scraps to the chickens or half-rotten apples to the pigs.

'You two scabby eejits, git in the house now and put yer useless selves to work.' She's found them out the back, playing with a piece of wood, hammer and some nails from the shed.

As George leads Rosa towards the house, she reaches down with no warning and thumps him on the back of his skull with a closed fist. He doubles over with the shock of it, clutching his head.

'That'll teach you to duck away from yer chores.'

George grabs Rosa by the hand, pulls her close so Maisie can't reach her.

'Gawd, as if you can keep her from me if I got a mind to give her a thumpin' too.' She screams with delight, giving him a shove in the back to make the point.

Roger, coming from the barn where he's tethered his horse and given it water, has witnessed the incident.

'You bloody harridan. I seen what you done. He don't deserve that.'

He pulls the two children away. 'What's she been doin' to you? Tell me.'

Rosa starts snivelling, pulls up her sleeve, where purple marks in the shape of pinching fingers line up like fence posts.

George pipes up. 'Look at her belly, her back. Maisie bin whacking her where it don't show.'

'And you, George? Same for you?' The boy nods.

'I'll bloody see about that. Where's Da?'

'Gone, went off a while back.'

Roger knows exactly where to find him and strides off to saddle the horse. Christ, got enough to do with soldiering duties and managing Porteous Mount without having to look out for these kids, this farm. If it weren't for the fact of being garrisoned at Parramatta he'd never have time to show up.

He finds Cuddy at the inn, already three sheets to the wind, and hauls him outside.

'You gotta pull yerself together, Da. The farm and those kids depend on you. Ma'd be the first to say so.' Roger's shouting in his ear, spitting fury.

Cuddy leans back a little, unsteady. 'Who the hell are you to be tellin' me what to do, you jumped-up piece o' shite.' He balls up his right fist and swings it at Roger, forgetting that his eldest, at twenty-eight years, is in his prime and sober. His son steps to the side and Cuddy is carried forward by the momentum of the punch to land face-down in the dirt, his hat landing nearby in a cloud of dust.

James Squire has seen the tussle as he walks from his brewery to the inn. Originally a lag himself, it pains him to see such an unedifying display, for it only serves to reinforce the prejudices of officers and officials against uncouth class-jumpers.

'Get him home, son. Take the brewery cart, you can leave your horse here till you get back.'

Roger manages to thank him while seething twice over, once for the wasted state of his Da, and secondly for the public humiliation as a respected settler and member of the Corps.

That afternoon, while his father is flat on his back on the bed, snoring loudly, he gives Maisie Brown her marching orders.

'You canna do that. Your father signed papers, agreed to victuals, clothes, a home for three years.' She tilts her chin defiantly.

'I don't care. Pack yer bags and get out, back to the Female Factory. Assault is a crime, and if you don't leave then the Flogging Parson be ordering you to the lashing triangle for mistreating these two. I'll be sure to take it up with him if I don't see the back o' you within the hour.'

When Cuddy surfaces, head pounding, mouth drier than a tanned cow hide and the taste just as foul, he enters the kitchen to the sight of Will frying something fatty and a tad burnt in the pan, the other three watching intently.

The sight of his hungry children hits him hard in the solar plexus, a pain greater even than the one in his head.

'Wotcha doin' there, son?' He tries to feign a normal voice, though the one that comes out of his mouth is scratchy, thin.

Will glances up, a fork in his hand. 'Fryin' up the last bit of bread.'

Cuddy can see the lad's soaked it in lard, probably hoping it will help fill their bellies. On the table four apple cores sit in a pile, and beside them a tin of treacle with four dirty spoons.

A wave of shame swamps him and he covers it by dragging a chair out from the table, noisily, the scraping setting his teeth on edge.

'Your big brother gone home, then?'

In the silence from Will, Luis answers. 'Yair, around midday. Said he'd be back later in the week.'

Cuddy tries to wrest back a little control. 'The men not about? Least they could bloody well have done is put some of their victuals the way of you kids.'

'Haven't seen 'em. 'Spect they're in their hut … .' Will looks his father right in the eye. 'Cookin' their supper, I reckon.'

His Da looks out the window into the yard, his brain starting to function so that he remembers they have a girl. 'Where's Maisie, then?'

Will lifts the bread from the pan. 'Roger sent her packing. She were getting stuck into Rosa and George.'

His father tries to salvage some pride, summoning a flash of temper.

'Least she coulda done was cook something before she left.'

With great effort he stirs himself from the chair, goes out to the shed to cut a piece of beef off a carcass that he got the men to dress the evening before, leaving it overnight to cool. He should have cut it down and salted it first thing, before the maggots could get to it. He hacks off a piece near the rump and returns to the kitchen, washing the meat down before throwing it into the pan and getting a pot of water boiling for pease gruel.

Next day, when he wakes, he gives himself a good talking to. Gotta buck up, Cuddy. Kids depending on you. He will never get over lamenting the loss of his dear wife and deserves the regret, sour in his gut, that he so often failed her while she remained steadfast to the end. For her sake, especially, he must go on.

After sun-up he goes in search of the men, needs to show them he is back in charge, get them preparing the fields for spring planting. One of them is mending a broken fence, the other two sawing the trunk of a tree blown down in recent high winds.

Satisfied they aren't idle, he arranges for the waged fellow, John Evans, to help in the barn later in the morning, a harness that needs repair. As he walks back to the house his hand goes to his pocket, feeling for the silver watch. Must be a good twenty-four hours since the last drink and the cravings are bad, but they are forgotten when he finds the timepiece is not there.

He doesn't feel the eyes on his back, Evans on one end of a cross-cut saw, watching his master checking his pocket.

Cuddy has been so addled by grog in recent weeks he can't for the life of him remember the last time the watch was on his person. Bound to be on the shelf in the bedroom, he tells himself, hurrying towards the house.

The shelf is bare, save for Melva's folded stockings, her sewing kit, brush set, and a nightdress. He looks away quickly, lest the grief get him in its tentacles.

The watch is not in the pockets of his Sunday best jacket or trousers, or by the washbasin. He calls to the boys. 'Anyone seen me watch?' They shake their heads. Back in the bedroom, he spies his tatty old work boots, still crusted from the last time he mucked out the cowshed, a space beside them where his new shoes should be.

'What the blazes, I bin robbed,' he shouts to no one in particular.

He springs into action, moving faster than he has for weeks, reaching the men in record time, but even as he approaches he sees the saw lying on the ground and no Evans.

'Where is he?' Cuddy roars at the other two.

One of them has a sly look about him and seems to suppress a smile. 'Took off not long after you was here.'

Despite farm chores waiting and hungry children, Cuddy leaves straight away for Parramatta to dictate a strongly worded advertisement for sending downriver to *The Sydney Gazette*.

STOLEN from my house at Kissing Point, with a Cypher M. C. on the outer case a Silver WATCH maker's name Bagwell, No. 1763; also, a pair of men's new Shoes strong suspicion falling on John Evans, who lived as labourer in my employ. Whoever will give information that may be the means of apprehending the said John Evans will be well rewarded by three guineas.

Back home, he sets the boys to work in the kitchen garden and leaves Rosa with them, on strict orders that Luis watches her. He wanders inside, thinking to cook something, but drifts instead to the next room, where he sits on the bed. His magnificent watch, the mark of a man who has risen despite the odds. It is lost to him, he knows it. He puts his head in his hands and weeps in messy gulps, the bed cold without the weight of his wife on the other side.

Despite the initials on the watch case, it is never seen again. In his heart Cuddy knew the minute he found it gone that he would never see it again, no doubt sold to a sailor and on its way to India or God knows where.

The stubble on his face is itchy, he's never liked it like that. He prepares to shave, propping a small, cracked mirror on a window ledge then hanging the leather strop on a nail. George is watching intently, recognising a quiet purpose as his Da performs the familiar ritual, each gesture slow and deliberate as he opens the cut-throat razor and runs it up and down the strop several times to sharpen the blade, flipping the flat back of the razor away from him on the up-stroke and towards him as he drags it down.

Then his Da lifts the razor in front of his face, holding the bone handle upright, pausing for a long time as he studies himself in the mirror. It bothers the boy for some reason, though he is too young to understand why. His father lowers the razor to the level of his neck, before angling the blade carefully, so it is poised, horizontal to his Adam's apple with the blade facing in.

The five-year-old is caught in the spell of the moment, a thick sensation closing in, making him muddle-headed, like when Maisie walloped him. A distant voice is saying he should do something, maybe call for someone, but all he can do is stand there mesmerised, unable to take his eyes off his Da.

The moment holds, stretches wide as the boy watches the hovering hand of his father, understanding that a great effort is under way. Without warning his Da stares at him, slowly lowering his hand. 'Mustn't forget to lather up first, son.'

CHAPTER THIRTEEN

TAM

SOUTHERN OCEAN, 1810

THE MONSTER IS BACK. THE roll of the ship, the lurching at the top of each wave before the bow thumps down the trough, cannot distract it. It thieved, lied, drew blood once or twice in the long, dirty months in Taunton Gaol, eating foul air, growing big on disease and death at every turn. Now it wants to steal a life.

One hundred and twenty like her loaded at Woolwich onto *Canada* and now nearly four months at sea, bound for Botany Bay. 'A pimple on the arse of New Holland,' Tam's cart-mate announced as they travelled the long road from Taunton to a future that could be no more seen than London bridge in a greasy fog.

The cargo includes five cases of hats, ten trunks of prints and five crates of earthenware. It's not lost on Tam that these items have far greater value than her own life, though the labour she can give will rate, likely not as much as the ones too smart for petty thieving and shoplifting, who have skills as forgers, counterfeiters, housebreakers, fraudsters. One of the women was even sent down for highway robbery, though her man got off scot-free, galloped off on their horse and left her with a pistol in her face, by all accounts.

Tam's mean streak flares when she's pushed too hard, though she's not alone, more than a few handy with their fists or quick to rip out a patch of hair if they've been strongarmed or slighted. But they scratch and bite like tomcats, while she sees herself as a rabid dog snarling at the end of a leash.

The Welsh washerwoman started it, taking Tam's hairbrush when she had her back turned. Her fist struck the thief in the belly, winded her, but two of her countrywomen felt the need to defend another from their homeland and soon there was a riot, hands slapping, boots kicking, mouths swearing and hissing. It took four soldiers to separate them, by which time Tam had her fair share of bruises and a ringing in one ear, spending three nights locked in the dark of the coal hole in the bowels of the ship, stuffing her ration of bread in her mouth to keep it from the scurrying rats.

Fresh food brought on board during their stop-over at Rio de Janeiro has not been enough to quiet her demon, thriving on cockroaches and fleas, tearing at her skin where bites itch in red welts by day and night.

Do it. Take a life to save a life.

The missing knitting pin will be noticed soon. Roughly fashioned from a partly straightened fishing hook attached to a length of wire, it has fallen from its hiding place under the skirts of the old woman they call The Queen.

Canada has battled the storm for days and most of the women are weak from sickness, some given over to the wish of dying, others willing themselves to go on. All too preoccupied with their own circumstances to see her withdraw behind one of the water barrels.

He has not been near Tam all week, needed on duty till the ship is in safer waters. She has counted three months since some part of him lodged inside. The sea wife, he calls her, though he laughs in her face because she is but a girl with no sense of how to make a man content.

The first time, forcing her to spread her legs, he pushed up her skirts and found his way into her woollen drawers as she struggled against his rough hands, a beast rising in her to fight him off, trying uselessly to kick him away with her boots.

It hurt, not just her nether regions but a scarring of her spirit from having to suffer the deal. The fact that it was worth it sometimes, for the butter from the firkin he shared with two other officers, the raisins, fat apricots preserved in jars, and lordy, the rum, made it somehow more painful. As though she betrayed herself in those small pleasures.

She is ordered to her officer's bunk whenever he decides, though he has made it plain she'll be discarded as a dirty rag when the ship berths at Port Jackson. He will join fellow red jackets at a reception at Government House, and she will go to a leaky convict hut in Sydney Town.

Behind the barrel, where she lies out of sight, the pain is fierce. She mustn't give in to it, has to stop what grows, for she has to kill this life to have her own. With a babe she'll have no chance.

She has waited for the moment, the ship steadying briefly as it crests the next wave, a huge hand of water lifting up the keel, holding it high into the belly of the storm as the knitting pin goes down inside her. Flesh of her flesh, it must end.

Soon a dark pool spills across the planking, drifts along a row of caulking, thick blood, the rich red of communion wine carrying its gift of sacrifice, while she is slipping away.

How long she's lain there is anybody's guess, as the ship thumps and rocks, every woman for herself in the chaos of bodies, pots and pails thrown about, sea water leaking through seams and flooding through the hatch.

When the lamps are re-lit it's a midwife who notices the blood stain coming from behind the barrel and tracks it to the girl, head lolling on the boards. 'Dear God, whatcha done to yerself.' She spies the hook near the girl's hand, knows in an instant what's happened.

'Oh, you done yerself some terrible harm,' she mutters, looking over her shoulder. 'None o' youse have seen anything,' she shouts, tearing some strips of cloth from Tam's skirt. Best not to bring this to the surgeon's attention or the girl will be clapped in irons, sent to gaol when they land, if she lives that long.

She sets to work examining the girl and doing what she can to staunch the bleeding. There's no guarantee how her patient will fare, but there's one thing she knows for certain – she's butchered herself so badly she'll never be troubled by babies again.

When the storm dies down the officer's servant comes to fetch his concubine. The midwife can hardly contain her glee when she hears that the fellow flew into a rage at the news that the girl's not in a fit state to bed.

'Let his prick keep swelling till it bursts, I say.' She lets out a full-throated cackle as the others join in, a belly-shaking release from the torment of the storm and every man who's judged, mistreated or betrayed them.

Perhaps it was the salt in the sea water washing about as she bled, or the quick action of the midwife, but by some miracle Tam's bleeding slows and stops, and she remains fever free. When the ship moors close to Sydney Town, clinging to the edge of the harbour, she is still weak but able to climb down the ladder to be rowed to the wharf.

She barely sees Sydney and is given no opportunity to rest and recover. Next morning she is put onto a boat with a dozen other girls and taken to the Female Factory at Parramatta. All of them have been promised as domestics to the district's settlers, a few having the good fortune to go to wealthier homes, though Tam is not among them. Within days her name is read out and she's loaded in a cart for the hour's ride to one of the district's farms.

She has been standing in the Kissing Point kitchen for just a few minutes when she's ready to turn and run. It's not the filthy state of it that makes her shudder, fat spilled around an iron oven that's been recently knocked together by a smithy, mud and cow shit tramped across the floor. Neither is it the scowling boy, probably a year older than her, running his gaze down her chest, across her hips, nor the nine year old, feet planted, shielding his sister.

What arrests her are the big, brown eyes of the snotty little urchin, the six year old looking out from behind her brother's arm, her round face so full of hope that Tam takes half a step back to put a little distance between herself and the motherless girl with the devouring stare.

The master rounds on them. 'Where's yer manners, say hello to our new help.'

The thirteen year old by the name of Luis is confused about the correct degree of politeness, calling her 'ma'am'.

'There's no need for that, boy. She be Tam and that's all you need to call her.'

The master's an old fellow, looks worse for wear. Though his wife's been gone nearly four years, the bloodshot eyes and the slight tremor in his hand are the giveaway about how he has coped.

She forces back a sigh and arranges her face into a look she hopes will convey interest and enthusiasm. She must be patient, make the best of it. Most importantly, she must keep a keen eye out for any chink, a gap where a glimpse of opportunity may shine through. The awful circumstances of her life must be refashioned, made worth it by something new. She must do her best to find it.

Cuddy Ranse is busy explaining her duties: cooking, cleaning, mending, washing, and caring for the young ones, with help on the farm during harvests. As he gives direction his shoulders pull back, bringing him more upright than he has been for weeks, for the girl's arrival is lifting a burden. With a bit of luck she may bring some sorely needed warmth and heart to the centre of his family.

The girl they had after that terrible Maisie needed a nudge now and then but was an acceptable worker, till she got her ticket of leave and took off to marry. He was disappointed in her just the same because she was often sullen, always joyless, never one for a laugh or a kind word. It was a trial sometimes to sit beside her gloomy bearing at the table, spotless though it may have been.

This one looks livelier and despite her age will hopefully be more capable in a womanly way that he can't define. He knows he will recognise it when he sees it, as he did the instant he saw his dear wife on the cobbled street of Gibraltar.

The little ones have been lost without their Ma, little spinning tops wobbling about badly at first, though he'd like to think they are more settled in recent times.

They were very nearly without their Pa in the early months, a close call. His hand so badly wanted to slash away with the blade, end the pain. He remembers staring into the mirror and seeing Melva looking back, beckoning, smiling, waiting with open arms on the other side. He could feel himself readying, gathering the strength to go to her. What stopped him was the sight of young George looking up, his face rigid with fear. He made himself a vow then and there – he'd never again shave without someone nearby.

The convict girl has a pinched look about her, and he hopes she's not diseased, though she looks strong enough. He takes sheets and a blanket from a shelf in the bedroom then leads her outside, pointing out the outbuildings, the grain store, the kitchen garden, then leaving her to get settled in her room off the side of the barn.

'We be needing some dinner, soon. There's a bit o' pickled pork, you could do something with that.'

The eldest, Roger, will be here with his new wife on Sunday so there'll be extras for the midday meal, he informs Tam. 'Married back in January, me boy, after getting a discharge from the regiment. A good woman that Ellen, a hard worker, had a tough time growing up.'

He stops himself, can't understand why he is yapping to a stranger.

It's a good match his son has made. His daughter-in-law, siblings and their mother were abandoned by the father, who jumped ship back to England when he got his full pardon. Then the Ma was killed in a freak accident, a carriage overturning and the wheels breaking her back. All up, his daughter-in-law has proven she's solid, a hard worker, just like Melva, and just as loyal to family, raising her younger brother and sister.

'Roger's done well, no sign yet of the land grant he was promised when leaving the 102nd, but they've settled at Windsor, up the Hawkesbury way where Ellen grew up, and he still manages Porteous Mount.'

Maybe it's guilt making the teeth rattle in his mouth, Cuddy thinks. It should be him, not his eldest, keeping the supervisor on his mettle at the Field of Mars property. He relies on his boy to keep the place running well, then wants to take him down a peg or two because of it. Knows he shouldn't, it's not fair, but can't see what others can, that he resents his son for showing him how much he falls short of the man he should be.

Easier to drown in grog than have the courage to change, to do something to restore his pride. Melva would never have stood for it, which makes it no easier. Even in death he's letting his good wife down.

'I put a bolt on the door. Be sure to use it.'

There's only one woman for every four men in this colony, something this girl will find out soon enough.

After her master leaves, Tam sits on the mattress, kept a few inches off the floor by a hardwood pallet, and listens to the sounds of spring on the farm. Goats bleat, a few cows are lowing, chickens clucking and scratching outside. The rank smell of pigs tells her they're penned close by.

The room has a low table with a candle, an upright chair, a few nails hammered in the wall and one square of window up high, the size of a ship's porthole. She squints up at the brightness of it, then shudders. Her eyes are playing tricks, telling her it's a soaring blue wave bearing down when all that's there is clear sky.

She puts her bag in the corner, takes out her best boots and places them neatly under the table, then hangs her Sunday shift and jacket on the nails. Her most precious possession, the small leather-bound prayer book the ship's surgeon gave to all the convict women, she lays beside the candle. She won't part with it, unlike those who sold their books to sailors for bread or liquor. There is some comfort in the prayers, but far greater satisfaction in the fact of the printed words themselves, providing the pleasure of lines to read.

She takes a deep breath. She is still healing, not yet returned to full strength, but there's no point in dilly-dallying. Time to discover what God has sent by way of the Ranse farm and family.

After so much confinement in gaol and aboard the ship, Tam steps outside every chance she gets, relishing the softness of hills, the wide arc of sky, the river sluggish below. The space unwinds a tightness within, not requiring her permission or cooperation, unlike the walls of the house, a boundary wherein great effort must be mustered to impose order.

Despite the earlier servant girls' efforts, the presence of the late mistress seems to hover in the hand-sewn apron on the hook, in the woven basket that holds onions, even the half-cake of soap. Tam sets to work, a frenzy of dusting, sweeping and wiping, clearing out dirt, soot and grease, showing the woman's ghost that this is a fresh start, there's no place for her now.

What remains in the children's memories is another thing entirely. Their eyes follow her as she moves about the main room of the kitchen, tending the fire, getting a batch of bread under way with the ample supply of wheat flour. Tam senses them sizing her up, watching her closely to see if she measures up, but to what?

Luis is quick to make it clear who they're comparing her to. As she kneads the floury mix he lets her know that 'Ma don't do it that way'. Hands too sticky to give him a shove, she resorts to sharp words. 'Well look about, she ain't here, is she?'

The lad's face crumples and she feels a stab of pleasure that she's wounded him so easily, followed immediately by a wave of remorse. It's not that long ago that she was a young foundling at the mercy of cruel grown-ups, and her face flames that she has it in her to be a persecutor of children.

She stomps outside. 'She musta been a bloody saint,' she mutters to herself as she draws water to start boiling the meat. Saint Melva once cared for the family and now it is the job of a sinner. Them kids will just have to lump it with who they got now.

Mrs Bainbridge taught Tam well and soon the master and his offspring have been won over by her beef and onion pie, juices mopped up with freshly baked bread, followed by baked apples stuffed with raisins, sugar, and chopped lemon peel.

The pantry cupboard is left unlocked, containing the wonder of food that sits there for the taking. She gorges on a bung jar of Cape Gooseberry jam until her sides start to heave and she must run outside behind the woodpile, using the toe of her boot to nudge dirt over the shame of the sticky mess puked up in the dust, such waste.

Back in the kitchen she finds Rosa standing on a chair, in her hand a spoonful of jam dripping onto the table and a gooey yellow circle of it around her mouth. Tam is tempted to slap her till she sees the fear in the girl's eyes, instead taking the spoon and lifting her down to wipe the mess from her face. She is rough with it so Rosa struggles to get away, forcing Tam to pin her to the spot by one arm.

'What be this, then?' Mr Ranse's stern voice fills the room as his frame comes through the doorway. He has been gone since breakfast, Tam assumed to the inn at the wharf or into Parramatta, but grey streaks on his clothes show he's been burning timber felled in the far field.

'Just cleanin' her up, sir.' Tam lets the girl go and she rushes over to hug her father's legs, wiping jam on his trousers. He pats her hair absent-mindedly, still looking at Tam.

'Orright then. Just so's we clear, I'm not tolerating the little 'uns being beaten. They had enough of that with the first girl.'

'No sir, course not.' Tam breaks eye contact and busies herself putting the jam back in the cupboard, wiping the tabletop, and moving the kettle over the fire. 'I'll make you some tea.'

'Don't bother, just need some of that warm water to wash up. Gotta go to town, see the fella who does my letters.'

Tam fetches the kettle and is taking it towards the pitcher beside the basin when her quick mind grasps that the moment should be seized.

'Don't expect you been told, Mister Ranse. I know me letters, had proper lessons, did the writing for an employer in the Mother Country.' She is still holding the kettle, aware she looks pathetic, that there's pleading in her tone.

The master's eyes take on a shine, the first she's seen since arriving. He too welcomes an opportunity.

'Arithmetic, too?'

Yes sir, I'm good with sums, kept his books for him.'

Cuddy looks at the girl with new interest. If what she says is true, it would be an advantage to have someone to do writing, keep farm ledgers. He will test her. She can write the petition he needs and he will take it to the scribe at Parramatta to have it checked. No way will he let a young thing like her pull the wool over his eyes.

He stays at the farm, sending her instead to Parramatta to buy paper and ink. Next day they sit at the table and he dictates a request to the Governor for Will, as a free-born youth soon to be of age, to go on the list for a land grant when the next round of measuring is done.

She writes with a neat, steady hand, forming letters confidently across each spaced row, with no ink splodges or crossing out. As the paper is set to one side for the ink to dry before folding, a fuss draws their attention outside.

Will and Luis are hopping about, pointing at three riders coming down the track. As they get near Cuddy almost falls over. In the lead is the new Guv, Lachlan Macquarie, accompanied by Rev Marsden and the area's wealthiest landowner, Gregory Blaxland, a free man come from England.

Cuddy shouts through the doorway to Tam. 'Fold the letter and seal it, quick. We got the Guv right here.' She appears with it in time to curtsy to the arrivals.

The men greet Cuddy but do not dismount, the parson conducting the introductions and the Governor explaining they are short on time as they've been inspecting farms from the Field of Mars as far south as Kissing Point, and must return to town before dusk.

'A fine property you have over there, Mr Ranse. One of four principal farms at Field of Mars, I note, all prettily situated. Do you find any disadvantage that Porteous Mount is the only one not on the banks of the river?'

Cuddy is keenly aware that, though he has washed his face and hands, he is wearing filthy field clothes. 'No sir, if anything I find it an advantage so close to the forest, away from flooding, with shelter from strong winds.'

The Guv seems satisfied with the answer. Before the visitors bid them farewell, Cuddy takes the letter from Tam.

'If I may beg your indulgence, sir, I have just this day written you a letter.' He holds it out. Marsden dismounts and accepts it on behalf of the Governor. 'I will ensure the Governor's secretary receives it, Mr Ranse.'

Within minutes the trio are riding away. Cuddy looks over at Tam. 'You better have done well with the writing. Too late to get it checked now.'

'It were well presented, master.' She might speak rough but she was taught how to write properly.

After eating, Cuddy returns to his workers, breaking up clods on farrows turned over weeks earlier.

'Uppity lot,' one of them mutters to the others.

Cuddy is curious. 'Wotcha mean? They say somethin' to you three?'

'Not so much to us, but about us,' the taller one complains.

'Go on then, what did they say?'

The three riders evidently made no attempt to lower their voices as their horses trotted past. 'Heard 'em complaining about houses round here bein' miserably bad like the folks livin' in 'em, every one of 'em poorly clothed and fed.'

Cuddy shakes his head. The cheek of the Guv and his hangers-on, making a man bow and scrape then bad-mouthing him and his farm anyway. Let them see how they'd fare in starting from scratch, and without the steadying hand of a wife. Mind you, the convict girl might be handy to have about the place.

CHAPTER FOURTEEN

KISSING POINT, 1810

WILL HAS BEGUN HANGING AROUND the house more than he should. Tam is at great pains to discourage his attentions, partly because she doesn't want to raise her master's ire by having him think she's making a play for his son, but also for a more important reason.

The lad makes sure to brush against her when he passes, takes every opportunity to hand her a milk jug or plate for a chance to get close to her hand. She feels the heat of him when he's close, a bull seeking a cow to mount, and she the only one in the field.

It's not that his barely concealed fervour doesn't move her. Sometimes when he is close or looking at her with a flush on his cheeks she feels excitement, too. But she finally has a safe sleeping place to herself, plenty of food, and an employer who treats her fairly, none of which she wants to jeopardise.

Then there's the other matter.

Will is almost a man, full of vigour, with a bright future. He will want children, will need to build a family to help him on the land. She cannot risk getting attached, only to be rejected when he finds she's barren as a wheat field parched for want of rain.

In some ways it suits her that she can't have babies. It will free her, she can dare to be different to the colony's other convict women, needing a man to save them from the effort of striking out to make their own life. The fact that most do it as a means of protection is something she too easily dismisses.

Twice now she has refused to unlock her door when Will came knocking in the dead of night. The third time she hissed at him to go away, only to have the voice of the waged labourer, Blister Blackburn, speaking quietly on the other side of the door. 'Come now, Tam, be a good girl, open up. I got some fine stockings you'll be sure to like.'

Will only told her a few days earlier how Blister got his name. 'Turns up after the work is done, if he can get away with it.' Well he's not getting away with anything tonight.

'Go away, afore I shout for the master.'

'Don't be like that. You an' me, we could make quite the pair, look after each other good and proper.' She can hear his heavy breathing.

'Don't need you lookin' after me, Blister. Go back to yer hut.'

Silence. A few minutes pass.

Then a voice that is lower, a touch more sinister. 'Just watch yerself, me girl. It might be orright when you got a locked door at night, but there's plenty of hours in the daylight for trouble.'

She shivers, hearing his feet padding away. Impossible to make friends in this bloody place but easy enough to make enemies. After that night, the open spaces around the farm and the shadowy outhouses and corners no longer hold appeal. The trapped animal within begins to come alive again.

Roger, Ellen and the two young siblings she's raising have come for a meal after church. The ten of them squeeze around the table, Cuddy at the head, all of them tucking into heaped plates of roast pumpkin, potatoes, native spinach, and goat braised with onions, all of which it has taken Tam the better part of a day and a half to prepare.

Cuddy delights in telling his family they're eating the ornery billy goat that head butted Rosa a few days earlier.

Tam clears the plates, lifts the kettle across to the hot oven top, then slides a tin of molasses gingerbread into the centre of the table. The tension between the master and his eldest son is on full show and while the water boils for tea the pair, already a couple of glasses of rum in them, go outside. Tam excuses herself to dash to the privy, not because she needs to move her bowels but because it's within hearing distance of father and son.

Their voices are muffled through the privy walls, so hot from November sun that Tam fears she will bake. As she fumbles with the door to get out, Roger raises the volume.

'It ain't fair, Da. I got the other farm now. You need to step up at Porteous Mount, put in a bit more over there to keep the place going.'

She hears Cuddy reply but can't catch the words. Roger is still wound up.

'Ma's been gone a good while, Da. What's yer bloody excuse now?'

Their voices rumble on. Tam noisily opens and closes the privy door as though she doesn't know they're nearby and returns to the mess in the kitchen. Ellen has made tea, sent the children out, and begun heating water for the dishes.

Tam is left to wash up, Ellen slinking out to the shade, while the kitchen servant gets ever redder in the face with the marathon of dirty dishes and cutlery, and the repeated heating of water to cut through the grease.

Roger's talking-to has had an effect. Cuddy is off to Porteous Mount at first light after spelling out chores he expects Will and Luis to do before he returns; Will to chop enough wood for the oven and pile it on the verandah, sand back the wooden plough, milk the cows, while Luis must fill the water barrels from the well, feed the penned animals, and do as Tam says.

Late in the day Tam sends George and Rosa to the vegetable garden, wilting in the heat, to pick the rest of the beans for supper. She's deep in thought about how best to talk to the master about George starting school. Irish convict Matthew Hughes teaches reading, writing, arithmetic and a large dose of the gospel in a slab hut less than a mile away, a curtain separating labourers' children from those of the settler employers.

She is still mulling it over in the privy, how the teacher was a corporal in the Irish militia, supposedly involved in a murder and sent here to serve a life sentence, but it's all for the good if George can get some learning. She has been showing the boy a few letters, can see he has a quick mind, though the master seems set on keeping him for labour on the farm.

She is hurrying from the privy to check George and Rosa aren't eating the young peas when Blister springs out from behind.

If the two other men are in sight they don't make a sound or a move, well-versed as they are in ignoring what doesn't concern them. Will's gone to mend a broken bit of fence where five ewes escaped early morning, and Luis is topping up water in the hog pen. Blister's chosen his moment well.

Caught by surprise, Tam's easily toppled and is scrabbling in the dirt, one of his calloused hands clamped over her mouth, the other shoving between her thighs. She tries to push his hands away, writhes as he pins her down so tight she can't even raise her knee to hurt him.

'Bastard, bastard,' she is screaming, but it comes out as a strangled groan.

'Lie still,' he hisses, foetid breath in her face. 'Sooner you stop fightin' the quicker it be over.'

Her boots are kicking up dust, heels uselessly scraping at the ground, unable to get purchase. Fury bursts from her limbs and chest, blocked against the strength of a man who's worked the fields for two years. She is trying to bite the hand jammed over her mouth when Blister's weight lifts away. For a brief moment Tam is stunned, then rolls over onto her knees, standing to stagger back.

Her master has Blister by the neck, spins him around, punches him in the face. He says not a word as he keeps punching, laying into him even when the man's nose is clearly broken, blood gushing across his mouth, a split appearing beside one eye.

Blister, strangely, is now the prey, stepping away as the master pursues him.

'Run, you coward, run.'

Blister clutches his crooked nose, screaming., 'You all saw it, he gone mad.'

Will comes running around the corner, sizes up the situation and steps close to his father. 'Let him go, Da.' The lad's quiet, urgent voice breaks Cuddy's violent spell.

The labourer slopes off, not stopping to collect his belongings at the workers' hut.

George and Rosa have heard the ruckus and are watching. The fear and confusion on their faces, watching their Da thrash the fellow, spurs Tam into action. She gathers her wits, spits out dirt, and takes them inside without bothering to shake the dust off her clothes. In the kitchen she hugs them for the first time, for her own sake, needing the comfort of their innocent, warm bodies.

Cuddy could have killed the rotten fellow, it was a near thing. The sight of him on top of the girl, her powerless beneath him, touched a scabby, unhealed place within, the buried sense of uselessness when the one you so badly want to save is beyond your help.

In Blister's face he saw all that he's raged against in the years since Melva died, lashing out at the pain, the waste, the terrible loss that had grown bigger, not smaller, with time.

It shocked him, the frenzy of hurt he wanted to inflict, a nasty boil that had been lanced and the pus, the poison pouring out through his fists. All the rum in the world has done nothing to stem the desire to do damage, make someone pay for the absence of his wife and the ballast she brought to his life.

He doesn't bother going into the house to check on the girl, instead speaking to Will and Luis, voice gruff. 'C'mon, enough entertainment for one day. We got work to do.'

The next afternoon the constable shows up, just as Cuddy expected. 'Got a complaint you abused one of your servants.'

The fellow is sympathetic enough when he hears the circumstances, quizzes Tam, then takes down a statement from her master. 'The law is the law, just the same. You'll have to go before Marsden next week.'

Cuddy knows how it will go with his men. Sure enough, they're suddenly struck blind, didn't see a thing. His little ones and Tam are the only witnesses.

He fronts the Magistrate at Parramatta the following Wednesday, in a courthouse as dilapidated as most public buildings in the town, not that it's what exercises Cuddy's mind, anxiously rehearsing how he will lay out his case. Once the clerk reads out the charge and he pleads not guilty, the constable recites the particulars as given in statements taken from Blister and Cuddy.

He doesn't need to have concern or call a single witness. Though once a soldier and a convict, all that matters to Marsden is the fact that he's now a settler, which means his word on what happened is good enough for the Flogging Parson. The case is dismissed, Blister skulking from the courthouse before Cuddy takes his leave.

The incident has left a sour taste in Cuddy's mouth, proving a more unforgiving mirror than the one in which he shaves. It is inescapable that he is a mess.

Roger is right about the farms, much as it pains him to admit it. He can no longer ignore their circumstances, the fact that they could slip through his fingers just like that if he fails to stay on top of things.

Melva knew how to work the land, what new crop to try when conditions changed, alert to replenishing the soil or letting it rest, always a step ahead, and keeping an eye on money going out and coming in. Such a fool he's been, never understanding what she gave to farming, doing more of the managing, the thinking things through, than he ever did.

The autumn rains have been lighter than needed, the wheat crop likely to be a poor five or six bushels per acre, while the early maize crop is struggling to take hold. Time to face his responsibilities.

The attack has shaken Tam more than she'll admit. Mr Ranse informs her that he's given the other men a talking to and there'll be no more trouble, but she finds it hard to believe. She goes about her days aware that she's a soft animal and any shell she's grown is no more protection than the one on a snail when the sole of a boot is coming down.

The master seems to notice her more, his keen eye finally lighting on Will's attentions in the kitchen and out in the yard. Once or twice he admonishes him, telling the lad to get out of Tam's way and let her do her work, which only causes Will to resent his father's interference and try even harder to win her over.

Luis is sent to the wharf to collect new chisels and an order of nails from Sydney Town, returning with mail that delights Cuddy. The Guv has confirmed that Will is on the list for land as soon as it can be measured, at Cabramatta, on the other side of the river, eight miles south-west of Parramatta.

'We done well,' Cuddy tells Tam, and she has the good sense not to go mouthing off about who did the writing, gave proper order to her master's thoughts.

The letter marks a turning point on two fronts.

For Will, the resentment of his father spirals like a dust devil, out of control. Blind Freddy can see, day by day, their closeness fracture, splinters flying off on anyone nearby in shouting and foul language.

The young stallion paws the ground, spoiling for a fight with the old one. It goes on for days, more heat in every encounter, as he fights against the future his father is busily mapping out for him.

Tam hears them on the verandah late one afternoon, after Will returns from an unexpected absence on the farm. He is the first one to raise his voice.

'Nothing but bloody hard graft, and for what, Da? These farms, all we do is get by, never any gain. Look around ya, you're getting older by the day. Do you think this is what I want for meself?'

'Steady on, you ungrateful little bastard. Who do you think kept yer in food, clothing, give you shelter? Makes me bloody sorry I bothered.'

Tam sneaks a look out the window as Will pushes his father in the chest. 'Well you don't need to bother yerself anymore, old man. I've signed on.'

Cuddy's so confused he fails to shove his son back. 'What the hell, where?'

'Geez, Da. Times are changin'. Better money to be made sealing over New Zealand way, and even that's not far enough away from you.'

He is spitting out his words. 'Got meself apprenticed to the master of the *Perseverance*. I be gone in the morning.'

He is up at first light, leaving with a hug for his brothers and sister, slinging his bag on his back and marching off with not a word to his father. Cuddy covers any hurt with bluster as he speaks to Luis.

'Time for you to step up lad, do a bit more on the farm.'

He sits at the head of the table to breakfast in sullen silence, Tam tiptoeing from fire to table with his fried eggs, willing him to leave soon and take his dark cloud with him. He goes to the fields when the sun has risen, returning late morning to wash up and eat, before departing again. She knows from the look of him where he's headed. Best have a heavy meal ready to soak up the grog when he staggers back at dusk.

Meanwhile, the second change is slower to unfold. Tam begins to notice Mr Ranse commenting on her cooking, addressing her more often, once even asking for her views on whether or not they could afford a new mare when the old one succumbed to the strangles.

She has begun to unscramble the Kissing Point farm's finances, recording what is spent and earned in neat columns in the green covered ledger Cuddy bought in Sydney. On Friday evenings, the little ones in bed, Luis laying out cards for a game of patience, Tam sits at the head of the table with the master, going through the numbers.

The two heads, glossy brown hair on the fifteen year old and the other grey and thinning on a man well past sixty years, lean close as she runs a finger down the columns, reading out each figure, pausing when he queries one or remembers something he paid for and forgot to say.

Weeks pass before the awareness dawns that he's thawing towards her, in a way that might be unseemly. Tam is overcome by the realisation that she is caught again, not by a cruel ruffian with a hand up her skirt, but by the attentions of the man she depends on for her survival.

At night she tosses and turns on her pallet off the barn and wishes with all her might that Nance was here and she could ask her what to do, but then she remembers that Nance, in her own way, betrayed her too.

She sits upright in her night shift, the air still warm so she doesn't need a shawl, and quietly slides the bolt from the door. In the barn the milking cow lies stretched out on the straw, eyeing the interloper. She remains there as Tam runs a hand down her back, then curls against it.

'I know, girl. They took yer calf from you. It's what they do ain't it, take, take, take.'

She drifts off to sleep, comforted by the rise and fall of the cow's breathing even when the cow lifts to a sitting position, its head motionless. Tam wakes only when the cow gets to her feet as dawn breaks.

CHAPTER FIFTEEN

KISSING POINT, 1810-1811

O N CHRISTMAS DAY THERE'S PLENTY of room at the family's table. Roger and Ellen have chosen to spend it at Windsor, not wishing to travel with their newborn daughter, while Cuddy's had no word of Will since he went to sea.

Tam has cooked a goose, Luis' first kill, though he resisted as long as he could and only chopped off its head when his father stood over him. She boiled the goose for half an hour before roasting it so the flavour wouldn't be too strong and stuffed it with potato mashed with sage, finely chopped onion and butter. A jug of apple sauce is on the table next to it.

Cuddy carves the bird, placing generous helpings on each plate, giving himself and Tam each of the legs with some of the thigh meat. They eat quietly, save for the clatter of knives and forks. Once Tam has cleared the table, retrieved the Christmas pudding from its water and started slicing it, all hell breaks out.

Rosa starts bawling and snotting, making such a commotion Tam can't understand a word she says. Cuddy is laughing, which makes the girl more hysterical.

'What, Rosa? Tell me what's the matter?' She wasn't near the girl, hasn't accidentally nicked her with a knife or caused any harm, though there've been times when she wanted to just to stop her whining.

George takes it upon himself to explain. 'You forgot to put the pudding doll in when you cooked it. Ma always did.'

Tam throws her hands in the air. That damn mother seems to haunt the place, keeps worming her way into everyday moments. Sometimes she could scream that it's time they all let the woman go.

She stops the thoughts. The girl's distress is real to her, and Tam knows what it is to be in pain and treated badly for it, her own vulnerability closer to the surface since Blister's attack.

'Rosa, Rosa. Close your eyes. I'll fix it, promise.' The six-year-old stops the racket, which abates to snivelling, as Tam removes the pudding. George gets in on the act.

'Everyone close yer eyes, you too, Da.'

Tam finds the white china doll on the shelf, wipes off the dust and jams it into the uncut part of the pudding. Back at the table, Rosa opens her eyes while Tam cuts through, pretending surprise when the knife finds the naked doll. She gives Rosa the piece containing the charm and is rewarded with a smile.

It feels unexpectedly good that the simple act has made the girl happy. She fetches the fresh cream, passing it to Cuddy with the thought that she's getting far too weak in the head. If she's not careful she'll go the way of Eileen Sullivan.

The convict servant struck up a friendship with Tam six weeks or so earlier, at Sunday service. The Methodist

Missionary who's been preaching has gone to Tahiti and Marsden was in full flight at the front of the room.

Eileen, who happened to be sitting beside Tam, spoke loud enough for those nearby to hear. 'Dunno why we're even here. The good reverend says God decides the rung where we fit in this mess they call society. Reckons us convicts have lost our place and can't get it back, so why bother.'

People turn to glare.

'Shh, you be gettin' us in trouble,' Tam whispers without moving her mouth.

Eileen giggles and lowers her voice, nudging Tam. 'Fat face, no neck. Blown up like a puffer fish, just as many spikes.' Tam gulps back a giggle herself, conscious that the Ranse family is only two rows closer to the front.

As they file out, the girl hooks an arm through Tam's, insisting they spend their afternoon off together, an appealing suggestion when she's a lively one, maybe two years older, and it's been a long time since fun came along.

Every Sunday afterwards they meander through the brewer's hop fields running down to the river, sometimes stealing into his large orchard to nick an orange or two, or they idle around the wharf, skipping stones on the river, watching the comings and goings while Eileen delivers fine commentary on locals, settler and convict alike. She works at the Shepherds' farm, closer to the tavern, and hears a great deal more gossip than Tam.

Then a couple of Sundays earlier, Eileen didn't show. Turns out she has been locked up in the Female Factory's room above Parramatta gaol.

'Tied down, the master says.' The young woman works on the farm with Eileen. 'She were crazy. Never seen nothin' like it. She were sick in the head.'

Tam struggles to understand. Her friend is impetuous, spirited, prone to breaking into a dance or song for no reason but nothing like this.

'She were strange, used to talk as though someone were answering, but it were only in her mind. Then the food thing, that were queer.'

'What do you mean?'

'She'd eat nothin' for a week, then stuff herself like a none-such, big handfuls of food shoved into her gob till she choked.'

Tam is beginning to see how little she knew of her friend.

'It went south when the mistress told her to do the dishes one night after supper. I tell you straight, I were there gathering the little 'uns to get 'em ready for bed when it happened.'

Eileen had gone into a frenzy, smashing plate after dirty plate on the floor, then starting on bowls before the master came roaring into the room and held her back.

'She were spitting at the mistress, screaming. Oh the awful things she called her.' The woman is enjoying reliving the spectacle, grinning as she talks.

'Stop. I've heard enough.' Tam knows, without a shadow of doubt, there'll be no coming back from this for Eileen. She is ruined now her mind has cracked, a fearful thing.

If she doesn't keep rowing the current will sweep her away, too; she'll lose all sense or reason and be just as damned as her friend. There are girls who kill when they break, usually themselves, though there was the one a while back who stabbed her master's son, he said for no reason but who can believe that.

It would be easy to let go the hope of a way forward but she mustn't let it happen. You start by smashing one plate then there's no stopping till they're all in smithereens.

Mr Ranse's voice jolts her from such thoughts.

'This one's for you.' He hands Tam a small drawstring bag. With a start she realises he's been handing out treats to the family.

She pulls the string wide, shaking the bag into her hand. What tumbles out is a small hatpin, in the shape of a blue tit with a tiny blue stone for its eye.

'Same colour as yer eyes, I reckon.'

She doesn't like the way he's looking at her, stammers her thanks, and jumps up to clear away the pudding dishes.

The New Year arrives with its lie of bringing anything fresh. Tam still works from sunrise till well past sunset, only now she does her best to avoid Mr Ranse, especially when he's on his own.

Since Will left the master has largely stayed away from the inn, though he hasn't the fire in his belly for farming, like the eldest son. She can see it.

As Easter approaches, Cuddy announces an outing. They will take the cart and go to the opening of the new road from Parramatta to Sydney, the entire route paved in stone by convict chain-gangs.

'It's progress,' he tells them. 'We be as much a part of it as any of them bigwigs.'

He turns to Tam and gestures to the children. 'Make sure they look their best. We're a respectable settler family now.'

When the day arrives Cuddy does a quick inspection of fingernails, behind ears and the back of necks, satisfied his three offspring are in their best clothes, Luis wearing a pair of long pants left behind by Will, making up for a growth spurt.

'Yer Ma would be proud.'

Tam takes a breath and holds it to stop a loud sigh. Their Ma did nothing to get this lot ready.

Cuddy insists she sit in the front of the cart next to him, and they bump and sway the eight miles to Parramatta, the three children laughing and giggling the whole way. They arrive in town to raised eyebrows from some who've gathered.

Tam casts her eyes down, uncomfortable at how it appears, old widower Ranse with his young doxy. She slips into the crowd as Cuddy talks to a drinking mate; probably should have kept hold of Rosa's hand, but George will keep an eye on her.

Fifteen miles to Sydney, how she longs to go there. The road is little more than the width of cartwheels, curving gently out of sight through forest on the edge of town. She imagines it threading on into silence, how it follows the winding river to Sydney, where people reinvent themselves, shake off their past, while she is stuck here.

Folks living on the eastern side of the river will still use the watermen, quicker when they have ready access to the shore. The road will mainly take agricultural produce to Sydney from burgeoning areas in the west, a delighted Guv tells the crowd. Tam is applauding with the others after he's finished his speech, when she spies George and Luis but no Rosa.

She picks her way through the throng to the boys. 'Where's yer sister?'

'Thought she were with you.' Luis doesn't want any trouble. It's a grand day out and not to be spoiled.

'George, you seen her?'

He shakes his head, worried now.

'You go that way, Luis, be quick about it. George, stay here, keep an eye out for her. I'll go to the river.'

Tam strolls to the edge of the crowd, not wanting a fuss. Once clear of the group, she breaks into a sprint, scanning the street as it dips down towards the ford. No sign of Rosa's green dress or her pale brown bonnet.

Her feet are slipping on the steep slope of marsh rolling down to the river, where the tide is rushing in across exposed mud. No sign of the girl on the footbridge upstream.

'Rosa, Rosa.' She is screaming the girl's name, panicked that she might be trapped in one of the muddy holes filling rapidly with surging water. A vigorous tide in this part of the river, where denser saltwater roils underneath fresh, can become a raging torrent in no time.

The child's dress and bonnet will be hard to see in so much green and brown on the slopes and in the dark river sludge. Tam runs along the foreshore as the water rises. She can't swim and if it gets much higher the girl will be beyond her to save. She should find Mr Ranse, get help, but she's hurrying to the footbridge, to see past the bend of the river. Not a soul in sight. She sprints back downriver.

The water heaves and swells, a sinister gurgling in its rise, covering animal tracks, any sign of a five year old's boots. Frantic, Tam skids in mud, landing on her side, hat askew. She wants to cry, instead scrambling to her feet, lungs burning, and hurries off, driven by visions of Rosa's black hair floating as the girl sinks from view.

She hears her name called from behind but can't stop. 'Rosa, Rosa,' she shouts, a ragged sound from her throat. But it's her name that echoes back, and she slows to glance over her shoulder. Luis is at the bottom of Church Street, close to the ford crossing, the unmistakeable shape of Rosa in his arms.

At last Tam stops, bends over, gasping. When she recovers and gets to Luis the girl is crying because her brother has scolded her. She reaches out her arms and Tam takes her, Rosa wrapping legs around her like a monkey.

Tam should put her down, she's getting mud over the girl's dress, but even as she has the thought her body is enfolding the child, melting against her. A foreign feeling floods her chest, uncomfortable, unable to find its place for a moment, then settling around her heart.

It's been so long since Tam's felt the emotion. It seems Mrs Kent did her job well, stamping her with an ability to love that's not been destroyed, despite every harm. It's a scary thought, for it has a tender belly.

In May she discovers that Eileen's been sent to the new Castle Hill Lunatic Asylum, in what's been an old granary, stuck in the middle of nowhere, seven or so miles north of Parramatta.

It pains her to think of the weight of those stone walls bearing down on such liveliness, for her friend has been declared mentally deranged and will never be set free.

As days go by, Tam's mind returns often to the moment when she stood in the Old Bailey dock, eyes searching for a glimpse of Nance, only to find she'd been abandoned. She cannot let it happen to Eileen. She waits till Friday, after she and the master have done the ledger and he's knocked back a few tankards of ale.

'Beggin' your pardon, sir. I would sorely like to put my mind at rest about a friend sent to the lunatic asylum.'

Cuddy leans back in his chair. 'How do you propose to do that?' They both know she's a convict, has no rights to visit without the master's say-so.

'If you would give your word for me to go see her, I be most grateful.' The grovelling, she hates herself for it. Always a beggar at the table.

He considers the request, the first time she's asked outright for anything, a pleasant shift between them, a touch personal. He overlooks the fact that it's an exchange between master and servant, choosing to see a girl needing his help. It's been so long since he shared anything at all with a female companion.

'Get the paper and ink. I can give you a letter.'

The Superintendent in his written reply refuses the visit, claiming that Eileen is a danger to herself and others, though he does give a brief description of her circumstances.

The young woman is fed and clothed well, with all care given. The Governor himself requires that every provision humanity could suggest has been made for the accommodation and comfort of those, such as Miss Sullivan, labouring under the affliction of mental derangement.

Tam reads out the response to her master, saddened that she is barred from offering comfort to Eileen or the chance to see her condition for herself.

'You did yer best,' Cuddy says, kindness in his tone.

She nods, takes herself outside, pretending the need to get something from the vegetable garden so he doesn't see her eyes welling up.

He is on the verandah when she returns, stopping her as she goes to the door. 'Things could be different, you know.'

He's not looking at her, instead squinting into the distance.

'We could marry. I'd see you right, make sure you're cared for, even get someone to help in the house.'

He is laying out the terms, hears himself speaking like he's trying to get a customer to buy something in a shop, so different to the first time, a young man overcome by such a flush of attraction it smoothed his thoughts, charmed his words.

'O' course I expect you need time to think about it. I be much older, I grant you, yet it's a fine enough offer if you want to get set up. The ways of this colony can send folks mad, like yer friend.'

Tam stands there dumbstruck, caught in the surprise.

Her master presses on.

'Take all the time you want to decide. We can't wed anyway till the end of the year, after you done your twelve months good behaviour.' He is pleased with himself that he's carefully avoided using the convict word, hasn't played up her lack of circumstances, for he still remembers the way that scalds.

Finally, he dares to glance at the girl, then is immediately sorry he did. Right now she looks marooned, less than her fifteen years or so, a mere child. A shaky feeling sweeps through him, as though he's sickening with an illness.

For her part, Tam badly needs to get away from this awkwardness, yet can't afford to offend the master.

'Thank you, sir. I shall think on it.'

'No need for the 'sir' business. Call me Cuddy.'

CHAPTER SIXTEEN

KISSING POINT, 1811-1814

COME THE START OF WINTER, two weeks have passed and Tam still has not given her answer, the question causing her so much bother she can't get her head straight.

Roger arrives unexpectedly early one afternoon. He and his father are meant to work together next day at Porteous Mount, so the timing is odd.

Tam has been wrestling wet work clothes onto a sagging rope strung up at the side of the house, a sharp westerly making it difficult. She is struggling with the wooden prop, shaped from a tree limb, trying to push the fork at one end into the middle of the rope and dig the other end into the ground so she can lift the washing and keep it from dragging in the dirt. Intent on the task, she hasn't heard Roger's horse.

She is striding to the door when she sees the men through the window, Roger standing while his father sinks onto a chair, leaning heavily on the tabletop, one hand covering his face. It's clearly not a conversation to interrupt. She busies herself cleaning out the chooks' roosting box, dragging out straw laden with droppings and piling it at the edge of the vegetable patch, then layering fresh straw for the hens. Better to hold the image of pale eggs waiting on clean straw in the morning than the sight of terrible news arriving in the kitchen.

George and Rosa have joined her and are playing with the hens, catching their favourites to stroke their dusty feathers. When George goes to run inside she calls him back. 'Stay with me. Give Roger and your Da some peace.'

An hour passes, maybe more, before Roger comes out, ignoring Tam to speak to the boy. 'Go to the maize field and fetch Luis. Da needs to speak to him.'

As George takes off, Roger faces Tam. 'Any trouble, get word to James Larra at the Freemason's Arms, corner of Back and High Streets in Parramatta. He'll fetch me from Windsor.'

He is on his horse and riding off before she can marshal any questions about what kind of trouble.

She stays outside with Rosa. Whatever's going down is for family, and she'll do well to stay out of it, though she's jittery just the same.

When the boys return, Cuddy gets them seated around the table, insisting that Tam be there too. 'I got some news. It ain't good.'

The shuffling of feet and the fidgeting come to a halt, every child's eyes locked on their father.

'Seems Will won't be coming back.' His voice is shaky; he clears his throat. 'He'd been working on the *Campbell Macquarie*, him and a few of the crew got into some bother with the natives in Feejee. They was under orders, sent to land a boat and get sandalwood.'

He stops then, unable to go on, the clock ticking loudly on the mantel above the fireplace, each beat piercing his temples.

'What happened, Da?' Luis can't stand the silence. 'They kill 'im?'

Cuddy nods. George starts to howl, Rosa joining in.

Their father stands, needs to walk away for a bit from the wreckage of his family, but Luis is dogged.

'We be havin' a funeral for him, Da. Won't we?'

Cuddy shakes his head, doesn't have the gumption to put the awfulness into words, that there was nothing for the Captain to retrieve, despite his efforts to pay the natives a ransom for the bodies of his three men.

He says the words in his head, needs to make them real.

The natives ate his son.

The five short words explode between his eyes and he charges from the room, not stopping till he's well clear of the house and can let himself double over, puke up his guts between his feet, and bawl. It's his fault, if he hadn't been so hard on Will he'd never have stormed off. What he'd give to have Melva here, she'd have smoothed things over with their boy, nothing bad would have gone down.

Inside, the three children are still at the table, faces white at the loss of their brother and, worse in some ways, the distress of their father.

Tam should do something, every instinct in her says so, though she can't think what. Rosa breaks the frozen scene, coming to Tam and climbing on her lap, burrowing against her chest.

Tam knows nothing of family ties, but she has experienced the confusion of sorrow, a pain so big it shatters all in its path and the pieces must be patched together into something new, not always better.

Her hand automatically goes to cradle the girl's head, as if to shield her. Only then can Tam summon the wits to take charge.

'I am so, so sorry, boys. It be a dreadful business.'

George can't hold back a moment longer. 'I wish Ma were here.' His chin trembles with the effort of staying strong; he doesn't want to cry in front of Luis.

'Come, give me a hug, George. Think we all be needin' one on such a day.' The boy hesitates then goes to Tam, letting her wrap an outstretched arm around him.'

She can see that Luis, now fourteen, would like to take comfort but can't because he is caught at the crossroads, where boyhood is the path that's been travelled but the one ahead, to manhood, must start today. It doesn't help that Tam's not much older.

'Someone needs to see to the firewood.' He ducks out the door and soon the loud whack of axe on wood can be heard, a thumping rhythm that goes on for some time.

There's sadness in Tam's heart, too. For a seventeen year old with fire in his eyes who barely got a taste of life.

Will Ranse, born in the colony, son of a settler, such bright prospects ahead of him. At Sunday service Rev Marsden takes it upon himself to give thanks for the boy's life and regret his demise, calling on the congregation to pray for his eternal salvation. The gesture makes Cuddy want to rise up from his seat, curl his fists and smash that pudding face to kingdom come, for what could such a hypocrite know about how deep the cut when a bond between father and son is rent asunder.

It haunts Cuddy. Two beautiful boys gone now, each alone across a wide ocean far from him, no chance to say goodbye, wish them Godspeed. Or ask for forgiveness.

In the darkness of a sleepless night the faces of Will and Danny float above, circling, merging into one pair of eyes that stare down from the ceiling, accusing, though the crime is unclear, other than the fact that he failed them both.

Weeks pass. There is no mention on the master's part of the arrangement he offered Tam and she has no wish to raise it. The family skates through its days, each person careful not to cause a crack in the ice beneath them lest someone, especially the master, fall in and drown.

Rosa is too young to grasp the way grief pulls at her father and brothers, so tight that they snap and snarl among themselves. She becomes Tam's shadow, seeking shelter from the black moods that come from nowhere. Even George hasn't the wherewithal to be his sister's protector.

The farm is struggling without a firm hand to guide the work, crops wilting in the drought that's lasted for months, cattle and sheep listless and thin with little feed in the fields. Tam wants to hide the ledger till the master is more recovered. Going through the figures is akin to kicking a dog while it's down.

He catches her unawares a couple of Fridays later, his voice weary. 'Let's not bother with the book tonight, Tam. We'll pick it up next week.'

He pours two glasses of brandy, with no mention of how he came by the bottle. She's drunk ale with Eileen but never this burning water, tart yet sweet on her tongue, each mouthful coursing slow as honey through her limbs.

They're alone in the kitchen, the three children all abed, a gentle glow in the room from a bright moon outside, the dying fire and the lone candle on the table. She should go to the lean-to off the barn, slide the bolt. Yet the act of standing is beyond her. She folds her body into the shape of the chair, sinking into the seat with each sip, melting against the back, the chair rocking a little where one leg has been mended, tapping softly on the floor each time she leans for the glass.

Tap, tap, tap. The clock ticking. A sheep bleating in the distance.

'I bin thinking.' Cuddy speaks to the ceiling.

'If you're in agreement, we should wed December.'

Tam sets the glass on the table, a little too hard. Her life seems to run on a loop that closes in on itself, dooming her to the rules and decisions of others. First Matron, then the Governors telling her what to do, who to be, and the Old Bailey judge, now Mr Ranse.

Little consolation, no commiseration, absence of mercy. A puppet not a person, and two more years to her freedom.

She clears her throat, a sound reminding her that she has a voice. It comes out tinny, lacking conviction thanks to the brandy and the fact that it would not be wise to rile the man on whom she depends for survival. 'It be a generous offer, Mr Ranse, though it's best you know I am not good wife material. You would do better to look elsewhere.'

He seems calm, evidently expecting her to decline.

'I'm of a different view, Tam. Yer a hard worker and the little 'uns have grown fond of you. You will do very nicely, to be sure.'

She shudders. He has ignored the prospect of them sharing a bed or any intimacies.

He takes her silence as assent. 'It's settled then, we'll make it official at St Philip's in Sydney, I think, before Christmas.'

Her head is stretched tight, she is outside her body, wants it to stop. Did she not speak, decline? Surely this is a dream, her throat closing up, mind clouded, as she watches her hand push her heavy body up from the table. She plunges out into the night, reaching her room only to sag against the rough-sawn timber wall, dragging her hand down it again and again, wanting to feel splinters under her nails, anything to drive away the deadness.

She lies on the pallet, laying out one path then the other, imagining each, over and over as the moon sets and darkness deepens. The convict servant who dares refuse the master, sent away to the Female Factory and maybe worse. Or the settler's wife, bound by the church, the law and the old man who is her husband.

Somewhere during the night the demon in her stirs. *Do as he says and bide your time, bide your time, bide your time.*

Suddenly she's unable to breathe and sits up, gasping. The knife in her hand, Mrs Bainbridge near its blade. The finger pointing crooked on the whore's hand when she broke it at Taunton Gaol. A noose around the master's neck or a rock smashed against his skull and dumpling Rosa screaming for her Da.

Who knows what this demon can do?

She dozes for a few hours and wakes groggily at dawn, remembering what has transpired.

Bide your time.

The sense of it hits like a sharp summer squall. Marry the man, at least there won't be any need to share the secret of no babies. Marry the man, do the time. A deal with the devil she knows rather than another who may show up at any time in this godforsaken land, where there's nowhere to run or to hide, except in the woods where bushrangers are armed and hungry for female flesh.

If she's sent to the factory she'll be lined up with the others, a sale yard not of fatted cattle but girls and women made to stand there while Marsden leads each settler or ticket-of-leave man down the line. If the fellow gets a fancy for the curves of a woman or a look in her eye, drops a scarf or handkerchief at her feet and she picks it up, the pair are hurried to the altar and wed there and then.

She's heard the stories, whispered behind hands in church. A game of chance, throwing the dice to escape the misery of the factory, only to be beaten by husbands, treated like slaves, sometimes forced into whoring to keep a man in rum.

Marry her master. At least he's not cruel.

Who knows, he's getting decrepit, his days probably numbered. A widow, she likes the sound, it has a respectable ring to it. The ticket-of-leave will come through in two years and she can take off from here, be her own woman and a free one at that.

When Cuddy announces the marriage, George and Rosa are happy to be getting a new Ma. Luis, on the other hand, does not intend to have some girl his age lording it over him. He had a mother, one remembered in full bloom, and he resents the weedy replacement his Da plans to plant in her place.

He waits till she is alone in the yard. 'Don't be gettin' ideas, Tam. You charmed Da into this and he may be actin' like a fool, but I see through you.'

The boy turned fourteen a couple of weeks before Easter and has landed hard into growing up. She hears the venom he will carry into adulthood and understands he will never grasp that she and his father have made a deal, the best that either can.

Meanwhile, she must seek the Governor's permission to marry. When it arrives, the condition is that Tam remains bonded to the master till she's served her time. Another convict saved by the sanctity of marriage, rescued from moral depravity and rampant cohabitation.

Cuddy speaks to Rev Marsden about the marriage banns. Allowing for the announcements to be made in church on three occasions, the wedding date is set for the twenty-second.

Tam will be a bride by Christmas. She pushes the thought from her mind.

Her husband-to-be has decided on a Sydney wedding for a reason. He may be a Catholic, but public mass is forbidden and any services in the faith are hidden from official eyes and this wedding needs to show off his respectability. The churching at St Philip's will have more clout than at Parramatta. Besides, all the children were baptised there.

As for Tam, the foundling hospital required her to worship according to Church of England rites, but the religion in which they marry is the least of her concerns. Mr Ranse insists she call him Cuddy now. She avoids it for days, doesn't want to encourage familiarity. He calls her to task about it.

'We be husband and wife soon enough. It's only right you use my Christian name.'

She wants to look away. Flustered, she wipes the table down again, having done it not two minutes earlier. 'Sorry, master.'

He breaks into a broad grin. 'That's worse than sir or Mr Ranse. Come on, let's hear you say it.'

Dear God, let this not be happening. A yawning chasm opens before her and she is falling in, can see no bottom.

'Cuddy.'

Satisfied, he takes his hat from the hook on the door and leaves for Porteous Mount, where he will share news of his upcoming marriage with Roger, whose own wife is three years older than the girl who'll be her mother-in-law.

They take the cart to Sydney. Ellen showed up an hour earlier to stay with the children, giving her father-in-law and his servant a terse congratulations as they left.

Cuddy doesn't want to waste the trip, he and Luis loading up bags of the new wheat they've trialled, red lammas grain to be milled while they are in Sydney, while Tam watches on.

'Can be a touch bitter as flour, so let's hope it grinds into good stuff.'

Strange wedding day conversation, is her only thought.

They have left the farm, bellies full of eggs Cuddy insisted upon instead of the usual porridge and are taking the rutted track upriver. Tam concentrates on the horse pulling the load, dragging her ever closer to the moment she's been dreading.

From the ford they leave Parramatta behind, stopping for Cuddy to pay the fourpence toll at the new gate near A'Beckett's Creek, then they are rumbling down the stone road towards Port Jackson. The heat of the summer's day has already drawn sweat patches under the arms of her Sunday dress, the red of the Indian cotton faded into pink from so many rounds of the washboard.

Other than an occasional greeting for a passing horseman or a bird flushed from the tall woods by the noise of the wheels, they travel in silence. Tam steals a look at her master, swaying on the seat beside her, jaw as slack as the loose reins in his hand, no sign of the nervousness she feels.

Not once has he mentioned his first wife, a love match it's clear. The second wife a common pedlar, no goods to barter but herself.

After an hour or so Cuddy starts to whistle a tune that's unfamiliar to Tam, and soon they crest a rise to see Sydney clinging to the edge of a lazy harbour sprawling in every direction. The view sings with such beauty that she smiles despite herself, sun bouncing on the water, scattering bright diamonds of light on its surface.

Beyond the small though busy town she spies three ships riding in the bay and six lascars rowing a boat from the closest one, flying a foreign flag. People worse off than her, she consoles herself, the story passed from convict to convict of the time a few of them felt so sorry for a crew of Indian sailors that they gave them clothing and blankets, an act of humanity prompting the authorities to punish her kind severely.

Soon Parramatta Road turns into George Street and minutes later the cart is slowing in Church Street. She must turn away from the distraction of the harbour, stomach tightening, as they reach their destination. She instantly sees why the stone church has been called the ugliest in Christendom. Its rectangular body squats heavily against a tall circular tower so big it dwarfs the rest of the building. The absurdity of it, so fitting for this marriage, gives her the only stab of pleasure she'll get from the day.

'Got an hour or more afore meeting the reverend, enough time for refreshments.' It's the first full sentence Cuddy's spoken since they left Kissing Point. She must gather her thoughts, focus on climbing down from the cart, keep willing herself forward.

At the inn they are served ale, slices of jellied tongue and bread. Cuddy, aware his bride has been far too quiet, raises a glass. 'To us, Tam. To a fruitful union.'

She clinks her glass against his. Fruitful. A terrible word, the most ill-chosen he could find. 'To us.'

They enter the cool gloom of the church at eleven o'clock to an enthusiastic welcome from the preacher. Their two witnesses are waiting, a husband and wife Tam's never met. If the woman's eyebrows shoot up, Tam's in such a state she doesn't notice. A voice in her head is saying 'run'.

Cuddy introduces them, tells her that the fellow arrived on *Scarborough* with him and the woman on *Neptune*. He stops himself abruptly, sentence hanging in mid-air.

With my wife. Tam knows exactly how that sentence was meant to end.

They are led to the altar, footsteps echoing in the empty chapel. She is dusty from the cart ride, hair hanging limp beneath the cream cotton bonnet with its soft crown and stiff brim. She tugs a little at the ties under her chin, fastened too tightly, and wishes she could undo them and throw the bonnet off.

She wears no lace, carries no flower, not even a bible. Her shoes are so scuffed the boot polish has failed to cover the wear.

For a moment she is hovering at the rear of the church, looking at the sorry scene. A girl out of options, a man older than a grandpa, the bluster of an over-blown preacher, two witnesses stiff as blades of grass in a hoar frost.

She returns to her body as Marsden pronounces them man and wife. Cuddy leans in, and for a horrible second she thinks the thin lips of this old man will meet hers, but he veers away to peck her on the cheek. The woman gives her a hug, whispers in her ear as the men shake hands and slap each other's shoulders.

'You'll be fine, darlin'. Just keep him happy.'

They depart to the inn, two married couples. Cuddy buys a round of rum to thank the witnesses. After a second round the men go outside to smoke pipes. Tam grips the chair to calm a dizzy spell.

'You done the right thing, marrying 'im.' Tam watches the woman's lips open and close, slow as molasses, the room starting its own gradual movement, the walls beginning to rotate. The woman clutches her arm, saving a fall from the chair, and jerks her upright.

'There, there. Us women got to do what we can to get by in this godforsaken place. C'mon, some fresh air'll bring you right.'

CHAPTER SEVENTEEN

KISSING POINT, 1812-1814

UDDY LEFT HER ALONE ON the wedding night. It was a blessed relief to get to her room, slide the bolt, and slide it again to make sure it had caught, that the door was properly locked.

Next day he got her to move her things out of the barn lean-to and into his bedroom, his first wife's brush and comb still on the shelf. She had stared at it, a mix of dark and grey hairs on the bristles of the brush. Cuddy rushed in front of her, scooped up the hair set.

'Sorry. Cleared Melva's things out a while back, forgot these.'

The woman is here, as in everything, for the first day as man and wife. Tam looks in the corner of the ceiling, half expecting her dark face to be looking down. As if to cleanse the room she strips the threadbare sheets off the bed, washing them so vigorously she has to mend two patches after they've dried in the sun.

Later, they undress facing away from each other, he throwing on an old shirt and stretching out on his back as she slips a nightshift over her head.

The temperature has climbed to eighty degrees during the day and the bedroom walls radiate heat. She lies stiff on the bed, her skin beading with sweat, and hopes it's good reason to keep their distance, but he reaches for her as soon as he's blown out the candle.

He has none of the ardour of the ship's officer, fumbling with her shift while she is rigid, unyielding, his sour smell making her turn her head away. The rubbing, stroking, the attempts to poke her seem to go on forever but never amount to much, leaving her disappointed because it would be over for the night once he'd emptied his seed.

Eventually he grunts, rolls onto his back and swears. She waits in the dark, motionless in case a movement excites him and it starts all over again. Soon she hears him snore and it is safe to roll away and sleep, too.

He is chirpy enough when they stir at daylight, running his hand down her hair, pulling her against his chest. Gradually, as the nights pass, she comes to see that affection, the comfort of touch, is enough. He doesn't seek to go further and repeat the failure of his manhood after the first time.

It takes a while to get used to the labourers calling her Mrs Ranse, causing her to look over her shoulder, expecting to see the first wife standing there. Other than the new sleeping arrangements and Luis' hostility, little else has changed in the monotony of her days.

The lad remains sullen, despite the months passing. Any hope of him softening has evaporated by autumn and Tam has given up trying to appease him, which only seems to inflame his rage. He tempers it around Cuddy, of course, but finds opportunity aplenty to get her on her own and put her in her place.

Efforts to sway Luis are pushed aside in June by the numbers carefully lined up in the ledger. The farm is going broke.

Two thirds of their flock of sheep have died from black disease, spreading quickly after heavy rains kept up for two days. Cuddy has started drinking again, was going to the inn at the wharf when he should have been moving sheep out of damp ground to the higher, drier field. Without the sheep there'll be no lambs this spring, no money coming in from meat to pay for seed and worse, to keep the debtors at bay.

Roger puts his foot down, refusing to let the steadier fortunes of Porteous Mount prop up Kissing Point.

'We do that, Da, and we lose both farms.'

His son standing over him incenses Cuddy. 'I'll thank you to bloody remember who owns the place.'

Despite further heated words, they reach an understanding that they'll use money from the next citrus harvest at the Field of Mars property. Alas, it proves too late. The Provost Marshal, acting on court orders, takes charge. By December Cuddy's forced to surrender a cart, mare and harness, a few pigs and a field of standing wheat, the harvest to be auctioned off to repay debts. It will all go under the hammer the same day as a blacksmith's shop, the effects of a tannery, and the belongings of a fellow farmer.

As the date of the auction nears, Tam sees her husband collapsing in on himself, leaving her feeling helpless and saddened. It would be going too far to say she's become fond of him, but he treats her kindly, cause for loyalty.

Luis is now fifteen years and George eleven. Cuddy calls them onto the verandah late one afternoon, along with Tam.

'The time's come, boys, to settle your future, and it won't be this farm.'

They wait to hear what it coming, a slow storm approaching, and when their father's next words rain down who knows what damage they'll bring. Cuddy pauses, shudders as though someone just walked on his grave, and with a start he thinks it's Melva, wanting to stop what he's opening his mouth to say.

'As you know, I bin to Sydney this week. Put out feelers, seein' what work might be around.' George's face has gone pale, his brother's not giving anything away.

'Luis, got you a fine position, apprenticed to Captain William Case on the *Samarang*.' Everyone's heard of the Government sloop, recently arrived from Madras with forty thousand Spanish dollars badly needed for the colony's currency. The lad nods enthusiastically, keen as he is to get away from Kissing Point.

'George, you bin bound over to the *Perseverance*, the sealer your brother did start on. You be a cabin boy. It'll toughen you up, young 'un.'

Mention of Will sends a chill through Tam, though the fate of the youngest son hurts far worse. It will be a brutal life for one still such a child, and she has a soft spot for him.

Rosa, on a growth spurt at seven years, is coming towards the house after carrying water to the goats when her younger brother brushes past, knocking her shoulder.

'Why's George actin' like a wasp in a jar?'

The eleven year old is gone within a week of his father's announcement. He lets Tam hug him for a long time as they make their farewell, then embraces his tearful sister. Cuddy slaps him on the back, wanting badly to throw his arms around his boy, tell him how much he loves him, but can't.

Luis, so brittle for months, is warm with his younger brother in saying goodbye.

George can't bear having anyone walk him to the ferry. As soon as he leaves, Cuddy and Luis scatter to find whatever farm chore will keep them busy. Tam and Rosa stand in the yard and watch the lad's back grow smaller until he merges with the hills.

'Your brother's a strong boy, he be orright.' She pats the girl's shoulder, her heart aching. 'Let's go, we got bread to make.'

As they measure out the flour, the girl gone quiet, it occurs to Tam that she's split in two, each half wrestling with the other. The dark corners within still throw shadows of meanness or spite, yet George and Rosa have brought some light and, dare she admit it, a little kindness to her ways.

Luis's turn comes at the end of November. He too is gone before the shame of the auction, marching off without a backward glance. Cuddy relents this time, thinking of other boys with no goodbye, and hugs his son before he leaves, holding on a fraction longer than Luis can bear, forcing him to pull away then cover it with false good cheer.

'No need to get soppy, you be seein' me again soon, Da.'

Tam keeps her distance. 'All the best, Luis.' She'd have been better off talking to a fence post for all the good it does.

The house is now calmer, more settled with Luis gone. Tam can breathe easier.

That night she and Cuddy are woken by shrill cries and squawking from the hens. Hurrying out with the lantern they find a hole dug under the henhouse and two bleeding birds on the ground. Cuddy swings the light around in time to see a pair of spotted quolls running into darkness, one of them dragging a limp hen.

Christmas looms a sorry affair, made bearable by an invitation from Roger to join them at Windsor, where the Guv's seen fit to grant him thirty acres. Tam busies herself in the two days beforehand, finely mincing beef, cooking it in suet with the last of their raisins, cinnamon, cloves, nutmeg, grated apple and a splash of brandy. The filling goes into a dozen pastry coffins she hopes will withstand the journey.

Their men have the day off, and animals fed and watered, the Ranses leave at first light on the thirty mile journey, Cuddy hitching their remaining mare to the light, two wheel cart from Porteous Mount.

The act of departing the farm brings on a mood for Cuddy, but Tam's determined that she and Rosa will enjoy the novelty of a day out.

From Parramatta the cart slogs its way along optimistically named Windsor Road, little more than a wide, rough track. Almost three hours later they reach a series of sloughs, where the cartwheels are bogged. Tam must take the reins while Cuddy heaves himself against the back of the cart, mud up to his ankles.

At last they rattle over the floating pontoon bridge across South Creek and pass through the scattering of public buildings, the troops' barracks and a handful of cottages that form the new town. Near the wharf on the Hawkesbury River, Cuddy points out the cottage for the commanding officer, the most substantial of them all, with weatherboard walls and a shingle roof.

A few minutes later they pull up at the front of a long hut. Ellen, babe in arms, waits out the front to greet them. She kisses her father-in-law on the cheek, seems unsure how to welcome the mother-in-law younger than herself, and settles for a touch on the shoulder.

'Roger's just washing up. Come in.'

Tam enters their home, cooing over the baby, a red-faced thing she chooses not to hold. Fortunately, Rosa is taken with the baby and fusses over her like she's a living doll.

Later, after they've eaten and celebrated with rum, Roger takes his father for an inspection of his property. Rosa plays outside with the shaggy farm pup, a Welsh Grey that Roger has high hopes will be a good herding dog.

Ellen seems to be warming to Tam. Unaccustomed as she is to female company and loosened by a couple of drinks, Tam finds herself sharing some of her misgivings about marriage. Ellen feeds then cradles her daughter, listening intently to Tam as she heats water, plunges plates into suds and wipes them dry.

'Ya know, Tam.' Ellen clears her throat. 'The first wife got the young Irish soldier with a mouth fit to charm. You got old timber, love. You got to expect there'll be some rot setting in.'

Tam drops knives and forks into hot, soapy water. Maybe she's imagining it, but she hears a touch of pleasure in the woman's voice.

Ellen, for her part, wouldn't admit such a thing, that she's playing out her grievance about her stepfather doing her out of her rightful inheritance, taking over the family property lock, stock and barrel, the farm thrashed from forest by the sweat of her late Ma and Da. Now Cuddy's new wife will likely get some of Roger's share of his inheritance when the old fellow's gone. Maddening, but it would be uncharitable to wish this slip of a girl ill, of course she wouldn't do such a thing.

As Tam finishes doing the dishes she sees the flash of scorn that Ellen's unable to hide. There'll be no kindred spirit here; what a fool she is to think there might be.

The visitors head back up the track mid-afternoon, Rosa grubby and happy, soon dozing against Tam's hip despite the cart jolting. The trio is jammed together on the seat, and Tam feels her husband's heat as they sway and bump, smells the rum he and his son kept drinking through the afternoon. He has drawn into himself since he went off with Roger, says nothing about how it was with his eldest. She contemplates asking then immediately decides she's too weary, that one rebuff is enough for the day.

Once through the marshy area, he speaks up. 'A hard life, farmin'.' His jaw is set. She wonders what he's holding back.

The cart rocks onwards.

'So much work Roger's got ahead of him. And there's Porteous Mount.' He flicks the reins softly. 'Hup, hup.' They jolt along for a few more minutes.

'It ain't in me anymore, Tam. Thought about it long and hard, I'm sellin' Kissing Point. If we keep goin' the way we are we lose it anyway.'

She should have seen it coming. He lost interest in farming months ago, probably longer, and the farm's been withering along with his motivation. She has saddled herself to a man in decline, and dammit, she knew it at the time.

'We be movin' to Porteous Mount, then?'

His head jerks around to look at her, as though he's just remembered she's there. 'We'll see.'

There's no will to fight left in her. She'd rather the demon rise up than be caught in the chokehold that grips her, a sense of powerlessness that makes it hard to breathe. But the demon has bowed down to the bond with George and Rosa, with a sense of belonging, and it has left her undefended.

The sale happens swiftly. Their neighbour's daughter, Mary Brown, has married a fellow who was a sergeant, a tailor in Cuddy's old regiment, and he is at their door within days of word going out that the property's on offer.

The deal is done within a week. Eighty-five pounds and a month to pack up, sell unwanted stock, and drive the rest to Porteous Mount. The wheat's been harvested to cover debts and Cuddy's arranged to share the proceeds from the late barley and small oat crops still in the fields with the new owner.

Letters are written for Luis and George to collect next time they land. Cuddy sends them to Sydney's postmaster, a new appointment to stop ships being mobbed for mail or nefarious individuals impersonating folk to steal parcels.

With so much to do the borrowed dray is packed high, the load lashed, and they're on their way before Tam has time for regret. The following days are even busier, for the overseer's been living in the Porteous Mount cottage amid mouse droppings and scum on every surface.

The place is smaller than the house at Kissing Point, with little maintenance done since it was built by its first owner. She gathers her cleaning rags and sets to work.

Roger comes and goes as the months unfold, sometimes staying overnight in one of the convict worker's huts. She is slicing hearth-baked bread for the midday meal when he appears in the doorway one Friday.

'Da's gone to Rouse's place, half a mile over.' He gestures with a thumb to the east.

'Oh, thanks Roger.' She keeps slicing.

'That bloke's got an illegal still. Your husband, he's drinkin' gut rot, Tam. You need to get him to settle down, do more round here.'

Slowly, carefully she lays the knife down. Rosa needs a mother, Roger needs a keeper for his Da, Cuddy needs … what the hell does he need, she no longer has any idea, just like she no longer knows what she might need.

'I can't stop 'im, Roger. Case you haven't noticed, he be near sixty-five now and I'm seventeen.' Her voice is rising as she speaks.

'Well you need to try a bit harder. He'll be dead soon if he keeps going.' He turns away, his face like thunder.

After he's gone she falls onto a chair. Christ, who is she, what has she become, other than a failure as a wife? In a year and a half she'll no longer be bound to her master. She'll still be his wife but no longer his servant, least not in the government's eyes. She needs a plan, not as a runaway, tempting though it may be, because there's Rosa to think about. She's grown too fond of her to bear the thought that she'll end up with the orphans and unwanted children in Sydney. Ellen's unlikely to want the burden of yet another responsibility.

As if on cue, the girl enters the kitchen, complaining that she's hungry. It's a relief for Tam to busy herself slathering some bread with newly churned butter, slapping on marmalade made the day before from the new crop of oranges and lemons.

Luis hasn't yet put to sea, it turns out. The *Samarang's* journey was aborted when she had to return to Port Jackson for extensive repairs. Since then the Captain's been in dispute with the Guv over convicts he recruited without permission. Now it's April and Luis has deserted, a gaoling offence.

The first Tam hears of it is when Cuddy returns from Parramatta with a copy of the *Sydney Gazette and New South Wales Advertiser*, getting her to read it out to him, as usual, after supper.

Her eyes almost immediately light on Luis' name.

'What is it?' Cuddy waits, expecting it's about a bushranger or more conflict with natives in the outer areas.

'It's Luis.' She reads the Captain's notice:

Luis Ranse, aged 16 years, 4 feet 9 inches high, of a pale complexion, has green eyes, light hair, is speckled in the face, and is a native of Kissing Point. Deserted on the 31st of March 1813.

All persons are cautioned against harbouring the above deserter on pain of prosecution; and all Constables and others are hereby required to use their utmost exertions to apprehend and lodge them in gaol, or bring them on board His Majesty's ship; whereupon the usual reward will be given.

Cuddy's furious. 'Stupid boy. Needs to give himself up, else they'll hunt him down and it be far worse.'

Next day he goes in search of his lad, to no avail, concerned the ten guinea reward will make him a target. A few days later Luis turns himself in to face the Captain and a hefty fine.

The Captain, meanwhile, is embroiled in another conflict, this time with the Captain and officers of the brig, *Governor Macquarie,* which causes a lengthy delay.

Cuddy continues to worry about Luis, lamenting that the *Samarang* needs to sail, give the boy a proper chance to test himself. Then in November Roger arrives with worse news. Luis has been shot in the back at Lane Cove, near the convict timber-cutting camp, where riff-raff gather for all the wrong reasons.

'What the bloody hell's he bin doing there?'

'Don't know, Da, but we need to see he's alright.'

Cuddy insists Tam go with him to the hospital at Parramatta, though she waits outside in the cart. He returns half an hour later. 'He'll live. A musket, only small shot, lucky for him. The doctor's taken it out.'

Luis has refused to say why he'd gone to Lane Cove. It hangs in the air between Cuddy and Tam, why he went there instead of coming to see his father at Porteous Mount.

Late November the incident is in the newspaper for all to see, how a fifteen year old, uneducated and neglected, had shot Luis. Despite Magistrate Alexander Riley declaring the boy an imbecile, he is charged with intent to murder or do bodily harm and Riley sentences him to five years' gaol at Parramatta, the first six months in solitary confinement.

Cuddy has gone to the hearing, hoping to find out more about Luis' reason to be in rough company. He arrives home with no further understanding, disgusted by it all.

'No winners there,' is all he says.

Life has a strange way of twisting back on itself or turning left when you expect it to go right. Months pass in a blur through the harvest, Christmas, Easter, the start of winter, and then they slam to a halt one night in August.

Cuddy arrives at the supper table stone cold sober, with a plan.

'Bin thinkin' about the future. The agreement signed with the Guv ends next month and yer a free woman.'

It's the way he says 'free' that startles Tam.

'I got eyes in me head, seen it's not been easy with me and the family. Truth is, I need to get out o' farming altogether, got no stomach for it. Not sure I ever did.'

She is set to be cast out again. Condemned always, it seems, to repeat her past. 'What are you sayin', Cuddy? You getting rid of me? I know Roger won't want me staying on.'

A pained look creases his face. She sees she has hurt him in some way.

'Course not, Tam. I might be many things, but not a waster who runs from obligations to his wife. I intend to do right by you.'

He rests his wrinkled hands on the table, as though it's a card game and he is showing his hand.

'Here's what I propose. I get a job as a constable somewhere round Parramatta, mebbe even the Hawkesbury, you helpin' me with the letter. And I get you a position, I reckon in Sydney, away from the gossips round here.'

He misunderstands why she's mute. 'I still got money from the sale, so I can pay for lodgings, o' course. Roger will keep managing things here, which will bring in a bit at harvest time and when stock gets sold.'

'But … but what about Rosa?'

He sighs long and hard, ignoring his daughter's big, round eyes turned up at him.

'You her Ma now. She'll go with you, get into school, keep on with the learning you started.'

Tam leans back in the chair, relieved. She's already feeling the lure of freedom after the confines of the farm, and can't wait to have a little independence, especially a bed to herself. Better still that Rosa can go with her. She has grown to love the girl.

The nine year old clutches Cuddy's sleeve. 'No, Da. I wanna stay here with you, and Tam stays too.'

'Hush now, girl. I won't be here in this house no more, be workin' elsewhere. You'll still see me, I'll make sure of it.'

CHAPTER EIGHTEEN

SYDNEY TOWN, 1814-1816

THE FAMILY HAS ERODED, CRACKS widening as the flood of events sweeps through. Tam can't help but feel she is to blame. Cuddy never says it, but Roger and Ellen have made their views clear, that she was never a patch on the wife who created the family, held it together with sturdy stuff, as though Tam was only up to paper and a few dabs of glue.

Cuddy is true to his word, and when September comes and she's no longer bound over to him, finds her a place as a maid in a Sydney home, with two rooms rented nearby for her and Rosa.

A week before they depart Porteous Mount, George arrives without warning, on leave from his ship. The boy's nearly a year older, and when he walks through the door Tam can barely hide her dismay at the change in him.

The boyishness is gone, his voice deeper. When he hugs her she feels how youthful pliability has been replaced by new contours ending in hard edges. His face shows little expression and worse, the light's gone out of his eyes.

Tam turns her back to fetch some cold meat and bread for George and reaches for a plate and knife. By the time she's back at the table, Cuddy has disappeared to the barn. As the pair in the kitchen talk, they don't see him feverishly forking hay into a handcart, anything to stop himself from falling to his knees and asking Melva's forgiveness for what's happened to her youngest son, to the family they shared. Soon the cart is full but he can't stop swinging the pitchfork, in the end hurling it so hard at the wall that the prongs stick into the timber, the handle vibrating from the blow.

In the house, Tam deliberately takes a casual stance. 'How are you, George?'

'Good. Glad to be back on land for a bit.' He is looking out the window, a plaintive look on his face saying more than any words can.

'You know I'm fond of you, George.' He looks at her then, the corners of his mouth turning up a little. 'There'll always be a place to stay with Rosa and me in Sydney.'

During his visit he doesn't say a word about the brutal, ugly life into which he has plunged. He is gone to his ship a few days later, bound for months away in the icy waters of the Southern Ocean, to the endless bludgeoning and bleeding of slick creatures on the new sealing island named after Macquarie.

He doesn't so much as leave Porteous Mount as drift away down the track. Tam watches him, bag dragging from his shoulder, her heart aching.

Their lodgings are with a widow in George Street, two dim rooms out the back. At least Cuddy's spared her and his daughter the dire boarding houses around The Rocks, where drunken seamen are quick with their fists and nests of criminals work dark alleyways.

The landlady, Meg Dods, not only lacks a husband but also her front teeth, gums smacking a little as she talks. She keeps a tidy house though, cooks decent suppers, and at last there's a stroke of luck for Tam. The ample-bosomed woman takes a fancy to Rosa and is happy for Tam to pay her a few pence extra a week to keep an eye on the girl when she's not at school.

Cuddy has arranged a domestic position for Tam with a friend of the fellow who bought Kissing Point. One of the few to be granted a liquor licence, her new employer, James Chisholm, has a thriving business importing wine and spirits sold from his premises in Spring Row, where his house is next door.

Tam knocks at the rear entrance, rapping at six o'clock sharp on her first day. The cook shows her in. 'Too early for the mistress. She bin poorly a few days now. I'll send you up in a while with her breakfast tray.'

Mrs Curran is toothpick lean, odd for one who spends all her time in a kitchen, and far from a young woman. She sets Tam to work laying out a tray with a supper cloth, egg cup and plate for toast, all the while reciting a long catalogue of chores the newcomer must get through each day.

The woman punctuates the list with frequent belches and breaking of wind, a stormfront of gases passing through the kitchen, assailing Tam's nostrils, her fingers quivering with the urge to ignore politeness and pinch her nose shut.

'You get paid quarterly, but the mistress might give you a loan to get proper clothes.' Tam looks down at her Sunday best, faded and patched in several places. Another household where the master and mistress are fashioning themselves into gentry.

As it happens Cuddy turns up the following Sunday, handing over an extra six shillings, enough to buy a new cotton dress. He has secured a job as a district constable at Parramatta, with an annual twelve pounds salary.

'You'll not be wanting to hit the drink so hard then, Cuddy. Can't be staggering around yerself then arresting others for bein' drunk in the street.' Oh, the sweet feeling of her vinegar words. She's never spoken to him like that.

If he is surprised he doesn't let on.

'C'mon Rosa, let's go buy a bag o' barley sugar.' The girl takes his hand.

'Don't be stupid, you know shops can't trade on the Sabbath.' Tam is strident, can't seem to be kind.

Cuddy leans close to her, hisses quietly. 'Mebbe I deserve your scorn, but not in front of the girl.'

Her anger, leaking out like poison when he stood before her, rushes through after he and Rosa are gone. She could easily turn into a madwoman, fists tight, bruising him, drawing blood, or it let it turn on her, rusting her soul like a piece of old iron left out in the weather.

Stop, Tam. Stop. The demon speaks, a different creature to the one she's known. *Take the anger and use it to make something good.*

After being shut away on a farm, Tam's shocked at the unwanted attention from men, whether lags, tradesmen or those who aspire to have esquire after their name. Any woman still breathing is fair game in a town where males still hugely outnumber the fairer sex. She must deter them at church, in the market, even when she and Rosa go strolling on her day off. She takes to wielding her married status as a talisman to ward them off.

Cuddy visits every month, showing up sober, his daughter always excited to see him. Then in March the following year he doesn't appear. 'Got poorly I expect, Rosa. Not well enough to ride here.' A hangover, more like.

From then on his visits are erratic, disappointing the girl. Tam distracts her with beach walks, picnics by the harbour, teaching her needlework and how to press flowers, grateful that at least Cuddy pays for their lodgings six months in advance.

In spring, George is the one to unexpectedly arrive. Now fifteen, he's no longer a cabin boy, has been taken on as one of two apprentices on the *Rosetta*, another sealing vessel. He is fit to burst with a story for Rosa about an encounter in the far south on his first trip on the colonial-built brig.

They had moored at Hobart Town, on the southern end of the island of Van Diemen's Land, needing supplies for their journey home. The Captain sent him to one of the inns with a message.

'I knocked on the back door, Rosa, could hear a celebration in full swing. An old woman answered, tried to send me away 'cos it were a christening party, but I weren't having it.'

George introduced himself to the woman, insisted on seeing publican Joe Ferrion. Turned out she was a Ferrion too, Maggie he thought the publican called her.

'You never guess wot, sister. She knew our name, met Ma when she first landed here in Sydney and Da were in such a bad way. The woman were a nurse, remembered Ma well.' He beams at his sister. 'Said we should be proud of her, imagine that.'

He omits the fact of the old woman's penetrating eyes, how they bored into him, has no idea that she saw something of the future even though she couldn't name it. George himself can't know that the screaming baby he heard that day will eventually be his wife.

Tam listens to the lad's story, grasping finally that what ties this brother and sister together, maybe the others too, could never be her. It's not the oft drink-addled father, either, but their experience of a mother who loved them so hard they can never be completely lost to each other.

What might it be to have that kind of love? She will have to be content with imagining it. She smiles at the pair, chatting amiably together as they always have.

The next she hears of her husband is that he's been appointed a town constable at Windsor. He shows up late winter, in time to pay the rent for the next six months. He needs her help with letter-writing, is once again chasing the thrill of acquiring land.

She writes the memorial, scraping the nib across the page as he makes his case. 'Some time back your excellency promised me land at Windsor muster. I only seek a small farm, enough to grant me a living or otherwise put me in some situation.'

Tam pauses to rest her hand. For the first time in a long while Cuddy's eyes are alert.

'I was once in good circumstances but have been unfortunate in that it slipped through my hands.' He waits for Tam to catch up. 'I would be thankful to your Honour to leave me in some situation to gain me a living, for I am an aged man, or otherwise grant me a farm of land.'

She studies him, a fading purple bruise on one cheek, mottled skin, veins snaking across the back of his hands. Her husband must be at least sixty-eight, was well on the way to his grave when they met. A chill passes through her.

'Did ya get that, Tam?' She focuses again as he repeats the ending.

'I will in duty ever pray. Cuthbert Ranse, Constable, Windsor.'

Tam blots and folds the paper, presses on sealing wax, then writes the address.

On her husband's next visit, three months hence, he is delighted to tell her he's been listed for fifty acres at Windsor. 'Not only that, the Guv made me Constable In Charge of the house built for him on the riverbank in town.'

She congratulates him, for Rosa's sake. If she could she'd shake her head, shout at the injustice of it. What hope does she have to get ahead when this old drunk can land on his feet because he's a man.

It becomes a pebble in her shoe, niggling through all the days of running, fetching, cleaning, all the thankless chores. Her prospects are confined by the boring, dirty tasks that those with privilege don't choose to do.

She grows spiky as an echidna, Rosa sometimes bearing the brunt of her irritation, causing Tam such sorrow she must apologise to the girl, try to make it right, but then falters and is short with her again.

She is lost in thought one afternoon, sent to buy Brazilian tobacco for the master 'and be quick about it'. The shop is one of the first dedicated buildings slowly replacing the front rooms of cottages for dispensing goods.

The assistant lays the wrapped tobacco on the counter and drops the change into Tam's outstretched hand.

'Excuse me, sir. That's a shilling short.'

The man shuffles, draws himself up. 'You're wrong, miss. It's correct.'

A deep voice behind speaks. 'I beg to differ, sir. The lady is quite right; you owe her another shilling.'

Red-faced, the assistant hands over the coin.

Tam turns to see a fellow about the same height and age as her, clothes dusted with sawdust and wood shavings. He gestures for her to pass and follows her out of the shop.

'Nothing wrong with your arithmetic, miss,' he laughs. She should flourish her badge of marriage, let him know she's a Mrs, but smiles instead.

'Thank you, Mr … ?'

'Goddard, Robert Goddard. Newly-arrived shipwright.' He tips his hat.

Tam is aware eyes will be upon her, loitering at the shop door with a strange man, yet she badly wants to stay, find out more about this fellow.

'Much appreciated, Mr Goddard.' She scurries off.

In June 1816, Cuddy transfers ownership of Porteous Mount to Roger. At the end of winter he arrives with news of the deed, long overdue for the son who has been running the place for years.

His daughter is twelve, growing tall, not a beauty by any means but attractive in her way, black glossy hair tied up under a bonnet shielding bright, dark eyes. He watches her strolling ahead on their way to buy her new shoes, gait that's awkward, bumpy, not gliding as a young lady might. She has the look of Melva about her now she's filling out, the recognition setting off a band of pain between his temples.

'She'll need a position, soon.'

'Surely she's too young, Cuddy.' Tam's long let go of any need to act like his servant.

'Anyone tryin' to court her?'

'No, she's still a girl.' She doesn't tell him about the incident a while back, one she and Rosa have vowed to keep secret. How the tallow man had his greasy hands on her, pinning her against a wall and it was only that Mrs Dods heard her screaming that she was saved.

Regardless, Cuddy's already formed the view that the sooner she's married off the better. She needs a protector. As with so many other decisions, he says nothing of this to his wife.

Tam's world-weary at twenty years old, can read her husband's mind. She will take matters into her own hands, for a woman knows best what a girl might need. Rosa is clever, has schooling. She needs a position where she can flourish, maybe even make a good match. No reason for the girl to live like the worn-out handmaid that's her stepmother.

Mrs Curran may be in charge of the Chisholms' kitchen, but her real talent is staying on top of Sydney's web of gossip, waylaying other servants and every delivery boy knocking at the back door until they spill what they've heard or been told. Tam risks sounding her out about suitable men with a vacancy for a bookkeeper or housekeeper.

The woman is wary. 'Lookin' at finding new employ, improving your prospects, are ya?'

Tam hasn't confided her circumstances but no doubt the cook's already ferreted out the story, is hoping to have lighted on a new scandal.

'My stepdaughter needs employment. I want to set her up as best I can.'

The woman leaves off peeling potatoes and warms to the task of sharing from the store of scuttlebutt and titbits she's so diligently gathered. She runs through a few names, working through a list that only exists in her head., 'and then there's a young shipwright, Robert Goddard, not been here long, already doin' well for himself, so they say.'

With a start Tam remembers her encounter with him.

He rents a cottage his employer owns in Cumberland Street, near the docks, according to the cook, has no one to keep house or cook supper and is waiting for the next transport ship to bring more convict girls.

On her afternoon off after church, Tam goes to the dockyards in the hope that a man with ambition might be there. It's eerily quiet, not a hammer or saw to be heard, the men gone to their homes, the bottle or a card game. She inhales the crisp smell of shaved ironbark mixed with pine pitch, closes her eyes and breathes it in, a forest filling her lungs.

'Can I help you?'

She jerks back. 'Sorry, don't mean to be intrudin'.' The fellow she met months earlier has materialised before her. His clothes shout that he is a free man, no need for the convict's blue woollen jacket and white gurrah trousers.

He wears moleskin pants and a dark waistcoat, a red neckerchief tied to stop sweat running down his shirt.

'I remember you. Bit of trouble with the tobacco seller's assistant, as I recall.' He is smiling, leaning against the ribs of a whaleboat, while she stammers her way through an explanation about her purpose in being there.

'Your ward, you say.' He pauses, looks around him as though he's lost interest.

'And you? Already in a position, I expect?'

She is taken aback at the turn of the conversation. 'Yes sir, I am.'

'No need for the 'sir', miss. Let me think on it.'

'Not miss, I be married.'

His eyes widen then shift to a queer side-glance. 'Give me your address, I'll get word to you.'

Within the week a note is waiting with Mrs Dods. Rosa can start work the following Monday, with lodgings supplied. The girl is delighted she'll gain some independence, while Tam is already hoping the arrangement will be an advantage. Goddard has skills sorely needed in this colony, is a man going places, will be able to properly support Rosa if he takes a fancy to her.

So caught up is she in imagining Rosa's future that Tam has already forgotten the look in the fellow's eye when he addressed her.

She thought Cuddy would be best pleased, yet despite Rosa presenting it as her idea he's keen to let Tam know he's miffed, once they're out of his daughter's earshot.

'She's still my family. Least you coulda done was ask me.' There's no fire in it, an old bull obliged to paw at the ground, kick up a little dirt. Both he and Tam know it.

He cuts his visit short, saying he's paid for her lodgings for another six months but after that, with Rosa gone, the rent's up to her.

She watches him pull his hat low and ride off, head sagging on his shoulders so that the folds of his chin are tucked into his neck. She is twenty-one years old or thereabouts, saddled with a husband in name only, no less than the horse that carries him away.

CHAPTER NINETEEN

SYDNEY TOWN, 1820

TAM AND ROSA ARE FANCY free for a change, heading to Parramatta for Friday horse races. They've arranged a special day off as Rosa's keen to see her father after a long absence.

Cuddy's still suffering from the disgrace brought on by Luis the previous year, caught with two others stealing ten bushels of maize and sent to Newcastle to work in the coalmines' chain gang. The idea that his flesh and blood must endure the kind of deprivation he once did, shackled in ten pound irons, tied together with others like oxen, has been a trial and he has stayed close to Windsor.

The woman and girl take a passage boat upriver, the skipper sailing her until the wind dies and he must row. The boat has four oars in case a customer wants to lean on a pair to hasten the trip, and Rosa takes to the novelty of the task for half an hour or so, till breaking out in a sweat and sinking back on the seat, exhausted.

In the past four years she has grown into an exuberant sixteen year old, thoughtful at times, her dusky face breaking readily into a smile. Rosa has said little about the goings on between her and Robert Goddard, if there are any. Tam has tried several times to probe, but the girl steadfastly avoids giving anything away, other than the fact that he is kind and fair.

George visited a week earlier, returning from the Hunter River with coal and cedar before his schooner, *Elizabeth and Mary*, headed south to the sealing grounds. The nineteen year old gets regular work on merchant Robert Campbell's vessels, causing Tam to joke that he'll be a master of one of them soon enough.

The day is mild, autumn casting a sheltering dome of clear sky across a river that beckons them around every winding turn, past cove after curving cove. Tam stretches, her body relishing a sense of space, knotted muscles loosening, eyes softening to the view. She has forgotten how good it is when there's no jostling, no eyes watching your every move, no buildings cheek to jowl.

A flock of rosehillers burst from a stand of swamp oaks, the parakeets flashing crimson and gold as they dart over water, flashing into the darkness of eucalypt forest. The impression they leave is light, joyful, as if she held one of the birds in her hand and felt its fragile body tremble.

They are running with the tide and making good time. As they pass Homebush Bay Rosa whispers she is queasy, so when they land they don't loiter but head straight to the corner of Back and High Streets, ordering an ale at the Freemason's Arms. They wait there for Cuddy, as arranged.

Tam's hoping to meet the scandalous publican, former French forger James Larra, friend of her husband and Roger. Once a respectable stalwart of the district, his rapid fall from grace a few years earlier was played out in a gawking public court, where he was acquitted of causing his wife's death by improper marital relations.

She scans the room, a little guilty at her morbid curiosity, but Cuddy is the only man to approach. Her husband lopes in the door, rocking a little where one knee is giving him pain.

'Good to see you two.' He kisses Rosa on the cheek, makes no attempt to touch Tam.

They order roast turkey, a treat as the birds are new to the colony.

'Seen George lately?'

Tam fills him in on his son's whereabouts, unable to ignore the sadness that descends in a damp fog across his face. She figures he must be seventy-four now.

She doesn't bother mentioning she has taken up using her maiden name and is Tam Ranse no more. Wouldn't want people to confuse her with a woman of a similar name, the notorious Parramatta whore, Tamar Ranse. At least that's the reason she'd give Cuddy if he asked. Far more potent is that claiming her own name is a way of owning herself again, of holding onto one thing that's hers alone.

Cuddy gives Rosa the latest news on Roger and his family, still based at Windsor and doing well with their land and the Porteous Mount property, then falls silent, the mention of the farm stirring raw memories of a woman he loved, a partner in every sense. He pushes them away. They're a hole he falls into, the sides so steep he can't scramble out, worse than being deadened in the forgetting.

Rosa does her best to cheer her father while pushing food around her plate, few morsels forked into her mouth.

Tam watches the pair, their talk stilted, words sawing back and forth with no cutting through. It's as if they are strangers to each other.

Cuddy throws back the last of his ale. 'Let's go, or we'll miss the first race.'

A throng has gathered by the rough racetrack, convicts, settlers and families in their best dress, though separate from the gentry in a marquee near the finish line. The wealthiest, Wentworths, Macarthurs, Lawsons, a handful of others, own highly bred horses, sired by thoroughbred or Arab stallions. Tam's never seen such spirited creatures, muscled bodies up high on long legs, elegant necks, sides heaving in anticipation of the starter's gun. Scratch, Chance, Abdullah, Councillor, the names are far too pathetic for such marvellous beasts.

When the gun fires they spring forth as though they've sprouted wings. The thrill of it, their hooves vibrating the ground, is such a rush that Tam almost misses noticing Rosa leaning over to clutch the rail.

'What is it, my dear.' Tam's having to shout above the roar of the crowd, looking about for Cuddy but he's gone, no doubt to a drinking tent.

'A bit dizzy is all.'

Tam hooks her arm through the girl's elbow and guides her to a quiet spot off the nearby market square.

'Are you sickening, Rosa? Let's get you back to the inn.'

She shakes her head, tears welling up. 'I'm so sorry, Tam.'

'My dear, nothing to be sorry 'bout. You can't help it if you be unwell.'

Rosa begins to sob, spluttering before she can speak. 'I've not bled for three months.'

Before Tam can respond the girl grabs her arm. 'You mustn't tell Da.'

'Oh Rosa, he has to know. Your Da'll need to speak to Mr Goddard, see he does right by you.' She draws the girl into a hug, her head against Tam's chest.

The girl whispers. 'It ain't him.' She refuses to say who the father is.

Tam doesn't know what's worse, the anger that a day out's been ruined or the despair for Rosa, whose fate is now writ large.

An hour later they go in search of Cuddy, pretending they must get an early boat back to Sydney as Rosa's employer expects her to cook supper.

'Write soon, Rosa. They say I'll soon be moved here to this town's Government House. They be makin' me a porter at the gate.' He puffs up his chest a little. Something to make his daughter proud, not bad for an old fella.

Tam and her charge make their way to the wharf and wait in nearby shade till the next vessel is ready to depart. They say little on the boat, not wanting to speak in front of a third passenger travelling with them downriver.

As Tam walks Rosa back to Goddard's, she tries again.

'You must say something to your Da, Rosa. This ain't something you can do yerself. It needs to get sorted and be quick about it.'

The girl's shoulders sag. 'Maybe there's another way. I was thinkin' I'd get someone to fix it.'

'No.' Tam shouts so loudly a passerby pauses to ask Rosa if everything's alright. Once the woman has walked away, Tam is calmer.

'It's too dangerous. And don't you be tryin' to protect Mr Goddard, Rosa. He plants the seed he pays the price.'

The girl nods wearily, still looking a bit green. 'I need to go for a lie down, Tam. Thanks for seein' me home.'

On her next day off Tam goes to the shipyard on the western side of Sydney Cove, where four dry docks have been carved out of the sandstone shore. She scouts past the blacksmith's shop, storehouses and wharfinger's hut, betting on the fact that the watchman's off carousing.

Though it's the Sabbath, she is hoping Robert Goddard will be onsite, his propensity for spending most of his spare time there being something Rosa's commented on in the past. When she gets to the wide doorway of the workshop she's not disappointed.

'What can I do for you?'

He asked a straight question; she'll give him a straight answer. 'You can step up, Mr Goddard, is what you can do.'

He lays the plane at his feet, perplexed. 'What are you talking about?'

'Rosa, of course.'

Now he's more puzzled. 'She's not happy in her employ with me?'

Tam's getting riled. 'Not happy in the state you've left her.'

He matches her anger. 'Maybe if you stop speaking in riddles we can sort this out.'

'For God's sake, as if you don't know. She's with child.'

He blanches. 'I'd no idea. Do you know who the father is, if he'll care for her?'

For a second Tam wonders if it could be someone else, but now the demon's bristling and she can't stop. 'It's you, o' course. Who else could it be?'

He steps up quite close, his tone strident. 'I swear on a stack of bibles that I've never so much as touched her. If she's saying it's me then she's covering for somebody.'

He hasn't the look or the sound of a liar. She stands mute, a firecracker with the bang gone, fizzling out.

'I can see this is no easy thing. It's admirable you take responsibility for her, but the identity of the father lies elsewhere.'

Two weeks it takes to wear Rosa down. 'It's complicated, Tam. You wouldn't understand.'

She wants to shout it in the girl's face, just how much she does understand. Instead she plays her best card. 'I'll have to tell your Da if you don't fess up.'

The baby's father is a shoemaker, an older man with a woman and child. 'I love him, I want to be with him. Please, don't make trouble.'

Tam will confront him next day off, but before it comes round a messenger arrives at the Chisholms to fetch her, saying Rosa needs help.

At Goddard's cottage he is the one to answer the knock, showing her to the girl's room. A midwife is bundling up bloodied sheets and whispers to Tam. 'Act of nature, poor child.'

Rosa is sobbing into her hands. 'I saw it, Tam. A curled up grub of a thing.'

The midwife administers laudanum to settle Rosa and as the girl dozes off Tam promises to come back later to check on her. Goddard's putting on his waistcoat to return to work and shows her out.

'I must apologise, Mr Goddard. Rosa's now said who the father was. Please forgive me for thinkin' badly of you.'

His face creases in a smile. 'You aren't the first and you won't be the last. I'm just glad she's come to no harm.'

The experience fails to cool Rosa's attachment. Clancy Nation tells the girl early the following year that he's making a fresh start, going south to Port Dalrymple on the northern coast of Van Diemen's Land. It's a new settlement, plenty of work for a fellow with tools and a bit of nous. He wants her to go with him and she agrees.

Nation's woman and child will stay in Sydney and he will send money home to support them. Tam already feels sorry for the poor woman. Though Cuddy shouts and seethes, Rosa refuses to back down.

The farewell leaves Tam more heart-sore than she expects, Rosa teary, her mother's silver rose brooch pinned to her bodice. Cuddy turned up with the brooch days before the departure, bereft of words, the silver rose left to say how he felt.

Since Tam waved off the couple after Easter, the teeming streets of Sydney have become a lonely place. What does she have to show for her twenty-six years? The town crier passes by, bawling out the latest orders from the Guv so none may say they are ignorant of them, though she hears not a word of it. Melancholy seems to block her ears.

She can't shift the mood that descends, a bad case of the morbs, Nance would have said. On her days off she starts lying in bed for hours, staring in the gloom at fly spots on the ceiling.

The doldrums worsen when she gets a letter from Rosa. The pair have found their feet, Clancy's skills in high demand, while Rosa has a maid's position at a grand home on Launceston's outskirts. It's a town on the move, she reports, a wave of free settlers driving progress.

You been a Ma to me in all but name. I would be so very cheered if you were to join us, dear Tam. You would find many opportunities round here.

One Sunday stretches into the next, then another and another. Tam sprawls on the bed, lacking energy to read the book in her hand loaned by her mistress. *Persuasion*, penned by a woman, no less. She is berating herself for ignoring the novel when Mrs Dods knocks.

'A gentleman caller for you.'

Tam rises, combs her hair up and fastens it tightly, then goes out to the parlour expecting to see Cuddy.

Robert Goddard stands as she enters, hands holding the worn brim of his hat in front of his waist. 'I have a matter I'd like to discuss. Perhaps we could go for a stroll.'

Mrs Dods fusses with the curtains while listening to every word. The last thing Tam wants is to walk with this man, but it's far worse to tickle the eavesdropping ears of a snoop.

They head in the direction of the dockyards, Goddard's feet forever taking him that way.

'How is Rosa?' He asks despite knowing the answer. She has written to him too, thanking him for the small loan he advanced so Clancy could set up his workshop.

Tam recounts the letter she has received, painfully reciting every detail rather than let Goddard speak. Eventually she fades to a stop.

He decides against further small talk, not because of her discomfort but due to his own. He has a proposition and is not entirely sure about his motivation.

'The girl I've had since Rosa has proven to be rude and slovenly, so I've had no recourse but to see her on her way. It would be a great relief to me if you'd agree to take the position.'

They are facing the water and she is grateful he's not looking at the red flush staining her cheeks.

'Surely it would be folly on your part, after my behaviour.'

'Nothing wrong with a woman who stands her ground.' It should be a compliment, but she receives it as a criticism, perhaps a comment on her failings, uncouth woman that she is.

She continues to amble alongside him towards the wharf. Starting over in Van Diemen's Land, so far south it's the last place before the South Pole, holds no appeal. This change might be the tonic she needs, jolt her into brighter spirits. She quells any thought about the heat in her face that's spreading through her chest.

'What do you say?'

'I accept your offer, with thanks.' To salvage some self-regard she quickly adds: 'Of course I'm more experienced than Rosa, which is worth eight pounds a year, Mr Goddard.'

She doesn't see his grin as he accepts, a man well aware that with lodgings supplied he ought by rights pay her less, not more, than she currently gets. There are no secrets among domestics in this town.

They say goodbye, agreeing she will give two weeks' notice to the Chisholms and Mrs Dods. The minute he has gone she's at sixes and sevens, and when she reaches her lodgings is too unsettled to go in, veering away into the next street for a long walk to calm herself.

She will send a note to Cuddy, give him her new address. Someone will read it to him, if he even cares.

After a while her steps tap out a familiar rhythm, one-two, one-two, vibrating in her bones where the girl still lives, the one who walked away from the hospital believing she had a chance, that she might set her own course.

She carries the girl and all the other versions of herself that have come before. They spring up one by one with pleading eyes and outstretched hands, saying she owes them more than the beaten dog of a life she inhabits now.

Soon her chest heaves, billows out, a sail catching the wind, waiting for a hand to take the tiller. This might be the slim moment she gets before the weather turns nasty or worse, her days remain becalmed.

She will make it turn out right this time. She must, or all the wasted years will fill her lungs and she'll drown on dry land, gasping for air, defeated.

CHAPTER TWENTY

SYDNEY TOWN, 1821

TAM ARRIVES AT GODDARD'S COTTAGE, two conflicting forces competing for attention. The desire for a bigger life is raging within yet is dampened by the certain knowledge that she's still no more than a hapless servant.

The friction sets her teeth on edge in the following days. She catches herself grinding them and starts walking around with her tongue pushed against the roof of her mouth to stop it.

After cleaning for a busy household the bachelor's cottage is no challenge, except for clothes that need a hard, long scrubbing to remove tar stuck with oakum fibres. She hardly sees the fellow, who works from dawn to dusk repairing damage from rough seas, fire or accident on growing numbers of ships with strange flags, and sealing and whaling vessels.

After his supper, often eaten late on his own due to meetings or drinking at the inn, he attends to paperwork. She mostly retires to her room before he gets in.

The man's desk has a drawer with a lock but layers of drawings and papers spill haphazardly across the top. She tells herself she's dusting as she studies the lines of ink and text and the letters with customers' specifications.

At the bottom of a tray, buried by documents, is his green bound ledger. She lifts it in one hand. She could open it, run an eye down the columns of figures, see for herself the state of his financial affairs. The book balances easily, though is heavy after a time. She brushes her fingers down the cover and when its coolness has a tone of chiding, puts it back as she found it.

Late in the second week, Goddard announces he'll be going to Richmond on the Hawkesbury River for the next month, working on the finishing and fit out of a new vessel under construction for Robert Campbell.

'There'll be little need here for cleaning and cooking, with me gone.'

She'll be without work, she knows it, after throwing in a steady job at the Chisholms.

'What I'd like, if you're agreeable, is for you to take care of my papers.'

In her mind she's already packing her bag, storming out, and good riddance to him, playing her like a fiddle to get his own back.

'Tam, are you alright?'

She realises she's only half-heard him.

'Yes, I'm fine thank you. What do you mean?'

He explains a bit more, how he needs some organisation, a proper system so he can find things, and if she might familiarise herself with his ledger she could take over keeping his financial records.

'So are you up for it? I realise it's different to domestic duties, but I know you've learned to write well and do figures.' He omits the bit about Rosa filling him in.

He has caught her by surprise, leaving her floundering in equal parts pleasure and ill-ease.

Over supper that night, out of the blue, he asks her the strangest question. 'Where do you see your life going, Tam?'

She doesn't remember giving him permission to use her first name, though more importantly his question assumes an awful lot, gets her back up yet again.

'Do you think, Mr Goddard, that a woman of my standin' dare have such things as expectations, let alone in this place? You, on the other hand, are a fellow with a respected trade, can claim the right to a future as easy as takin' in the air you breathe.'

She exhales hard, almost blowing out the lamp nearby.

'You make a good point ... and call me Robert, please, I keep thinking you mean to speak to my father. I merely inquire about what you might draw you, hold your interest if you had the chance.'

It's a trick question, surely. He is up to something and she doesn't like the feeling that he toys with her.

'Perhaps, Robert, you would care to be more direct about why you ask such a question.' So formal, the effort of shaping each word tires her tongue.

He bursts into raucous laughter, reaches for his glass of ale. 'Well that's surely put me in my place. Truth is, I was only wanting to know if you have any leanings, so to speak.'

For his part, he explains, he intends to buy property, follow in the footsteps of the man who's employed him, William Foster, and make a success of himself.

'Generations of my family have lived at Dover, worked in shipyards. Forty acres of English oak woodland to a ship, you know.' His hand passes over the tabletop in front of him, as though he's running it along steam-bent timber.

'Where we lived we saw the havoc of privateering and smuggling, the violence, and for so many, the poverty that is the bastard son of greed. In time I hope to help those less fortunate.'

Tam has never heard anything like this loftiness, someone ordinary having such thoughts, that they might give aid to the poor or needy. This man doesn't come from the dog-eat-dog places she's been, might as well have come from the stars. Unless he's a pretender, working on her in some kind of a ruse.

'Had you the chance, Tam, what would you choose?'

She's tired of this game, blurts out what comes from deep in her belly. 'I'd choose to matter, to have a life that means more than being a slave.'

The smile fades from his face and she is shocked at her brazenness, then immediately fearful. When he hoists his heavy glass she knows he'll throw it at her and gets ready to duck.

'A toast.'

She lifts her glass, trembling. She has known the class of men capable of sudden cruelty or false charm leading to harm, but this fellow's a breed of his own.

'Here's to choosing the life that we want.'

She thinks it over in the days he is gone, as she reads his papers and starts to understand the breadth of his work and its value, sorting letters in order of dates, buying folders and carefully naming them for the contents. Finally, she picks up the green ledger.

Within minutes she gauges that a shipwright has it all over a farmer, steady work and no worrying about the vagaries of weather. No fretting about the size of the harvest and the purse it may or may not bring, for money flows as a fountain each time Robert Goddard makes effort.

He has been here but a year, yet she sees the sums that he's banked, regular figures for the income columns and fewer on the expenditure side. Here and there she notes an amount with a mark, a small red dot. She scans the name beside each, unsure what it means.

Turning the page she scans further columns. There's a red dot again. This time, though, she recognises the name beside it: Rosa's fellow, the expenditure dated the day before they sailed. So he has given or loaned them money to get set up.

She sits back in the chair, the ledger still open before her. This man is confounding, unlike any she's known. It scares her that she can't read him, how she keeps trying to shape the clay of his character with the only tool she has, a lifetime's learning gathered about men, what they want, how they inflict hurt.

It keeps her off balance when he is home, wary because she doesn't know what to make of him, while he remains steady in his interaction, and her attempts to paint the canvas of his personality with dark colours have come to nothing.

Perhaps, it occurs to her, he is not the one who is unpredictable. It's like he holds up a mirror, showing her that any fickleness might be lodged in her own behaviour.

The thought lands in her as squarely as any truth. She must chip away at the hard shell she's built, find a way to look for the good, even though the idea of opening out seems to hurt more than the pain that's caused her to close.

She must not keep living from her past or it will devour any hope of a future.

She closes the ledger and puts it away, her body heavy as she stands. How to start, what path to take? It all seems too hard. She gathers bucket and brush, rolls up her sleeves, and goes to mindlessly scrub the front step.

He returns tired but jubilant, the Hawkesbury job finished and Campbell quite satisfied with the quality of the work, to announce he's invited his friend, William Foster, to supper the next night.

'If you could make a special effort, it would be appreciated.'

He is delighted with the way she's tidied and ordered his desk, suggesting that she take over the paperwork and accounts from now on.

'Used to go through the accounts every Friday with my husband on the farm, maybe we can do the same.'

The mention of her husband jars Robert, though he hides it with his thanks.

Tam has managed to buy curry powder to make a lamb dish, fashionable as a first course, the Chisholms' cook says. For the main dish she makes a beef pie, grinding the meat and chopping in onions and potatoes. Strawberries arrived that day from Parramatta and she was at the market early enough to get some. She sprinkles them with a little sugar and places a jug of thick cream on the side.

William Foster arrives wearing knee-length breeches with stockings, hessian boots and a waistcoat topped with a silver cravat. Boyishly good-looking and about ten years older than Robert, he catches Tam staring and winks. 'Usually in my old work clothes. Thought a change would do me good.'

Robert greets him warmly and the pair settle into a glass of rum while Tam finishes the cooking.

The Chisholm's cook filled her in on their visitor after dispensing advice on curry. Tam sneaks the odd look at the guest as she works, wondering what it took for his wife to pack up their son a few years earlier and go back to family in Van Diemen's Land, never to return.

She stops herself. Now she's doing it with Foster, looking for what's wrong, what may be bad, instead of simply listening, seeing for herself what's revealed.

Despite herself she's drawn to the fellow, not by attraction, which can only be a nuisance or lead to disaster, but because he too has a living ghost for a spouse. When she serves the meal and Robert insists she eat with them, she fancies their guest will be one for the whores at the inns or cottages around The Rocks or maybe has a woman he keeps in his bed and no harm to his reputation as a married man, while the woman must hang her head in shame.

The ease between the friends puts her in mind of Nance, forgotten for so long. Ten years ago now, the girl was never one to grow old and fade away. Gone to worms or water, more like, dumped in the Thames when her keeper had enough of her.

She swallows the last of her ale, declines the offer of rum, fearing it might bring forth the spectre of Nance in her mind. The food is comforting in her belly, the fire at her back burning bright in the grate, throwing yellow light on the lively faces of the men, while she is in shadow.

'Mighty fine fare, miss. So good I ate too much.' Foster pushes his chair back a little, undoes a couple of buttons on his waistcoat.

Tam's eyes flick to Robert to see if he'll set his friend straight but he is looking at her, echoing the compliment.

'A missus actually, Mr Foster.' Why must she insist on making it clear?

'William, dear girl. You must call me William. My friend has clearly found a treasure.' He chortles, slapping Robert on the arm. 'Make sure nobody lures her away.'

Tam's cheeks burn at the hidden suggestion.

'A good cook and reliable, indeed a treasure in these parts.' Robert says it firmly.

Foster sensibly grasps that his friend has laid out a public boundary for what goes on between the young woman and her employer, and rightly so. He accepts the rebuff in good part and the conversation turns to business. Half an hour later the two men gather their jackets and leave for the inn, while Tam sets to work on the dishes.

Next morning Robert sleeps a little later, is slower getting ready for work, the effect of his night out showing in dark circles under his eyes.

'I hope William didn't offend you, Tam. He is a good soul and the best of friends.'

She sets porridge in front of him. 'I could see he were just bein' friendly.' *And hinting at things he knew nothing about.*

'He misses Maria and especially his son. Took it out of him letting her move south, back to her folks.'

Tam's mouth flies open. She swiftly shuts it, doubly astonished, that Foster cares so deeply he was willing to let his wife and child go, and that Robert would share such a thing when he hardly knows her.

On his side of the table Robert reins in his tongue, awareness knocking his headache up a notch that the woman opposite is also wed and may well have feelings about that fact.

They go on day after day in a kind of dance, neither sure of the steps, Tam unable to question the awkwardness that exists from her side. He moves forward and she retreats. She holds her ground and he circles. He is unfailingly kind, even when short-tempered about problems with a big job at the dockyard, at pains not to take it out on her.

One Sunday morning she dresses for church, looking forward to having the rest of the day away from the cottage.

As she leaves the front door he appears from the path. 'I'm going to St Philip's, might walk with you.'

It's the first time she's known him to go to her church. He usually worships elsewhere.

The carmine red dress bought with her last wages is in the newer style, the waist dropped lower than under the bust, sleeves a little fuller, the skirt flared, a row of appliqué around the hem. Altogether showier than the old Sunday best, it hugs her curves in what now feels like all the wrong places.

'Such a beautiful day for early spring. Thought I might take my gig out on the water after the service. Be delighted if you'd join me.'

He is matching his pace to hers, walking a couple of handspans from her shoulder as they hurry up Church Hill at the sound of the bells starting to peal.

'I might just do that, Robert, as long as I don't have to row.' The cheek of it, so bold she hardly knows herself, flashing like a firefly at dusk.

Rev William Cowper isn't known for energetic sermons, and even Robert Campbell once remarked that the cleric was so dependable with the gospel that he could safely doze off in the pew during the service. Tam dearly wishes she could do just that today.

Sitting down the back with the other maidservants, she watches the back of Robert Goddard's head alongside Foster's and regrets accepting his invitation. The excitement has turned to irritation, prickling her skin, chafing in her chest. She wants it gone.

She waits outside at a distance as the church empties out, her employer one of the last to leave, perhaps by design, for heads will turn at the sight of them together. Foster spots her first and makes a beeline in her direction.

'Good to see you, my dear.' He tips his hat.

She watches him keenly to see if he is mocking, though there is no sign of it.

'I hear you're going out on the harbour. I must say, you're in safe hands for such an outing. Now I must be on my way. Good day to you.'

When Robert arrives at her side they follow the street around the harbour to a shed on the edge of Campbell's dockyard, between The Rocks and Dawes Point. Inside is a lightweight rowing boat on a trolley. The gig's honey-coloured timber, curving gently, is so inviting Tam reaches out to stroke it.

'Beautiful, isn't she? A labour of love.'

Within minutes they're on the shingly beach and the boat is off the trolley, its bow in the water. He rolls up his trousers, hands her his boots and socks and gestures for her to step into the boat from the gritty sand. He pushes off, leaping in to land so lightly in the stern that the boat barely rocks.

The harbour, glassy earlier in the morning, is a pattern of whirls and ripples where a gentle breeze has picked up. Robert rows to a silent beat, muscles working the oars smoothly, deftly, saying little.

Up the harbour he follows the coast around to the long finger of Cockle Bay, its swampy shore and shallow waters opening up where New Market Wharf has been built for unloading Hawkesbury produce. The steam-powered flour mill sits in Sabbath quiet, the slaughterhouse too.

Robert rows the gig onto a small reach of harbour sand near the head of the bay and helps her out, dragging the boat to shore. From under the seat of the rowboat he retrieves a pannikin. 'This way. I'll get us a drink.'

Freshwater creeks run into the bay and he dips the tin mug into the closest one, handing it to her. As she gulps it down he wipes sweat from his brow. After his turn they sit on the sand, watching a pair of white ibis digging nearby in the silt.

'I don't know much about you, Tam, except that you're devoted to Rosa.'

Devoted. She rolls the word around on her tongue. It makes a strange shape; she can find no place to put it.

'You know the girl, Robert. It's easy to have care for her good heart.'

She is thinking that if she wants she can leave the bay now and walk back into town. Market Street runs off the new wharf and only a mile along it, maybe two, she'll be back at the house.

'What about you, Tam? When did you arrive?'

'Eleven years soon. Sometimes feels like yesterday.'

The two ibis strut several feet down the shoreline then spread white wings wide and take to the sky. She watches them glide, all thought of walking away gone. She is wistful, relaxing in the sun of this man's attention.

Soon they are chatting, sharing stories, though she is careful to choose only the bare bones of hers.

'Your life and mine, they've been so opposite. I can hardly imagine how hard it's been to survive.'

No, no, no. She will not let herself cry. Too late, the tears are flowing. 'Sorry, not used to blubbering like this.'

He searches the inside pocket of his jacket and pulls out a kerchief. As he passes it to her his face, full of gentleness and concern, is close. He has ocean blue eyes drawing her in. She wants to reach up and stroke his cheek, the urge causing alarm, the two combining to make her freeze so that his hand with the scrap of cloth is suspended between them.

'Here, please take it.'

She dabs at herself with the kerchief, breaking the spell, handing it back quickly because it smells of his sweat and she wants to bury her face in it. Whatever has come over her? Maybe this is what others call joy, though she can already feel the sorrow it drags behind it, and she fears the loss when the happiness is gone will leave her sorrier than if she had never known it in the first place.

They haven't brought any food, and eventually hunger signals it's time to leave. He takes her hand to help her up, brushes sand off the hem of her dress, so natural with it, while she stands ramrod straight, wishing, oh wishing, to be a sapling, able to bend and sway, meet the gentle gusts of his regard.

They return down the harbour to the dockyard, where she helps him drag the boat into the shed, not minding that her shoes are full of sand. She takes the bent arm he offers as they walk off, leaning together and laughing as they near his cottage mid-afternoon. She doesn't see the bent figure till she's almost upon him.

Cuddy, eyes narrowed, has watched them all the way up the street.

Tam introduces the two men, Robert excusing himself to go back to the dockyards the minute he's shaken Cuddy's hand.

In the kitchen, Tam, needing the habit to calm herself, stokes the fire and gets the kettle boiling. Her husband looks wretched. She hasn't seen him for months and has forgotten how old he's become.

'You're goin' well then, I see.' It's snide. He pulls himself up, no need to go punishing the girl, though it stings to see her happy with that fellow.

'What is it, Cuddy?'

'It's George.' His head falls into his hands and he rubs his eyes vigorously.

'Left a while back on the sealer *Success*. Got word they bin forty days or more and haven't made it to Hobart. Him and eight others on board, all missing like.'

CHAPTER TWENTY-ONE

SYDNEY TOWN, 1821-1825

A SLEDGEHAMMER OF GRIEF STRIKES TAM, worse than she's known. If ever she had doubts about loving George they are swept away in the torrent of sorrow for the boy she first met, now the man who lies drowned at twenty years old.

Cuddy leaves the Goddard cottage a shrunken man to return to Parramatta, unable to do anything but wait in the hope that, unlike other sons, he will have a body that can be laid to rest.

When Robert appears at supper time he is careful not to pry, taking his time removing his jacket and hanging it on the hook behind the door. Tam pulls herself together and tells him the news.

He goes immediately to her at the fireplace, where she's attempting to fry pork in a pan, and for a moment she thinks he will wrap his arms around her. He stops short, instead reaching out to lay a hand on her upper arm.

'I am so very sorry, Tam. I can see you loved him as your own. What can I do?'

As your own. Whatever does he mean? The boy was never a child of her scarred womb. She shakes her head at the inference, a gesture he interprets as indicating there's no action to be taken.

If this is what it means to love, she's not sure she can ever let it get its claws into her again. The knowledge that George is gone is fit to burst her chest, disturbs her mind with images of a round face and puppy eyes, fingers curling in hers, of a boy leaning in close to his sister, singing as they played pat-a-cake.

Reluctantly, Tam writes to Rosa, now bearing another child of Clancy's, a terrible time to be causing upset. The ink spills as she writes the word 'drowned'. She screws up the sheet of paper, throws it in the fire and starts again, referring to him only as missing.

The weeks pass with no sign of the vessel or crew, not the first time Bass Strait has swallowed a ship whole, yet the world insists that life must go on. In Hobart, a court declares the ship's master, John Mace, dead, and a proctor begins the process of advertising for debtors so the estate can be settled. Rev Cowper has heard the news and in his next sermon asks the congregation to join him in prayers for the safe return of George and fellow crewmen.

A fortnight passes and Tam is wrestling sheets onto the clothesline late morning when Robert comes running up the hill, panting.

'The docks are buzzing with the news. George is alive. All the men bar an Otaheitian, poor sod, made it to shore. Been stranded since.'

The news has come on a brig berthed an hour ago, how a sealing ship found the men, thin as rake handles, on a tiny island in the Kent group, their schooner wrecked on rocks nearby. 'He's well, they say Tam, resting up in Hobart Town.'

She can hardly believe it.

'It's true, come with me and they'll tell you to your face.' Overcome with excitement, it's an effort not to scoop her up, embrace her tightly.

'No, no. I believe you. I must stay here and write to Cuddy, send it with the next messenger boat upriver.' It's a miracle, the first she can ever recall, melting away the weight she's been carrying at the lad's loss.

It puzzles her then, as she settles in front of the inkwell, that it's not George rising up in her memory but the sensation of walking up from the dockyard weeks ago, laughing, feeling light and free in the company of a man, then dashed back to earth at the sight of Cuddy.

At the Kissing Point farm the spectre of Melva seemed always in the way, clouding how Cuddy and the children saw her, how they summed up her worth. Now it's her husband who blocks any chance of sun.

She pushes the thoughts aside, dips the quill and begins scratching it across the paper. This is not about her, it's George's moment to stand in the centre. The young seaman had a nautical star tattooed on his forearm last year and clearly it's guided him home.

Three weeks later, her stepson appears at the door, face cracked and peeling, clothes hanging off his frame.

'Any chance of a cuppa?'

Tam's never done it before but it's involuntary, her body moving instinctively as she throws her arms around him, holds him tight until he struggles free, laughing.

'Geez, survived a shipwreck only to be done in by you squeezin' me to death.'

They talk until the second pot of tea is empty, the leaves gone cold in the bottom, as George tells what happened, how he thought he would die. Not one of them could swim, like most sailors, and the rocks cut them up bad as they struggled to the shore. He takes off his rawhide boots and socks, shows Tam his bandaged feet where, in the panic and flailing to get to land he got tangled in ribbon weed, had to kick off his boots as a vicious swell gripped him again and again, bashing him against the rugged coast.

'The Captain thought we was safe in Murray Passage, mostly sheltered in there. We were tryin' to beat out of East Cove on Deal Island when a fierce wind came from nowhere, whipping up waves like a sea serpent gone mad. We had no hope.'

The survivors lived on some wheat washed ashore, the occasional fish they could catch from the sand patch where they sheltered, and what they could forage. A gang of sea rats found them the second week but refused help.

'We had nothin' fit for 'em to steal and nothin' to pay for food so they took off in their boat to their camp, the buggers. Worse than animals, them kind of sealers, had a couple of native girls with 'em, no doubt kidnapped.'

When his tale comes to an end the pair sit in companionable quiet, undisturbed by a bullocky out in the street, hollering at his team hauling a dray. The telling of his ordeal has exhausted George, and he takes his hat from the table, makes his farewell.

'I'll go upriver tomorrow, catch up with Da. He's bin worried, I reckon.'

Tam holds the door open for him, her throat swelling with the need to say something, an urge so great it aches as it catches in her throat. Her stepson is disappearing, almost out of sight at the end of the street by the time she can open her mouth and whisper it.

'I love you, young George.'

Robert comes home early for a change, insisting a celebration is called for. 'Get your good dress on, we're going out. William's invited us to an early supper. He's having a few people over at his new house, specially requested you come.'

Foster's a jovial chap. She knows she'll have a good time, though it will set tongues wagging if she shows up with Robert.

'Is it wise for me to go?'

'Whyever not, Tam? Any friend of mine is a friend of yours.'

The familiarity in what he says sets off a thrill, followed immediately by nervousness. She is steering into new waters and like George, could easily be dashed on the rocks. She goes to change, regardless.

They are heading into Pitt Street, with its rows of small shops, when Robert shares a little of his friend's background. 'Doing well, he is, Tam. Do you know he was sent out as a boy, barely eleven? Caught housebreaking, trying to help his family. The Guv took pity on him and put him in an apprenticeship at the docks.'

Robert is busily extolling his friend's diligence and ambition when a familiar voice interrupts.

'Fancy seein' you here.' Ellen has her back to the milliner's shop where she has been browsing in the window. She looks at Robert, runs her eyes over Tam's smart dress.

'You're lookin' well.'

'How are you Ellen, how's the family?' Tam wants an earthquake to crack the ground right now so she can fall into the fissure.

'All well, yes. Except my old aunt, on her last legs. Came yesterday to pay my respects. Heading back to the Hawkesbury first thing tomorrow.'

Ellen's in no hurry to move off, she's enjoying herself too much. Oh the gossip she'll have for Roger, not that his stepmother's any threat now he has Porteous Mount.

'And you'd be?' She stares at Robert.

'Sorry, Ellen. This is my employer, Mister Robert Goddard.'

Ellen's eyebrows shoot up, a look of amusement rearranging her features. 'Oh, the employer, I see.' So cool and pointed.

'Mr Goddard, this is my … my stepson's wife, Ellen Ranse.' Robert dips his hat, has already summed up the situation.

'Pleased to meet you, Mrs Ranse. Now if you'll forgive us, we mustn't delay. My friend is waiting.'

Undeterred, Ellen smiles at Tam, all teeth. 'Sorry to have neglected you. As we're family, we must make more of an effort to stay in touch.'

Robert sweeps Tam up the street.

Clever Ellen, no need to say it straight, that Tam needn't think of remarrying. Plenty take the chance of finding a parson who doesn't know them, telling him they're single so they can wed, but they only get away with it if no one turns up to say otherwise. Roger's wife has made it plain that there's those who will.

A man can leave a woman, maybe a family, shave off his beard or grow one for disguise, move away, marry again; can get a divorce if his wife's caught in a single act of adultery. Yet the woman must prove more than adultery, that there's aggravating circumstances, cruelty, desertion, bestiality. Cuddy would have to beat her to within a dying breath, or someone see him having relations with his horse for the marriage to be annulled.

Oh yes, the law sets limits, might say a man can thrash a woman with a cudgel but can't knock her down with an iron bar. Yet the extent of a beating isn't what counts but the fact that marriage gives a husband every right to control his wife.

She is tied to Cuddy, has no hope of getting free.

The realisation has been slow to arrive. In Sydney up till now it hasn't been a bother that she's wed, can't choose a union with another, but the warmth growing between her and Robert has changed that. Now the fear, lurking within happiness at being around him, is pressing against her ribs, and dear God it will crush her, she knows it will. Ellen has played her cards well.

It continues to distract her as they reach the house, where William pours them a drink and introduces his friends, a delightful couple in their late thirties. Tam's still thinking about her circumstances over supper and on the quiet walk home, Robert insisting she take his arm so she doesn't stumble in the dark.

She is trapped in a marriage that offers no comfort, not a jot of support. It's not that she hates Cuddy. Knowing him, she expects he hadn't thought it through, had been caught up in needing a companion, a mother for the little ones, saw her as the easy way out. She'd done the same, convincing herself she had a good plan, not grasping that it might lead her to sacrifice her chance at happiness. *Stupid, stupid Tam. Should have seen it coming. Will she ever bloody learn?*

At home, when she says goodnight, Robert tries to kiss her on the cheek. She brushes him off and goes to her room, shutting the door tightly and wedging a chair under the doorknob. Impossible to trust another when you can't even trust yourself.

Robert, flushed though he is with his friend's best wine, hears the chair drag and knows what it means. He is hurt she's misunderstood, though who can blame her. He resolves to find out more about her past.

Sober again at breakfast, he watches how she moves, graceful as a foal at times but mostly awkward as though she hasn't yet properly found her legs.

'Your name, it's unusual. Were you called that when you were born?'

She squints as she puts a plate of toast on the table, as though a small thorn has stuck in her hand. 'I were told the proper name is Tamsin, but me Ma only ever called me Tam.'

He butters toast and dollops on marmalade. 'Tamsin, such a pretty name. It suits you.' Her face is impassive. *Steady on, Robert.*

She pours the tea and he waits till she has the cup balanced in both hands, taking small sips of the steaming liquid.

'You know what, I think I might call you Tamsin from now on.'

She makes no attempt to deter him.

'Yes, that's what I'll do. It's too beautiful a name to go to waste.'

Tam's nerves are shot, never mind the business about her name. Half an hour later he's off to work and she is glad to see the back of him.

She can't shake it, the awful feeling in the pit of her stomach. Like Dickson's steam-driven flour mill over at Cockle Bay, a fire's been lit and a wheel's begun grinding away. Robert keeps piling on coal, and she is terrified she'll burst under the strain.

He makes it his mission to ferret out more about her. In the following weeks he goes slowly, sneaking in a question here and there when they eat together or cross paths, gradually understanding that she grew up in a loveless way, so different to him, arriving in this harbour young and beggared. Probably fortunate, as it happened, that old Cuddy Ranse married her, saved her from marauding men.

She has a force about her, is made for more, he's sure of it. He doesn't know the harms that befell her in prison or the crime that brought her to Sydney, she won't say and that's her right. There's a spirit about her, worth any wait, and he will do all he can to see it thrive.

It has been there from the first time he clapped eyes on her, the recognition of a flame that burns in her the way his own aspirations light up his days, yet hers flickers often, must not be let die down, go out. He's not stupid, knows every person is their own flame-keeper. Yet he had a father who was the chimney that shielded his lamp till he could keep it alight for himself. This woman had no one.

In the meantime, he must resist the urge to hold her, caress her hands, her face. She has the wildness of an alley cat under the surface, and if he makes a wrong move she's likely to bite and scratch.

She is not the first attraction he's known. There was a woman in Kent his parents dearly wanted him to wed, an engagement for six months until he came to understand the bond lacked the strength to see him through the slings and arrows of a lifetime. The light in Tamsin, though, draws him as a moth to a candle, its brightness breaking through shadows and no way to know if it may turn him to ash till too late. If that be the case, he will take the risk.

He is also, in his own way, a pious man, believing that God has a plan for him, and in the ink flowing from a divine hand is the name Tamsin. He is grateful he works hard and falls exhausted into bed each night, dozing off immediately. At the shipyard he relies on drawings every day, skilfully bringing them to life in the ribs of a vessel, the curve of a keel. This plan, on the other hand, has no path for execution and worrying about it, trying as a mere man to fathom it out, will be no help.

For her part, Tam, despite herself, begins eagerly awaiting his arrival home at the end of the day, noticing it is earlier than before. Robert has far more questions than Cuddy ever did and she should resent them, push back at such trespass, cool his interest, but the way he holds her with his eyes as he listens is addictive as laudanum, soothing every limb as they sit at the table.

The muster for the census of 1825 rolls around, Robert Goddard, shipwright, still renting in Cumberland Street near The Rocks, a few doors from his friend William Foster's fine home.

Tam Pummell is listed in the servant column as his housekeeper.

In the front room of the sandstone Goddard house, its verandah overlooking the harbour, Tam has finished cleaning the grate in the parlour. She shakes out the newspaper Robert discarded that morning on his armchair. Leaping from the Government Notice on the front page is Cuddy's name. He never got the land promised at Windsor, instead new Governor Thomas Brisbane has announced he'll get a hundred acres at South Colah, up towards the Hawkesbury.

She snorts, tosses the paper away. A hundred bloody acres and the only ones to live there will be koalas, plentiful around there.

The injustice of it rankles. He's been given regular work despite heading towards eighty, principal messenger to the Guv at Parramatta, and now he's done it again, begging for more land and getting it despite his past. Not for farming, of course. There won't be an ounce of sweat from his brow to mark the place.

No coincidence that the Guv's brought in new regulations requiring purchasers to pay five to seven shillings an acre when land is sold. He'll be getting forty-five pounds or so when the time comes. Enough to buy a shop, get yourself a future, though not a penny of it will come her way.

No such chance. It stinks.

She throws her apron on the table, needs to get out for a walk. She'll go down for a visit at William's place, where his new partner has moved in, a lovely girl, only fifteen years, quite a to-do on the part of her parents up Middle Harbour way before they gave consent. Be good to check on her, given she's already in the family way.

Anastasia answers the door, skirt already stretched tight across her belly when it's only June and she's not due to birth William's babe till December. Plenty have tut-

tutted at a man of thirty-six taking a girl for his mistress, though thankfully it seems a love match.

Tam likes the girl, a gentle, cheerful soul who's had the good sense to go with a man who will stand by her, no matter what. She has come to know William in recent years, considers him a friend in her own right and is fond of him, despite the fact that he can't understand why she and Robert haven't partnered. She's not even sure she understands herself.

Perhaps William is the reason Robert arrives home so nervous that evening. Their meal eaten, he lays down his knife and fork. 'We need to talk, Tamsin. I can't go on like this.'

He reaches over, lays his fingertips lightly on hers. She wants him to take her whole hand, pull her onto his lap, kiss her neck, hold her close. She aches for it, but it must not happen. She gently pulls back her hand.

She must leave, seek a different maid or housekeeper position. There is no other way.

'I bin thinkin' the same, Robert. It's a trial being in the same house with you, given the way we are growing close.'

He lets out a sigh. 'I'm so glad you feel the same. I want to show you how much I care, want you to share my bed.'

She shakes her head. 'That's not what I meant. I think it best for both of us if I seek employment elsewhere.'

He is thunderstruck. 'But why? Have I made you unhappy?'

The flirting, the touch that's supposedly accidental, downing ale and sharing stories at the table late into the night. She has been drunk on the thrill of it, on his appealing character, the way he looks at her like nothing else in the world exists.

And now it will end.

'You're a young man, enterprising. You'll go on to do big things. You need a proper wife who'll give you sons, an heir, maybe daughters to look after you in old age.'

'What I want is you, can't you see, even though you're already married. I don't expect your situation to change. I want to be with you, just the way things stand.'

Her shoulders start to shake and she presses her knuckles against her mouth to hold back a raw sound that seems to spring from the corner of the room yet is escaping from her lips.

'It can't come to pass. Please, you don't understand.'

'You're right. I don't.'

Sorrow plucks at her, sticky and heavy. It was always going to come to this. She begins to cry. 'I'm damaged, Robert, did it to myself. I can't give you children.'

He rubs his forehead, suddenly weary.

'What do you mean, did it to yourself?'

CHAPTER TWENTY-TWO

SYDNEY TOWN, 1825-1828

S HE CLAMMED UP, REFUSED TO answer any more questions the awful night of honesty. Since then they've tap-danced around each other, Robert unable to reconcile the woman he's come to know with one who could cause herself serious harm, Tam quarrelling with herself about leaving for another employer or staying.

She is the one to break first, cracking in the tension. She must go, it's the only way she'll find peace. The Chisholms' cook has retired. Tam searches her out in the quest to find new employment.

'Ah, had a fall from grace have we?' Mrs Curran is sunning herself on a bench out the front of her small cottage, enjoying her own humour.

Tam ignores the jibe. 'Better suited to a family, I think. Know of one in need o' help?'

She endures a good twenty minutes of idle gossip, collects a few names and departs.

That night Robert is quieter than usual. She would have preferred to leave in the morning after he'd gone to work, her letter propped against the salt pot on the table, but she's grown up now and that would be the coward's way.

'I've made up my mind.' She clears her throat. 'I am giving notice.'

He keeps chewing on the chicken leg he has in his hand, unable to hide the flush of anger that crosses his face. When the bone is clean of meat he lays it down.

'This is madness, Tamsin.'

He says her full name in such a way that her stomach does a small somersault and seems to land much lower down, causing heat. It's distracting, though she presses on.

'There's no future for us, Robert. Best we part ways now.'

'Us? You're acting like you're the only one here who matters.' He's suddenly shouting, gripping the table with one hand, leaving a greasy smear of chicken fat. She stares at it, thinks she'll have to wipe that off later, use the polishing cloth to buff the surface.

'I can't know what's best for you, but I surely know what's best for me. Why are you so intent on destroying what we share. Is it me you're trying to harm or is this another way for you to cause damage to yourself.'

He's gone too far, knows it immediately in the frozen face on the woman opposite.

Tam pushes her chair back so hard it teeters, rocks a couple of times, legs banging on the floor, but doesn't fall. Her body has disappeared in the spin of light-headedness; she can't tell where it is and throws out a hand to find a surface she can grab. The hand meets Robert's.

'Steady now, steady. Sit, please Tamsin. I'm really sorry.'

He fetches water and she gulps a few mouthfuls down, still floating a little above where she sits. He is right, and she hates that he can see what she's denied to herself. The demon has not been subdued, has not gone. She feared for years it would hurt others, instead it has become sly, turning on her, not striking or cutting to make blood flow, but blighting hope, crippling her character, causing hurt without landing a blow.

She gulps more water, its cool flow passing down her gullet, drawing her back to the pressure of her thighs on the chair.

'Are you alright?' Robert still holds her hand. She nods, unable to speak. She has pictured herself in a particular way and now the paint on the canvas is cracking, peeling, old brushstrokes lifting away, revealing who she is, and she doesn't at first recognise what's there.

It's the same as light reflecting off an image and hitting the eyeball, causing a person to see what's in front of them, and in the same way it can never be unseen. She grasps, in all its enormity, how she has undermined herself most of her life, been her own scourge.

The Matron, the times she was beaten with a stick, the Magistrate, hardened women in the gaol, the officer on the ship, all intent on causing her harm, searing her heart with a portrait of what she deserves. She has taken it into herself, grafted it on like a spare limb, believing it to be the essence of who she is, then used it against herself because the hurt, the pain is all she is worth.

Tam lands back in her body, heavy as a rock. She leans over the table, head in her hands, and sobs, no longer aware of Robert, half-eaten food on plates, the clock ticking, noise out in the street, overcome by the abominable knowledge she has been her own punisher.

When she is spent she sits up, surprised to see him still there, a calm figure, head cocked to one side.

'I can't pretend to know what just happened, though I see it ran deep.'

She purses her lips in agreement. 'You got any brandy?'

He returns with the bottle and pours two glasses. Twice he tries to ask questions and she halts him with a raised hand. She is half-way through the glass of firewater before she's ready to speak.

'It ain't a pretty one, my story, Robert. I will tell it and I'll not hold it agin you if it changes anything.'

She begins, leaving out nothing, the mother who was a whore and gave her away never to return, cruelty at the Foundling Hospital, losing the Bainbridge's protection. Nance's hopeless life and betrayal, the mockery of a court hearing, violence in Taunton Gaol. As she nears the time on the *Canada* she falters for a moment, but the story is a bloodletting, releasing what's built up for years, and she must see it through.

Robert, listening intently, winces as she explains what the officer made her do. She looks away from him, towards her feet, shaking as she tells how she used the knitting pin to puncture her own flesh and the child.

'Oh God.' He has tried so hard to be quiet but the sound escapes, causes her to pause.

'Please, go on.' She was only fourteen or so, he keeps thinking, a defenceless child.

'No more to tell, really. You know most of the rest, about bein' sent to Kissing Point, to Cuddy's farm. How it were for me there.' The marriage, she means, hoping he understands why she agreed.

'It's a lot to carry, Tamsin. You never said before just how wretched it was in your early days.'

The brandy is finished. Slowly she lowers the glass to the table, an oval one, a proper dining table in shiny red rosewood, solid on its pedestal. She gets up and walks around to where Robert sits, and lightly touches his arm, gestures for him to stand.

She's an inch or more shorter than him and must tilt her head up, but at last she can give in and stroke his cheek, move her hand to the back of his neck and pull him towards her in a kiss.

Afterwards, he folds himself around her, holding her chest to chest.

'If you still want me, Robert, I'm willing to share your bed.'

He says nothing, his face soft as she waits for his response. It comes in the form of a hand against her cheek, the palm somehow holding her entire body in its heat. When he bends and kisses her, he is the moon drawing the tides and she has found the shore, arriving with relief.

At the next muster Tam Pummell is listed at Robert Goddard's address as householder. Tam hadn't meant to say the word when asked for occupation. She should have said housekeeper but that's not what came out, her mind thinking of the way her body hums at his touch, of early mornings entwined with Robert, whispering as the sun rises.

Robert doesn't care how she described herself. What they do in the privacy of the house is their business only, he reminds her. Plenty of scandalous liaisons in Sydney, convict, free people and officials alike, despite the Guv's efforts and the ranting of church ministers.

They build bridges between each other with affectionate gestures and words, and long nights of exploring each other's bodies, Tam marvelling at the way love colours everything around it in vivid hues. All that she touches seems precious, even the lowly salt pot on the table or the loose button she stitches on Robert's shirt.

Their lives also increasingly include a delighted William and Anastasia and their baby daughter, Elizabeth. The two couples have become fast friends, William taking a paternal role with Robert, mentoring him, and protective with Tam as much as his young wife.

Tam returns from a visit to Anastasia late one afternoon, having spent an hour with baby Elizabeth in her arms so her friend can drink tea in peace. The young mother is a child with a child, and the broken nights have left her frazzled, worn out from relentless responsibility.

Before she left, Anastasia asked on behalf of her and William if Tam and Robert would be the girl's godparents. The request has sent Tam home with a worried mind.

'Robert, at some point I'll be free to marry.' She has waited till the supper dishes are washed and they're sitting side by side in their armchairs in the parlour, a lamp burning low on the side table between them.

Cuddy's taking far longer to age and fade away than ever she had imagined, but that's not the problem.

'It bothers me I can't give you babies. You never really said what you think 'bout that.'

He puts down the book he's been reading and studies her, an intelligent woman, one who has started to share ideas of her own.

'I've been tied up with other things over the years … my mother dying six years before leaving, Pa the year before, then fixing on getting myself to Sydney, making something of myself. Being a father hasn't come up.'

'Surely it must rankle, Robert.'

'I'm about to be a godfather. Good enough for me, Tamsin. If I can't have a child with you then I don't fancy having one, and I can live with that.'

The lamp flickers, throwing stripes of shadow across his face. She searches for any sign that he is consoling her, kidding her along, but sees none.

'If ever you change your mind, you must tell me.'

He nods, then reaches for his book but thinks better of it and goes to her, leaning down to kiss her forehead. 'It will not happen, Tamsin. I promise.'

'I'd understand if you did change your mind, Robert. I never want you to pretend.' She means what she says, but the pain of losing him over it would be impossible to bear.

The baptism is a quiet yet joyful occasion, Elizabeth asleep in her mother's arms and oblivious to Rev Cowper anointing her with oil then sprinkling cool water on her forehead, while Anastasia's parents beam beside her and William. Tam fully expects Robert will take his vow seriously, to encourage the little girl in her faith. He will be a good godfather, a steady hand for the child as she grows, while she questions what she has to offer.

She and Robert take turns in renouncing evil and declaring faith in Christ on behalf of their goddaughter. When the parson faces Tam and she agrees to guide the child in her Christian life, she consents with all her heart and it moves her unexpectedly, happy tears welling up. The baptism marks a new sense of kinship, family coming together and growing bonds, not through shared blood but the natural flow of love and respect. She is godmother, a link in a chain of care that wraps around the baby girl.

The group makes the short walk down Church Hill to the Fosters' home, where the servant girl, recently employed to take some of the load off Anastasia, has laid out food and drinks. Tam walks behind the cheerful group, gazing across the town where modern multi-storey buildings devour rotting old huts, then over the glistening harbour, ignoring puffs of dust kicked up by the feet ahead.

The world has begun to look different, more forgiving. Her mind is less inclined to the narrow path of what might be difficult, cause harm. Sometimes she can bear to consider what she deeply desires, might bring genuine reward. Being there for Robert is a pleasure, but the charring, cooking, and washing she could do in her sleep. They are merely chores, not granting fulfilment, a glorious word, once so utterly out of reach, now coming to her often. The idea of it has awakened, rousing from its long slumber since childhood, perhaps called forth by the new experience of a man who delights in seeking to protect her and does his utmost to make her happy.

Next day, as she walks along Pitt Street, her eyes alight on a small notice in the window of the music store, advertising the services of the woman who teaches piano in a room at the rear. Tam passes the bootmaker's shop, recalling that his boot-binder is a convict girl, then the milliner's where two sisters make hats.

Walking into George Street, she gazes in the window of the bookseller, where a woman stacks new publications on a shelf, then notices the jeweller's, his widow now free to openly claim the pendants, bracelets and mourning brooches as her work. Why hasn't she seen this before, the women who toil without fuss in small shops, make goods or trade, some under the names of men, a few in their own right, doing what they love?

Not one of them publicly wilful but resisting stricture just the same.

It's a revelation, a word Rev Cowper uses often in his sermons. While this is no religious enlightenment, the sudden understanding is uplifting and her compass shifts and trembles, swinging back and forth. She must trust it to find true north.

That night the new rush of energy is overtaken when Robert shares his news. He has taken William's advice to be bold, to back himself. He will pledge all he has to build a vast storehouse, three storeys high. Robert Campbell has already made a commitment that his business, Campbell & Co, with the busiest wharf in town, will lease it.

'Already got the land in George Street.'

Tam grasps it's a canny move. The street, emerging from the bush track worn by the feet of Eora people long before the British arrived, is developing rapidly with shops and inns, and the road to Parramatta veers off it.

'Been a battle to get the finance, but with goods coming in from Parramatta and imports coming from the docks I know it'll prove its worth.'

Plenty have gone bankrupt, Captain John Piper for one, lost everything after building his grand home. Tam's seen it with Cuddy too, how easy it is to lose what you've made from nothing after years of work. If Robert's wave of enthusiasm dumps them when it crests, she'll be going down with him.

'Congratulations, Robert. I know you'll make a success of it.'

She ponders it for hours that night, unable to sleep. How men think to the future, don't wait for someone to give them permission, encouraged to think about what they can do, not forever being told what they can't, so often that they dare not crack open the door to the possible. A woman must struggle against endless rules to have an independent thought, let alone do anything to push against the tide.

When she wakes after a few hours' sleep, the thoughts are still pestering, needling as she dresses, washes her face and makes their breakfast. They refuse to leave her alone when she goes to the market, the butcher, returns to chop vegetables and clean the fireplace.

She is pondering Robert's accounts, how much comes in, what's paid out, how he moves money around, sees it taking form, no different to his wielding of an adze or chisel to shape timber for a new vessel. Something magnificent arising from nothing but an idea. The wonder of creating.

She pictures him running a hand along timber he's smoothed, the look of satisfaction he gets when the grain runs just right, while her hands leave nothing lasting.

Her back aches from bending to whitewash the back of the parlour fireplace. She stands to stretch, flings the brush into the pot so hard the contents splash. She could cry or rage, lash out; she's been here before, the surge of reaction that wants to burn itself up, no good to come of it but exhaustion when it's done.

She keeps standing, feels the power building, wanting to move out of her in a scream, or pass through her fists to punch the wall, and she wants to do it now. Yet she holds it in, and as she watches a small gap opens, a flicker of curiosity emerges. The whitewash needs cleaning up, yet she remains standing there utterly still until into the gap a flash of understanding arrives, perfectly complete, landing hard in her as a migrating bird might when reaching its destination.

She knows what she will do.

Like Robert, like William, Cuddy in his time, too, she will prepare for the future.

Her plan will start with one simple step, and she needs to keep it close, make it completely hers until she feels it is so. She is given a generous housekeeping sum each fortnight and with a little care should be able to set some aside, along with her savings, kept in the drawer with her stockings and underclothes.

Never before has a pot of whitewash seemed so glorious. She wipes up the splashes from the hearth bricks and puts the pot back on the shelf in the washhouse out the back.

The first time, the small act of keeping back some coins has a big effect on Tam, one she hasn't predicted, the gesture beginning as a small ripple, then each fortnight that passes, each sum squirreled away, growing into a gently rising tide. It's as though she has been dipping into Robert's brandy, her feet dancing through the days, light and joyful.

She trusts Anastasia, wants to tell her what she's doing, but it doesn't feel right, as though sharing the secret will weaken the scrap of sovereignty she's wrested from circumstance. Besides, her friend is mired in domesticity, already expecting her next child.

William, aware that he is twenty-one years older than Anastasia, wants to make sure his family is provided for if something happens to him. His first wife had a daughter and remarried in Hobart some years earlier, William turning a blind eye. Now it's time for him to flout the law and marry.

The wedding in spring is a small affair but a happy one, Rev Cowper showing the respect owed to a successful businessman and his young bride. Easter falls early the following year and Anastasia gives birth to a second daughter, Ann, soon after. Tam and Robert are godparents again. Parents and godparents delight in calling the cheerful child Annie.

Tam holds the newborn, surprised at the way her heart swells with as much love as she has for the baby's two-year-old sister. It comes rushing, unbridled, not begrudging, held back like it was with George and Rosa.

The year is burning itself out, the end of 1828 shuffling towards history, when Cuddy shows up at the house. Tam hasn't seen him for years. He is thinner, more bent, his voice getting frail. Whatever he is here to say she doesn't want it said on the doorstep.

'Come in, Cuddy.' She ushers him into the parlour, where he looks at the table and matching chairs, the fancy tea set on the side table, the richly patterned rug on the floor.

'You done well for yerself.' The remark is grudging, and she frowns, irritated, waving a hand to offer a seat on one of the armchairs.

'Wanted you to hear it from me, not from tittle-tattle. I'm leaving fer good, off to Van Diemen's Land, get closer to George, maybe see Rosa.'

She's taken aback at the news, then quickly recovers. 'Thought you had Roger and Ellen for family.'

She avoids mention of Luis, who's not been heard of for a long time, since he racked up big debts with publican Thomas Woolley at Parramatta's Tollgate Hotel then took off, despite a written agreement he'd work for the fellow to discharge what was owed. Woolley was so incensed he paid for a newspaper advertisement, warning others off employing Luis. Humiliating for his old Da, fetching and carrying for the Guv in the same town.

'I do, but I miss the other two.' Cuddy sinks a little on the chair, sadness turning his face greyer.

Tam's ready with a barb but reminds herself she's not hard-hearted these days, instead searching for some benevolence. George is based in the south of the southern island, now works for a leading whaling operation run by Captain James Kelly and the fellow's business partner Joe Ferrion. They've put her stepson in charge of one of the bay whaling stations, according to his recent letters.

'George's Ma, your Melva, would have been proud o' him.'

She cannot help but think it's probably best the first wife doesn't have to see her husband looking like this, sagging, the burnt out stub of a candle, nothing but downhill for years. She wants to hate this old man, taking advantage of the young girl she once was, but it's not in her these days. He was kind enough, kept her from wickedness in every corner, and in this hard-edged colony it matters.

Cuddy looks at Tam like he's seeing her for the first time, the girl he took for a wife, who never had the chance to be that because the space was already taken, stayed taken.

'Sold some land at South Colah, wanted to give you this. Not much, but it's yours by right.' He reaches in his pocket, gives her ten pounds.

She runs her thumb across the stack of bank notes, strong black ink yet the paper surprisingly soft and thin where it's been printed on a local newspaper press. They are no measure against what she's lost in a past shackled to Cuddy. Tam looks at the old man, aware there's no point in making him suffer just because he had shortcomings and she was the one who paid the price.

'When you see George, Rosa too, give 'em my love.'

His face quivers a touch. 'If I caused you harm, I hope yer able to find some forgiveness in yer heart.'

Though he mumbles it, she hears every word.

'Nothin' to forgive, Cuddy. Just the way o' things.'

He pats her on the shoulder as he leaves. He must be at least eighty now, has the smell of deathly decay about him, and she knows that soon enough she'll be a widow. A sense of unexpected sadness lingers for a long while after he's gone, not born out of love, for there is none, but history that has been shared.

CHAPTER TWENTY-THREE

SYDNEY TOWN, 1830-1831

ROBERT STILL PAYS TAM'S WAGES six-monthly, an uncomfortable transaction. He insists it's only right as she works so hard and deserves the recompense, though it seems another way to keep her in the servant role and she has said so.

'Then I'll seek out a maid and you can be mistress of the house.' He's smiling as he says it, and she can't tell if it is a joke.

'No need. Idle hands an' all that.'

She has counted her savings. With the money Cuddy gave her, she has more than sixteen pounds. His gift, if she can call it that, has been in the drawer all this time but now he has died the money seems cleaner, and she is finally ready to put it to use.

He took his last breath on his own in rented rooms near Hobart Town's Ship Inn the previous December. Thinking about what George wrote, she manages a smile. Seems Cuddy was the opportunist to the end, petitioning the Van Diemen's Land Guv soon after arriving, asking to be found a position as the pension of one shilling a day, provided by the Governor of New South Wales, was insufficient for his support.

An official recommended that consideration be given to anything suitable that could be found for an eighty-three year old, on condition information on his character was obtained from New South Wales.

That were the last he heard of it, Tam. Within months he were gone. I had him buried in St David's Cemetery a few days before Christmas. Thought you should know. He could be a right old bugger with the drinking though I miss him just the same.

Robert can't hide his delight at the news. 'We can marry, Tamsin, make it official, maybe next year when the storehouse starts paying its way.'

It's odd, she thinks, that she loves him dearly yet is unmoved by the suggestion.

Anastasia has given birth to a son, John, though he arrived a few weeks early and is poorly. Tam spends the mornings at the Fosters, caring for the baby and the two girls while Anastasia catches up with sleep.

She is cradling the baby the next day, crooning to settle him. He's tired, should be napping but instead is throwing little fists back and forth, his face scrunched like a balled up piece of paper.

'Shh little one, shh.'

Suddenly the tiny body stiffens, begins to convulse, his head lolling back. Tam lays him in the crib, pulls away the swaddling cloth, swallowing down panic. He is breathing, his colour blue, but when she touches his forehead there's no sign of a fever.

She shouts for the convict maid. 'Fetch the surgeon.' The girl comes in, sees the baby jerking, throws her hand over her mouth. 'He got the devil in 'im.'

'Don't be ridiculous. Run for the doctor. Now.' The girl rushes out.

Anastasia enters the nursery, dazed from being woken by Tam's voice. 'What's wrong?' She sees the way the boy is stretched out, now strangely limp, and begins wailing. 'John, oh John.'

'He's alright, Anastasia. Had a fit but he's peaceful now. The surgeon's on his way.'

Tam places her hand gently on his chest, feels it rise and fall, then swaddles him for his mother to hold. Anastasia lifts him, leans her ear to his mouth, checking that he breathes. The baby boy suddenly gags, as though he will vomit, does it again then seems to settle.

The maid returns, breathless. 'Bland's man says he's workin' up at the dispensary this morning. He'll get him down to the babe soon as he's done.'

William Bland has a private practice but, having been a convict himself, gives free medical care in one of the Rum Hospital buildings in Macquarie Street, on the eastern fringe of town. Anastasia starts to cry. It'll be a good hour before the surgeon gets here.

John's colour has returned and he is sleeping in his mother's arms when Bland arrives to examine him.

'No sign of a fever beforehand, you say?'

Anastasia nods in reply.

The surgeon checks the baby's vital signs, quietly notes that his breathing is noisy, a little shallow, then moves the limbs, checking how the muscles respond.

The examination over, he gestures for Tam to swaddle the boy, then takes Anastasia out to the parlour.

Tam is reluctant to leave the babe in the crib and keeps him against her chest as she waits to hear the surgeon being shown out. Afterwards, she goes to Anastasia, bent in wretched fashion in a chair.

'Says he suspects the falling sickness, probably have it for life. What have I done, Tam, to harm him?'

They sit, bearing the sadness together. Little John, if he survives frequent seizures, will grow up to be a social outcast.

'You mustn't lose hope, Anastasia. You will give him good care, we all will. He has a purpose, bein' born this way. Maybe you'll see it as time passes.'

Tam has no interest in trying to get land, attempting to gain power through farming animals and crops. She has set her sights on a different kind of cultivating, the kind that might help a woman to rise.

The Bank of New South Wales won't advance loans to women on their own, yet there are plenty with skills going begging and many have children to be fed and clothed. The colony's women are derided, but by and large they're not the shirkers the papers blame for disorder and depredation. Most of them do makeshift work, Tam's seen it for herself, offering services where there's a call, as washerwomen, needleworkers and menders, hawkers, taking in lodgers, anything to earn a crust. She has decided it's not good enough. The colony has a rising merchant class and it's only right that women can share in the opportunities, not be shut out.

Tam is ready to make a mark.

Soon after Robert leaves for work, she takes her basket and walks briskly up Pitt Street towards its corner with Hunter Street, past an eating house, shops, and surgeon Bland's rooms. She slows near the parchment manufacturer, checking street numbers. Next door is the shop she seeks, but at the last minute she's too nervous and goes past to the haberdashers, pretending to study a sign in the window advertising special prices for coloured sewing silk.

The business with baby John has rattled her more than she cares to admit, and now she hides a secret from Robert. An image comes to her, of the water skink that dropped its tail when trapped by her careless boot in the garden. In time it will grow a new one, shape itself anew. She's working at doing the same, except the effort leaves her skittish.

A loud rhythm of hammering starts up at the wheelwright and blacksmith opposite, startling her from such silly ideas. The reflection in the window glass is a grown woman who should be above such childish thoughts.

Have courage.

Inside the mixed goods shop, a neat older woman is busily arranging a display of soaps.

'Mrs Eager?'

'Yes. May I help?'

Tam's throat is dry. She clears it rather too loudly then introduces herself and explains what she wishes to discuss.

The woman smooths her skirts, and for a moment Tam thinks she will evict her from the shop. A young assistant hurries in, taking an apron from behind the counter and tying it on. Mrs Eager gives the girl some instructions, then turns back to her visitor.

'Come through. I think it best we chat over tea.'

Jemima Eager, proprietor, is hospitable, accustomed by now to most of Sydney knowing her business, that her merchant husband Edward returned to England a decade earlier never to return, leaving her to raise their four children while he soon met a sixteen-year-old and went on to have another brood.

Tam questions her over the challenges of starting a shop without backing from a man.

'Ah well, the business were his, my dear, given over to me. I try to use it wisely, lease the stores, dry cellars and sheds out the back. The marble masons, Clewett and Patten, are one of my tenants. Reputable businesses only on my premises.'

Tam's disappointed as the picture emerges, not least because the woman's husband made local newspaperman Edward Smith Hall a trustee for property left to the children, which means the woman's still confined in how she runs her affairs.

'What interest is any of this to you?'

Tam lays out her plan, how she has a small sum that she hopes will grow and she seeks to make modest private loans, give one woman at a time a leg up.

'Many have skills, as you know, I dare say. Though not the means to start a small enterprise. I'm tryin' to decide how best to proceed, Mrs Eager.'

The woman has a puzzled countenance. 'Call me, Jemima, if you please. I understand your Mr Goddard is already benefactor to some needing training or starting in business.'

Tam shuffles in her seat, her face pricking with a flush of disloyalty.

'Yes, he helps out capable men wanting to get set up. I see a need, though, to help women, those who bin in circumstances I've known. And to be honest, Jemima, this is somethin' I want to do in my own right, prove to myself I can do it without a man.'

Such an outrageous thing to say out loud, quite ridiculous, giving herself airs. Enough to make a stuffed bird laugh. As a smile spreads across the shopkeeper's face, Tam prepares for her to start chortling, though she remains composed.

'I see you're a good woman. There's plenty of our sex who could make a future for themselves with just a little bit of help.'

Soon Mrs Eager must return to work, but only after the two women have agreed Tam must start quite small. The proprietor knows someone, an orphan she grew up with, wants to start a servants' registry office. All she needs is a loan for a few months' rent.

Her host farewells Tam at the door, hand on the knob, standing half out in the street. She lowers her voice. 'Bit of a surprise, you are. You'd do well with your own shop.'

'Not for me, Jemima. Haven't got what it takes.'

The first loan is paid back promptly at the end of the three months. Next Tam loans a small sum to a poulterer needing rent for a stall in Market Place, then to another ex-convict for furniture to start a boarding house. When those funds are paid back she helps a needlewoman, mother of two little ones, who needs equipment to start a business from a room in her house.

Tam is discreet, seeks out women with reliable character, noting down names and sums in her own green ledger, bought for the purpose. Caution is needed, of course. Merchants and wealthy landowner moneylenders are publicly pilloried for living off the labour of others. A woman who's a moneylender would cop it far worse, and men would roll their eyes if they discovered she doesn't charge her women interest, like the twelve percent they slap on.

The satisfaction is not in making money for herself. She is giddy with pleasure at creating change, giving others like her a chance. It's a strong elixir, running hot in her veins, such a rush that she begins to add a few shillings here and there from Robert's funds to the money she sets aside.

Meanwhile, baby John is growing stronger, though more seizures have confirmed the falling sickness will blight him always, maybe cause him to die young. Anastasia is red-eyed each time Tam visits, inconsolable for weeks, while William walks like a man who's been walloped, spending longer days than ever at the dockyards and warehouses.

'Can you talk to William? Anastasia needs him.' She is clearing the supper dishes from the table.

'He's dealing with it the best he can, knowing him. Not sure talking to him would make any difference.'

Tam props against the table, plates in her hand. 'Please try. Breaks my heart that she's so lost.'

Later that evening Robert is rifling through papers in the wooden set of pigeonholes on the desk. The correspondence he seeks isn't there and he searches the desk drawers.

She has hands in hot soapy water when he enters the kitchen.

'What's this?'

She looks over her shoulder to see he holds up her personal ledger.

'Keepin' a record of household expenses, is all.'

'Don't lie, Tamsin.' His voice is icy.

'Alright. Bin makin' a few small loans from the money Cuddy gave me, and my savings, maybe a bit left over from housekeeping. Just to women of good character.' Being made to explain has quickly doused the pleasure of her little scheme.

Robert slams the ledger down on the bench, thrusts his face in front of hers. 'What the dickens are you up to?'

The harshness of his tone smacks against her. Without thinking she is on the balls of her feet, the old fighter surging up. She wants to strike him, shove him backwards, yet she wills herself to give a reasoned response.

Haltingly she gives her explanation. Perhaps he might have a little pride in her efforts, given his donations to the orphans' home and the benevolence he dispenses to men starting out in business.

The more she tries to present her position, the greater his fury.

She can control herself no longer. 'No bloody need to get worked up, Robert. I'm bein' careful. Just trying to help a few women have more in their lives except poverty, motherhood and housework.' She spits out the last sentence.

He leans towards her with what she fears is menace, and she cowers. 'You think it right that you're the one angry with me?' His eyes glint in the light of the lamp.

'It's not the money that disturbs me, Tamsin, though some of it, dear God, is mine by rights. Don't you get it? It's the damn deceit.'

He pivots on his heels, gets to the kitchen door. 'We're meant to marry early in the New Year. Hanged if I know what's the point when you still don't trust me, and plain as day you're showing me I can't trust you.' He grabs his jacket, set to storm out.

She should keep her trap shut but it's too late, she is shouting at his disappearing back. 'I won't be governed by you.'

The door bangs shut. She finishes the dishes, quaking a little in anger and the fear at her own impudence. How dare he ruin the excitement at what she's been creating.

A couple of hours later, Robert still not home, her fury cooling, she is climbing into bed when a hot wave of shame cuts through. She's been seduced by the novelty of gaining wings and not had a single thought about damaging their trust. Self-reproach pins her to the mattress as she sees what she's done.

Being loved, loving people back is harder than she ever thought in all the years she yearned for it. Opening her heart to Robert, the Fosters, their girls, little John, leaves her raw, exposed as a wind-swept hill and no protection but her own outstretched arms.

Others do it as easily as breathing, while her love twists inside like tangled rope, and when she pulls at it oh how it hurts, a mess of pain tied up with tenderness and affection. The very thing she wants to give others, wants from them, rubs like a rasp at old wounds deep inside. Will she ever be free of them? She asks it over and over till exhaustion numbs her mind and body and she sleeps, alone.

Robert emerges from the spare bedroom next morning to say he'd been with William, managed to talk to him about spending more time with Anastasia. He tells her about it as though it's an apology for shouting the night before. He is shocked by the strength of his anger and only in cooling off overnight has he seen it was a cover for hurt feelings, that she had not seen fit to confide in him about a matter of such great importance to her.

His remorse worsens her mortification. 'I'm truly sorry, Robert. I spoke harshly when there were no need, and I don't like myself when I get like that. You bin nothing but considerate to me.' She searches the wind-burnt lines around his eyes but can't see a frown.

'No more secrets, promise. Can you forgive me?'

'Already have.' He gives a half-smile before his mouth turns down. 'I meant what I said, though …' he pauses '… about trust. If you're not able to give me that, best you tell me now and we go our own way.'

She gives him every assurance to which she can lay her tongue, desperate to make him happy, the whole while doubting she can ever live up to her word. Maybe the damage to her foundations can't be fixed and in time the house of their relationship will fall down.

'What about the loans I give? Can I keep going?' Demeaning, asking for permission when she wants to have authority like Jemima Eager, sure of her worth.

'Of course, Tamsin, long as it doesn't get out of hand. If it's a help, we can discuss how you're going each week when we review my accounts.'

Her little jig no longer feels like her own creation. The relief that he's willing to overlook her behaviour is immediately replaced by a confusing rush of dread. It takes all her effort to keep it at bay while Robert eats breakfast and leaves for work. The minute he's gone she curls on the bed, knees tight against her chest.

She is barren, will never make a baby, badly aches to have one with Robert. The knowledge is a hollow, lonely emptiness in her innards. The moneylending scheme was meant to be a dream she brought to life instead of a child, an unmet need for creation that sought to be realised, making her more whole before they married.

Their wedding is in February. The day brings a hot breeze, dust eddying around their feet and the wheels of carriages and drays as they walk hand in hand to church, William and Anastasia behind them. Though now the Fosters have a nursemaid for John, William has had to cajole his wife to leave the house.

At the altar Tam looks up at Robert, wide shouldered, slim-hipped, his back upright, and marvels that this husband is one she can admire. A man whose hands she yearns to have hold her, touch and stroke the curves of her body when the candle's been blown out. She stands proudly beside him, content to become his wife.

The year is made more glorious with Robert's promotion to wharfinger at Robert Campbell's operation, in charge of receipt and delivery of all goods coming and going. As overseer he's provided with a cottage at the wharves, where he can delight in being in the thick of it.

The cottage, at the northern end, faces the water, barely twelve paces from the wharf edge. It is a rectangle stretched a hundred and twenty feet long but only twelve feet deep to allow for rows of storehouses stacked at the rear.

'A big improvement on the old wharfinger's hut.' He laughs as he says it, remembering the first day, more than a decade earlier, when she threaded past the building to find him in the workshop.

The cottage is handsome enough, he tells Tam, in brick with a shingled roof, a big parlour and dining room downstairs with stone-flagged floor, a semi-detached kitchen at the rear, and upstairs two decent size bedrooms and one small one.

With the news, Robert has decided it's time to insist. 'We're getting a maid, Tamsin. You're a wife now, don't want you doing the dirty work no more.'

She is thirty-six years old the first time anyone scrubs a filthy floor on her behalf. She watches the maid on her knees and feels shiftless, like she no longer belongs here.

CHAPTER TWENTY-FOUR

SYDNEY TOWN, 1839-1841

THERE'S A SAYING PEOPLE USE, that disaster strikes as though it's a bolt from the blue. Tam's wiser than that, knows it creeps in, often disguised in the mundane, worms its way in, and before you know it your life's been overtaken, turned inside out.

The day begins as any other. William has sailed to Van Diemen's Land in the hope of helping bail out William junior's struggling farm. His son is married now with a young daughter, but debts have piled up as he tries to get established at Kempton, about thirty miles north of Hobart Town.

Tam is on her way for the daily visit to Anastasia and the children, now in greater numbers with the arrival in recent years of Sarah, now five, Thomas, four years, and toddler Harriet.

The maid half opens the door. 'You can't come in, Mrs Goddard. Mrs Foster says so.'

'Why ever not?'

'She's sick, got catarrh bad and a fever, four of the children too. Don't want you catchin' it.'

Tam doesn't hesitate. 'Tell her I don't mind. I'll take my chances.'

'No, she says if I let you in I have to pack my bags and go. The doctor's been, so's you know, told her no visitors.' The girl holds the door firmly.

'John, how is he?'

'No worse than the others. Now I have to go.' She shuts the door in Tam's face.

Influenza has been raging in Van Diemen's Land, many have died, and ships have brought it to Sydney, where its rapid march from the docks through narrow-gutted tenements, squeezed together in go downs and passages on the lower slopes of The Rocks, has advanced into the rest of the town.

Newspapers have proclaimed the disease has an atmospheric origin, hot winds occurring before it begins to spread. Treatments include purging and herbal remedies to reduce inflammation and fever, though Tam can't help but wonder if medicos say such things so they don't have to confess they're helpless.

It plays on her mind, her friend lying ill. She keeps picturing the little ones sick in their beds, moaning and tossing, or worse, bedclothes neat as they lie still. Surely Elizabeth, now fourteen, helps care for the others.

Maybe the doctor suggested it, Tam doesn't know. But when next she knocks the maid tells her that Anastasia has put Annie and Harriet into the Female Orphan School to save them from the deadly disease.

Tam trudges home, hurt that her friend did not consider sending the girls to her. Robert is just as put out by the development when she tells him that evening.

Tam goes to the Fosters' front door every day, guts twisting, for an update from the maid. All still very sick, she reports, failing to mention that Anastasia, weak and fevered, has directed that's all she may say for fear of panicking her friend.

On the fifth day Elizabeth opens the door a crack, influenza now confining the maid to her bed. 'Hello Aunt Tam. Mother's doing a little better, the others too. No need to worry.'

The girl's eyes are sunk in her head, and she leans against the door as she thanks Tam for offers of assistance in a grown-up voice, while her face is that of a child in over her depth.

Tam forces herself to thank Elizabeth, turn her back to the closed door and walk away while every instinct says to force her way in, see the situation for herself.

For two weeks the family battles illness till finally Tam is allowed to enter.

Anastasia weeps in her arms. 'Please, stay with the children. I must go to fetch Annie and Harriet home.'

Tam has become angry, in the intervening days, that the girls have been dumped with cold strangers, especially the toddler, far too young to have her spirit blunted in such a place. She says nothing, though; her friend is too vulnerable now to make her feel worse.

Her disturbance is nothing compared to the fury of William on his return, when he discovers what his wife, with best intentions, has done.

The following Sunday after church, Robert and Tam go to the couple's home. They have decided it must never happen again.

Elizabeth and Annie are with them in the parlour when Tam speaks up.

'Anastasia, I know you was only wantin' to protect the two girls and spare me and Robert from illness, but they should have come to us by rights, been with those who care about 'em.'

Robert chimes in. 'In fact, God forbid it happens again, we insist. We don't have children of our own, true, though we will always do our best by yours if they're in need.'

Anastasia, apologetic, downcast eyes flicking up to her husband, agrees. Annie, unable to contain herself a minute longer, rushes over to hug Tam, who holds on tight, unexpectedly finding she doesn't want to let go of the girl.

For almost seven years Tam has loaned money interest-free to enterprising women. Robert is surprised that only one ever failed to pay back what she borrowed, taking off to try her luck at the new settlement on the south coast at Port Phillip. Tam, on the other hand, has always trusted that the women would see it was a privilege, wouldn't want to deny others the same chance, understanding that the funds must keep circling, paid back then loaned to another.

She has become friends with many who've benefitted, enjoys visiting, seeing how they flourish, their children healthy, some even getting an education. A walk down the western side of George Street takes her past Bessie Graue the fruiterer. At the corner she turns into Bridge Street, where Ann Howarth 's store boasts her sign as a bonnet and corset maker, while nearby Sarah Hay, pastry cook and widow, has sweet treats displayed in the window. In Pitt Street, Maudie Quinn, abandoned wife, has a business weaving richly coloured shawls.

Though it bothered Tam at first, collaborating with Robert has proven fruitful, not the least because he values her advice in his own benevolent activities. They have become a partnership, stronger now that Tam has learned to quiet the worthlessness often close to the surface.

Her money lending has come to an end with the talk of new usury laws being introduced soon. She has no wish to be caught up in legal matters and it seems a good time to let the scheme go.

One of the women she's helped has a knitting business she runs from her home. Tam is thinking about it as she strolls late one morning, how life starts off like an unravelled ball of wool, all knots and kinks and no sense of how the stitches will come together. Then somewhere along the way, if you're lucky before the end, the pattern emerges in all its brilliant design.

The tracery of her life has started making sense, she thinks, as she tugs the front of her woollen coat closed against the biting late winter breeze. What a fortunate woman she has become, valued and loved by Robert even if she struggles to value herself, landing in comfortable circumstances, close to such a true friend as Anastasia. So why, oh why, does it not feel enough?

True, Robert's business affairs are more complicated these days, the storehouse going well, with him in talks for two more deals to expand his investments. An accountant recently took over managing the financials, and maybe the gap it has left is what makes her feel uneasy, a bit empty.

Pull yourself together, you miserable cow. You've everything you need to be happy. She forces up the corners of her mouth and picks up the pace, suddenly wanting to be in front of the parlour fire and leave her unsatisfied self out in the cold street.

She arrives home to a letter from George, bringing cheer. Now married, he writes to tell her that his two-year-old son is thriving and his wife happy in the brick house he's had built. His years at sea have borne fruit, he is now a ship's master.

Tam reads the letter twice, smiling the whole time, heartened when he says he hopes to visit soon, as he has done occasionally when his ship berths in Sydney for supplies. She hopes so, too.

In a quirk of fate, George's wife is none other than the granddaughter of the nurse who helped save Cuddy so many years ago.

It's a strange kind of miracle, even George says so. God went to great lengths to give him his wife, making sure Maggie Bloodworth, midwife to many, was in that Sydney sick tent with his Da, never knowing she was saving an ailing convict so his son could stand at the altar and make his vows to her own flesh and blood.

The thought of it gives Tam goosebumps.

She picks up his latest letter again and reads it a third time, hears his affection for her remains undimmed. Despite his busy new life it radiates out from the blue ink on the page. Rosa also has not forgotten her, though she has drifted away under the weight of family responsibilities and the correspondence is now limited to a letter received each Christmas.

Two years later, as January is getting started, Anastasia births another son, George. Still weak from the birth, in May she catches scarlet fever, the latest scourge to spread through Sydney. Soon six-year-old Thomas is feverish and vomiting.

William is at the Goddards' door with the news. 'Please, can you take the others?'

When he's gone to organise the children and their belongings, Tam remains standing in the hallway. The nearby clock tick, tick, ticks. She will remember it always, the last moments of a house that's utterly silent.

For two weeks the children live at the Goddards, pining for their mother, Tam floundering in all that must be considered – making beds, extra shopping, meals, washing, mending, cleaning shoes, making sure they say their prayers. The tasks are straightforward enough, aided by William's contribution of funds for their care and Robert swiftly hiring a cook. The children's emotions, running high, are another matter and Tam is caught in them, a whirlpool that some days sucks her under and by bedtime she fears she may drown.

Baby George is the worst affected, frequently screaming at the sudden separation from the mother who's been his whole world. William, fearful the baby might die, has scoured the town for a wet nurse and sent her to the Goddards, where she announces she wants to take the boy to her home.

'No, he needs to stay with his brothers and sisters.' Tam sees the dirt filling the creases of the woman's hands, the face that hasn't seen a washcloth for days. She can't bear to let the boy go to filth.

Instead the wet nurse trudges to the house three times a day to feed George, leaving a little breastmilk in a jar in case he wakes hungry overnight.

In the small hours of morning a day or so later, George stirs, miserable and squealing. Tam holds him upright against her shoulder as she goes to the kitchen for the milk and a teaspoon. She has seen Anastasia feed many times and gets the babe in the crook of her arm, hoping it will encourage him to take the milk from the spoon.

He tries to latch onto it, pushing it away when metal touches his lips. Tam tries again and again. The boy's eyes are shut tight, his face the colour of a crushed mulberry as his shrill cries fill the room. She touches the spoon against his lip, hoping to dribble in some milk, but the baby turns his head and the precious milk runs down his neck.

Elizabeth appears in her nightshift, long hair tousled in great strings over her shoulders. 'Let me try, Aunt Tam.' She holds out her hands for her brother, by now tense with rage.

His sister lifts him against her chest, sings a lullaby in a low voice, swaying in time to it as he gradually calms. 'Try now, Aunt.'

With the girl still holding him, she spoons small pools of milk into his mouth. His eyes widen at the familiar taste, but his mouth still moves in a sucking motion and he keeps turning, nuzzling at Elizabeth in the search for his Ma.

'Keep going, get as much as you can into him.'

The inky sky out the window is growing pale, the night thinning as the rising sun nears. George gulps and chokes occasionally but takes enough milk to settle the edge of his hunger. Daylight will soon be upon them, though Tam only feels a darkening within that a girl not yet fifteen knows more about mothering than she ever will.

John seems to concur that afternoon, when a seizure knocks the eleven-year-old to the floor and he smacks his head on the corner of the hearth. For a split second Tam, entering the room with a tray of biscuits for the children, is frozen while Annie rushes to her brother's aid.

A lump the size of a goose egg is already showing above his temple. Annie grabs a cushion and puts it under his head while he recovers. She sees Tam's distress. 'No need to worry, he's coming good.'

Even a child can do better than her.

The days melt together, moving fast. William brings them to a sharp halt when he arrives on the twentieth, slumped on the doorstep, struggling to speak. He whispers with Tam in the kitchen, asking her to gather the children together in the parlour.

'I got bad news.' He looks around at the five sets of eyes fixed on him, Elizabeth holding a dozing five-month-old George. He is their father, their strength, and doesn't want to say the next words, certain if he does he'll break down. He looks across, nods at Tam to take over.

'Your Pa has talked with the doctor.' She pauses, lets the children grasp the situation is serious.

Thirteen-year-old Annie reads her father like a book and is already crying, John too.

The tick of the clock intrudes as Tam draws breath and she wants to snatch it from the mantel, smash it to pieces in the grate.

'The illness has taken its toll on yer Ma.' Anastasia's heart and lungs are failing fast and she is unlikely to make it through the night, but Tam can't bring herself to voice the awful truth to these dear ones.

'Get your faces washed and tidy yourselves. It's time to go and see her, give her a little cheer.'

Dear God, she will go to hell for keeping it from them, that their Ma is dying. It will be the only chance they'll have to say goodbye and she's so bloody weak she can't tell them.

'I'll see you at the house shortly.' William levers himself up from the table, forgetting his hat, and goes home bare-headed and empty-hearted.

Robert arrives home just as Tam's leaving with the children, gutted by the message William sent to him earlier.

'What can we do?' His lips are so close they brush against Tam's ear.

'Be here for them is all.'

'And you, Tamsin. I'm here for you.' She steps away. It's too much for her to think about what it means to lose her dear friend, seems a trifling thing against the loss for these young ones.

At the Foster house she and Robert stay on the doorstep, William demanding they remain there as the children file in. 'I need you two to stay well.'

She and Robert dither in the street. They should go home, but they can't. Stupid to stand around, people passing and staring, but they can't bring themselves to leave.

Elizabeth is the first to come out, inconsolable. When Tam throws her arms around the girl she sobs into her shoulder. 'Don't tell the others, I beg you. Pa pretended otherwise but Thomas is also fading fast.'

The door opens soon after and William leads the rest of the children out, four-year-old Harriet on his hip, as Elizabeth quickly separates from Tam and composes herself.

They make a sorry procession on the short walk back to the wharfinger cottage, fear striking them mute as they walk towards the harbour. Harriet, usually chatty, is up on Robert's shoulders, clinging on quietly, her chin resting on the top of his head.

Anastasia, light of William's life, devoted Ma, the truest friend Tam's ever known, slips away at dawn. The Foster maid knocks to let them know, William unable to lay down his wife's hand and leave her bedside.

Thirty-one years is all God's given her. Tam thinks of Cuddy and knows it isn't right, that such joy and goodness can be snuffed out so young while others go on forever. She can't afford to wallow in her own grief, though, must think of the children, clinging together on the settee and the floor in front of it, tied together on a raft drifting out to sea.

Less than a fortnight later their brother Thomas joins his mother at the burial ground.

William, bowed under the load of loss, spends hours on his knees praying. He would give away all that he owns, the five homes in Cumberland and Cambridge Streets, the business premises, to have his darling wife smiling before him and his solemn little boy pestering to be taken to the docks.

Tam can't seem to warm her hands for weeks after Anastasia's funeral. They carry the coldness of her friend's skin when she washed her, combed her thick, walnut-coloured hair, powdered the face to hide its ravaged greyness.

The body seems so thin, light, as she works, carefully cutting Anastasia's favourite bodice and skirt to get them over rigid limbs and torso. William has agreed the clothing is more in keeping with the spirit of his wife than a shroud.

Tam steps back when she's done, casting around the room for a sign. She aches with the need to sense her friend's presence, have a visitation, a chance for a proper goodbye.

'Are you there, dear Anastasia?' She says it softly, pleading, but the play of light and shadow is from the flame of the nearby lamp and the air is lifeless.

'Where are you, dear friend? It's miserable without you.' She studies the face of the corpse, unyielding in death's grip. Anastasia can't be called back. It is done. The pain is a blade thrust into her chest and her hand flies to her heart. She can't breathe, doubles over, no longer a woman but an animal, its primitive, raw howl taking over. She swallows it back, gasps for a minute or two till she can stand.

Tenderly, she smooths the sheet over legs and hips. 'Don't you be worryin' about William, my friend. Me and Robert, we'll watch out for him, and the children, of course. Dear Anastasia, please know we'll give them all the love and care we can.'

She places a small prayer book and posy of forget-me-knots on the body. 'You was the best, the dearest friend I ever had. Wherever you are, in heaven by rights, go softly and know you was loved, will ever be.'

Tam stands back, satisfied with her work, then runs her fingertips down her friend's cheek one last time.

William has decided the children should see their mother, say goodbye. They arrive to a bedroom with curtains drawn, the room thick with gloom broken only by the flickering candle on the dresser and another on the bedside table, Tam hoping the low light might bring a little softness to the scene.

The children cluster to one side, overcome by the reality that their lively Ma, full of warmth and laughter, has been replaced by the stiff, waxen body on the bed.

Immediately Harriet breaks free from Elizabeth and runs to the bed, thrusting a hand-me-down rag doll at the corpse.

'Mama, mama, get up, come play.' The girl throws the doll Anastasia made years earlier for Sarah, maybe Annie, and it lies crooked, sprawled on the pillow, arms and legs akimbo, grotesque beside the neat parcel of flesh and bone that was the girl's mother.

She calls out again to her Ma, then instantly is agitated, scrambling quickly onto the bed, where she kisses her mother's cheek again and again.

'Get her out.' Tam jumps at William's loud roar, fearing he's lost his temper. Before he can get to the four-year-old Tam scoops her up and carries the girl from the room, howling worse than an animal with its leg in a trap, still calling 'Mama, mammaaa … .'

Harriet will not be stopped. She throws herself about in Tam's arms, fists flailing, head tossing, writhing fast, and Tam must kneel so she doesn't drop her. 'Harriet, Harriet, shh now, shh darling, it's alright, it's alright.'

It's an utter lie, Tam condemns herself for it. Nothing is alright, not a single thing, and this blessed girl is the only one honest enough to shout it out, scream out the injustice, the pain, the turmoil covered by the pretence of peace in that dim bloody bedroom.

She stays on her knees, hugging and rocking the little girl, their tears joining together on their cheeks.

Two days later they all gather again outside the bedroom. Tam arrives early, leaving Robert to follow with the older children while their maid cares for the baby and Harriet.

The undertaker arrives, a short fellow with pudgy fingers and a parish pickaxe of a nose that seems to lead him and his tall, thin, black-clad assistant through the front door. As they proceed towards the bedroom Tam glances over her shoulder, half expecting Anastasia to be standing there, chuckling at this pair, agreeing it would be far more fitting for them to be on the stage, fooling about, making audiences laugh.

The body is already in the cedar coffin, William seated beside it where he has maintained a vigil overnight. Tam longed to be there too but chose, in the end, to be with the children. She enters the room with the undertaker, goes to the grief-stricken husband and places a heavy hand on his shoulder.

'It's time, William.'

They lean together, arm in arm, as the lid goes on the coffin. The sound of the first screw going in sets off an impulse in Tam. She trembles with the urge to yank the screwdriver from the undertaker's hand, rip the coffin lid off, as though it's the closed box stripping her friend of any humanity, robbing seven children of an adoring mother, not death itself.

As the box is carried to the front door, it's Sarah who makes Tam's tears well up, the girl reaching out tenderly to caress the wooden side as it passes towards the hearse.

The family follows the coffin up Church Hill in a mourning coach pulled by black horses, Tam and Robert in a gig behind.

At the church the Minister, up in the pulpit, reassures them it was a good death, a release from the pain of the world into one that is pure, unending. He looks pointedly at the family. 'Your loving wife, your mother, your friend is in heaven and when the time has come there will be such a joyous reunion, for this is the way of God's greater plan.'

Tam casts her eye along the pew in front, at the children lined up beside their father, John and Sarah slumped together, Elizabeth and Annie as upright as their Pa. How can there be homecoming when their home is broken, the heart of it torn away?

Thomas' death soon after deepens the sense of disintegration. Tam weeps as she cleans the body and prepares him for the undertaker, the only time she can cry at the boy's passing. So much grief that all of them soon are strung out and irritable with each other.

CHAPTER TWENTY-FIVE

SYDNEY TOWN, 1842-1846

I N THE LOWER PART OF The Rocks, the terrain has made it impossible for successive governors to lay down orderly streets. A maze of lanes, blind courts and narrow paths spread like a spider's web through sandstone shelving on the harbour's edge. Criminals do a roaring trade, prostitutes openly tout for business, and in dark inns the frequent fist fights are entertainment for labourers and coal-lumpers.

Beyond the chaos, at Campbell's Cove, life seems more orderly in the wharfinger cottage, though it is mere pretence. Recent events have worked their way into the fabric of the days, worse than borers tunnelling through wood, the children spending a good deal of time with the Goddards and growing more fragile.

William, lost in the fog of grief, decides that Tam should take charge of his brood. Along with Robert they come to an arrangement – the children will live with their father on Saturdays and Sundays and with the Goddards on workdays.

Annie and Sarah continue to go to school, unlike half the colony's children, while John is too poorly to attend.

He and Harriet, along with the baby, are in Tam's care during the week, aided by Elizabeth.

Tam wants badly to give them all a good life, even John, who she has been teaching his letters. She doesn't for a moment kid herself that she can be their Ma, heal them, give them back a Pa who is capable and attentive. She can feed them, keep them in clean clothes, give them routines, hold the little ones when they cry, but these children need so much more and she feels, to the marrow in her bones, that she is hopelessly inadequate. She may be the only Ma little George knows, cause for panic when she wakes at three in the morning.

She is a dried out woman on her way to fifty, one who once did cut her own child to pieces, then failed others on a farm at Kissing Point. She will let them down, is fearful she may leave them stunted for lack of what they need to flourish, as she was at their age.

The thoughts loop endlessly through her mind. Only the image of the little ones, scared and crying in a dormitory at the orphanage, propels her to keep going, which is sometimes the best that can be done.

The childless couple that is the Goddards now have a house full of children through the week, with all the noise and disorder it brings. Tam has a second maid to help with George and to keep an eye on John, but her weekdays of work still stretch from daylight till the candle's snuffed out at bedtime.

She and Robert fall exhausted into their armchairs after the children are delivered to William's house on

Fridays, though by Sunday morning Tam is yearning to see the five older ones at church.

Elizabeth, now sixteen years, has begun drawing back from the family, worrying Tam. She catches the girl looking across the aisle at church, locking eyes with a fellow sitting with a stout grey-haired woman. The man, in his late twenties, gives the slightest nod, a secret communication passing between the two of them.

On the Monday Tam carefully questions the girl.

'How do you know the fellow from church?'

Elizabeth, never a good actress, attempts to feign ignorance. 'What fellow?'

Tam laughs, an unexpected snort because it's brought to mind the way she and Nance loved to bat each other's questions away as a tease.

The response throws Elizabeth, who has expected a rebuke. In the surprise she blurts out the truth. 'Someone I met at the market.'

Tam wants to jump in, berate her, warn against liaisons that can lead to a knitting pin and a lifetime of sorrow. Instead she nods, stays quiet for a minute.

'It's a hard time for you, Elizabeth. Remember, though, you got lots of years ahead of you, plenty o' time to make a good match.'

A match? It's like Tam tossed a lighted one into bone dry kindling. The girl, not one inclined to a hot temper, flares into anger.

'Like Ma, you think? How much time did she get?'

Tam knows instantly she's made a mistake.

'What would you know, Aunt Tam? Every bit of this place and Pa's is covered with sadness. I sometimes forget which house I'm in and reach to a shelf for something, only to find what I need sits on a shelf in another house, yet it doesn't matter, not one whit, because the sorrow, it's everywhere.'

Tam's never heard the girl raise her voice, but she seems unable to stop.

'This damn glue of grief, binding your place with Pa's, I can't stand it. I want a life of my own.' She sinks onto a chair, emptied out, waiting for punishment to be delivered.

The outburst has rattled Tam, and she is desperately trying to think what Anastasia would do or say right now, but there's no sound of her friend's voice. She will have to find her own.

When she opens her mouth, she's as surprised as Elizabeth that compassion is what pours out.

'I see how it is, dear girl. You want something for yourself, more than this broken way you're livin'. It's the best there is for now, and I'm sorry it ain't enough.'

She questions Elizabeth for a time. The fellow is Edward Fitzgerald, an only son who goes to church with his Ma. He is a market vendor, purveyor of fancy goods, intent on making more of himself. 'He's a man who plans to go places.' Quite likely, Tam thinks, by courting a girl whose father has means.

With Christmas approaching and all it entails, she's failed to notice the girl's frequent trips to the market and now realises, with a start, that the pair have been meeting up.

'I think it time, Elizabeth, that your Pa has a talk with your fellow.'

'Please, Aunt Tam. Will you talk to Pa, bring him round?'

William, with all that's happened during the year, is defensive, up in arms that some lad has taken advantage of his vulnerable daughter.

'William, you probably haven't had the chance to consider it yet, but she is of marrying age. Don't you think it best you intervene, at least find out what the man's like?'

William meets Fitzgerald and still resists. Christmas passes, then the New Year, Elizabeth pleading, crying, the fellow coming to the house to see William, followed by a visit there from the mother, pleased to aid her son in marrying into success.

By Easter William's been worn down. It's not the husband he wanted for his energetic eldest daughter but he feels he must give in, not the least because he has no desire to risk her having an illegitimate child. The colony is changing, attitudes tightening up about woman birthing out of wedlock, as his dear wife once did.

In October the pair marry, going to live in one of the houses William owns, over at Black Wattle Swamp, where industry is creeping around the foreshore. Edward works at the cooperage near his home, his father-in-law securing him the job rather than see him spend his days in blood and guts at the abattoir there.

Tam misses the girl, so like her mother in many respects, capable of knowing her own mind and just as exuberant as Anastasia. She finds herself standing in the kitchen sometimes, wishing only the best for the new couple yet full of misgivings.

John's seizures are more frequent, wearing him out for longer so that he lies in bed, limp, for a day after, occasionally two. Tam takes him beef broth, arranges the pillows so he can sit up to spoon it in.

He takes a few mouthfuls, leaves the spoon in the bowl. 'Why must I be like this, Aunt Tam? No friends, no hope of working or growing up to marry, have a family?'

The wretchedness in his voice tugs at her heart. 'Only God knows the answer, John.' She rubs his arm. 'Take a little more broth.'

The spoon rattles a little against the bowl as he begins to sob. Tam puts the tray on the side table and climbs on the bed beside him.

'It's an awful thing to say, the Reverend would scold me for it ... .' He gulps, splutters out the words. ' ... but I'd rather die, go to Ma and be healed.'

Tam wraps her arms around him, lets him cry out his despair, a dark place where no one else can go. All she can do is hold him tight, keep holding on so it can't claim him for good, so he can find his way back. At least she hopes so.

That night in bed Tam tells Robert about the boy's anguish.

'We have to start locking away the medicinals.'

'Surely, Robert, he'd not do such a thing.' The dear, gentle boy. She can't imagine him committing such an act. It's too horrible to even think of it.

'We can't know that, Tam. How can we understand how desperate he feels, trapped in a body that's outside his control?'

She goes out first thing next morning to buy a box she can lock. She must be vigilant with John now. It would destroy William to lose another son.

The boy is twelve years old. She has been negligent, caught up with the baby and little Harriet, must find a way to help him gain purpose. He needs a reason to live. Surely there is a role for the boy, even though he remains at home.

'It's tricky, Tam. Much as I care about him, you know what people think.' Robert sighs. Divine punishment, possession by demons, Tam's heard it all, sometimes from God-fearing people.

'It ain't his fault, it's not fair.' She slaps a hand against her forehead.

'I know it isn't, but he'll only be shunned. Folks think he should be in the asylum.'

Robert warns her against speaking to William. 'He's still finding it hard to cope. Please, don't make it harder.'

She is not giving up on the boy. Next morning, as she shows nine-year-old Sarah how to knead bread, she is thinking how particular John is at cards, in his letters, in all he does.

'More flour, Sarah.' Suddenly, she knows what to do. She calls the maid. 'Help Sarah finish off here, if you would.'

Within minutes she has her bonnet on and is striding towards the far end of George Street. Ruth Wheeler is in the workroom at the rear of her shop, clock parts laid out carefully on her table, a tiny screwdriver in her hand.

'Still doing well, I see, Ruth.'

She laughs. 'Thanks to you, Tam.'

Such a joy to see the woman's business still thrives, that the skills her watchmaker father taught her back in the old country haven't gone to waste.

'I got a favour to ask.'

William is open to the proposal but puts his foot down about John being anywhere other than in either of the

Foster or Goddard homes. It was to be expected and Tam is not deterred.

Ruth agrees to spend an hour a day at the Goddards training John up for cleaning, polishing and basic repairs, for a small sum of money that William won't need to know about.

The sticking point is John himself, still dispirited. 'Can't see the point of it, Aunt Tam.'

Ruth is the one, with three sons herself, to excite the boy about the possibilities. She has taken the back off a watch, is showing him its innards.

'See, John. Every watch, every clock is a puzzle to itself, wants to run, be alive. We are like surgeons, tickling this, adjusting that, cleaning away the dross that's getting in the way, so that it hums and sings the way it's meant to.'

She smiles at the boy. 'Nothin' better than getting a broken watch, seeing it come back to life. Here, hold it in your hand.'

John takes the gold watch, heavier than expected.

'Can you hear it, the heartbeat?

The boy holds the watch near his ear, breaks into a grin. 'I can, for sure I can.'

John is bright, learns fast. Twice a week Tam sends the maid to Ruth's shop and she returns with a small bag containing instructions and clocks or watches needing cleaning, polishing or adjustment.

Robert buys a small work table and they put it in a nook off the kitchen, where the boy can work away from his siblings, stay warm from the cooking fires, and the cook and maid can watch out for him.

William is astonished at the change in his lad, grateful the boy feels more useful.

Robert insists on celebrating Tam's birthday each year. She doesn't have a date so in their early days he nominated the first day of spring. 'It's fitting, don't you think?'

At first she indulged him but over time she's come to look forward to it.

Four years have flown by since Elizabeth married and moved out, with eighteen-year-old Annie embracing her new role as the eldest. She blocks the doorway when Tam tries to enter the kitchen, Sarah giggling behind her sister.

'What's this?' The girls shoo her out.

'Why can't I come in?'

'None of your business, Aunt. You have to leave.' Sarah's in stitches, usually the one taking orders, not giving them.

That night, after supper, the girls emerge triumphant with a two-tiered lemon cake. Once it's cut, Robert pulls out a small box, hands it to Tam.

'Happy fiftieth, my love.' The children all cheer, giving a rousing rendition of the birthday song, faces shining in the lamplight, even John's.

She opens her husband's present, a small gold watch hanging from a chatelaine. She knows instantly he has purchased it from Ruth, a gesture full of meaning for a wife he knows so well.

Her heart overflows.

'Why are you crying?' Harriet loves her birthdays, can't understand.

'I'm filled up with happiness, Harriet, is why.'

Next morning, she leans on the back door jamb, enjoying the balmy day and the view across the wharves and Campbell's Cove, tucked into the North-West side of Sydney Cove. She sips a steaming cup of tea in her hand, a few minutes to relax before going back inside to a multitude of need.

Robert, ever restless, has continued to do well. He's never more at home than here, still uplifted by exotic faces and foreign tongues, the excitement of new cargoes, the hubbub of goods coming and going.

He has his eye on land at the elevated end of George Street and plans to build them a new house, near where mansions have sprung up on Bunker's Hill; a home better suited to a child-filled life.

He's also pursuing new opportunities on the edge of the town, has bought land on a section of South Head Road running east along the ridgeline above, where there is space to build three shops with dwellings above.

Tam doesn't see the need for it, though she supports his ideas, understanding that he is driven to create the life of material substance that his own father aspired to but could not.

As for her, how she would like to talk to the ten-year-old girl, tell her to have faith, life would sweep her away, bring pain, but she would wash up in a good place, wanted by a good man, perhaps loved by many, a mother of sorts.

Through the house she hears an urgent knocking at the front door and leaves the maid to deal with it. Another hawker, no doubt. There's a salty tang in the breeze off the harbour and she breathes deeply, unaware that in a minute the maid will be beside her with words that will wipe away the peace of the moment, and soon she will be flailing again, unable to find her feet.

CHAPTER TWENTY-SIX

SYDNEY TOWN, 1846

THE MAID IS CALLING. 'Mrs Goddard, missus.' She appears in the doorway with five-year-old George on her hip and a sound of panic in her voice.

'You're needed at the Foster house.'

The three girls have followed the maid and cluster behind her, faces lined with worry, Annie insisting she goes with her aunt.

'I'm sure all is well, Annie. Look after the others. I'll be back soon.'

The bedroom is darkened and for a terrible moment Tam thinks it's Anastasia's corpse in the bed. Instead it is William, ashen, his large frame seemingly shrunk. He reports that the doctor has diagnosed lung fever and given instructions for administering Fowler's arsenic solution.

Tam draws up a chair. 'How long have you been ill, William?'

'A couple of days, is all.' His breathing is laboured, the words slow. 'Thought it was a springtime cold, but in the end I couldn't get myself to the office.'

It's been evident for some time that he never regained full strength after Anastasia died, as though she took some of his stamina with her to the grave.

'I'll be up and about soon. Can you keep the children tomorrow and Sunday? Give me a chance to rest up.'

Despite his protests, Tam insists she will visit daily and supervise his care. He doesn't want the children to see him weak and prefers them not to visit. When he fails to improve the following week, Tam sends for Elizabeth, who arrives promptly that afternoon. She has a son now and a neighbour is looking after him.

She whispers with Tam outside the door as she leaves. 'I want to stay, care for Pa, and it pains me that I can't. He must let Annie come and stay, Aunt.'

As he becomes weaker William finally agrees. Annie moves in as his nurse and eventually persuades him to let her siblings visit. 'It's worse for them to imagine you sick than to see it with their own eyes, Pa.'

Tam leads them up from the wharves, a wary eye on Harriet, so distressed when her mother lay in the same bed.

Annie has pulled the curtains open, done her best to make the room cheery, and has propped up her father on pillows. He's been bedridden for a couple of weeks and it shows in the lethargy of his movements, the smell of stale breath in the fug of the room.

Their father summons up energy he doesn't have, questions them one at a time about their progress in learning, their behaviour with their godparents.

Five-year-old George, doted on by his sisters and brother, has spent recent days perfecting cartwheels so energetic that Tam has banned them from the parlour and dining room.

'I'll show you, Pa.' The boy glances around the room, sees there's not enough space. He plucks at his father's sleeve. 'Come on, I can show you outside.'

The effort of sitting up has exhausted William, his breathing shallow though he manages a semblance of a smile. 'Another time, dear boy.'

Annie swoops in, shepherding them all from the room. As the maid helps them on with their coats, Tam draws her goddaughter off to the side. 'The doctor, what's he say?'

The girl's lips are pursed. She shakes her head.

William remains bedridden, sinking slowly as his lungs gurgle with fluid. By the beginning of December, Tam and Robert can see he hasn't long, his muscles shrinking, his once solid frame merging with the bedclothes. They stay at his bedside, helping Annie.

On the evening of the third of the month he grips Robert's hand, lifts his head a little and stares into his friend's eyes. 'The children …'

The effort is too much. He slumps back on the pillow. Robert knows exactly what his friend tries to say. 'Rest now, William. We are taking good care of them. We won't let you down.'

After supper the older children join them, Elizabeth, John and Sarah part of the semi-circle of chairs around the bed. Dawn is breaking, John and Sarah dozing, when William unexpectedly rallies.

'Open the curtains, would you.'

Annie leaps to her feet, pulls the drapes wide. The lamps reflect on the glass so it is difficult to make out first light breaking over the harbour. She knows that's what her Pa wants to see and hurriedly snuffs out the flames.

It's peaceful in the room, quiet and still as they all look to the window, where a wider world is slowly taking shape in lines and lumps, called forth into form by the rising sun. Only when Tam glances back does she see, in the soft golden glow, that William has slipped away, determined to avoid any fuss to the end.

Elizabeth, holding her father's hand, is the first of the children to register it, a mournful, raw lament emerging from her at the sight of her Pa's blue lips, no attempt to hold it back, big sister or not, the sound rising, filling the room.

The wave of it reaches Tam in a sensation so strong she must clutch the seat of her chair. It's as though she can feel the Earth slowly turning, carrying them forward, her and Robert, the children, the bed with their friend, all frozen where they sit yet propelled by the passage of time never-ending.

The Earth turns, will keep on turning, seasons passing, circling around. However much she tries, it cannot be slowed or stopped, must always move forward no matter what she might wish. Like William, she will be engulfed by it one day.

Elizabeth's wail is spent, while her siblings cry quietly. Tam stands behind the eldest, now a woman herself, a hand on her shoulder to steady them both.

Grief has circled the room and has chosen Elizabeth, now fully in its grasp. The twenty-one year old, once seeking to flee from the pull of sorrow, is now bound forever to it. She will come to birth more children, all to die young; her husband gone too, Edward falling ill on the Turon River goldfields, inland near Sofala, still trying to seek his fortune.

Beside the bed, Tam senses the shift in Elizabeth without understanding where it will lead, to an empty brown bottle of chlorodyne, the end of years of dosing herself with the addictive mix of laudanum, Indian hemp and chloroform, her goddaughter dying at her own hand.

In the moment, though, the mistress of the Goddard home is focussed on the immediate concerns of orphaned children distressed anew, of the mountain of her own grief she'll need to scale.

The funeral is a big affair, fifty mourners, maybe more, on foot behind the family in the black carriage on its way to church.

Robert is an executor of the will, along with Robert Campbell junior and his brother, John. William has left a big estate, eighteen houses to be divided between the children and a hundred pounds for his son in Van Diemen's Land, with Robert a trustee for properties bequeathed to the youngsters who are not yet of age.

The Goddards have been made full-time custodians of the dependent children. In the murky days after the funeral, Tam talks to her husband to see if he can bring forward his plan to build a home for them in George Street.

'We need to get the children away from the waterfront, the swearing, the constant goings on, give them a calmer place to recover.'

It's never been a bother for her. Like Robert she enjoys the action, the liveliness around where they live, coloured sailors, down-at-heel drovers and foul-mouthed lumpers thronging only a few paces from their doorstep, but she worries about how it influences the broken Foster children.

Robert has had the same thought and swings into action, getting plans drawn up for a trio of three-storey brick houses, shops below and dwellings above. They can live in one and rent the others to cover the mortgage.

The days unfurl in tears as she and the older girls pack up the Foster home. There's never enough of Tam to go round. She is stretched as thin as a shoe lace, one moment soothing a sad child, the next organising the cook, supervising the maid in cleaning the Foster home or arranging a cart to bring the children's chosen furniture and possessions to the wharfinger house.

After supper one evening, John and the younger ones abed, she and Annie work on the quilt she's been teaching the girl to make. A starburst pattern spills out from a centre of blue cotton and gold velvet pieces, broken by the embossed white from a section of a coat once worn by Annie's Ma and slips of green satin from an old waistcoat of her Pa's.

Tam aches to be in bed herself, but she's promised to show the girl how the next row of the pattern should be placed.

'I haven't said before, Aunt Tam, how very grateful I am.' Annie lays down the pin she was about to stick into the fabric.

'No need for gratitude, dear girl. You know me and Uncle Robert's happy to take care of you all.'

The eighteen-year-old shakes her head. 'That's not what I meant. What I'm saying is I'm truly thankful that you're raising the family, for I'd have been the one to shoulder the burden.'

She takes Tam's hand. 'I know it's a wicked thing to say, but it wasn't in me to do it.'

Robert is busier than ever, what with organising plans for his new buildings, and working late in his office on new ways to stop carters and owners removing goods without paying the wharfage fees. He tried having George with him for an hour here and there, introducing the boy to the world of work, but the proximity to the water's edge was a dangerous thing for a five-year-old with a fascination for ships. Better he stays at the house.

Month on month, the hour or two in the pew at church becomes the only quiet time Tam has with Robert. He is tetchy on occasion with her, short with the children too. Her patience is tested when he issues commands to one of them, or to her, expecting obedience in an instant, not his usual character at all.

Sitting in church one Sunday, John on one side and Harriet on the other, she glances over the nine-year-old's bonnet to Robert, on the other side of the girl. He looks wan and it occurs to her, in that instant, that he's not well. He has been tired lately, weary at the supper table, going to bed earlier than usual. She thought it was the stress of work combined with the fact that he's turned fifty, but now she's not so sure.

He has promised George he will do a little more work on the toy sailing ship he's begun making for him, and back at the house takes off his Sunday jacket and goes for the glue.

'Robert, can I have a quick word, first.'

'Of course. What is it?'

Tam tips her head towards the parlour, where the children have gone. 'Upstairs would be better,' She lays her bonnet on the bed. 'You don't seem well, my love. I notice you've been tired a lot, have complained a few times about headaches.'

'No more than usual.' He pushes back a run of hair that's fallen over one eye, and she sees many strands of grey.

She suggests he sees the doctor, maybe get a tonic to perk him up.

'If it will make you happy, though I myself don't see the need.'

She can't let anything bad happen to him. The thought alone makes the weight of concern for the Foster youngsters a vice across her shoulders.

The fever strikes a week later, a piercing headache arriving with it. Food passes straight through him, and water rushes from cup to bedpan. Typhoid, the doctor determines, likely picked up on the wharves, dormant at first, its tiny shoots putting down roots till it has become strong, flowering in urgent symptoms.

Everyone knows the harbour is polluted: blood, fat and chemicals from tanneries, wool washing, soap and candle making, slaughterhouses, joining with the contents of cess pits in an unholy soup. Yet it's the sailors who get the blame for spreading disease.

The doctor recommends the cold water cure, the best course of action for typhoid, helping immerse his patient in a hip bath filled with unheated water. A large ice block, part of a cargo shipped in insulated boxes from a frozen lake in North America, has been left to melt in it first. Robert must stay submerged for up to four hours, but after half an hour he is begging to be helped out. The doctor insists for another quarter hour, his patient clinging to the side of the tub, pleading to be finished.

Tam can't take any more. 'He needs to get out.'

Later, with the doctor gone after demanding Robert be admitted to hospital, Tam refusing, she helps a shivering yet feverish husband into a fresh nightshirt. 'A cruel thing to do to you, my love. I hope you'll forgive me.'

He looks up at her from the pillow, face slack as though she's a stranger, before a wild look sparks in his eyes and his mouth stretches taut. 'Get away, you black-hearted devil spawn.' His arms thrash and she steps back in alarm at what he might see at her centre.

'It's me, Tamsin, your wife.'

He is agitated, mumbling, soft sounds accompanied by the waving of one hand then just as suddenly harsh grunts, jumbled sentences, his head thrown from side to side. He is gone from her, demented. She speaks softly in a soothing voice, trying with all her might to call him back, for the whole colony knows delirium in enteric fever is usually a death sentence.

He continues thrashing, refusing to take the opium tincture that might give him some peace, and she can do nothing but sit beside him, keep him safe from the bed rail, from falling on the floor. Eventually he slips into a stupor, worn out from his exertions.

She rubs his hand, whispers how much she loves him. In the years before meeting her man she was a paltry creature, made of air, anger and spite. Any substance she's grown will go with him if he dies.

She puts Annie in charge of supervising the younger ones, the maid and the cook, and quarantines herself in the bedroom with Robert and his medicines: opium to calm the delirium, worse at night; oil of turpentine for the loose stools, ten or fifteen drops on a spoonful of sugar, given every two to four hours. The oil makes his urine smell of violets, though does little to overpower the stink in the room.

Annie and the maid cart pail after pail of water to the door, and soap for Tam's relentless washing of her hands and cleaning her husband. She refuses to let them take away soiled sheets and nightshirts, dumping the foul linen in a wicker hamper, to be burned at the first opportunity so there's no risk to others in the house.

'It's such a waste, Aunt Tam. Please, let us wash them.'

Instead Annie is sent to buy more and when they are gone, fresh ones again.

Over and over Tam sponges Robert down to cool his temperature, cleans bloody discharges, rolls him to check for ulcers on his skin. The doctor has warned that his tongue must be wiped carefully to stop gangrenous lesions and minimise swelling of the gums. In the first attempt he willingly opens his mouth, puts out his tongue but then suddenly bites her fingers. She tries again and again, till she can no longer hold herself up by the bed and must doze fitfully on the floor beside him.

With the curtains closed, brass oil lamps burning around the clock, she lives in an endless twilight, a fugue where she is neither asleep nor fully awake, sometimes forgetting the food Annie's left outside the door. A week bleeds into another and her mind begins to wander, searching out frailties, the many reasons why she is unworthy.

Annie, John, Sarah, Harriet, George … they're all down in the parlour, gleeful at the uselessness of their aunt, never once believing she could do the mothering they need, laughing at the pretence they've kept up that she might bring a bit of good to their lives.

Tam wonders if she is dreaming and pinches herself but it hurts and she thinks she must be awake. She rolls onto her back and looks up from the floor to see Robert floating above, his face accusing, voice like thunder. 'You never could be the wife I needed, a sorry excuse for a woman, with your crippled womb, your blighted soul. Get out, get out now.' He points at her, his glare a shard of ice in her chest.

She staggers to her feet, can't tell where to find the door and stumbles as she tries to get her bearings. She is suffocating, must get out, can't stay a minute longer. The wall is hurtling towards her face and she steps back sharply, bumping into the round table with the lamp, knocking it over.

Glass breaks and oil spills to the flame, bursting into yellow, a mere flicker that licks along the fuel now leaking across the floorboards. Within seconds it flares up in a hot wall before her.

She is in hell, it makes sense, was always on her way there, has known it since she first had memory, that the fires of hell are the only way her soul can ever be burned clean.

The flames dance before her eyes, beautiful, beckoning, and she is dancing, swaying with them, then falling through air, forever falling, passing out before she hits the floor.

CHAPTER TWENTY-SEVEN

SYDNEY TOWN, 1846

THE FIRE IN THE WHARFINGER cottage is the talk of the town, how the children fought the flames in their nightwear, even the boy with strange fits, the glow of the bedroom window seen from ships moored nearby.

Fire volunteers rushed to buckets and ladders the insurance company kept on the wharves, storming into the house. By the time the horse-drawn engine arrived, its bell clanging, hand pumps at the ready, the flames had been doused, leaving acrid smoke and the smell of charred floorboards.

'What about the sick fellow, Goddard?', the gossips ask. 'And his wife, she were in the room with 'im I hear?'

'Dead,' someone says, and the word spreads like its own fire through kitchens and shops in the town.

By the time the rumours double back on themselves and reach the overseer's cottage Robert has begun a slow recovery. He greets the news with grace as he sits at the oval dining table, Annie passing on what she's heard from wagging tongues as she hands him a bowl of porridge.

'Folks will say anything for a bit of attention.' In her mind the terror of the night still looms large, running up the stairs with slopping pails of water, bare toes stubbed in the hurry, troubled by guilt that she was not the one to raise the alarm. It was John, often sleeping badly because of restless legs, who heard the thump of the side table hitting the floor.

'Let them, Annie, if that's what they take for entertainment.' He stirs sugar into the bowl. 'Did your Aunt eat?'

She shakes her head.

Tam has been sleeping in the girls' room for three days, affected by the smoke, but the doctor says there's been a collapse of spirit as well. Once she knew Robert was safe she had taken to bed.

He pats the girl's arm. 'Don't worry, I'll see to her.'

He climbs the stairs slowly, his legs still inclined to weakness, in his hands a tray with tea and toast. The door is ajar and he nudges it a little wider with his elbow so that it swings open into a darkened room.

'You can't go on like this, Tamsin.' He speaks softly, places the tray on the bedside table and goes to the window, flinging the curtains wide so that bright light searches out every nook and cranny.

Tam throws her arm over her eyes. They hurt. This is cruel.

The bed creaks a little as he eases himself onto the edge. 'This isn't helping. It's time to move on. Surely you know the children need you?' His voice drops to a whisper. 'I need you too, dear wife. Please, I beg you, eat a little something and come downstairs.'

Her eyes are still covered. She gives no sign of hearing him, not even a murmur.

He sighs. 'The men will be here this morning to replace the floorboards in our room. It will be far too noisy to stay in bed.'

The tea goes cold, the toast hard. He sits awhile longer, resists the urge to grip her by the hand, force her to her feet, maybe even give her a sharp slap to shock her out of the morass.

'I don't understand. You're the strongest woman I know. You saved me when I was so ill, have cared so well for Anastasia's brood. What is this about?'

A stripe of sun moves slowly down the wall, unnoticed by the man. After a time he stands, a little unsteadily, and quietly leaves the room.

I lie here, asking over and again, what's wrong with me, why do I bring harm? Pictures run through my mind, torturing me. The beating stick bearing down on the back of my legs and the slow fall to the floor, the cold eyes of Matron, Becca's blue face, the fish staring up from its dead eye, Nance rubbing shoulders, the grip of the watchman, the stupid wig on the beak, bright blood spilling across the ship's planking. On and on, only to start again.

I'm forsaken; it was always so. I'm slipping through the fingers of time, must face my fate. I can do naught more.

Within the week Robert returns to work with much to catch up on, though his offsider has made a reasonable fist of it in the month of absence. He remains troubled by his wife's sorry disposition, concerned that he is failing at loving her back to her full self, while the younger children drift about the house, Annie doing her best to keep up their routines.

Upstairs, Tam has refused to move back into her bedroom with its smooth new floorboards, and grows thinner by the day, ignoring the busy thrum of dray drivers, sailors and labourers on the wharves, unmoved by John, Sarah and George's attempts to draw her from bed.

Nine-year-old Harriet refuses to go near her aunt, remembering another woman lying still on a bed in a darkened room.

Robert comes home each evening to a house once a well-oiled clock, now juddering about, too fast or too slow, out of rhythm with itself.

The days continue to pass till early one morning Annie hears a loud rapping at the front door. She opens it to the wind burnt face of George Ranse, clearly a little worse for wear with the drink but smiling broadly in the certainty he will be welcome,

'Your Aunt in? Haven't seen her for a while.'

Annie takes him into the parlour, explains the situation, and offers tea.

'I'd much rather see her, if you don't mind.'

The girl hesitates but decides any intervening event, even a visit, is better than going on as they have. 'Follow me.'

In the bedroom she speaks softly to her Aunt, opens the curtains half-way and ushers George in, pushing a chair near the bed before backing out of the room.

'What's this then, Tam?'

He ignores the silence, presses on. His head, foggy from celebrating the previous night when he berthed the *Frances* with a bumper cargo of black oil and whale bone, is quickly clearing with an urgent sense that he must throw out a line and reach this woman.

He understands blackness, the pull of it, the way it can come to you as a warm blanket, treacherous in wrapping around a person so tightly they can't see any light. He grasps immediately that his stepmother is in the grip of it.

'Thirty-six years ago it were, do you remember?' He pats her arm as if to remind her he's still sitting there.

'I recall it so clearly, never forgot that first day you stepped into the kitchen, me and Rosa terrified o' what was coming.'

He pauses as though in the space between them Tam has replied.

The chair has a straight back and he leans into it to stop the familiar feeling of the sea rising and falling, the rocking of ocean swell beneath him these past two months of whale chasing, a rhythm that always persists for the first day or two back on land.

'Pretty soon we was glad you were there, glad to have a kind heart about the place at last. Luis, he didn't come easy to accepting our Ma was gone, and Pa ... well, you know good as me, he weren't a lot of fun to have around when he were in his cups.

'You became Ma to Rosa and me. I'm a father now and I can see how hard it would have been to take that on when you was just a girl. I never thanked you but I am now, Tam, for binding yerself to us two when no one even asked if you wanted to.'

The room is getting warmer from the sun and he wipes a sweaty palm down one trouser leg, anxious not to stumble with his words when he needs to see this through. 'I lost a boy, a few years back. He were only a lad of two, such a dear little fellow.' His voice chokes a little as he says it.

Tam turns her head towards him, pushes up against the pillow so she can see George better.

'You never let me know.'

'Not for the want of it. I couldn't write it down, hard letters on a page would have made it more real. Betsy and me, we buried him and never spoke of it again.' Or maybe it was him who never did the speaking, hard to tell these days.

'Oh George, how terribly sad. I'm so sorry.'

'I ain't mentioning it to make you sad, Tam. Guess what I'm saying is that whether you come by motherhood in giving birth or by taking on the children of others, the measure of how well things fare for you is forever coloured by their fate.'

She's never seen such vulnerability in him and wonders why it's shown up now.

'I got eyes in my head, always been able to see that you never thought you was up to the job of being a Ma to us back then. But you was, and I can see from the faces of Annie and the young ones downstairs that you're doing alright by them, too.'

He scrapes the chair back and leans over to kiss her on the cheek.

'I don't know what story's got in your head, trapped you there, but it ain't true, Tam. I know about such things, believe me. You got to cut them loose, free yourself, for your sake and the sake of the ones who need you.'

She sees in his weather beaten face, the grey hair at his temples, that soon he will be growing old, but she can't mistake the sound of the soft five year old speaking through the armour surrounding the man.

It touches her as nothing has done since Robert got sick, a gift of sorts from this salt bitten seaman, parcelled in the old string of memory, wrapped in torn paper and stuck with paste, yet holding all that she gave him as a small boy, returning to her as an unexpected act of grace.

She squeezes his hand and they stay like that for a moment, her looking up from the pillow, him reaching down. Then he pulls away gently and leaves the room, taking with him as much of the darkness as he can gather around him. She remains propped on the pillow till her back aches. George is right – the future has no pull because she's captive to the past.

Annie brings up beef soup a couple of hours later and when she returns for the bowl it is completely empty. It's hardly the stuff of miracles, but it is a turning point.

George's visit is working on her in strange ways, has jarred something loose, and Tam can't work out what. She's never seem him like that, made pliable by loss, wisdom growing out from the roots of pain.

In the coming days she observes she is no longer asking why she always hurts the ones she loves. Instead, she finds herself pondering George's words and asking a new question, maybe a better one: why can't I let go the story I tell myself about who I am?

She has exiled herself for years, always an invisible fence between her and others. A wild dove in a cage will do the same if kept there long enough, staying in its confinement though the door has been left open.

Robert greets her return to the supper table with delight, buoyed to see her sitting there when he arrives home a few evenings later.

As Annie rounds up the children, the cook brings in steaming plates of roast potatoes, tripe in white sauce and onions, and lamb sweetmeats with peas. Tam leans across to touch Robert's arm. 'I've moved back into our bedroom, though I'd rather we use candles instead of a lamp.'

A few hours later she is curled against his chest, enjoying the weight of his arm pulling her close.

'I'm happy of course, Tamsin, though a touch bewildered. What changed?'

She wonders for a moment if she should say it's like she walked to the edge of a cliff, not knowing if she would jump or stand there frozen till a gust of wind forced her over. That one way or another she must go forward.

'I figured it was time I stopped thinking only of myself.'

She has said it as a comfort to her husband, though the truth is the opposite. She is being pulled within ever more deeply, called to examine all the old ideas she's seen as the sum of herself, turning them over, looking underneath for what they hide.

George's visit has set in motion a wheel from the top of a hill and it is rolling, gathering speed, and all she can do is to watch what's unfolding with curiosity, fearful about what will happen when it reaches the end.

The motion is taking her somewhere, without needing her involvement, and it is stripping her bare, even the soles of her feet feeling tender, unprotected from the ground.

'Are you alright, Aunt?'

John is standing in front of her, and she becomes aware of leaning heavily on the back of a chair. 'Yes, I'm fine thank you. A bit dizzy, is all.'

She decides to go for a mid-afternoon stroll on her own, but Harriet determines she will go with her.

'No, my dear. I'll be far too slow for you. Best you stay here with Annie.' The girl bursts into tears.

'She's missed you,' Annie whispers in her Aunt's ear.

Tam relents and sends the girl to fetch her bonnet. As they pick their way along the wharves, between heavy wooden boxes being loaded onto a cart and a stack of nearby casks, Harriet takes her hand.

It seems the most natural thing in the world, the way the young girl curls her warm fingers in her Aunt's. The surprise is that Tam finds it so steadying, as though the girl is holding her fast, tethering the two of them against winds no one else can see or feel.

They walk north up George Street, stepping to one side as an omnibus and its pair of horses rumble by, continuing past the General Post Office with its doric columns and people chatting on the front steps.

Harriet misses nothing, exclaiming over what she sees, though Tam must shush her when she loudly points out a turbaned fellow in a bright blue uniform, his sabre slung from his hip. 'Now, now Harriet. He will have business here, probably buying walers for Indian royalty. They're fond of our rugged local horses.'

Tam lengthens her stride, her legs welcoming the chance to properly stretch, until Harriet complains that she can't keep up.

As they round the corner a familiar voice causes her to turn. Jemima Eager hurries to catch up. 'Glad to see you out and about, Tam.'

Tam braces. The last thing she needs is a conversation about the fire.

'It's been ages and I've not had the chance to say how much you've helped so many women in this town.' She is puffing a little after her exertion. 'Your husband too, of course, though his benevolence is of a different kind. Far better, I think, to help a woman make a living so she can raise her children rather than donate funds for them to be kept at the orphans' home.'

She realises she's accidentally given offence to the woman's husband. 'Begging your pardon, that were a bit forward.'

'No harm done, Jemima.'

They chat briefly before Mrs Eager must depart to the Post Office.

'Did you help other children? Harriet's question is innocent, curious.

'I … I suppose I did.'

They walk peacefully until they're approaching Moore's wharves and warehouses at Miller's Point. 'Oh look, Harriet. A flying horse.' A mob of walers is corralled on the wharf, one swinging in a sling across the deck of a ship.

They watch as it is loaded and another secured for the crane to lift. The sight of the creatures being taken from the solid feel of land for rough seas is making Tam queasy and she is suddenly tired. She begins to lead Harriet home, the vigour of the outing emptying her mind, and the girl going quiet.

Nearing the house, it occurs to her that she's no longer fallow ground. Harriet's trusting hand in hers and Mrs Eager's reminder about what she's given other women; they're signs that a harvesting is under way.

'Oh.' She stops without warning, startling the girl.

The mothering, so much of it amounts to something, amounts to nothing. A force that comes out of nowhere, rises, falls away, maybe a little of it lodging somewhere in another girl, another woman, urging her on to do her best however broken she may be. Because the damage, the parts that are wounded or scarred are not the source but the grit in the shell, from which the pearl of love may lay itself down, day by tedious day, week by difficult, hurting week.

Her story for so long was shaped by others, people who were cruel, neglectful, who exploited her, kept her downtrodden. Even the ghostly presence of Cuddy's first wife at Kissing Point, in the silences, the spaces, the troubled eyes of the children, has caught in the corners, lodged in her understanding of herself.

She has embraced the story, owned it with such fervour that she couldn't see its falsehoods or the bursts of true spirit shining through. She may be broken in some fashion but was never beyond repair, and the knowledge of that is a strength.

She can release her story of harm, cruelty, violence. Let go the raging demon. She will not die, become nothing without it, because it was never her, the awareness made possible by a glimpse of a truer self. Waiting inside, below what the world once reflected back, beyond the pain she carries, is her real nature:

It has been there all along, intact, crowded out by the lies she's believed, waiting for her to make space to meet it. She cannot describe it yet, trace the outline of it, but it carries compassion. For her.

She is still rooted to the spot when she finally understands. Loving herself is what will make her who she's meant to be, is the only thing that can do it.

Harriet has lost patience with her Aunt and pulls free, running on ahead. Tam's eyes follow the girl to the wharf entrance, where Robert is at his office door talking to a drover, writing something on a clipboard. He sees her, smiles and waves, and her heart swells as she waves back.

Annie waits anxiously in the cottage, keen to see Tam is okay, and Sarah, John and George are expecting her return. The maid will be beating rugs, the cook will have the kettle singing in the kitchen.

She hurries towards the front door. It has taken a lifetime, but at last she is coming home.

On the other side of the world, at the mouth of the Mediterranean, it is early morning, and a restless wind swirls around The Rock of Gibraltar. It forces its way through a narrow street where a British sergeant's wife walks downhill, head bent in a flurry of grit.

She is passing a cracked stucco house where they say an old Catalan once lived, supposedly a seer, when the wind suddenly drops. Just as quickly it picks up again and rises in a shape that catches her eye.

It may be a trick of the dust, but she will always believe what she saw was much more, a blur at first shapeless, then just for a moment swirling, shifting into a face, shoulders, a young woman in a hooded cloak suspended in the air, dark, piercing eyes fixed on her, head thrown back in a laugh, hovering for mere seconds then gone.

AUTHOR'S NOTE

Until the lions have their historians, tales of
the hunt shall always glorify the hunter.
African proverb

Those judged weak by society are often denied a voice. In colonial Australia, ruled by the world's most powerful nation at the time, to be a convict made you the lowest of the low, despite the fact that most were transported for crimes arising from poverty. If you were also a woman there was a special place for you, lower still. Free women married to a convict fared little better.

Yet some were brave enough to defy the restrictions of a deranged society. Women dared fight against the rules, both visible and invisible, and were sent to the hard labour of the Parramatta Female Factory, locked up for good in the asylum, or found drunk in a gutter and thrown in a gaol cell. Others, by character or sheer luck, built a future for themselves brick by brick, falling down and getting back up, full of pain and loss, conforming and rebelling, doing what it took to go beyond surviving to thrive.

Threading through it all for these women was domestic life and work, of little import to early historians yet at the heart of the society that developed, shaping the next generation and giving far more than ink on official records kept by men will ever show. Some were also skilled artisans, farmers, businesswomen, though their contribution was often hidden behind the name of a husband.

Their forgotten lives were important. They mattered.

My four times great grandmother was there, mired in the needs of others, giving care in sickness, passing on stories, loving and grieving, contributing to the substance of community and connection. A family story suggests Elizabeth Connor was Spanish, and possibly met my four times great grandfather, Michael Connor, in Gibraltar when he was fighting in the American War of Independence.

After Elizabeth died and he was well into his sixties, Michael married sixteen-year-old Harriet Parker, who was thrust into raising his children while still a child herself, and later, willingly this time, the children of friends. There is no record of her ever having babies of her own. Both women had colourful lives and they have inspired this story, which draws on known facts though is a work of fiction, condensing timeframes and events to suit the narrative and altering names to avoid confusion.

From these two women the flawed, damaged, sometimes weak, often wonderful women, Melva Ranse and Tam Ranse, were born in my imagination. I hope I have proven an adequate midwife.

Elizabeth's cause of death and the date are unknown, though she disappears from colonial records in 1806, about five years before Michael weds Harriet.

After Michael's death, Harriet went on to marry shipwright George Atherden, who was a similar age to her.

It is likely they were partners for some time before that as census records show she was his housekeeper the year after he arrived in the colony, and both were godparents to Anastasia and William Foster's children. They did, indeed, become full-time carers to the Foster children after Anastasia then William died.

Harriet died in July 1875 at the George Street house in which the couple spent their later years, from 'senile gangrene' after a fatal fall at home. She was about eighty years old. George died four years later, by which time he owned several commercial and residential properties in George, Oxford and Gloucester Streets in Sydney. The Atherdens left substantial assets to the Foster children, as well as their tenants and a number of charities.

ABOUT THE AUTHOR

Anna Housego has always been fascinated by the currents that ebb and flow in us, and in our lives, bringing strength or creating havoc, depending on how we meet them.

A former journalist, she has worked in a range of jobs, from roustabout at a frontier pub to political adviser, and for two decades was a freelance communications consultant. The storytelling gene comes from Irish ancestors. Growing up in a wilderness town full of eccentric characters switched it on.

She lives a long way south on the island of lutruwita/ Tasmania, off the south-eastern corner of Australia, close to her two adult children and their families.

The Two Wives of Cuddy Ranse is her fifth novel and is a companion to *This Savage World*.

ALSO BY ANNA HOUSEGO:

The Way to Midnight
One Small Life
Crows on the Roof
This Savage World

www.annahousego.com
@annahousego
@annahousegoauthor

Made in the USA
Middletown, DE
20 January 2026

27378056R00230